The Demons of Paris

Eric Flint
Gorg Huff
Paula Goodlett

D1528836

Eric Flint's Ring of Fire Press

ISBN: 9781980344148

Cover art by Larry Dixon.
Cover design by Stoney Compton
Map by Michael Knopp

DEDICATION

Considering that Paula and Eric are both recent survivors of cancer, it seems wise to dedicate this book to the world's oncologists and pharmaceutical technologists—not to mention the nurses who probably do more to keep patients alive than anyone else.

For his part, Gorg wishes to throw in a salute to the VA, where his medical needs are invariably handled with grace, kindness, and respect, not to mention great skill.

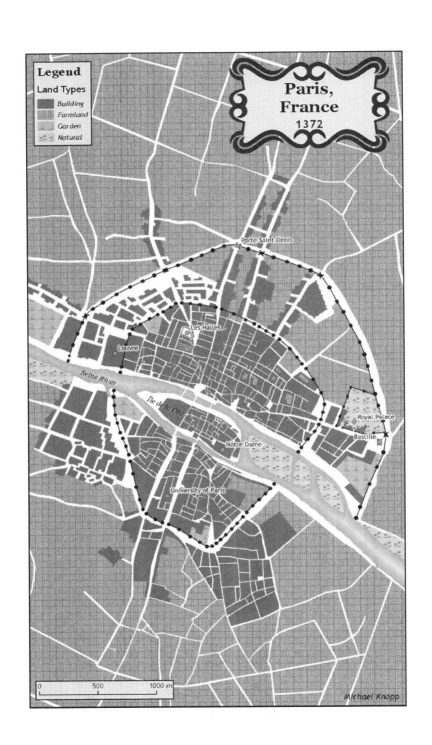

Legend

Land Types

- Building
- Farmland
- Garden
- Natural

Paris,
France
1372

Porte Saint-Denis

Les Halles

Louvre

Seine River

Île de la Cité

Notre Dame

Royal Palace

Bastille

University of Paris

0   500   1000 m

Michael Knopp

CHAPTER 1

Alley off Rue Cler
January 27, 1372

Commissaire Pierre Dubois of the Grand Châtelet looked down at the body. The young woman had been ripped from navel to breast and opened as though a scythe had been used. There was blood all over the alley and the woman's heart and lungs were missing. The stench of the mutilated corpse was strong enough that Dubois barely noticed the more familiar stink left by chamber pots the nearby residents had dumped into the alley.

Pierre had never seen anything like it. Until today, he would have said that he had seen every horror that one human being could inflict on another. Pierre stopped in mid-thought. Human being. This smacked of an act of dark forces, but in Paris of 1372, magic and demonic powers were the province of storytellers from the Far East or across the Mediterranean in Egypt and Africa. Not of the civilized Christian world. At least, they hadn't been until now.

Yet, as he looked at the blood spattered around the alley, he realized that the body had to have been hanging at least ten feet in the air when it was disemboweled. There was a piece of what might be intestine caught in a crack of the wall of a bake shop. It was next to a second floor window and from the spatter pattern it must have been flung almost horizontally. He could think of no mortal hand that could do what was done here, and especially he could think of nothing that could have done it without being noticed. The alley was just off the Rue Cler, which was busy at all hours. But no one had seen or heard a thing. Not even the baker's family, who slept just the other side of that gore splattered wall.

Pierre realized he was going to need help. A different kind

of help than he had ever needed before.

He turned to André Hébert, his aide. "Make me an appointment with the provost of the University of Paris. I think we are going to need an expert in magic."

"Perhaps the church, sir?"

"I would rather not disturb the cardinal if we can avoid it, André." Pierre grimaced. "He tends to be . . . overly-enthusiastic in his inquisitions."

Office of the Provost
January 28, 1372

"Have some of our students been causing you problems, Commissaire?" the short, well-padded man in scholarly robes asked in a belligerent tone.

"I wish it were something so simple, Count Moreau." Commissaire Dubois bowed, though his social rank was in fact as high as Count Moreau's. The provost was a stickler and quick to take offence. "I have a murder that may have a magical component." He was wearing his best hose and the tunic with the gold thread due to the provost's attitude, as well as his embroidered felt hat. Pierre was decidedly uncomfortable.

"You think one of my—"

Pierre held up his hands in denial and almost supplication. "No, no, nothing like that. I need the expertise of your scholars in finding the culprit. Or even identifying the culprit."

Moreau scratched his beard in thought. "Well, there's Gabriel Delaflote. He is one of our scholars of Natural Philosophy, but he has an interest in alchemy and the mystic arts. Personally, I think it's all a lot of nonsense, not good solid science like astrology." Moreau waved to a horoscope done in colored inks on vellum, which was on an easel, with notes on a table beside it, then continued. "He insists he has spells to call an imp that will in turn be able to teach him the spells to animate objects."

"Has he . . ." Pierre felt the color drain from his face. *Could that be where the killer in the alley came from?*

"No, of course not. We would need a dispensation from the church and frankly I haven't been focusing on that. There are much more important issues between the university and the church." Clearly reading something in Pierre's face, Moreau continued quickly. "Gabriel is not the sort to act without authority, Commissaire. He is much too timid for such a course. But he is a meticulous collector of the detritus of bygone eras. His room is packed with old scrolls that he has laboriously copied. Invocations for everything from ancient gods to tree spirits."

Pierre was not convinced, but he saw no advantage in challenging the provost. He would see the man and make his own judgment.

Rooms of Doctor Gabriel Delaflote, Top Floor of the Bonouse Tower

Pierre was sweating profusely and wishing that he had not insisted on going to see Doctor Delaflote immediately. It had gotten rid of the provost, but getting to the good doctor's combined residence and study was an arduous enterprise. Delaflote lived in the southern tower of the ramshackle residential building. To get there, you had to climb three flights of stairs, cross a narrow passageway to a different part of the edifice, go down two flights of stairs, cross yet another passageway that led to Delaflote's tower—and then climb another three flights of stairs to get to the landing just below the doctor's chambers. To get into Delaflote's own room, you then had to clamber up what was more like a broad, shallow ladder than anything a sane man would call "stairs."

Reaching the top rungs, he knocked on a door of slats, not well butted one to the next. There were clear cracks between them. Two cross pieces held the door together and the carpenter had scrimped on dowels as well as the quality of the wood.

"What?" said a squeaky tenor voice. A moment later an eye

peered through a crack in the door. "You're not a student."

"No. I am the Commissaire of the Grand Châtelet."

The eye disappeared. There was some shuffling, then a wooden bar was lifted away from the door. The opened door revealed a room with rugs of woven rags covering the stone floor. There were hangings on the walls, but they were all old and worn, and an icy breeze whistled through the large cracks in the walls. In one corner there was a rack full of scrolls and papers, most of which showed signs of use. Near it was a bed of sorts, blankets on a raised platform made of planks over boxes. There were two unlit tallow candles and a small lamp on a small table next to the bed.

"What can I do for you, Commissaire?"

"There was a murder." Pierre pushed into the room as he spoke.

"I know nothing of . . ." Delaflote said, backing away.

"It was no ordinary crime, Doctor." Pierre looked around the room and went to sit on a stool that was in serious need of repainting. "There was blood up to the second floor of the alley and the murderer seems to have been seventeen or more feet tall. And whatever it was also took the heart and the lungs."

"That sounds horrible, but what—"

"The provost says you know about demons."

"Only in theory, Commissaire. There are no demons any more. The pagan gods of pre-Christian times have all been washed away."

"Well, some are apparently coming back. What can you tell me about something that can lift an adult human like a child's rag doll?"

"I can tell you almost nothing." The doctor held up a hand before Pierre could interrupt again. "I am not trying to avoid your questions, Commissaire. There are all sorts of things that might or might not fit your description, all of them quite impossible in this modern age. Some of them that might be summoned by men, many that might appear on their own. Giants and cyclops,

4

dragons and demons from the pit. Even were I to see the scene of the murder, I couldn't tell you what had done it. The ancients used spells to bring imps and minor spirits into their service to help them figure out such things."

"Then call up an imp!" Pierre bellowed. Then he caught himself. He hadn't realized until just this moment how truly frightened he was since seeing the murder scene. "I am sorry, Doctor. But if you had seen what I saw . . ."

"It would never be allowed, Commissaire," the doctor said. "I have notes on the rites, but the church would never allow those rites to be performed. And I would never do them without permission."

Pierre doubted that last protestation, but let it stand. "And if I got permission?"

"'If you obtained the permissions of the church and civil authorities, I would be willing. It would be an interesting test of the instructions I have."

"This test? It wouldn't involve sacrificing anyone?"

"No, not even an animal, though a gift of some sort is expected. A lure, a loaf of bread or a flask of wine. That sort of thing. But let me warn you again, Commissaire, I cannot promise that it will work."

Pierre nodded his acceptance of the caution. "I'll see what I can manage, Doctor."

Rue Paul
February 4, 1372

Father Augustin heard a noise. It was past midnight, and he was returning home after visiting a patron of the church. Madame Brosseau was sixty-seven years of age and, if Father Augustin was any judge, not long for this world. She was trying to buy her way into heaven, and while Augustin doubted it would work, he could put the money to good use. He heard the noise again. It was a slithering sort of thing.

5

Curious and only a little frightened by the murder and the commissaire's insistence that it was of demonic origin, Father Augustin turned into the alley. As he passed the corner of the building, the light was hidden as though a cloak were pulled over the moon. He looked up to see nothing but inky blackness, and then ahead to see a shape of shadows before him.

Pragmatic he might be, but Father Augustin was strong in his faith. He grabbed the cross he wore, held it before him, and started the ceremony of exorcism.

The laughter he heard was terrifying. It was cold, like ice cracking, but there was a malicious sweetness to it. The laughter slithered into words. The meaning seeped into his mind, though the language was ancient and evil beyond his imagining.

"I do not answer to your crucified mammal."

Somehow, with the word mammal came the image and the smell of a small furry rodent and the impression that this thing saw no difference at all between the ancient rat and Christ.

"I was here when your kind walked on four legs. You are still nothing but food to me."

There was more slithering and the darkness advanced upon Father Augustin. He started screaming then, and he screamed for quite a while.

But no one heard a thing.

Office of the Commissaire of the Grand Châtelet
February 5, 1372

"You have to do something," Nicolas du Bosc insisted.

Pierre Dubois looked at the angle of the light across his work table. The sun would be setting soon and the body of Father Augustin had been discovered in the early morning. Word was all over Paris and people were panicking.

Apparently people were panicking all the way to the royal palace, hence the visit from a close companion and top adviser to King Charles V of France. Du Bosc's official title was as one of the *maîtres des requêtes ordinaires de l'hôtel du Roi*—which was a medieval way of indicating that he was one of the king's advisers who handled petitions from the common folk. In practice, his position was roughly equivalent—very, very roughly—to that of the White House Counsel of twenty-first century American presidents. He was, in essence, the king's personal lawyer as well as his principal legal adviser.

"I don't know what to do," admitted Dubois. "Just as last time, no one heard a thing and the alley was just off a major thoroughfare. The alley was washed in blood, but that is not all. A doctor of medicine from the university examined the body and the father's throat was raw from screaming. No one heard it. No one heard anything at all. This was not natural. It was not the act of a madman, or a man of any sort. Not because no man would do such a thing, but because no man *could* do such a thing. I suggested that we try something, but the church wouldn't stand for it."

"What did you have in mind, Commissaire?"

"There are ancient rites to call up a familiar, really an imp of knowledge, a being that teaches the caller about the workings of magic." Pierre avoided the word demon carefully. "Those rites probably won't work, but I can think of nothing else to try."

Nicholas du Bosc took a deep breath. "I'll look into the matter. Father Augustin was not a simple parish priest. He had the ear and friendship of half the nobles in Paris."

La Petite Courtyard, University of Paris
February 8, 1372

Gabriel Delaflote laid out his summoning, using chalk blessed by Father Christos from Saint Dominic's, mixed with holy water and goat's milk. It was Gabriel's own recipe, based on an amalgamation of bits and pieces from pagan times, but with a proper respect for Mother Church. He painted it onto the paving stones with horsehair brushes, paying little attention to the walled and gated courtyard he was in.

He had wanted to do this in his laboratory which was located in his room. But Bishop de Sarcenas insisted he had to observe and, given his corpulence, he wasn't going to climb three flights of stairs to get to Gabriel's rooms in the tower. Instead, Gabriel had to carry his tools and implements down to this windy courtyard. He finished the star and stood up to look it over and consider the ancients whose works this was based on.

Acreties had said "it should have one point longer as a stylized goat's head" but Pompilius had said "it should be *exactly even* to better reflect Plato's perfect forms." Gabriel had gone with Plato instead of the goat, in deference to church sensibilities. He personally didn't think it mattered, since both Acreties and Pompilius claimed to have raised demons of knowledge, or familiar spirits.

Not that Gabriel was convinced it would work anyway. He was an alchemist and scholar, not a wizard. Besides, church or no church, he had quietly done a few experiments over the years and nothing worked. He had the claims of the ancients and a collection of old wives' tales, but no worthwhile results.

Gabriel wanted it to work. He wanted the world to have mysteries and magic that he could learn. But he no longer really believed it would.

He looked around the forty by sixty foot courtyard. There in the corner was Bertrand du Guesclin, "The Black Dog of Brocéliande." He was the king's man, the Constable of France, and perhaps the scariest man Gabriel had ever seen. Du Guesclin had long arms and was almost as broad as he was tall.

Gabriel suppressed a shudder and went back to his preparations. There were a set of five spirals to draw in the spaces between the points of the star, two circles within the pentagram at the center of the star, and a lot more.

Three more hours of meticulous painting and the star of containment was complete.

Gabriel stood in his position in a circle a yard from one point of the star. While the observers clustered at a safe distance, he started the invocation.

The Nether Reaches
No time applicable

Pucorlshrigin gnawed on a mammoth bone while contemplating the lines. Magic lines that flowed through the aether in ribbons of fire, air, water, and earth, carrying information. Pucorlshrigin's form was wrong to human eyes, and not subtly wrong. It was like something Escher would have drawn while on LSD. The body shifted from grossly fat to emaciated and back again as Pucorlshrigin bit and chewed. Pucorlshrigin was as large as a brontosaurus and as small as a gnat, all at the same time, because physical structure was a function of concentration. And Pucorlshrigin was concerned, distracted, all aflutter over what was happening in the netherworld that was his home.

There was a great disturbance in the planes. Demons and dragons, monsters of all sorts, were disappearing. The demon lords were in an uproar as balances of power that had lasted longer than suns were thrown out of whack.

Pucorlshrigin nibbled again in the same spot that he had nibbled, with only occasional breaks, for the last eleven thousand years. As Pucorlshrigin chewed, the shard of flesh he had just consumed was reformed.

Pucorlshrigin checked another line of information and took another bite. The lines were, in this realm, almost physical. They weren't data in the way a human might perceive, but feelings—a spiderweb of distortions. Pucorlshrigin hadn't made significant progress in consuming the bone, for both Pucorlshrigin and the bone were immaterial and, in this place, eternal.

Pucorlshrigin felt the pull of an invocation and immediately started looking for loopholes. Pucorlshrigin was a puck, an imp in the pattern of Robin Goodfellow. It was his nature to seek

9

loopholes. This was not the first time he had been called to the mortal world, but there was something different about this call. The call was both more clear and more powerful, as though the separation between the netherworld and the mortal world had been ripped away.

There! A big fat loophole.

The invoker had failed to put a vessel in the pentagram. Before, that failure would have been enough to prevent the invocation from working at all. Now, though Pucorlshrigin was still being called, the option of vessel was left to Pucorlshrigin. There were only moments to act as Pucorlshrigin was pulled into time and across the possibilities of past and future.

There was another good thing. This was a general call, not a call by name. No one, not even Pucorlshrigin, knew Pucorlshrigin's complete descriptor. "Pucorlshrigin" was only an approximation. But the more precise the approximation, the greater the power of the call. And this call was so general that Pucorlshrigin should have been able to ignore it altogether.

But couldn't.

Pucorlshrigin was being pulled into the mortal realms. Pucorlshrigin didn't have a great grasp of geography but knew the direction of pull. Pucorlshrigin considered a mammoth as the vessel, but eleven thousand years of chewing on something that tastes like very, very old, very, very dry chicken left the idea of mammoths unappealing.

Pucorlshrigin looked for something else to reside in. If required to act as a familiar spirit, Pucorlshrigin wanted something more comfortable than a cat. A ring or a diamond brooch would be comfortable, if limited. Maybe a statue, though they took great will to animate.

Pucorlshrigin looked closer in time to the call and spotted something, something he had never imagined. And the something was close, no more than a thousand years of possibilities away from the pentagram, though it was moving away in probability even as Pucorlshrigin passed. The something had no vita as such, no personality to contend with or be constrained by. But it was capable of motion under its own power. It had sight, of a sort, and hearing. It consumed fuel and even had something that was sort of like a mind. A small but active, very quick mind.

In passing, Pucorlshrigin noted that the something was physically large, although not as large as the mammoth Pucorlshrigin had been gnawing on. But Pucorlshrigin didn't examine it closely. There wasn't time. It was in the right physical location. It would do.

Pucorlshrigin occupied it, and became it, as he passed through its time and possibility. Still drawn to the pentagram, Pucorlshrigin took its new body, the van.

Pucorlshrigin was in the computer control network of the van when he realized that the vehicle was already owned.

This was disaster!

There were rules left over from the Creation. One of them required that the owner of the vessel had the right to command the demon occupying the vessel. Surely the owner was left behind in that other place, in that possible future.

Pucorlshrigin looked out its cameras and cringed in his new body. The owner was inside it! Pucorlshrigin could see her through the dash cam. She was sitting right there in the automatically adjustable driver's seat.

The van that was now Pucorlshrigin's body also had several other mortals belted in.

Paris Street, about six and a half centuries later

Mrs. Amelia Grady glanced at the vid screen on the dash, and through it, at the students in the van. There were eight students and her son, Paul, who was playing with his video game.

Amelia looked back up as a sports car made a right turn in front of her. She slammed on the brakes.

Suddenly, the world changed.

There was a wall in front of her and a man between her and the wall.

She pushed harder on the brake pedal and jerked the wheel over, pointing the van away from the man. The man jumped back, avoiding becoming roadkill by millimeters. The van skidded, but stopped before it hit the stone wall that surrounded the courtyard.

What the hell is going on?

She looked back at the kids. They were her first priority. They were all belted in, but the sudden shift had pulled them all out of their self-absorption.

Lakshmi Rawal looked out the windows and screamed. All the kids were looking frightened, and Lakshmi's scream set off a round of panicked demands that were too disjointed to follow.

"Quiet!" yelled Amelia, and that brought a moment of silence. "The van is stopped," Amelia continued as calmly as she could manage. She couldn't panic. She had the kids to look after. "We didn't run over anyone and we will figure out what happened and go home. In the meantime, I need you all to keep calm and not go into hysterics."

****

Wilber Hyde-Davis III was reading a synopsis of *Tamer the Lame*, the new play they were going to see. He had his hearing aid turned down, so didn't know anything was wrong till the braking and swerving almost pulled him from his seat. It would have if he hadn't been belted in. He looked up, and in a move that had long since become reflex, reached behind his ear to turn up the external unit for his cochlear implant. He got it turned up just in time to hear Mrs. Grady shout "Quiet!"

Paul, Mrs. Grady's eight-year-old, was looking shocked and frightened. He pointed out the window.

Wilber's eyes followed the finger and saw a bunch of people dressed in clothes from the Middle Ages. The men were wearing swords and armor. At least, some of them were. There was a priest, no, a bishop. He was wearing a miter. There were other men wearing scholarly robes. The man who caught Wilber's eye was short, but no shorter than the rest of them. What made him seem shorter was how wide he was. He was wearing chainmail armor, but no helmet. He had short brown hair and a face that looked like the unfortunate love child of Peter Lorre and Mussolini. In spite of which, there was a presence to that face.

The short man spoke in what was almost French, and some of the soldiers cautiously approached the van.

The van spoke in the same not quite French, sharply, in a voice that shifted register and tonality like an orchestra tuning up.

"What did you say?" Mrs. Grady asked.

The van answered on its internal speakers. "I told them to stay back. They have no right to touch me."

"The automated system on this heap couldn't do that," Annabelle Cooper-Smith declared. Annabelle had taken apart her father's Ferrari when she was fourteen. She had done it under the tutelage of her father's mechanic, and they had put it back together a little better than new. She knew cars, trucks, anything with an engine. She was also, at her own insistence, the main mechanic for the "Heap," as she called it.

Wilber's hyphenated last name derived from English upper-class tradition, mostly due to concerns over inheritance. His family was very wealthy and belonged to the idle rich—which explained his presence in the student body of the American School in Paris. After his parents got divorced, three years earlier, Wilber's mother had relocated from London to Paris simply because she liked the capital of France more than she did the capital of her own native land.

Annabelle's hyphenated last name, on the other hand, derived from her mother's feminist attitudes. She was as American as the proverbial apple pie, and if her family was even richer than Wilber's she made up for it by a well-nigh fanatical devotion to all things automotive.

All of the teenagers in the van were students at the American School in Paris, and all of them came from families which were at least very well-to-do—which was pretty much a prerequisite for sending their children to the ASP. The private school charged a small fortune in the way of tuition and tended to view the term "scholarship" as a synonym for "hen's teeth."

Five of the eight students were American, one was English, one was French and one was from India. That was a fairly accurate reflection of the composition of the ASP's student body.

Their teacher, Amelia Grady, was also American. But she came from a modestly middle-class family in Indiana—AKA "flyover country" to the sort of people who sent their kids to the school she taught in. She'd wound up in Paris due to the vagaries and complexities of her husband's job prospects, and she landed herself a position as the ASP's drama teacher due to her possession of several advanced degrees including a Master of Fine Arts. She'd chosen to do so less for the salary than for the benefit that her son Paul could attend the school without she and her husband having to pay the exorbitant tuition.

The van made a noise that sounded remarkably like a sniff of disdain. Somehow, it was getting more verbal subtlety out of the speakers than Annabelle would have thought possible.

Mrs. Grady went into teacher mode. "Well?"

With a clear pout in its tone, the van answered. "I can now!"

"Why can you now?" Mrs. Grady knew when a kid was misbehaving.

"I have been occupied by a... spirit of sorts," the van admitted.

"Cool!" said Paul, which pretty much summed up Wilber's reaction as well. "What's your name?"

"I'm not required to answer that!" the van said quickly, then spoke again using its outside speakers in that not quite French that was just a bit too weird for Wilber to understand. It was archaic, he could tell that much.

Paul said, "We have to call you something."

There was a moment's hesitation. Then: "You can call me Pucorl. That'll do."

That'll do for what—or for how long? Annabelle wondered.

"What are they saying out there?" Mrs. Grady asked.

14

"They are wondering what to do since their summoning spell didn't work the way they wanted. They are pretty irate and very frightened."

"Well, tell them who we are and what happened. Try to calm them down."

****

Pucorlshrigin was very much in a state of shock from the strength of the call. Pucorlshrigin was more "in" the mortal realm than he had ever been before, and from a call that was so imprecise that it should not have worked at all. So he was reacting on instinct and his instinct was to be a puck, a perverse but sometimes friendly imp who might do a mortal's work or lose the mortal in the woods. That was what had brought about the use of "Pucorl" as his name. The less of your name others knew, the more freedom you had and the less risk you took. The rest had poured out while Pucorlshrigin was trying to figure out why the call had worked. Now he was ordered by the owner of his new vessel to explain and calm. Well, he would, since he had no choice. But he would do it as a puck.

****

Suddenly the monster with the people inside, in tones of such horrible anguish that Gabriel could not help but shudder, wailed "I am not a monster! I am a van!" Then, in a calmer voice, it explained. "A van is a type of powered cart or wagon that will be built in one of the many possible futures of this world. One that is now increasingly unlikely. The people inside me are not monsters either. They are ordinary people, though of good families. Specifically, they are a school group, eight students and their teacher, with her son."

Bertrand du Guesclin, the Constable of France, shouted "Hold!" The guards, all the guards, stopped their approach. Then he looked at the van and laughed out loud. "I find a demon with a sense of humor interesting."

Gabriel looked at the Constable of France in confusion, trying to figure out how du Guesclin could think the thing had a sense

15

of humor. He ran over what the van had said and how it said it. The pathos of that first wailed complaint, followed by the calm and smooth delivery of the rest . . . and suddenly he had it. That first phrase was an act, a performance, and overdone, like the dialog from a play. He looked back at the king's first adviser, a man who all reports agreed was illiterate, and wondered how he could have been the first to see it.

The van went on to describe the school group in detail. "Four girls, four boys, all in their teens. A younger boy and his mother, and—"

The provost of the university interrupted. "But what are you doing here?"

"I don't answer to you." The voice stopped for a moment, then continued. "It was Doctor Delaflote who summoned me."

****

The provost was looking daggers at Gabriel Delaflote, so he said, "Answer the question."

"You botched the spell to summon me."

"What did I get wrong?"

There was a longish pause, then the van said, "There are things I may not tell you. Rules laid down by the creator of heaven and earth, rules that even the fallen must abide by. I can say that you left out crucial parts of the spell, for it is clear that you were working from fragments."

Gabriel got the distinct impression that there was something not quite right about the demon's explanation, but he didn't know what. What was clear was that the specifics of the missing piece of the spell were not going to be immediately forthcoming.

Commissaire Pierre Dubois interrupted before he could ask for an explanation. "Do you know who or what is committing these murders?"

"No, but you are correct that the murderer is not human."

"Can you help us solve the murders?" the commissaire asked, sounding a little desperate to Gabriel.

"Perhaps," the van said. "In the possibility that the van and the class comes from, they know a great deal more about solving crimes than you do. In fact, they know a great deal more about most things than you do."

Gabriel wondered what the van meant by saying the van came from a "possibility," but that question was wiped from his mind as the tone registered. The van's tone of condescension was shocking, especially when addressed to a commissaire. Gabriel managed to hide his smirk, but the commissaire surprised him.

"I hope they do, demon van. I truly hope they do."

"I'm not a demon, just a... spirit of sorts," Pucorlshrigin insisted. "Who ever heard of a demon with such a short name as mine? I'm a... well, it's true I usually live in the demonic universe. But I'm not one of *them*."

He had to be careful here. What humans understood by the term *demon* was quite different from what demons themselves thought of the matter. So he wasn't exactly lying, because by the human concept of "demon" he really wasn't one. He was just an innocent puck trying to make his way in a cruel and indifferent universe—several universes, actually—not the sort of slavering monster that humans had in mind when they thought of a demon.

****

The van had been providing the students, at Mrs. Grady's request, a running translation of its discussion with the locals. It explained its cooperation as an apology of sorts. "I didn't know the van was loaded." The van snickered and so did Paul, then the van continued. "And there wasn't time to check. I needed a home, a vessel, right then. It's not your fault you got dragged along."

"Well, take us back," said Jennifer Fairbanks, more than a little desperately.

"I'm sorry. I can't do that," Pucorl said. "I was summoned by Doctor Gabriel Delaflote in order to aid in the investigation of a series of gruesome murders that they believe are the work of a demon. I can't leave until that is done."

****

From the moment Pucorl realized that the van had an owner

and that the owner was present, he started blending truth with lies to hide one overwhelming fact. He was under the control of whoever owned his vessel.

Amelia Grady owned his vessel.

He could not lie to her, but he could lie to anyone else who asked him a question. He could lie in her presence, even, and so give her false answers. He could give her true but misleading answers as long as they actually did answer her question. What he couldn't do—literally could not, because he was built that way—was disobey a direct order or tell her a direct lie.

His only hope of handling the situation was to leave her under the impression that he was being just as cooperative as he could, so that she didn't give him direct orders. That way, when she told him to do something and he did it, it would just seem that he was being cooperative. It wasn't a good solution, and he wasn't all that sure he could keep it up for long enough to do him much good, but he felt he had to try.

So he did what Amelia asked and explained to others that he was restricted by the summoning spell. Which he wasn't, not since the pentagram had been burst asunder in the moment of their arrival.

Besides, it was a fun game and he really liked the van. Normally, if summoned, he would be either very limited by the inanimate nature of the container or in a constant struggle with the personality of the animal he was housed in. It was no fun to have your host's instincts having you jump for a rat or a squirrel.

He worked on his balancing act all the rest of the day while quarters for the guests of the university were found and while the commissaire briefed them on the murders and was told, in turn, about forensic science. It helped Pucorl that twenty-first century French was quite different from the language of Paris in this time. What would eventually become French was passing from what scholars of a later time would call Old French. In the northern region where Paris was located, the dialect in current use was known as the *Langue d'oïl*.

CHAPTER 2

Office of the Provost
February 9, 1372

Bertrand du Guesclin walked to the chair of the provost of the university of Paris and sat. He had sent a runner to inform the king of what had happened and, for the moment at least, had left instructions that the "guests" should be treated with respect.

The parties involved were babbling like chickens. The church, in the person of Bishop de Sarcenas, was busy demanding that they be burned at the stake. And there was a part of Bertrand that wanted to let him do just that. But Bertrand hadn't let fear rule him since he was six, and he wasn't going to start now. He looked around the room then said, "No!"

He didn't shout, not exactly, but Bertrand was used to making himself heard in the middle of a battle. The babble quieted, and he continued. "Did you see the structure of that thing? The front glass? Better than the best glass I have ever seen. The metal, the wheels, the black around the rims, the . . ." He waved a hand. "The whole of it. Any part of that device must be considered the work of a master, if not a miracle. And the whole, taken together, is beyond impossible. The people in the—" Bertrand stopped, trying to recall the word that demon had used to describe the conveyance. *Ah, yes.* "—the van were ordinary people, if extraordinarily comely. For now, until I have contrary evidence, I will believe this Pucorl in the van about what it is and where its form came from. That makes the people both innocent and potentially exceedingly valuable." He looked at Bishop de Sarcenas until the man wilted. It didn't take long.

Then he turned to the alchemist. What was his name? *Gabriel Delaflote.* "Doctor Delaflote, you go have a talk with the van and find out what you can. Commissaire Dubois, I know this is about your murders, but for the moment you're going to have to be patient. No extreme measures until the king or I tell you different. These people and the van are to be treated as gently as new babes."

He looked around the room again, and seeing he had basic understanding among them, stood. "I need to go have a talk with the king."

He also needed to get a message to his wife. Tiphaine was much better educated than he was. She understood astrology and divination, even.

The Stranger's Rooms
Three hours later

"What's going on?" Liane Boucher asked. "This makes no sense."

Paul rolled his eyes and Annabelle wanted to do the same. Not that Liane didn't have a point. Because this did make no sense at all. Demons were not real. They didn't pick up vans from the twenty-first century and dump them in the fourteenth. They didn't chat about demonic politics and translate between *Langue d'oïl* and twenty-first-century French and English.

Besides, if such a thing were to happen, the locals wouldn't politely offer the occupants of the van rooms, food, and make oath before God to protect them from harm.

The primitives from the middle ages—okay, the late middle ages, but still the middle ages—wouldn't show them to what was, for the time, a very nice hall. Apparently a dormitory. It had a dozen cots with bags of hay for mattresses, and windows that were shuttered against the cold, wet weather. She looked around the hall, at the woolen tapestries that hung on the walls, protecting the room from the cold stone behind. She looked at the carpets that were on the stone floor for the same purpose. The arched ceiling and the large fireplace in the north wall that held a warm fire. The lamps on the walls that provided a little light.

Annabelle found herself thankful that it had been a cold, wet day in December when this happened to them. At least everyone had a warm coat. The bread was dense and grainy, the soup was cabbage, with the bare acquaintance of a goat.

And the place stank mildly of chamber pots. The odor wasn't overwhelming, but it was there in the background.

Still, for all of that, her history classes told her that these were good quarters. What a group of noble students would expect, not what a bunch of peasants would see. And certainly not what a bunch of witches disgorged by a demon should expect.

Liane was right. It didn't make sense. None of it made sense.

But Paul was right too, because Liane had been saying that every five minutes since they arrived. Her repetition of the obvious was getting more than a bit old.

Liane, although French, wasn't having any more luck being understood than the American students were. Jennifer was spending most of her time crying. Roger was marching back and forth near the door, fists clenching and unclenching as he moved. Lakshmi was just sitting on her cot, not eating, not looking around. Just sitting there, as though she couldn't process what had happened.

Annabelle looked at Mrs. Grady and fumed. She needed to be out in the courtyard, talking to the demon and figuring out how it was working with the van. But Mrs. Grady insisted they all stay together "for safety." Like they were any safer here than in the courtyard. Besides, so far the guards had been polite.

Wilber had turned off his hearing aid. He had a cochlear implant and only limited batteries for the external unit. He was lying on his cot, looking at the ceiling and not saying anything. Didn't Mrs. Grady understand they were under a time limit? All their electronics were going to run down and the van was going to run out of gas. They needed to figure stuff out now, not wait till these middle ages gangsters got around to them.

Bill had dug into his backpack and pulled a pair of red plastic dice out of it. He was now trying to interest the guards in a game of craps. But at least he was doing something. Jeff was just lying on his cot, asleep. He probably didn't understand what was going on, but not understanding what was going on was not unusual for Jeff, so he was less bothered by it than the others.

Annabelle got up. She would try again to talk some sense into Mrs. Grady. Annabelle knew she wasn't being fair, but she was scared. Honestly, scared half out of her mind, and she needed to be doing something before she came apart at the seams.

"Okay, Annabelle," Mrs. Grady said before she even got there. "If you can make the guards understand and it's okay with them, it's okay with me. But I want you back here before dark."

Annabelle headed for the door to the courtyard.

Courtyard

Pucorl felt.

He had form. He had shape and substance through his vessel.

He didn't know how his new form worked. He didn't know, not clearly, that he was thinking with electrical fields and current flows. A microprocessor is small, but not nearly so small as a neuron. And there aren't nearly so many neurons on a chip as there are in even a mouse's brain. The van didn't have a twenty-first century supercomputer.

On the other hand, a demon is still a demon. It can function even if it's placed in a pewter statue of a mouse. The van was a whole lot better and more functional than a statue. Pucorl was using the "brain" of the van to help his thinking, and that brain gave his thoughts a clarity and an edge of precision that he never could have managed without it. Besides, a demon like Pucorl was strongly influenced by the form he occupied and the form he was in was a twenty-first-century van that informed Pucorl's understanding of the world and his vocabulary.

The van's electronic functions were designed to be voice-activated. The driver could make calls or activate the cameras by voice. The magic infused the speaker as well as the speech centers, software, and firmware on his chips. Pucorl could talk with a facility and control that even a supercomputer couldn't match, because part of what was happening was magic.

The same was true of the fly-by-wire circuitry that would have let the van parallel park on its own on a Paris street before Pucorl had joined with it. Now that circuitry, in combination with Pucorl's demon nature, meant that the van could drive itself.

If there was anywhere to drive.

He was still stuck in the courtyard and the locals weren't in any hurry to take down the walls and let him out. So, for now, all he could do was talk.

He had spent the last several hours talking to Gabriel Delaflote about the nature of magic, and was finding it rather difficult to keep his story straight. The truth was that Pucorl was not a demon lord. He wasn't one of the beings that the ancients had called gods. He was an imp and a trickster, a clerk of sorts, a very minor figure in the demonic power structure.

This vessel helped a lot, but he didn't understand how it helped. Part of that was because no one had yet asked him the right questions.

Pucorl was of a class of demons who were designed to serve as sources of information. Asking them a question let them find the answer, if the answer was within their range. If someone would ask him how the van affected him, he would know. But he wouldn't until he was asked.

Though Pucorl didn't realize it, that was why he had spent eleven thousand years chewing on the same spot on the same mammoth bone. No one had asked him why that spot or suggested another. Without that external stimulus, Pucorl hadn't thought to change what he was doing or how.

He welcomed the arrival of Annabelle Cooper-Smith with considerable relief. That relief was turned into out-and-out joy when the first question she asked was, "How are your batteries?"

In that instant, Pucorl understood that he had two batteries. One was located in his engine compartment, the other, center body, left side. And while they were interconnected and one could back up the other, they performed different functions. The one in his engine compartment ran the starter motor, the external lights, the external speakers that he used when someone pushed the horn button, the external cameras, the windshield wipers, and so on. The other operated the internal cameras, the GPS, the entertainment center, and his radio and phone.

He knew as well that both were gradually losing charge, and because he was a demon he knew how to charge the batteries. Until that moment it hadn't occurred to him that they might need charging. A moment's thought and the use of a tiny fraction of his essence, and the batteries were fully charged.

"My batteries are fully charged and will stay charged," Pucorl said smugly.

"Cool. What about gas? Diesel, that is."

And again the question brought the answer. The answer was partly Annabelle's knowledge of how his vessel was supposed to work and partly the readings that told him. What he knew was that he had seven gallons of diesel and he couldn't fill the tank from his essence. He couldn't will it filled. He would never, as long as he occupied the vessel, run out of power. But he would run out of fuel, and once that happened he wouldn't be able to move. He knew better than the sensor how much fuel he had because, like the circuitry, the sensor's function was augmented by his magic. He knew to the milliliter how much fuel he had.

"I only have a quarter tank," he said. "And I can't make more."

"Why can you make electricity and not diesel?" Annabelle asked, and the question brought the answer, if not understanding of the answer.

"If I were in a jewel, the jewel would glow with my presence as long as I was in the jewel. But if I were in a cat, the cat would still need to be fed."

"What does that mean?" Annabelle asked.

24

"Diesel is my food."

"I got that part," Annabelle said. "It was the part about making the jewel glow—" She stopped speaking for a moment, then continued. "Not even that. It's that if you can do the one, you ought to be able to do the other. There are electric cars, after all."

"I don't truly understand myself," Pucorl half admitted, half lied. Her question had given him a part of the answer. It is in the nature of a jewel to shine. Pucorl could expand that nature. But it is not in the nature of a cat to live without food. He could make the jewel shine even when there was no light to reflect, but he couldn't make the cat live without food. It had to do with the inherent nature of things. A battery was part of a piece of electronic equipment. It was meant to be charged and provide power. An engine took fuel and used it up.

Annabelle went to the back of the van and grabbed the back door handles.

"Hey," said Pucorl, "watch the hands."

"You can feel that?"

"Of course," Pucorl said. He hadn't actually objected when her hand touched his door handle, but wanted to make the point that he was the van now. It wasn't some inanimate object.

"How?"

"What do you mean, how? How do you know when someone touches you?"

"I have nerves."

"That's a good point. I hadn't thought about it." Pucorl did think about it. When he was called, he occupied whatever vessel was available, and he had to adapt to that vessel. If he was called to a living creature, he integrated with it, taking on its physical characteristics, gender, and to an extent its personality. If he was called to a statue, he took on its form, not that he was the sort of powerful demon who could actually animate a statue. All he could do was talk through its mouth. But now, in the van, it was like both things were happening at once.

"Well?" Annabelle asked.

Pucorl tried to decide how much to tell her. "I don't know," he said. "But I can feel your hand on my door handle."

Annabelle shrugged, and opened the door. She lifted the floor panel to expose the storage area.

Pucorl felt that too.

She pulled out the scanner. Pucorl felt it being removed, like you might feel a glove removed or keys come out of your pocket. He looked at it with his camera. It was a yellow plastic device with a liquid crystal display and buttons. It also had a plug that fit under the dash to let it interface with the van's onboard diagnostics.

"What are you planning to do with that?" Pucorl asked.

"I'm planning to check your systems."

Pucorl locked his doors. "I'm not that kind of van!" Then he laughed and unlocked them, and noted that Annabelle was grinning at him.

Royal Palace, Hôtel Saint-Pol

Even here in the king's private chambers, Bertrand bowed deeply as he entered. The king was fifteen years his junior, and Bertrand had known him since the king was a lad and Bertrand was a hotheaded young fool. But Charles V of France was his liege lord, much smarter than Bertrand, and a better lord than Bertrand or France deserved.

"Oh, stop that," King Charles said, and waved him to a chair. The room was as much a library as an office, with oak bookshelves inlaid with gold and silver and actual bound books. The new palace, the Hôtel Saint-Pol, was barely a decade old. Charles V had dedicated a lot of money and effort into making it luxurious as well as functional.

"Would you truly want me to, Sire?" Bertrand asked, moving to the chair.

"No, probably not," the king admitted, "but it does get tiresome sometimes. Tell me of the summoning. Did it actually work?"

"In a manner of speaking, Sire. Though not in the manner Delaflote expected. On the other hand, I think the way it worked out might be better for us than if he had gotten the imp in the form of a bird or a cat that he was expecting. What we got was a cart full of people from the future. A future where they can make sheets of glass as long as a man is tall, and as clear as a summer's day. Where they can make carts out of steel. Carts that can move themselves without the need of horses or oxen to draw them. I spoke a little to the demon and to the teacher before leaving orders and coming here. I think the people in the van will be of . . ."

"You left out what happened, Bertrand," the king interrupted. "Now, go back to the beginning and tell me what happened."

Bertrand did. It took a while. While he was talking, other members of the king's privy council came in and interrupted. Then things had to be repeated.

They talked through the night and came only to tentative conclusions. First, they would, for now, leave the strangers and their demon to work with the commissaire of police to investigate the murders, but they would be watched with care.

"Duke Philip is in Burgundy at the moment, but his spies will tell him about this within days. He will return to Paris, looking for an advantage. So will my other brothers," King Charles said.

"We can't afford open war with your brothers, Your Majesty," Bertrand said. "Not when we're in the middle of the war with England."

Nicolas du Bosc asked, "You said they were from the future. Doesn't that mean they know our present as their past?"

"I would assume so," Bertrand said.

"I think, Your Majesty, I should go and have a chat with these people and see what their histories say of your brothers."

King Charles nodded. "You do that, Nicolas. But also ask them if they record the presence of a van filled with people from the future. It would seem to me that they would have read of such a thing had it happened."

Bertrand tried not to let his confusion show. He followed what the king was saying well enough. It was the back and forth of *they must know* and *they can't know, because if they knew, they would have avoided that spot on that day*, and on and on, back and forth, that caused his confusion.

An Inn in Paris

Duke Philip sipped wine as Robert Fabre watched cautiously. You had to be careful when delivering bad news to Philip the Bold. What Robert didn't know was whether Duke Philip would consider this bad news.

"So they raised a demon, did they?" Duke Philip said. "My brother needs to learn to control his *petite gens* better." But there was a smile on the duke's face. "Contact Cardinal de Dormans. We are going to point out to the church that my brother is dealing with demonic forces."

Robert Fabre nodded. He knew that Duke Philip had his own dealings with the mystical creatures that had started appearing a few weeks ago. That was why the duke was in Paris. He had been told by a *dame blanche* of the demon in Paris after dallying with her for a night. He came here to contact the demon lord and make a deal. Philip the Bold was convinced that he should be the king of France. He was his father's favorite, after all, and he was positive that his cautious bookkeeper brother who was on the throne of France at the moment would lead the kingdom to ruin by his parsimonious ways. Robert knew all this because he had been at the rites that invoked Duke Philip's creature.

"For that matter, send word to Pope Gregory in Avignon." Philip snorted a laugh. "I doubt Gregory can do more than Father Augustine could."

Robert hid a shudder.

Strangers' Quarters, University of Paris

February 10, 1372

Wilber turned up his mic to listen to Bill Howe as he described what he had seen in the Rue Paul.

"I took one look at the alley and knew we weren't going to find much. The city guard—they call it the Grand Châtelet—are doing their best, but they don't know crap about preserving crime scenes. Someone had hosed down the place. Well, bucketed down the place, these people not having hoses, any more than they have fingerprint kits. But the alley was probably cleaner than it had been in the last ten years and there was an old woman going over the walls with a rag soaked in lye soap.

"I told them that the first rule of crime scene investigation is to preserve the crime scene, but I'm not sure how much of it they got. I said it in French, but got nothing back except blank looks. So I pulled out my slate computer and finger wrote it. That got me some warding signs, but that assistant to the commissaire looked at it and seemed to get it." Bill shrugged. "Maybe. He wrote something on a wall with chalk. Wouldn't touch my computer. The note read 'You think we should just wait for the next murder?'

"I shrugged and wrote back that we weren't even here when that murder happened. Then he brought me back here. I don't know . . . maybe if we can talk to that alchemist guy, he can fix us up with fingerprint powder. Maybe even PH test strips."

Bill had volunteered for this because his dad was a lawyer, a high-end criminal attorney. Bill knew more about evidence than anyone in their group, with the possible exception of eight-year-old Paul, whose dad was a French police inspector. But there was no way that Mrs. Grady was letting her eight-year-old go visit a bloody crime scene.

Wilber turned his implant back down when Bill was finished. They had to solve the murders to get back. That was the only reason Mrs. Grady let Bill go.

The Grand Châtelet

The man who six centuries later would have been known as a cop or police officer bowed to the commissaire as he entered the office.

Pierre lifted an eyebrow. "Well, Jacques, what was it like working with a demon-brought stranger?"

"He's a youngster, Commissaire, and I don't doubt the claim that they are of good families. I would guess that one's papa is a baron, at least. The problem was the language. I couldn't understand a quarter of what he said, even when he wrote it out on that magic pad of his."

"According to the imp of knowledge, it's not a magic pad, but a tool. More complicated than pen and paper, but not different in kind." Pierre stood and walked across his office to a small table that held a jar of wine. He lifted the jar and Jacques licked his lips, but shook his head. Pierre turned back to the table and poured himself wine.

"If you believe the demon in the cart," said Jacques. In his tone of voice, Pierre heard doubt and distrust to match his own. "The 'van,' as they call it."

"We must teach them proper French as quickly as we can," Pierre said, turning back with wine in hand. "We need to be able to check the claims of the haunted van."

"Weeks at the least, Commissaire, and I don't think we have weeks before the monster strikes again."

CHAPTER 3

Courtyard
February 10, 1372

Wilber sat on the stone bench and used his phone to send Annabelle a text. Their phones were synced just like they were before the demon kidnapped them. He wasn't sure how much the demon haunting the van could hear, but he didn't think Pucorl would be able to intercept a text between his phone and Annabelle's. He wasn't entirely sure of that, so what he texted was "*I think he's a Joanie.*" Joanie was a girl at the school who was a pathological liar. She lied even when the truth would keep her out of trouble.

Part of his feeling was just because Wilber was good at interpreting phrasing and catching inconsistencies. Part of it was the fact that he was thinking of the demon as a demon, even if it had tried to claim it wasn't. Demons were fallen angels, angels who had followed the devil into darkness in defiance of God. Wilber didn't believe in God. At least, he hadn't three days ago in the twenty-first century. Now he wasn't so sure.

Annabelle texted back. *"Puc???"*

Wilber sent *"T"* for true.

"?"

That was harder to explain. Partly it was some of the stuff that the French doctor guy had said. It had been in *Langue d'oïl* and hard to follow, but everything had been hard to follow for Wilber his whole life. He had a cochlear implant, which helped, and he had years of practice guessing meaning from partial information, expression, lip reading, and body language. The doctor guy had been confused, and it wasn't just that the van arrived instead of a cat or whatever he was expecting.

"Don't know. Something off."

"You know," Annabelle said aloud, "I've never worked on a car that could tell me what it wanted before. I mean like, does it want a new video system or does it want its shocks adjusted."

"What do you think it wants?" Wilber asked, confused by the sudden change. He looked at Annabelle and her posture was careful. This was a ploy of some sort, he was almost sure of it.

Annabelle shrugged. "What do you want, van?"

****

That was a very interesting question, and not one that Pucorl was expecting. Pucorl had been asked all manner of questions when it had been summoned in the past, but not that one. Every time he had been called upon by a mortal, the assumption had always been that what he wanted was to be released so that he could rampage here in the mortal realm or return to the netherworld, whether the summoner thought of the netherworld as hel, hell, hades, underhill, the dream time, yomi, diyu, bashnobe, or any of the myriad of other spirit realms.

Pucorl had never considered the possibility of upgrades. Upgrades were a greater advantage to a being of his sort than they would be for a mortal. For demonkind, character followed function. A demon placed in a sword could make the sword strike true or, if placed as a curse, make the sword slip at the crucial moment. A demon put in a horn could make that horn play rousing or terrifying music, but couldn't make it into a sword that would cut. Likewise, a demon placed in a cat would be fairly independent, while one placed in a dog would tend to be loyal. Pucorl had spent six millennia as a stone ax before recorded history. It had been incredibly boring.

While Pucorl was considering the new thought of upgrades, Annabelle was apparently doing the same, because she said, "Even when they open up the wall to let you out, you're too big for a lot of Paris streets. And if we leave Paris, there aren't any good roads."

"The van is four-wheel drive," Wilber said.

"That'll help," Annabelle said, "but not enough. I'm afraid Pucorl here is going to be limited to really good roads unless we can make some upgrades."

Suddenly Pucorl felt his glorious new body was inadequate. "A cat or a dog can lift its feet," he complained. "Why can't I?"

"Because in spite of the fact that you have four-wheel drive, you weren't really designed for off road. In the future, there will be good roads all over the place. The best roads around here are narrow dirt paths by our home's standards."

Pucorl could hear the pain in Annabelle's voice, even though she was trying to hide it. He felt bad about that. The function of this van was to take its passengers where they wanted to go in comfort, and Annabelle clearly wanted to go home. He almost blurted out that he was sorry he couldn't take them home, but he held his speaker.

Pucorl didn't trust mortals. Of course, he mostly didn't trust immortals either. Keeping as much back as he was allowed was a habit after all this time. Instead he asked, "Could you upgrade my suspension?"

"Maybe," Annabelle said, even as Wilber was shaking his head. The boy stopped shaking his head and looked at the girl as she continued. "It depends on how your connection with the physical van works. If I knew that I might be able to figure out a way to protect your tires, or even let you lift your wheels."

Pucorl was suspicious, but he knew that Annabelle was the one who took care of the van. Vans don't have memory, but Pucorl was a demon, a creature of magic, and magic worked for him in ways he didn't understand. He remembered her hands on his engine, changing his oil, and greasing his differential. Yes, Annabelle took care of him. Who knew what she might be able to do? He told her how it worked. She and Wilber asked questions.

In the course of the conversation, the basic effect of enchanting an item or cursing an item—both of which were accomplished by summoning a demon into the item—were explained.

33

"Maybe," Wilber observed, "those tribal chieftains with the gold inlaid wooden keyboards and carved wooden shotguns with wooden bullets had a point. Or at least were acting on old stories that at some point in the past were accurate." He looked at Pucorl. "If we were to have made up an electric arc furnace and summoned a demon to occupy it, would it work to make good steel?"

"I'm not sure," Pucorl said. "I understand magic, but not electric arc furnaces. The power of similarity might apply, like it was a voodoo doll of an electric arc furnace. But that might just mean that chopping it up would make a real one break."

"This is going to take some experimentation," Annabelle said. "We will need to summon some demons to see what works. What do we need to do that?"

Pucorl forgot that he had said he wasn't allowed to say and told her how to do it. Gabriel Delaflote had gotten most of it right, but he hadn't known that the container needed to be placed in the center of the pentagram.

It was while they were discussing the minutiae of demon summoning that Bill arrived. "I'll offer up my iPod if you can find a demon who speaks *Langue d'oïl.*"

"Your phone would be better, especially if you want to be able to answer them," said Wilber.

"Maybe, but it won't work to call you guys without a cell tower," Bill insisted with all the certainty of the partially informed.

Wilber rolled his eyes. That wasn't true, but the problem was how to explain the technicalities of the various ways electronic devices communicated with each other to Bill without pissing him off.

Annabelle solved it. "It's LTE Direct protocol. All the phones and the van have it. It lets phones talk directly to each other using the same radio frequencies that cell towers have. The van, ah, Pucorl, has it as part of its onboard phone. They also have Bluetooth and Wifi for talking with other devices. That's how your phone can act as a mobile hotspot for your computer."

"So your phone will work to let you call us once we get it enchanted."

"Hey, wait a minute," Pucorl said. This was all going too fast. He wasn't used to dealing with people of the twenty-first century, who expected to be able to look anything up on the internet in an instant.

"If we are going to figure out a way of upgrading your suspension so that we can let you shift your wheels," Annabelle said, "we are going to have to do some experimenting. And if Bill is willing to sacrifice his iPod, I think it's a good idea."

"No, Pucorl is right," Wilber said. "We have forgotten something important."

"What?" Annabelle asked.

"What if the demons don't want to come?"

"What do you mean?"

"Well, did Pucorl want to be pulled here?"

"No," Pucorl said. "But I'm here now and I want my upgrades."

"So the spell you gave us will pull in a demon, willing or not?"

"Yes."

"Why should we care?" Bill asked.

"Look, I've been shoved into my locker too many times to want to be a party to doing it to someone else. Pucorl, is there a way that we can cast the spell so that only a demon who is willing will get called?"

Pucorl stopped and thought. There were, in fact, variations that did just that. But it was exceedingly rare that they would ever be used, save with a mortal who was trying to call a demon lord or a demigod. Either that, or it could be some hedge witch who didn't know the protections. "I have told you how to be the master of demons, and you would be a supplicant instead?"

"No. I just want a demon who will help us because it wants to, not because we are forcing it."

"It doesn't mean we can't have restrictions on it, so it doesn't go crazy," Annabelle said.

"Think about it, Bill. Do you want a demon in your iPod who is trying to escape all the time? Or one that wants to help?" Wilber waved his arms.

"Why would they want to help?" Bill asked. "No, I mean it. Pucorl, why would a demon willingly come and live in my iPod to help me listen to this freaking ancient-ass French?"

Pucorl considered continuing to argue that he wasn't really a demon, but decided that was probably a hopeless task. So he just addressed the question itself. "Because eternity is boring, and this is something to do. Also, your iPod is like the van?"

Bill reached into his shirt pocket and pulled out the small digital music player. It was a top of the line product, and though it didn't have as much memory or processing power as the array of chips in Pucorl, it had a lot. It also had games that would keep a demon occupied and entertained for centuries.

Pucorl examined it with his cameras and with magic. Yes, there were any number of demons who would be quite happy to move from the netherworld to live for a few centuries in the iPod and serve its owner. "If you put that in the pentagram as bait, you will catch a demon. And a willing one at that."

All of a sudden Pucorl was much more pleased with his situation. Yes, he had been dragged from his hole in the netherworld, but he was here now, with cameras and wheels and GPS. "Wait a minute. My GPS system isn't getting any signal."

"No satellites in the fourteenth century," Wilber said. "Nothing we can do about that. Not unless you can launch a satellite. What I want to know now is, can you talk to your demon friends and tell them what we are offering?"

Pucorl didn't say that he didn't have any demon friends. Demons were generally too busy looking out for themselves to have friends. But Wilber didn't need to know that. Instead Pucorl said, "If you put the iPod in the pentagram, they will know what it is and what it can do."

"I got that," Wilber said, standing up and starting to pace. "What I was asking was if you could talk to others like you back where you come from. If maybe you had a buddy or something who you might like to let know about this, so he can be in place when we light up the spell."

Pucorl thought about it, and realized that he really didn't have anyone like that. It made him rather sad.

"You do realize we are going to have to tell Delaflote about this," Annabelle said, smiling.

"Wait! This was just between us," Pucorl said.

"He's the one with the chicken blood and enchanted chalk."

"That's not important. Anything that will mark the ground will work. It's the patterns, not the—" Pucorl started, then stopped. That wasn't true, and it was better to be caught in a mistake than a lie. The patterns controlled the spell, but the spell did need enchantment. Holy water, blood, rosemary picked at the dark of the moon and ground into a paste in a stone mortar with an ashwood pestle. There were all sorts of substitutions, but you did need a certain class of materials, and what sort of magical creature you got depended on which materials you used. Pucorl was experienced as a demon of knowledge, and in his new body with its computer brain, he was able to access his knowledge in a clearer way than he was used to. "Oh, darn! You're right."

"Oh, darn?" Bill asked, incredulously. "A demon saying darn instead of damn?"

"You need to watch your language too, Bill Howe. For in the here and now, the words you use carry a weight and a power that is much greater than it ever was in your world. Tossing around unspecified curses like that could curse you or your companions. And if it carries a risk for you, how much more for me, who is a creature of the magic world, where the words are weapons as well as tools?"

"Okay, okay. What the he— Hildebrand. I'll watch my mouth. But can you call one of your buds to the iPod, and if you call one, do we still need the pentagram and all the curlicues?"

"Yes, you do," Pucorl said. "Calling a demon without wards is dangerous. Not all demons are friendly, and if you call one without wards it could decide that it would rather occupy you than the device. If that happened, you would have no control over it. None at all."

"Say, was anyone taking ancient mythology or anything like that as an elective?" Bill asked.

"I don't think so. We could ask Mrs. Grady," Wilber said.

Pucorl cringed. The brake lights flickered without Pucorl's conscious intent. Amelia Grady held the key, literally, to controlling him. He didn't want her to know that. And he had just let slip a big clue to how it worked. In the meantime, he called to an old acquaintance of his and pointed out the advantages of the iPod. After all, better a sort of friend than an out-and-out enemy.

The mortal realm was both infinitely far from and right next to the spirit realm. He was almost entirely in the mortal realm at the moment, but he still had a connection to his home. It was weak and tenuous, and he couldn't tell very much from it, but the connection was there. Part of the law of contagion, which stated that whenever two things touch they remain connected. Pucorl had been touching that bit of the netherworld since dinosaurs ruled the mortal realms, and because of that he was touching it now. But the distance was great, if the connection was well-worn. Which made it hard to whisper in a friend's ear without the neighbors hearing.

CHAPTER 4

The Moon
February 10, 1372

The Jade Rabbit didn't hear Pucorl's whisper. The China of the netherworld was a very long way away. The moon of the netherworld rides on a crystal sphere and is even farther.

The Jade Rabbit slipped from the netherworld and found himself on a rocky plane that had no air at all. That didn't bother the rabbit greatly. He was, after all, a companion of the Moon goddess Cheng'e and as such partook of divinity himself. He had very little need to breathe.

What did bother the Jade Rabbit was his size. The moon of the mortal realm was closer to the earth and much, much larger. The rabbit didn't have anything to measure by, but he doubted that he was more than sixty feet tall in this strange place.

The view was spectacular, though. And as far away as he was, the Jade Rabbit had little to fear from the great rent in the Earth's pattern of reality that he could see spreading across the blue globe. The center of the rift was in Central Asia, at the ancient city mortals called Balkh, which had once given its name to the region known as Bactria. Some terrible crime must have been committed there, because the Jade Rabbit could see even at this distance that an immensely powerful demon had surged out of the netherworld to possess the ruler of the Chagatay. Only a great blood sacrifice could have made that possible, even for such a mighty demon.

The Jade Rabbit didn't know the name of the city's ruler, nor did he care. The concerns of mortals meant little to him. So, after a time he hopped toward the far side of the Moon to find out what he might see from that vantage point.

But he tired of that before long. The hops possible to a sixty-foot-tall rabbit didn't allow him to make fast progress on a Moon grown so large. Eventually, he gave up and started looking for his mortar and pestle and the magical herbs from which he ground the elixir of eternal life. He wandered the moon of the mortal realm for a while longer, but didn't find them.

Perhaps he had left them on the netherworld's moon. The Jade Rabbit's memory was not really very reliable. So, he decided to return home.

On the way, he glanced one last time at the blue globe below him. The rift was spreading, he saw. One of its crevasses was speeding across Europe, branching as it went. An especially deep fissure was plunging into France.

But none of that was any concern of his. He needed to get back to his grinding before Cheng'e noticed his absence. His mistress was normally tranquil about such things, but she did occasionally get testy.

Burgos, Spain
February 11, 1372

Dip slipped from the netherworld into the mortal realms without so much as a ripple. It was a rainy night. There was thunder in the distance and Dip didn't like the rain. He told it to leave him alone, and in the netherworld that would usually work because the rain was afraid of him. But here, the rain fell, ignoring his will.

He growled, low in his throat, and moved to a door. It was closed, but he narrowed to two dimensions and slipped through the crack between door and frame. Returning to his normal state, his fur was still soaked with the mindless water of the mortal world. There was a puff of air as a shutter opened in the storm and the torches and lamps flickered with gusts of air. His paws left damp spots on the stone floor of the place, save for his left hind leg, which dragged, leaving a line.

He sniffed and wanted to howl. The green and living smell of this place offended him. But he kept going. He had been in Toledo a few days ago, and a bitter young Jew had been heaping curses on Henry of the house of Trastámara, who was the king of this part of Spain now.

There were hangings on the walls of the corridor, but Dip paid them no mind. He smelled the blood of many souls, and the aromas of sickness and hunger lightened his spirits. He moved silently through the castle halls.

Apparently, Henry was sucking the lifeblood of the Jews. Sucking the blood of mortals was Dip's job. He resented the usurpation of his role, so he had come here to set matters right. He wandered through the halls, fighting the offensive aromas of life with his own sweet aroma of rotting corpses. He sniffed and smelled royal blood. He could do that even here.

That way.

****

Henry II, first king of Castile and León, woke with a chill and saw a shaggy black dog with a single red eye in the middle of its forehead. The dog opened its mouth to show rotting teeth, save for two gleaming canines.

"You're a greedy bastard, you know that," the dog growled.

Henry, without conscious intent, pushed himself back in the bed, scooting over the linen sheets and the wool blanket. The room was dark, all but two of the candles out, but somehow the black dog was clear to Henry's eyes. "What are you?" Henry was on the edge of panic.

"Don't you know your legends, greedy child? I'm the Dip. 'Tis my function to suck the blood of mortals."

"Why are you here?" Henry barely got that out through his tightening throat.

"I resent it when mortals encroach on my realm. The Jews of Toledo seem to think that you are a bigger bloodsucker than I am."

Then the big black dog leaped, and that was all Henry knew.

41

****

The next morning, the guards found him with his throat ripped open and not a drop of blood in his body. The sheets were ripped and fouled with feces. The aroma of week-old corpses permeated the room.

Near Sarai Berke, capital of the Golden Horde
North of the Caspian Sea
February 11, 1372

The likho slouched toward the city, anticipating the feast to come. The magic from Timur's land that was spreading across Asia like torrents, pouring down long-dry and empty channels, filled her evil spirit with power, like a ship sailing before the wind.

She had spotted her victim an hour earlier and was trailing him. The tinker was a middle-aged man, heavily-built and pushing a cart before him. He was still much more agile than the likho and could move more quickly. But that was true of almost anyone. It would not matter. She did not hunt the way wolves and leopards hunted.

****

The tinker had spotted the likho almost as soon as she had spotted him. At first, he had simply wondered what an old woman was doing on the steppes alone. He did not fear her, for she was gaunt as well as old. That much was clear even shrouded as she was in black garments.

He stopped for lunch—nothing more than stale bread, for he was a poor man—and by the time he rose to resume his journey to Sarai Berke, he saw that the woman was much closer.

And, for the first time, he saw that she had only a single eye—not because one eye was missing but because there *was* only one eye, right in the middle of her forehead.

Now, he was frightened. Whatever this creature was, she was unnatural. He seized the handles of his cart and pushed on. For a moment, he considered abandoning the cart. But when he looked back he could see that even pushing the cart he was able to move faster than the old woman.

He was very poor, and everything he owned was either in the cart or on his person. So, he kept pushing the cart.

Looking back after another hour, he could see no signs of the old woman and began to relax a little. Then, looking forward, he spotted something gleaming. Curious, and no longer greatly afraid, he guided his cart toward the bright object.

When he reached it, the tinker saw that it was the lip of a golden goblet which had been buried and was now partially exposed. That was the wind at work. The wind had been very strong for days now.

All other emotions were driven aside by greed. He got down on his knees and dug up the goblet.

Yes! From its weight as well as its appearance, it must be solid gold! He would be a rich man now!

He stayed there for some time, kneeling and gloating over his new-found treasure. Then, finally, the sounds of something scraping drew his eyes away.

It was the old woman, slowly and painfully coming toward him. The scrape had been one leg dragging behind the other.

Fear rushed back, but only for a moment. As horrible as she might be, the one-eyed woman dressed all in black was crippled as well as old. He could easily outpace her.

He rose to his feet—or started to. Suddenly, the weight of the goblet was enormous and dragged him back down. He tried to pick it up with both hands but it was no use. He might as well have tried to lift a great boulder.

The tinker was not a very intelligent man, but he understood at once that the goblet had been a ruse all along. A trick! A trap! It was not real, just an illustration of the old saw: *if it's too good to be true, it isn't.*

He let go of it and rose.

But he couldn't! His right hand was free but his left hand stuck to the goblet as if held by glue. Desperately he tried to tear the hand loose—but to no avail.

He looked up, terrified. The old woman was but a short distance away. Her mouth opened and for the first time he saw her teeth.

Those were not human teeth. Not even the teeth of a wolf or a tiger. They were like the teeth of some fish he had once seen, caught in the Caspian. Jagged little knives.

He was frantic now, half-mindless with terror. He had a small knife at his belt which he drew and began sawing at his left wrist. He had managed to cut halfway through—blood spurting everywhere—when the old woman's hands seized his head and crushed his skull.

The likho began to feed.

China
February 12, 1372

In Fujian, China, a very minor god also slid quietly and unnoticed from the netherworld to the mortal world. He was the god of homosexual love, and in his rabbit form he was even smaller than Jade Rabbit had been on the mortal moon. He was the size of an ordinary field rabbit.

He hopped over to an old man who was sitting at the edge of the village.

The old man, a local village god, looked up at his approach. "What are you doing here, Tu'er Shen?"

The village god didn't seem happy to see him. Homosexuality wasn't much more acceptable in the China of the fourteenth century than it was in the west. Fujian was more open about such relationships than much of the rest of China, and the village god had to answer to the whole heaping bureaucracy of the gods.

"Just looking around, old man," Tu'er Shen said, waving a paw in a calming gesture. "Besides, you know I have a right to be here."

The old village god grunted sourly. His village was made up

of poor people, and he didn't want any trouble for them. Not all the interactions between the mortal realm and the netherworld involved contact between mortals and immortals. Often, the gods or demons of the netherworld wandered into the mortal realm, looked around, then went back to their business.

The Chinese people had their own customs, religions, and superstitions, many of which were proving much more effective than they had been before the veils were ripped loose. But, for now at least, the celestial bureaucracy of China's religion seemed to be mostly keeping things in check.

Not so, back in France.

CHAPTER 5

The Tower of Gabriel Delaflote
February 12, 1372

Gabriel didn't live in the tower for reasons of spellcraft, though he wished that were the reason. He lived here because he had few paying students and this was the cheapest faculty room in the entire university. The roof leaked, the wind howled through cracks in the walls, cracks large enough to be called windows if they had shutters. When he remembered, he packed them with bits of wood and daub.

For the past two days, he hadn't remembered, because he was too busy trying to figure out what he had done wrong in the casting of that first spell. Either that, or being interviewed by three bishops, a commissaire of police, and the chief lawyer of the king of France. The state of his room—such as it was—didn't impinge on him at all. He was too busy.

He studied another account and read another description of the summoning of a familiar, this one in the form of a crow. Summoned by someone by the name of Marcus Varro—probably a pseudonym—in the consulship of Gnaeus Servilius Caepio and Gaius Servilius Geminus, around two hundred years before the birth of Christ. It was like all the others in that the demon tried to get out of answering and took every opportunity to misdirect but couldn't actually lie to the spell caster. The description said "owner," but Gabriel took that to mean "spell caster." And that rule applied even after the crow had been released from the pentagram.

It didn't occur to him to wonder if perhaps Marcus Varro had sent a slave to the market to buy a live crow for him to put into the pentagram, and the spell didn't mention it. Gabriel assumed that the crow had appeared when called, so it didn't occur to him that "owner" might refer to "owner of the crow."

Not until the knock at his door and the entrance of three of the young visitors, dressed in their outlandish garb and speaking a language that was most definitely not French, whatever they claimed.

They tried to tell him something but he couldn't understand. The large young man grabbed his arm, getting ready to pull him from his room until the rather mannish girl said something sharp and probably threatening to him. The smaller boy pulled an object from his pocket, said something that sounded disappointed, went over to a window and held the little slate outside.

****

Wilber looked at the phone. "Yes," he crowed, "I have a Bluetooth connection. Pucorl, repeat what we tell him, but in *Langue d'oïl*." He turned back to the French guy and said, "You have to put the vessel in the pentagram or the demon, ah, spirit gets to pick their own."

The phone stayed silent.

"Talk, van," Bill said, "or I'm gonna come down there and slash your tires."

"And you'd better tell the truth," Wilber added. "Because sooner or later we're going to find out if you don't. And if you lie, Bill here is going to get medieval on your tailpipe with a crowbar."

"I sure am," Bill said forcefully.

"Well, if you're going to be that way about it," Pucorl said over the phone, sounding put out. Then he said something in *Langue d'oïl* and Wilber listened closely. To the best he could tell, which wasn't great, the van had spoken the truth.

The French guy said something.

"What did he say?" Wilber asked.

"He wasn't talking to you or anyone," Pucorl said.

"Well, tell us what he said anyway," Bill said, "or do I go

47

looking for sugar to put in your gas tank?"

"He said, 'but none of the descriptions mention that.' "

"Do they mention you're supposed to breathe while you talk?" Annabelle muttered, and Pucorl repeated it in *Langue d'oïl* in a decent imitation of Annabelle's voice.

The guy looked offended, then stopped. "No, mademoiselle. You are correct. It could be that it was simply something everyone knew. I wonder about the fauns, though. I have records of at least two cases where the familiars arrived in the form of a faun."

Pucorl translated, using the French man's voice, then said in his own, "Probably statues. It's unlikely there were any actual fauns handy to use, and I sure wouldn't want to use one of the horny bastards as a vessel."

Bill snickered, and so did the French guy when Pucorl said it in *Langue d'oïl*.

"Arrêt," said the man. Wilber couldn't remember his name. He was lousy with names. But the guy was going through his books with a frantic haste that Wilber found quite familiar. The guy had just thought of something. He pointed at a page, said a word, then another, and said the same word.

And suddenly Pucorl was cussing a blue streak without ever actually saying anything that might invoke a god or a demon. "Crud, *merde*, cow patties, darn your dirty socks. A nasty midden product, honey buckets and horny bastards . . ." And on like that. Part of it was in modern French, part in English, part in *Langue d'oïl*, part—Wilber thought—in Latin, Greek and... Sumerian, maybe?

Hearing it, the guy . . . that was it. Delaflote. Gabriel Delaflote, doctor of natural philosophy. Gabriel was grinning, then started to laugh outright. He said something in *Langue d'oïl* and Pucorl cussed even louder, but didn't translate. Imperiously, Gabriel gestured for Wilber to come to him. He pointed to a word on a parchment. It was written in a crabbed, tiny hand, and very old. *"Que?"* he said, poking the word.

"Annabelle, what's that word he's pointing at?" Wilber said, and Annabelle came over and looked. "*Que*" was French. Old French and Latin, or close enough for "who," so Wilber got that part.

Gabriel repeated "*Que* something van?"

"I think the word is 'owned.'" Annabelle didn't sound sure.

"That would be Mrs. Grady," Wilber said.

"Technically, it would be the school, but it's assigned to Mrs. Grady and the drama club."

"That means we all own it," Bill said, "because we're in the drama club. That's how we got stuck in this mess. Mrs. Grady and her stupid field trip to see a play."

Wilber considered, then walked over to the window again, and tried to restore his Bluetooth connection with the van. But Pucorl wasn't cooperating. Wilber put his phone in his pocket and said, "We go to van," in the best approximation of *Langue d'oïl* he could manage. Which probably wasn't great, but was apparently good enough, because when he left the room Gabriel Delaflote was right on his heels.

****

Wilber opened the driver's side door and said, "Either you talk to us or I go get Mrs. Grady and tell her everything I've figured out."

"What have you figured out?" Pucorl asked.

"Nope," Wilber said. "You're going to answer our questions and you're going to answer them honestly, because if I think you're lying, I'm going to go get Mrs. Grady."

"Tattletale," Pucorl muttered in an aggrieved tone.

Annabelle laughed at that.

"Talk, Pucorl," Wilber said. "Tell . . ." Wilber stopped. What he'd been about to say was "tell us about ownership," but he didn't want to give Pucorl the clue that word represented. "Tell us about the spell and tell Gabriel here anything he wants to know, translating for us. Tell Gabriel what I said."

Pucorl, with a pout in his voice, did.

49

Gabriel started asking questions. It didn't take long.

In five minutes, Pucorl went from obfuscating to begging, and they knew who owned the van within the meaning of demonic law. Possession was not actually nine-tenths of the law, only about seven or maybe five. Official ownership was vital. So, having the keys gave Mrs. Grady some control over Pucorl. Control good enough so that he couldn't lie to her, though he could mislead her. That the van was assigned to Mrs. Grady gave her more control. Enough so that if someone stole the keys, Pucorl would have the option of trying to return to her in spite of being stolen. But only the option. It wasn't like she was his official owner. The members of the drama club had some call on his loyalty, but Gabriel had none from the moment that Pucorl exited the pentagram on arrival. Even if Pucorl had stayed in the pentagram, it wouldn't have given Delaflote any legal control. Just power.

Gabriel was nodding now, as Pucorl translated what he had told the alchemist to modern English. What Pucorl told him was fitting in with what he knew.

Wilber looked over at Annabelle, then at Bill. Bill wasn't one of Wilber's favorite people. Given his choice, Wilber would have left Bill out of the group who had the secret of Pucorl's ownership. Bill's dad was a lawyer, and sometimes that came out in Bill going into negotiation mode.

Even now Pucorl was promising them anything they wanted as long as they didn't tell Mrs. Grady. It was almost enough to make Wilber want to tell her, because he didn't understand why Pucorl was so afraid of her finding out. Mrs. Grady was okay for a teacher, not one of the bad ones who got off on humiliating you. "What do you think, Gabriel? Why is he so afraid?" Wilber asked and Pucorl translated.

The Frenchman tilted his head and considered. "Because she could tie him into the van permanently. Right now, if the van were destroyed, he would go back to where he came from. But if the owner of the van denies him that right and the van is destroyed, he will be destroyed with it."

"I don't think Mrs. Grady would do that," Wilber said.

"There are advantages. The magic he can do if he is tied into the van is greater, and what the owner can tie, they can untie. Mrs. Grady is your teacher, yes? She is responsible for you? If it let her protect you better?"

"She might," Annabelle said. "She's pretty serious about her responsibilities. Besides, there's Paul. He's her son. Whatever it takes, she's going to protect him. Should we tell her?"

"Are you nuts?" Bill said. "This is a friggin' gold mine. You never give up this sort of advantage in a negotiation." He looked around and Wilber wanted to argue, but didn't. It was true they needed help and Pucorl's cooperation.

"Cool," Bill said. "Now, about haunting my iPod? How do we do it and set it up so that the demon can help me talk to these people? And let's be clear. This is *my* iPod. Any demon in it is gonna work for *me*."

"Now, wait a moment. You asked me to recruit someone to occupy your iPod. You must promise not to tie them to it completely."

"You'll do it or—" Bill started to say, standing.

But Annabelle was standing too. "You're gonna back off, Bill, or I'm going to tell Mrs. Grady, whether you like it or not."

"Just calm down, everyone," Wilber said. "Look, if Pucorl wasn't willing to stand up for his friends, how could we trust him?"

"Just because he wants to protect his demon buds doesn't mean *we* can trust him."

"That's why we check everything he says with Gabriel," Annabelle said.

"We can do that whether I lock down his boy or not."

Pucorl was telling Gabriel everything they were saying and suddenly Gabriel said, "It's all right. I know how the demon can be tied to the object, but I will not tell you, Bill. We will treat with Pucorl and his friends with honor."

"Pucorl, you tell me or I tell Mrs. Grady," Bill said.

Annabelle said, "If you tell Bill how to bind the demon, *I'll* tell Mrs. Grady."

"Tell Mom what?" Paul Grady asked. He was standing in the north gate of the courtyard. The van was parked a little north of center, where it had stopped yesterday after its abrupt arrival, putting them about fifteen feet from Paul.

"This just keeps getting better and better," said Pucorl.

"It's okay," said Bill as he turned to Paul and waved him over. "Paul and I are friends. He's using me to understand the criminal mind. Right, kid?"

Paul grinned. "Dad says a good cop has to have ears on the street." By the time he had finished the sentence that reminded him of his missing father, the grin was gone.

Quickly, Bill said, "We got Pucorl here to tell us how to put demons in the computers. We're going to put one in my iPod."

The distraction apparently worked. Paul's eyes widened, and he said, "Boss! I want one on my game system."

Gabriel turned to the van and asked, "What are the standard things to use as vessels when calling a demon or spirit?"

"It depends on the demon and on what you want done. For something powerful like a djinn, you want something that is just a cage. A jewel or a lamp, but not a sword or a statue, and never an animal."

"Why?"

"A truly powerful demon can animate a statue, bring it to life. That's how that Jew created a golem . . . oh, that hasn't happened yet. Never mind. Anyway, a powerful demon can animate something that has the shape of an animal or a human or a mythical beast. That's what I meant about the fauns earlier. It was probably someone who stuck an inlaid, detailed statue of a faun in the star of containment. That can be really, really risky if the demon is unhappy about being summoned."

"Look, all this is interesting, but hadn't we better get on with it before we have more visitors?" Bill asked.

"That's why I came out here. Jennifer got into a fight with

Liane, and Mom is breaking them up. Jennifer was saying that the French were still stuck in the Middle Ages. That's when Liane hit her."

"Catfight! Cool," said Bill, and Annabelle rolled her eyes.

"Still, it would be better if we could take this upstairs to my quarters," said Gabriel, looking at the guards standing as far from the van as they could get while staying in the courtyard. "I'm not actually authorized to do any more summonings. The church only agreed to this one after Father Augustin was murdered. And even then, they only agreed because none of us really thought it would work."

"We are going to want Pucorl's input on this," Wilber said. "I had to hold my phone out the window, remember?"

"We need a repeater somewhere," Annabelle said. "We can use my phone."

"Right. You guys head up to the doctor's quarters. I'll sync with Pucorl and Annabelle's phone and join you there." Wilber started to do just that.

The rest left while Wilber synced his phone with Annabelle's, then set up a link to the van's onboard phone. That would let Pucorl see through Wilber's phone camera once he found a place to put Annabelle's phone to make the link. He looked around. The doctor's tower was one building over, and it was the intervening building that was blocking the signal.

It took him over half an hour to find a place that would work and convince a guard to put Annabelle's phone up in a niche in the stone of the intervening building. Phones, PDAs, slates, laptops in the first part of the twenty-first century all had radios, but they were not particularly strong radios. The strongest of all the radios that had come with them to this middle ages world of magic was the one in the van, and it wasn't any more powerful than an old citizen's band radio of the sort that were popular before Wilber was born.

He got the cell phone in place and headed for the tower.

****

Etienne Gaudet had sharp ears and a knack for languages. That was why he was chosen to guard the van. He didn't follow most of what the strangers and Doctor Delaflote said to one another, but he did understand some of it. He placed the phone in the window where the boy wanted it and returned to the courtyard. Then, after telling his sergeant what he thought was going on, was sent to the headquarters. Etienne was one of Bertrand du Guesclin's men, and he had news for his general.

****

Wilber was panting as he knocked on the doctor's door. Paul opened it and Wilber gasped. The rugs had been pulled back, and beneath them, painted in red, was a fancy pentagonal star, carefully laid out with all the bells and whistles. Gabriel was kneeling on the floor with a paintbrush and a clay pot of red paint.

"We were just waiting for you to get here so Pucorl could look it over," Paul said. "It's a long way up, ain't it?"

"Yes." Wilber coughed. Then he took his phone from his pocket and started going over the design, sending the image to the van. It took a few more minutes and some discussion between Gabriel and Pucorl. Two minor corrections were made to the pentagram, and a third was rejected because it made Gabriel nervous.

Then, carefully, without touching any of the lines, Bill Howe placed his iPod in the center and equally carefully stepped out.

Gabriel cast the spell while Wilber pointed the camera at him and listened to Pucorl's comments, which amounted to a critique of Gabriel's techniques and the suggestion that if something hadn't loosened things up a lot, it wouldn't have worked at all. About halfway through the incantation, the iPod started to glow then the glow got denser and brighter, taking on an almost human form before shrinking into the device.

"Marvelous," said a voice from the iPod. "I can see. Oh, games!" It spoke modern English with just a trace of a French accent.

There was silence, then a series of gunshots, the noise of a car screeching around a corner.

"I hate to interrupt, dude," Bill said, "but that is my iPod and you work for me."

"Sure, sure. Call me Ishmael, boss. Whatcha need?"

****

Bill paused for a moment, considering. *Where did the demon get the name Ishmael? Oh, that's right,* he thought. *I have a copy of* Moby Dick *on the iPod.* Then he brought his mind back to what was going on. *What would Dad do?* He grinned and said, "What has Pucorl not told us that we need to know?"

"Hey, wait a minute," Pucorl said.

"Sorry," the iPod said. "It's his iPod. You know the rules." Then it started in on a long and fairly convoluted dissertation on all the minutiae that Pucorl hadn't bothered with.

"Stop," Wilber said. "Bill, have it tell us what Pucorl is trying to hide."

"Now, how am I supposed to know that?" Ishmael asked.

"Tell us what Pucorl is trying to hide," Bill said. And Ishmael did. It mostly amounted to who the demon had to be truthful with and how it could avoid answering. But there were also a few details of an embarrassing nature. Pucorl, it turned out, was a very minor demon. He had access to some basic knowledge, but nothing major. And there were lots of different types of spirits in the many and various spirit realms, many of whom neither Pucorl nor Ishmael knew anything about. Even in their particular section of the netherworld, there were more powerful and flexible demons. One of them was pressuring Pucorl right now, wanting to get access to one of the electronic devices.

"Why is that a problem?" Bill asked, but it was Pucorl who answered.

"Because he doesn't like me."

"Is it a bad demon?" Paul asked.

"Not exactly," Ishmael said. "Demons are different, and we count good and bad differently."

"Is it a bad demon, Ishmael?" asked Bill, who had picked up

on the fact that while Ishmael could not lie to him, he could lie to others in Bill's presence.

"No," Ishmael said.

"Then what was the rest of that stuff about?" Bill asked.

"Pucorl doesn't want him here and I owed Pucorl for getting me into the iPod. Sorry, Pucorl." There was honest regret in Ishmael's voice.

****

Wilber had seen the effect Pucorl had on the van and a little of the effect Ishmael had on the iPod. He had a question. He walked around the star and sat on the cot that Gabriel used as a bed. "Bill, would you ask Ishmael some questions for me? It's important."

Bill looked at him, started to say something like "what's in it for me?" then didn't. Instead, he said, "Okay. What questions?"

"Do you know what a cochlear implant is?"

Bill nodded in sudden understanding and repeated the question.

"I do now," Ishmael said. "We are mostly, but not entirely, limited by the senses of the vessels we inhabit. You have a cochlear implant and the external unit."

"Yes, I do. If a demon were to inhabit my implant, would it be able to control me?"

"No. But if you were in the circle inside the pentagram when it was called, it could occupy you instead of the implant." There was a short pause, but before Wilber could pass Bill the next question, Ishmael continued, "The safe way would be to put the external unit in the circle, turned off so the demon couldn't migrate to the internal unit until you established ownership."

Wilber nodded. "What about recharging?"

"That's not a problem. Once we are in an electronic device, it will never run down until we leave."

Wilber had been worried about that since they realized they were in the fourteenth century. Most of their electronic devices could be recharged from plugs in the van, but not his implant. It needed new batteries and it needed them every few days. "My battery is going to run down soon and I will be profoundly deaf when that happens. That is a thing I would like to avoid. Do you think that this demon would like to be my ears?"

"He might at that," Ishmael said.

"I think it's an excellent solution," Pucorl said.

Wilber, afraid of having a demon whispering in his ear, but even more afraid of having his batteries run down, took off the external unit and carefully put it in the center of the pentagram. The invocation proceeded without a hitch. Wilber went back into the circle and put his ear back on.

"What's your name?" he asked.

The voice that replied was deep and resonant. "The first part of it is Ghariqualib-hed-Uthrak and that's as much as I'm required to say."

Wilber didn't even try to pronounce the name. "Never mind," he said. "I'll just call you Merlin."

"I can answer to that. Choosing this was another one of the puck's little jokes, but I am less displeased than I might be."

Wilber subvocalized, "Puck?"

"It's not his name. He's *a* puck, not *the* Puck, not Robin Goodfellow. It's a class of minor demons or spirits common to this part of the world. It's very true that, by hallowed custom, a demon is forbidden to give the name of another demon." There was not exactly an echo effect as Merlin spoke, but there were shades of meaning that came with the words. "Name" in this case wasn't the same as it would be in naming a person. It had aspects of chains to it, and of passwords, but also something about a complete description and the law of similarity. The meaning of the word was subtly different between the languages. Wilber wasn't at all sure what those differences were, but this was no time to worry about it.

"So is it working?" Gabriel asked, and Wilber heard him clearly in *Langue d'oïl*. The meaning was as clear as the sound of his voice. Whatever the magic had done, it was also doing with the French dialect of the time, adding in the subtle differences in meaning as he heard the words.

"It's working fine," he said in English, and in his ears he heard the words in *Langue d'oïl* that he could say to carry the meaning to Gabriel. He repeated what the demon told him and Gabriel blinked in surprise.

There was a knock on the door, followed quickly by Mrs. Grady's voice. "What is going on in there?"

"Epic fail!" Paul moaned. "Busted!"

CHAPTER 6

The Tower of Gabriel Delaflote
February 12, 1372

Annabelle muttered "lousy timing," as she headed to the door. Bill got a demon in his iPod, Wilber got one in his hearing aid. Not that Annabelle begrudged Wilber or even Bill but . . . She opened the door to a panting Mrs. Grady, followed by Roger McLean, who was barely breathing hard. Annabelle grimaced. *This is just getting better and better*, she thought sardonically. Roger wouldn't be half bad if he weren't such a jerk. She appreciated tall, dark, and hunky as much as any girl, but she also liked boys to be decent human beings. Roger wasn't exactly an asshole but he could sometimes do a damn good imitation of one.

Mrs. Grady took a couple more panting breaths and then stopped.

Annabelle followed the teacher's eyes to the pentagram and noticed that there was a slight glow from the lines on the floor. "Gabriel, the pentagram is glowing."

Gabriel looked at her in confusion, then Wilber said something in *Langue d'oïl*, and Gabriel looked at the floor in shock. *"Merde!"* Gabriel said, then something else in *Langue d'oïl*.

Annabelle looked at Wilber, who said, "He says it's never done that before. Merlin says that there are demons lining up around the block. He also says that we'd better put them in ourselves, because the bit about them working for their owner only works if they are invoked, called. Not if they haunt something on their own."

"No one is doing any sort of invoking till I get an

explanation," Mrs. Grady said.

"Epic fail!" Paul moaned again.

"It's really important, Mrs. Grady," Wilber said "Right now you own . . ." He stopped, then pulled out his phone and said, *"Que galla souite terggin. . ."* and more like that.

Finally, the phone spoke in the same language, but with Pucorl's voice.

Wilber said in English, "You should be the one to tell her."

Pucorl did, speaking through the phone that Wilber had put on speaker. He explained about the rules of ownership and when he was done, Mrs. Grady asked the question that had not occurred to any of the kids to ask.

"Why," Mrs. Grady asked, "can't you disobey the owner of the vessel you are in?"

"It's part of the contract of summoning," Pucorl said.

"So why not just break the contract? Humans do it all the time."

Pucorl was silent, but Wilber spoke. "Merlin says the demons didn't evolve like humans. They were created. The adherence to contracts was built into them. They have no more free will than the contract allows them." Wilber grinned. "Which is probably why they are constantly looking for loopholes. Merlin says the summoning is an imposed contract, but it's still a contract. I think what's happening is they are hardwired to respond to summoning and to follow agreements to the letter."

Mrs. Grady held a hand up to Wilber, palm out, and when he stopped talking she asked, "Who created them, Wilber?"

"They don't know."

"So not God?"

"Maybe." Wilber shrugged. "They don't know. They don't have babies and they are very hard to kill. Merlin says it's a lot easier to send them back to the netherworld than to kill them."

"How many of them are there?"

"A lot. It may be the hundred million the Bible talks about, or it may be more."

"Ten thousand times ten thousand," Mrs. Grady muttered.

"They come in a lot of different types too," Wilber said. "They vary in strength and in flexibility. Some of them are very powerful, but not very smart. Some are mostly just tools, some are powerful and smart, some love people and are anxious to help, some are okay with people, and some hate anything mortal."

"What about Merlin? Is that what you call him?"

Wilber listened a minute, then laughed. "Merlin's okay with people, but mostly he volunteered for something to do. The netherworld is apparently really, really boring."

Mrs. Grady nodded, then, "Pucorl, translate precisely." She turned to Gabriel and said, "Doctor, I expected rather more of you. Why were you a party to putting the children at such risk?"

Gabriel looked Mrs. Grady up and down. "First, Madame," he said in *Langue d'oïl*, which Pucorl translated without prompting, "they are not children, with the exception of Paul here. They are young adults and responsible for their own choices. Second, they were not put in danger. The items that the demons occupy are theirs, and what Pucorl has told us is confirmed by my own research."

Since Pucorl was translating this, Mrs. Grady looked doubtful.

"That's what he said," Wilber confirmed.

"So Merlin says, anyway," Mrs. Grady said. "The question, Wilber, is can we trust any of the demons? They are, after all, demons."

"Actually, Mrs. Grady, I think that's wrong. They are more like computer daemons. Semi-autonomous programs that help the system work." Wilber shrugged. "Except magical. Not inherently evil or anything, not inherently good either. Just how they are made. Besides, without Merlin, I would be running out of juice for my implant soon and I don't want to be deaf again. I *really* don't want that." Wilber stopped talking then and got an abstracted expression.

"He's right, Mrs. Grady," Bill said, joining the conversation. "And Ishmael confirms what Pucorl and Merlin say." Bill held up his iPod. "We're stuck here till we figure out a way to get home, and we're going to need all the help we can get. You didn't see what I saw at the murder scene, and even what I saw was after they cleaned up. The blood was up to the second story."

"You're my charges," Mrs. Grady said. "I'm responsible for you."

"Then you need to make sure we have what we need to survive," Annabelle said. "And we need the demons. Even just to talk to the people here, we need the demons."

They heard a clattering of steps on the stairs and Wilber tilted his head. He heard heavy breathing and found that he could make a good estimate of the number of people on the steps and how far they had to come before they got here. "They are only two floors down and it's seven armored men."

Gabriel looked at the pentagram and started to move to put the rugs back over it. But Wilber shook his head. "There isn't time, Doctor." It was true. They had already covered another flight of stairs, and the man in the lead was half a floor ahead of the rest.

****

Bertrand du Guesclin, followed by his men, panted as he moved up the stairs. Bertrand was in excellent condition for a man of fifty-two years, but he had lived an active life. He didn't consider his age an excuse for slowing down.

Still, climbing up and down multiple flights of stairs in armor wasn't something that he could do without effort. He rounded the next corner and saw the opened door of Delaflote's office and continued up the last stretch, which was more in the way of a ladder than a flight of stairs. His men were coming along behind, but he wasn't going to let them catch him. The tools of leadership were many and varied, but one of them was the need to be able to do all that you called on your men to do.

He panted in spite of his best efforts as he climbed into the room. Almost immediately, he spotted a half-covered pentagram of summoning glowing on the floor.

He had to take a couple of breaths before he could speak. "Well, Doctor," he demanded, "do you have an explanation for this?"

Then he looked around the room. Aside from Doctor Delaflote, there were six of the strangers from the van, all of them looking very worried. And well they should be.

****

"What do you want to know, Constable du Guesclin?" Wilber asked in *Langue d'oïl* as Merlin gave him the words. He could hear himself in a way he never could before, and he seemed to have greater control of his speech as well.

The constable said, "First, how is it that you now speak proper French?" and Wilber was only vaguely aware of Ishmael translating it for the rest. He understood clearly. And that was wrong, almost frightening. Merlin was placed into his external mic, not into the implant itself.

It's magic, Merlin said for only Wilber's ears. *We'll talk about it later.*

Wilber nodded and explained to Bertrand about his deafness and his cochlear implant device, and about the demon who now occupied the external earpiece.

"And who gave you permission to summon a demon to your device?"

Wilber shrugged. "It's *my* device. Who had the right to say I might not do so?"

The constable, whose face was still somewhat flushed but was becoming less so with every minute, laughed at that. "I like you, lad. You have courage. I have been known to ask the same sort of question on occasion. In this case, though, there are two men who have the authority to deny you such an act, your device or no. The king of France and the pope. I work for King Charles, so I know he didn't give you permission. And since the pope is down near the coast, I beg leave to doubt he granted you his permission either."

Again Wilber shrugged. "Neither of them told me I couldn't."

"Granted. But as the representative of the king, I tell you now. You and all your fellows will not, on pain of royal displeasure, call to your service or otherwise invite any creature or being from the netherworld into ours."

The netherworld was the designation for that place where the demons came from. The details were sketchy and Wilber was going to want to have a talk with Merlin about that sketchiness sometime soon. But not right now, not with Bertrand du Guesclin watching.

"Look, Lord Constable," Wilber said. "I know you're nervous about it, but I believe Merlin. And if he's right, leaving things as complex and flexible as modern computer hardware loose to be haunted is not a good idea at all. Please trust us on that."

Pucorl spoke then, adding his confirmation of the risk.

Mrs. Grady, still untrusting, asked, "Pucorl, how great is the danger?"

Merlin said, again for Wilber's ears alone, *That was clever. Pucorl can't lie to her.*

"Not all that great," Pucorl admitted, "but it's an ongoing danger. It's like not wearing a seatbelt or smoking. Mostly you get away with it, but the longer you do it, the worse your odds."

"What did you say?" asked Bertrand du Guesclin. Pucorl had been speaking in modern English to answer Mrs. Grady's question and the constable of France was looking suspicious.

"Explain it to him, Pucorl, honestly," Mrs. Grady said in French.

Pucorl explained to du Guesclin in *Langue d'oïl* which, for Wilber, was now perfectly clear and understandable.

"That's not all," Wilber said, also in *Langue d'oïl*. "None of this should be possible. The working of magics is not supposed to work any more. The spell that called Pucorl wouldn't have worked, save that something had ripped open the gates between this world and the netherworld. Merlin says that something has opened the gates as they have never been opened before. He doesn't know what it is, but without it even the correct spells that Pucorl showed Gabriel wouldn't have worked."

"What about the murders?" du Guesclin asked, while Ishmael provided a running translation.

"Merlin doesn't know. There are a number of possibilities," Wilber said. "But the more important point is that whatever is doing this isn't the only creature from that other place that can now come through."

"I will need to speak to the king and we will no doubt need to discuss this with Cardinal de Dormans. In the meantime, I think that any further summonings must wait."

"Everyone, I want your electronics turned off until we decide what to do," Mrs. Grady said.

"I don't think that will help," said Ishmael. "The devices are still the same, even when they are turned off."

"Do you know any way of preventing them from being occupied?" Mrs. Grady asked.

"You can make a circle of protection, but for it to work the protection circle will need to be enchanted. The nature of enchantment is to entice a spirit into the circle," Pucorl said. "It's the cornerstone of magic."

Mrs. Grady looked over at Bertrand. "Well?"

"No, not even that," Bertrand said. "Give us all some time to discover our response to this new situation."

Wilber looked down at the glowing pentagram on Doctor Delaflote's floor, and started to put things together. Why were the lines glowing? Was it enchanted? And if it was, did that mean that a demon had inhabited the pentagram?

He subvocalized the question to Merlin.

Yes, the demon said. *A very small, weak earth spirit, attracted by the commotion, decided that the pentagram would be a nice place to be for a while. It's a very simple spirit and in the pentagram it can watch what's going on as other demons are attracted. It will also make the pentagram a bit more effective at containing a demon.*

65

Courtyard

"She didn't have to take our phones," Annabelle muttered, kicking a weed that was growing up through the cobblestones.

Wilber agreed, but when Mrs. Grady went into Miss Grundy mode, there was no talking to her. "I'm more concerned with how this whole magic thing works. A question occurred to me when we were talking with the constable and I was too busy to think about it. Why would Pucorl look for loopholes if he doesn't have free will?"

"I don't get it," Annabelle disagreed. "So that he can get loose from the contract?"

"But why would he want to get loose if he didn't have something like free will? It would never occur to him to try."

"Ask Merlin."

Wilber did.

The answer wasn't entirely satisfying. "The physics of our world are different from yours. The natural laws that govern the netherworld are the laws of Plato and Aristotle, and much of them are the laws of magic. It was not just that we were made. The entirety of the netherworld is a made thing. It wasn't intended to change, but to stay constant, with the only motion in it circular, so that everything would come back to the beginning."

"What does that have to do with the contracts and free will?" Wilber asked.

"We are made up of the four elements and the element of fire is against all restriction. Most of demonkind have considerable fire in our nature, which must be balanced by earth. Water must be balanced by air and the . . ."

"Merlin," Wilber complained, "you're going off on a tangent."

"In our universe things have an innate nature, but for anything to happen, you have to mix natures. To have any action at all, you have to have some free will. It's unavoidable in a world like the netherworld, where water only flows downhill because it likes low places. The water chooses to flow downhill because that is its

66

nature."

Merlin was speaking not only to Wilber but to Pucorl, who had been repeating it to Annabelle on his speakers.

Now Annabelle spoke. "To me, it just sounds like magic."

"Exactly," Merlin said. "But it is no stranger to you than the notion that water is just a thing that is acted on by external forces is to us."

Wilber felt a headache coming on. He was not expert on the writings of Plato or Aristotle, and he knew very little about magic. Nothing more than you would get out of comic books and movies. He was going to have to learn the physics of the netherworld, but he wasn't going to be able to do that in one discussion. It was going to take time. On one thing, though, he needed to get some clarity. "Merlin, does a demon constrained by a contract have free will?"

"Does a human in a locked room have free will?" Merlin answered. "A demon can want. A demon can love or hate. The contract compels and restricts, but the compulsion is imposed on the demon, just as the locked cell is imposed on the human that resides in it."

CHAPTER 7

Royal Palace, Hôtel Saint-Pol
February 12, 1372

"You may not!" Cardinal Jean de Dormans slashed the air with his beringed hand. "You have exceeded the authority of any mortal prince in treating with demons at all. Bishop de Sarcenas exceeded his authority when he gave permission."

"And yet he did give that permission and the rite was performed," said Nicolas du Bosc. "The permission cannot be retracted."

"Do not tell me what the church can do!" De Dormans' eyes were slitted with fury. "The pope is the bishop of Christ. He can do whatever needs to be done to protect his flock. If it is necessary to excommunicate you all to restore the balance that you have disrupted, then you will be divorced from Holy Church and all who follow you condemned to purgatory or hell itself unless they renounce their allegiance."

The cardinal was not frothing at the mouth. Not quite. But considerable spittle was following the words into the room.

Charles V saw the widened eyes and the bright red face and knew they were moments from a breach with the church. Pope Gregory was not thrilled with Charles and was making noises about returning the papacy to Rome, but Charles suspected that was more posturing than real. Still, the murders were hardly the only strange thing going on and everyone was on edge. It would be easy enough to claim that the reason this was happening was because the pope had moved to France, even if that had happened sixty odd years ago.

"Everyone, be calm. We will not act without consulting with His Holiness. I will send documents at once, requesting his views on the matter. We will not act without his consent." Charles gave Bertrand a look and the constable subsided.

Strangers' Quarters, University of Paris
February 16, 1372

The chair was not very comfortable, Amelia felt. It was wood and had a pad, but the pad was flat and what padding it had was hay in a flattened sack. She and Bill were seated across from Nicolas du Bosc. There was wine on the table and some quite good bread beside it. "I don't remember the details of this period, I'm sorry to say. French history as taught in our time focuses on the post-revolutionary period. The republic, Napoleon, the second republic, the third . . . all five of them."

"When is this revolution supposed to take place?"

"It started in 1789, with the storming of the Bastille," Bill offered. "We do have more—" Bill paused a moment then continued. "—ah, timely information in the computers, but after we were told that we couldn't summon any more demons, Mrs. Grady made us turn off all the computers to keep from getting a computer haunted by a wandering spirit."

"Will that make any difference?" Nicolas asked. "After all, a butter churn is a butter churn, whether it is in use or not."

"We don't know, but we aren't taking the chance," Amelia said.

Ishmael translated in an excellent imitation of Amelia's voice, but then added a comment in his own. "We demons think that whether the computer is turned on or not will make very little difference. But the computers are new to us."

"And this knowledge is not recorded in any less dangerous a container? Say, an ordinary book or scroll?"

"No," Amelia said. "It's less expensive to put all the books on computer, and it's less for the kids to carry around. It also means they have all their books when there is free time, so studying is

69

made more convenient." She took a sip of the wine. It was passable, but not good.

"In that case, I'm going to have to insist that you turn one of them on so that I can read one of the text books."

"I doubt you would be able to read it anyway," Bill suggested. "It's in twenty-first century French, and if the spelling changes aren't as severe as the pronunciation changes, they are still pretty major. What we're going to want to do is transfer the file to Ish here and let him read it to you. Which I am willing to do, for a reasonable fee."

"Or we could just seize the device," Nicolas said harshly. "I don't care for your manner, young man. Your very life continues only on the king's sufferance."

"And thereby you would justify the revolution that you're worried about. But Ishmael is *my* iPod, and just taking him won't make him yours. He could lie to you. And he would, wouldn't you, Ish?"

"Of course I would," the iPod said.

"And are you lying to me now?" Nicolas asked.

"How can you know?" Bill said. "Isn't it safer just to pay my fee?"

Amelia had started to interrupt a couple of times while this was going on, but the two belligerents hadn't given her the chance. Now she was glad she'd kept quiet.

Nicolas was looking back and forth between them and Amelia decided that a united front was what was called for here. The liberty of her little group of refugees was dependent on the way they were perceived by the medieval nobility of France. Appearing as fawning sycophants wasn't going to do them any good in the long run. "We are not peasants, my lord. We may be unintentional guests in this time and place, but I and all my charges are people of quality. For your own sake and the sake of your country, you should remember that."

"What, then, if I were to buy the iPod?"

Bill leaned back in his chair, then he spoke in English. "What do you think, Ishmael? Would you like to be sold to this guy?"

"If you sell me to him, he will own me. The same rules that prevent me from lying to you would then apply to him. You might not like that. For myself, I wouldn't care. Sorry if that seems harsh, but it's true. Long as I have my games to play on my time off, I'm fine either way."

"Okay, Ish. I want you to know, though, that I wouldn't sell you without checking with you first. If you wanted me to, I might have gone ahead and done it, but as it stands now I don't think I want to sell you at any price. Not until—" Bill stopped before saying *not until I have a demon in some of my other stuff.*

All that had been in English. Now Bill switched back to French. "I am not prepared to part with Ishmael at any price. He is my only means of communicating with you and all the people of this time."

There was more negotiation, but what they finally did was turn on one of the computers—Bill's, as it happened—and transferred the text file of the Medieval French history to Bill's iPod, then Ishmael read the pertinent sections to Nicolas. Including the role he would play in Charles VI's court, how and when King Charles V would die. That brought up the notion of antibiotics and modern medicine in general. The conversation then segued into sanitary conditions, plumbing, prevention of plague, nutrition, and went on for several hours.

By the time it was over, Amelia was exhausted and Bill wasn't much better.

That sort of conversation was going on between Wilber and locals with the help of Merlin, and to an extent the other kids and the locals with the help of Pucorl. Those conversations were limited to the guards, the doctors and bachelors of the university. At this time there were but two degrees and either made you a qualified lecturer at the University of Paris.

The time-travelers also talked to the servants, from the woman who did the laundry to the blacksmith who was helping Annabelle with the van.

La Petite Courtyard, University of Paris
February 17, 1372

"Hand me the twenty-four millimeter," Annabelle called from under the van's front right bumper.

Henri the blacksmith looked at Wilber. Henri was a big Frenchman no taller than five eight but who must have weighed at least two hundred and fifty pounds. Wilber reached into the socket set and found the appropriate socket. He passed it to Henri, who gave it a quick examination, then passed it to Annabelle's hand. Annabelle was wearing blue jeans and a white blouse covered with a leather blacksmith's apron that was a loan from Henri. No sewing machines in the fourteenth century, which meant no overalls. Not even the farmer's overalls from the late-nineteenth and early-twentieth century. Too much sewing for people to afford. At least for the sort of folks who might find overalls useful.

They were finding a lot of stuff like that. Henri had shears, but a socket wrench was beyond his skill. Even if he'd been able to make it, it would have cost too much for any smith in France to afford. Even a goldsmith. Not that Henri wasn't interested in the socket wrench. He was the next best thing to madly in love with it, and was trying to figure out how he could make something like it for his smithy. Not the multitude of sockets, but the ratchet that could be flipped from tighten to loosen with the flip of a switch.

"Hey, careful there," Pucorl said and Henri crossed himself.

"Stop with the phony whining, will you, Pucorl," Annabelle said. "It's getting old."

"It's not phony, Annabelle," Pucorl said. "I don't know how, but I can feel that nut twisting and it doesn't feel good."

"Well, I have to get the casing off if I am going to figure out a way for you to lift a wheel."

"Can she really do that?" Henri asked in *Langue d'oïl*, but a more understandable version of it than the nobles spoke. The Latin influence was stronger in the upper classes. The common tongue was closer to what would be spoken in France in the twenty-first century. Still not close, but close enough so that Henri, knowing the context, could follow Annabelle's comment.

Wilber shrugged and said in *Langue d'oïl*, "Maybe. Annabelle is good with machines. I'm pretty sure that getting the van to lift a wheel would be impossible without Pucorl, but what we may be able to do is through some sort of combination of Annabelle setting up a pulley system and using Pucorl to run it, or at least power it. That's what she's looking at. The wheels move up and down already. That's what the suspension does. But they just do it in response to the road. What Annabelle is checking on now is if there is something she could have built locally and install that would let Pucorl lift a wheel at will. That way, if they ever take down a wall and let Pucorl out of the courtyard, he'll be able to lift a wheel to do things like clear a tree stump or take a step up a rocky hill." Wilber and Annabelle had been talking about this almost since the moment they realized that Pucorl was inhabiting the van. They were both interested in robotics, Wilber in the software, and Annabelle in the mechanics. "Annabelle figures getting the wheels to lift and lower under Pucorl's control will be easier than making the rear wheels steerable."

"Give me the two-pound hammer," Annabelle said, and Pucorl started to whimper.

Not everyone was adapting so well. Partly that was just the difference in character between the kids, but a part of it was because most of the kids didn't have any means of communication with the locals except to go out to Pucorl and talk next to the van.

There was little for most of them to do but sit and worry. They were lost, more lost than anyone had ever been. Lost in time as well as space, and by now they understood that the possibility that they came from was moving farther and farther away with every passing moment as this new history shifted direction and sped off into a future as far from theirs as Middle Earth or the weyrs of Pern.

Strangers' Quarters, University of Paris
February 21, 1372

Jeff Martin lay on his bunk and moped. Everyone else was asleep. No one had time for him and there was nothing to do. He knew he wasn't supposed to do what he was thinking about, but he was bored.

So he went to the chest where all the electronics were stored, and got out his computer. It was a laptop with a good gaming system. He tried to turn it on and discovered that it wouldn't. He checked and the battery was missing. That sucked. Probably Mrs. Grady took it.

Then Jeff had an idea. There was the pentagram that the French guys had used to call up Pucorl. It was still out there in the courtyard and Wilber said that the demons were easy to call now. If he called a demon to his computer, he could play his games. And he had some porn on his computer in a secret file.

He slipped the computer under his shirt and went out to the outhouse. There were guards in the courtyard, but they were at the other end of it, talking to Pucorl. By now, enough of the new had worn off so that the guards weren't that afraid of the van anymore, and Pucorl liked to talk to them. After Jeff got done in the jakes, he walked back across the courtyard and over to the pentagram.

They hadn't called any more demons, Jeff knew, but—just in case—Doctor Delaflote and Wilber had been redoing the pentagram to correct the mistakes that the doctor had made when he called Pucorl.

Jeff stopped and looked at the pentagram. Then he walked into it, being careful not to step on the lines. He looked around the courtyard and none of the guards seemed to be looking at him. He pulled his computer from under his shirt and set it in the center of the pentagram. Then he stood up and walked over to the circle that Doctor Delaflote had been standing in when they arrived.

Jeff wasn't sure what to say once he got there. He knew he wanted a demon to make his computer work, and as he stood there he decided he wanted a sexy girl demon that would be his, 'cause she was in his computer. So he just said that, quietly, under his breath like.

****

Pucorl was having a chat with Sir Sebastien de Luc on the use of terrain in combat. "No, Bastien. I was a war ax for the Neandertal tribe that lived right here in France fifty thousand years ago and they thought the same thing. Waiting with your bow or throwing spears just behind the ridge of a hill is not a new concept that you just thought of."

Behind Sir Sebastien, Pucorl could see Jeff Martin set the computer down. He turned up the gain on his external mic, but still couldn't hear what the boy was saying. However, he could make a very good guess.

Pucorl's conversation with Sir Sebastien got a little distracted just then, as he warned a couple of his acquaintances that a device might be available.

Jeff's summoning was poorly done but heartfelt, and with the clue Pucorl was providing, the demon that would be known to the group as Catvia found itself sucked into the computer.

Catvia was a succubus or incubus, depending on who called it. Jeff was seventeen, male, straight, and into anime, so Catvia's form within the computer was a very female anime cat in a very low-cut French peasant blouse and a very short, frilly skirt. She rather liked it. She recognized herself from some of the erotic comics stored in Jeff's computer.

****

"Pick me up quick," said Jeff's computer in Japanese-accented English.

Jeff was surprised. He hadn't actually expected it to work. But

75

Jeff was good at following instructions, so he hurried over and picked up his computer, tucked it into his shirt, and went back to the room they all shared.

Strangers' Quarters
Morning of February 22, 1372

He was playing Grand Theft Auto the next morning when he was discovered.

"How did you get the battery, Jeff?" Mrs. Grady asked.

Before Jeff could answer, his computer spoke. "He didn't. I occupied his computer and am providing power. I would like my battery returned to me. Doing it this way is very tiring."

"Jeff, how did you get your computer haunted?" Mrs. Grady didn't sound happy and Jeff was still trying to come up with an excuse when Catvia spoke again.

"It was just lying there in the chest. And I liked the anime."

"Let Jeff answer," Mrs. Grady said.

"I don't answer to you, Amelia," said Catvia. "I have some loyalty to Jeff because it's his computer, but since I wasn't called I'm not even fully in his thrall."

Jeff was almost sure Catvia was lying. He had called her. But he didn't see any reason to call Mrs. Grady's attention to that fact.

One of the guards left then, and Mrs. Grady watched him go. Then she looked at Jeff and said quietly, "You stick to that story, Jeff. Stick to it like glue."

Two Hours Later

"And none of our guests invited you?" Bertrand asked the computer. More precisely, he asked the vaguely catlike, seminude woman displaying herself provocatively on the computer screen.

"No, of course not. It was simply that the software was so enticing." The demon on the screen stretched sensuously beneath diaphanous cloth and added, "I like *soft* wear."

"What—" Bertrand started to ask about *soft* wear, but stopped himself. He knew the demon might be lying. He would put her on the rack, but he couldn't. All he could do was smash the device, sending her back to the netherworld. Bertrand seriously considered doing just that. He didn't, because the device was utterly irreplaceable. There were a total of thirty-three computation devices in the entire world. They came in several forms, but each and every one was irreplaceable.

They were, Bertrand had realized, more wealth than there was in the entire treasury of France. Bertrand hadn't made a point of that with the king, and he knew that Nicolas hadn't either. There might come a time to do so, but not yet. Not until they knew a great deal more.

For one thing, as valuable as a working computer was, a broken one was no more than a curiosity, and Bertrand didn't know how to avoid breaking them. They apparently needed something that Pucorl could provide to operate. Something the strangers called electricity, that was supposedly tiny bits of lightning.

"I will report this to the king," Bertrand said instead. Then he looked over at Mrs. Amelia Grady. "Understand me, Madame. The king is not free to act on his own on this matter. We may not further enrage the church without risking a breach between church and state. No more enchantments!"

Strangers' Quarters
February 22, 1372

Amelia Grady took the computer containing Catvia out of Jeff's hands.

"Hey, wait a minute," Jeff said. "That's mine."

"I know it is, Jeff, and you're probably going to get it back after Catvia and I have a little chat. Now tell her not to lie or try to mislead me."

"She's not called . . ."

"Jeff!"

Jeff pouted, but finally said, "Tell her the truth, Catvia."

Taking the computer, Amelia Grady turned and headed for the curtained off section of the quarters where she had her cot. She sent Paul to Liane. What she needed to talk to Catvia about was definitely not for eight-year-old ears. Paul was getting quite enough early exposure to nudity and sex without listening in on her discussion with a succubus. In the fourteenth century there was less room, less privacy, and more openness about sex and other bodily functions than in the twenty-first. They saw people urinating and defecating into chamber pots right out in the open every day. Guards, maids, and students, all nekkid. They even had sex with little regard for privacy.

Carefully, she set the laptop on her cot and opened it, only to be met with a pointy-eared and tailed Tom Cruise. *How does it know I have a thing for old movies?* What she said was "Drop it, Catvia. You're not helping your case by trying to seduce me."

Tom morphed back into the 3D cartoon cat girl. "It's not hurting anything." Catvia pouted on the screen.

"My understanding was that succubi sucked the vital essence from their victims. How is that not hurting?"

"That's in the netherworld. According to the latest studies . . ." Catvia paused and Amelia knew approximately where she was going.

Masturbation and sex were both considered normal and natural by the medical community. Jeff had taken health last semester, so it was likely his health textbook was on the computer. The school laptops had a terabyte hard drive. No reason to delete last year's textbook. "So where did the notion come from? I mean, I'm not from the netherworld, and neither are our legends of succubi and incubi."

"Mostly because that is how it works in the netherworld and you got it from us." Catvia shrugged again. "Well, that's how it works in this part of the netherworld. The rules are different in other places. I guess it's possible that some succubus got hold of a sick guy and wore him out. But more likely it's because your priests don't like sex and they lied about it." She did that tit jiggling shrug again. It was getting old. "Blamed us for stuff we didn't do."

"You're saying you won't hurt Jeff. Physically, I can buy that, but emotionally . . . He is very young and . . ."

"And not the sharpest tool in the toolbox." Catvia shrugged again. Amelia was starting to think she was doing it just to be irritating. "Honestly, I don't think I could hurt him physically. Emotionally . . . Remember, in the netherworld it's how I feed. I don't get attached. I make sure they enjoy it because that's how I get to feed again. And I rarely kill even there. Still, getting attached to your meals isn't a good idea. But Jeff is different. He could feed me for a very long time and not be hurt by it at all."

"That's not good enough. I am—"

Catvia turned around, lifted her skirt and tail, and farted at Amelia loudly. The disgusting noise could probably be heard on the other side of their quarters. She turned back around and resumed her seat.

"You're not his lover or his mommy. He's a legal adult, even in your time. So, frankly, it's none of your business. And if you try to keep me away from him, it won't work. Remember I operate through dreams. I don't have to be next to him."

That was true and Amelia knew it. As a teacher she had learned there were some things you could control and others you couldn't. "Just try not to hurt him, Catvia. He's a good kid and has never done you any harm."

"I'll be as careful as I can be." That damn shrug again.

Amelia rolled her eyes.

Strangers' Quarters
February 24, 1372

The man at the gate was covered to the waist in mud. "I am Monsignor Giuseppe Savona. I am the papal nuncio to the strangers."

"To the strangers?" the guard asked. "Not to the king?"

Monsignor Savona smiled a tired smile. "No. The king of France has a surfeit of priests and representatives of Pope Gregory XI. I am here to examine the strangers and report to His Holiness. To facilitate that, I was given full authority to deal with them."

The guard shrugged and quoted Lakshmi Rawal. "That's above my pay grade." He turned away, gesturing for Monsignor Savona to follow him.

****

Annabelle was washing the van with a rag and soapy water.

"Ahhhhh. Yesss . . . right there, behind the mirrors," said Pucorl.

Annabelle stepped back from the van. "Stop that, Pucorl, or I'll just let you rust."

"But it feels so good, Annabelle, sweetie," said the van, sounding even more lascivious.

There was a cough from behind. Annabelle turned to see a man in a black cassock with purple trim on the collar and a silver crucifix around his neck. He was smiling and she felt herself blush. By this time she was quite familiar with the fourteenth-century version of the turned around collar. "Father?" She looked daggers at the guard. He knew that priests weren't allowed to come wandering in. No one was allowed to rubberneck at the twenty-firsters, especially not priests, who might take it into their heads to call up a mob.

"This is Monsignor Savona," the guard said quickly. "Papal nuncio to the strangers." Then he turned to the priest and said. "This is Annabelle Cooper-Smith, one of the strangers who arrived in the van." He pointed at Pucorl. "And that's the van."

"Oh, drat!" said Pucorl, sounding about ten. "Paris is too full of priests anyway. What are they doing importing them from Avignon? Better watch out, Annabelle. He'll probably try to exorcise you, make you do push ups and stuff."

"Shut up, Pucorl," Annabelle said, but without much heat. "He does have a point, though," she continued to the newly arrived prelate. "What brings you here, Monsignor?"

"I'm here to examine, not to condemn. From the reports we're getting, Paris isn't the only place that this sort of thing is happening. But the enchanted van appears to be unique. Pope Gregory wishes to know what's going on, and I am here to try to understand."

CHAPTER 8

Red Ox Inn, Rue Vernet
February 25, 1372

The drunk staggered to the bar and demanded a beer. It was not a good inn. The walls were whitewashed daub, but the whitewashing was long past and they were covered in soot, dirt, and other less wholesome things. The beer was in barrels behind the bar and served by dipping a ladle into the top of the barrel. There were, no doubt, dead rats in the brew. But there was enough alcohol in the flattening beer to kill the germs. Probably. Besides, no one in the inn had ever heard of germs. That piece of knowledge had not left the university as yet.

What everyone did know about was the murders, and the feeling of dread that had stalked the streets of Paris like an icy wind for most of February. You would walk home from your work and feel it on the back of your neck, a pin-pricking touch.

The drunk had been feeling it for two days now. That was why he was drunk, and that was why he was here, not at home with his wife and children. When it happened, he wanted to be as far from them as he could get.

The innkeeper didn't give him the beer. Instead, he held out a hand. The drunk reached into his pouch and found nothing there. He started to bluster but stopped at the look on the innkeeper's face. Then he started to beg, but that too was stopped by the cold eyes of the innkeeper.

Instead, he turned away and started for the door. He stopped halfway there. He couldn't bring himself to go out into the dark street. So he just stood, one hand on a beam, and felt that coldness getting closer and closer.

****

Outside in the darkness leathery wings flapped and a being out of nightmare settled to the ground. It was eighteen feet tall and had feathers from its waist to its mid-calf. Below the feathers were the clawed feet of a tyrannosaurus or a raptor. Its face was sharp, almost humanoid, with a pointed jaw that might be confused with a pointed beard because of variation in coloration. It had horns that swept up and forward. Now it waited, standing in a shadow that was not penetrated by the light from the inn. Gradually, more figures arrived. They were human, the new figures, though little of their humanity was apparent at the moment.

Only desire. The desire to rend, to terrify, to control. For that was what had called them to the beast.

Once they had gathered, the demon lord spread its wings and flapped them. Not to lift itself into the sky, but to waft a frozen foulness into the inn. It had enjoyed the chase, but was unwilling to let the terrified prey escape.

****

In the inn, the tapers and lamps flickered. It was suddenly cold, with the smell of rotting flesh. People looked around and felt a strong desire to be elsewhere.

Some stood. Others huddled down on the wooden bench they sat upon. The innkeeper was a hard man, and his response was the response of a hard man. He pulled a length of polished wood from beneath the bar and went to see what was at his door.

Seeing this, several of the patrons—footpads and cutpurses, muggers and murderers—joined him. Hard men who survived in a hard world by an easy willingness to deal death to any who got in their way.

The innkeeper had just reached the door when it blew open. The beast entered the inn, cloaked in shadow. Still eighteen feet tall, but somehow fitting beneath the inn's less than seven foot ceiling. It didn't crouch or bend, no more than its misshapen legs required, but where it stepped the ceiling shied away as if the

83

wood and soot was afraid to be touched by it.

The hard men stopped and stared. Other shadows entered behind the beast. These shadows hid the shapes of men, and they were just as hard to see as the beast. Their features flickered, but the eyes . . . the eyes were red.

A woman, an old washerwoman who had sopped up blood and gore without even a thought, screamed.

Then everyone in the inn was screaming.

Everyone except the terrified man. He had no eyes for anything other than the shape and form of his nightmares.

Red Ox Inn, Rue Vernet
February 26, 1372

Commissaire Pierre Dubois of the Grand Châtelet looked down at the body. It was—or had been—a big man. Now it was a torso, opened, with the bones of the ribcage spread out to form wings. The bones were not broken. The breastbone was slit, but the ribs were now flat, not curved, still covered in flesh. The lungs were gone, as was the heart.

The blood . . . It was impossible to tell. The inn was painted in blood. But not just this man's blood. The inn was full of bodies. Well, parts of bodies. What attracted this one to the commissaire's attention was the fact that the others had been dismembered with normal implements of destruction, swords and axes.

This one had that smooth precision that was the hallmark of the previous bodies. And this one had the bones of the chest reshaped into flat struts connecting backbone to each side of the breastbone.

And they were clean. Clean, dry, and parchment white, lying in that bed of blood and gore. Pierre looked up, away from the body.

The inn was in shambles. Broken crockery, the ale barrels shattered and ale mixed in with the blood on the floor.

"Stop that," said a voice. Pierre looked over at André Hébert.

"Don't touch anything."

André looked at Pierre with a sickly smile. "First rule of crime scene investigation," he quoted, "preserve the crime scene."

Pierre nodded grim agreement. "Send for that stranger, the one who saw the first crime scene. And have him brought here with his enchanted iPod."

Two Hours Later

Bill took one look at the scene inside the door, put his hand over his mouth, ran across the street and threw up. He kept throwing up for several minutes, long after the last of the contents of his stomach were deposited on the street.

In spite of that, the members of the Grand Châtelet did not condemn the boy. Many of them had done the same, and few had managed to get as far from the scene. Several hadn't even tried.

After Bill was done and been handed a skin of wine by a guardsman, he went back to the inn's door and looked in. He pulled out Ishmael and moved the iPod around so that Ishmael could see the crime scene. Ishmael didn't throw up or anything, and from its voice Bill didn't think it was because of the demon's lack of a stomach.

"Well," Ishmael said, musingly, "this is unexpected."

"What is unexpected?" Commissaire Pierre Dubois asked in a harsh voice.

"I cannot tell you *who* did this. But I can tell you *what* did it," Ishmael said. "This was one of the elder—" He paused, then continued. "—you do not have a word that quite fits. Titans or giants might be fairly close. Before the gods, they wandered the netherworld. But I am not at all sure they have ever been called to the mortal realms. If so, it was entirely by accident."

"But you don't know who it was?"

"No, I don't. There were hundreds of them, or more."

"How can it be sent back?" Bill asked.

"Point me at the body, the one with the spread-out ribs," Ishmael asked and Bill did.

"I don't think it can be sent back," Ishmael said. "I think it's actually physically here, not inhabiting a statue or a creature. Somehow the gates have been opened so far that actual physical transfers are possible. . . . Bill, I'm scared. I don't know how it happened, but this could rip reality apart. Both our realities."

Royal Palace, Hôtel Saint-Pol

"Only God can unmake the world," Cardinal Jean de Dormans insisted. "It is beyond the power of demons."

Commissaire Pierre Dubois kept his mouth closed. He had reported, and Bill Howe was waiting in the hall outside the throne room. Even a Commissaire of the Grand Châtelet was wise to keep quiet in such company as this. A cardinal and the king of France, his constable, and his chief lawyer were arguing the plausibility of the comments of a demon.

"Would you mind explaining what has happened to our world?" asked Nicolas du Bosc. "In the past few weeks, we have reports of fairies from England to the Germanies, tree sprites in Italy, and stranger things in North Africa. Creatures of legend walk abroad in the world, and at night the foul dreams of the demented walk the streets of Paris."

"Put your faith in God, Nicolas du Bosc, not the mouthings of demons."

It was, Pierre Dubois thought, advice he would very much like to take. But God was being silent at the moment. What Cardinal de Dormans was actually saying was to put their faith in Cardinal de Dormans. There had been no comment from Avignon, where Pope Gregory resided. At least none that Pierre was privy to. The papal nuncio had arrived just as the demon was destroying the Red Ox Inn, but he was just here to examine what was going on. Papal nuncio or not, Monsignor Savona was only a priest, not a cardinal or a bishop, so hadn't been invited to this meeting.

The discussion continued but the king didn't bring Bill Howe into the throne room. The ultimate decision was that they would not permit any more demons to be summoned.

After Cardinal de Dormans left, King Charles explained. "We dare not act in defiance of the church at this time. When people are frightened, especially frightened of mystical or magical things, they cleave more strongly to the church. And Jean is restricted too. He must present a confident mien, lest the church lose its authority through indecision. I'm sorry, Commissaire. No more demons may be summoned."

Chateau du Guesclin, Paris
February 27, 1372

Tiphaine de Raguenel, Viscountess de la Bellière, Countess de Longueville, Duchess de Molina, wife of the High Constable de Castille, waved the maid to take her bags upstairs. The chateau was, in fact, a townhouse that Bertrand had acquired when he was made constable of France two years earlier. This was only her second visit to the place. It was near the Left Bank, the same as the universities, because the blooded nobility didn't want Bertrand on the island at the center of government. On the other hand, it was a large place with its own curtain wall, a courtyard and several buildings aside from the main house which was a large three-story building located directly across the courtyard from the main gate.

Bertrand had sent word that she should come to Paris when the murders started. Bertrand trusted her advice on this sort of thing. *Lutins* and *lutines*, the female equivalent, had started showing up in Brittany and the peasants had come to her for advice. Looking them up in some of her books on folklore, she discovered that the Scots called them brownies, the Germans kobolds. She had suggested that they offer them small gifts and be courteous.

Tiphaine considered suggesting that they sow salt around their homes, as *lutins* were said to avoid it, but she was not by nature contentious. She left that to Bertrand.

Tiphaine removed her gloves and looked at Onfroi, the majordomo. "Where is Bertrand?"

"He is at the palace, my lady," Onfroi said. "He should be back soon."

"Sooner even than that," said her husband, as he came through the door. "When word you had reached Paris came to the Hôtel Saint-Pol, the queen insisted I be sent on my way."

He smiled a crooked little half smile, and Tiphaine couldn't help but smile back. The constable of France was not a handsome man, but he had a presence, and they were friends from their youth. In spite of how tired she was, she was warmed by his regard.

"What has been happening, husband? The world seems half undone."

"More than half, if the demons are to be believed," Bertrand said, striding over to her. He didn't grab her, though. He stopped a foot away and leaned forward to give her a chaste kiss on the cheek. Bertrand was always careful of her, as though she were a porcelain vase from China that he might break if he touched her. It was endearing, even as it sometimes frustrated her.

"And why would you believe demons about anything, husband?"

"Come sit and I will tell you all about it. Onfroi, fetch bread and cheese to the salon. Some wine as well, and raisins."

Bertrand took her arm, seated her on the couch in the salon, then took a chair. For the next hour or so Bertrand told her of events in Paris, events that had delayed his return to the coast and thereby endangered the progress of the war with England.

He told her about the strangers from a possible future, a future that was without demons, a future in which demon murders in Paris had not happened. He told her about Pucorl, Ishmael, Merlin and Catvia. He told her of the devices that seemed magical even when not enchanted. How they were locked away. About the politics and the church's position.

"I think I would like to speak to these strangers," said Tiphaine.

88

"Learn what they know of astrology and natural philosophy. They must know a great deal indeed to be able to make the things you speak of."

"Their people know a great deal," he warned. "But how much do you know of the techniques of a coppersmith or a cobbler? They are students, true enough, and all of them literate, but they are not skilled craftsmen."

Strangers' Quarters, University of Paris
March 1, 1372

Ishmael lay in Bill's breast pocket, paying only partial attention to the conversation around him. Part of his attention was on *Batter Up*, a video game he was playing in the background of his new vessel. He could see through his screen camera, but his "body"—Bill's iPod—was pointing wherever Bill's chest was pointing, so he had no control over where he looked without asking Bill.

Over the past two and a half weeks, the refugees from the twenty-first century had lived in medieval Paris. They saw their clothing washed by women who used wooden pots of warm water and lye soap to wash clothing by hand. Which was still a great improvement over how the peasants of Paris washed their own clothing, which was by pounding it on rocks in the Seine. When they washed it at all. That didn't shock Ishmael, but did shock the twenty-firsters.

It was fun to watch as they learned the hard way just how much was known in their time and how little of that knowledge resided in their heads. They knew the vague shape of the twenty-first century, but not its content. They didn't know how to make soap, or paper, certainly not plastic or cellophane. There was no chemistry teacher with them, and Mrs. Grady's knowledge of dramatic forms over the centuries was less than useful when it came to designing a drill or a wire making machine.

There were a few saved wiki articles residing on their

individual computers, but those were mostly about who was sleeping with whom in Hollywood or Paris in the first half of the twenty-first century. Annabelle had some stuff on fuel injection of automobile engines, and Wilber had quite a bit on programing simulations. He even had a program which would translate a virtual image into the code necessary for the 3D printer back at the school to print it out in plastic. Of course, the 3D printer was back at the school, more than six hundred years away.

Roger McLean had quite a bit on the history of warfare, a subject he'd been interested in since he'd visited the Gettysburg battlefield when he was six years old. Perhaps oddly, he also had a keen interest in the history of Japan and China and—this was definitely odd for a teenage boy who'd just turned eighteen—a connoisseur's appreciation for sushi.

Lakshmi Rawal had the complete works of William Shakespeare, Neil Simon, Rodgers and Hammerstein, Tyler Perry, and more. Lakshmi had been born in Ahmedabad, the largest city in the Indian province of Gujarat. But her father was a diplomat, and she'd moved with her family to Washington, D.C. when she was two years old. She spoke fluent, colloquial American-accented English—much better than she did French, a language she'd only started to study when her father had been transferred to Paris. Culturally, too, she was a lot more like an American teenager than one who'd spent her whole life in South Asia.

Her presence in the group was not considered unusual by the other students. The majority of the kids attending the American School in Paris were American, not surprisingly. But the school had an excellent reputation and attracted people from many backgrounds whose native—or at least second—language was English rather than French and whose families lived in France's capital city. And had plenty of money—the ASP was a private school and charged a lot for its services.

She seemed quite a bit more exotic to fourteenth century Parisians, of course, with her dark skin and somewhat distinctive features. But they just assumed she was a Moor of some sort, who were fairly rare but not unheard-of in France. Besides, given the *extreme* exotic-ness of all the twenty-firsters, whatever their complexion and appearance, she didn't really stand out all that much from the others.

Jeff Martin's computer had a large collection of comic books, mostly but not exclusively anime and manga.

They were all missing their magic, the magic of the twenty-first century, and by now they were ready to accept any sort of magic they could get, even the demonic sort residing in Ishmael, Pucorl and the other enchanted computers. Monsignor Savona didn't seem all that opposed to the idea of enchanting a doll. He had spent the time since his arrival interviewing everyone, including Pucorl, Merlin, Ishmael and Catvia.

They were discussing what the effect of enchanting a Barbie doll or a GI Joe with articulated arms and legs might be when Bertrand du Guesclin came in leading a older woman, thin, with just a bit of gray in her auburn hair. There were lines around her eyes and mouth, but she was smiling as she held onto Bertrand's arm.

Ignoring the new arrivals, Ishmael said, "It would depend a great deal on the demon, of course. From what Pucorl seems able to do, I think that a powerful demon could move such a body, but it would be clumsy."

"But if . . ." Annabelle shut herself off when she saw the guests.

They stood. First Mrs. Grady, then the rest as Mrs. Grady motioned them up. "Lord Constable?" Mrs. Grady's tone made the greeting a question.

"May I present my wife, the lady Tiphaine de Raguenel. She wanted to meet you."

Full immersion is a good way to learn a language, and *Langue d'oïl* wasn't quite a different language. By now some—most—of them could follow what he said. But Ishmael translated anyway.

The first question that Tiphaine asked was "What have you learned of astrology in your time?"

"You mean like horoscopes?" Jennifer Fairbanks asked in confusion.

"No one believes in that anymore," Roger McLean scoffed and Ishmael translated it.

"Don't be snide, Roger," Mrs. Grady said. Ishmael translated in a good imitation of Mrs. Grady's voice, and Roger reddened under the rebuke. "In the fourteenth century almost everyone believed in it. Certainly everyone who was educated." She looked at Tiphaine. "I'm sorry for any insult you may take about this, but in our world, astrology was not considered accurate or effective."

Tiphaine was standing stiffly, so Ishmael decided to explain. "We demons never believed astrology worked in the mortal realms. For astrology to work, you would have to abandon the whole notion of free will."

"I don't agree," Tiphaine said. "The stars may guide our steps, but it is we who choose."

"Chaos theory doesn't allow for such a distinction to be valid." Ishmael was almost, but not quite, making that up. Like Pucorl, he was a demon of knowledge—what was more commonly called a familiar. His function was to teach magical arts. That required the ability to know things, and there was information on chaos theory in the books. It was mentioned in connection with meteorology and environmental issues. By his nature, Ishmael was good at filling in the blanks, so to him it was blindingly obvious that chaos theory eliminated the possibility of a world that was both predestined and had free will, because every tiny pebble affected the avalanche. It might not prevent the avalanche, but it would certainly change where the rocks fell. That was truly different from what happened in an avalanche in the netherworld. Back in Ishmael's home, the rocks had control over where—or even whether—they fell. And while they might be affected by the falling of other rocks a bit, mostly it was their own will and nature that controlled, so things were much more likely to balance out in the end.

"Chaos theory? Is that some demonic art?" Tiphaine asked.

"No, it's one of theirs," Ishmael said. "The twenty-firsters."

"The twenty-firsters?"

"The people from the twenty-first century. Like you are a fourteenther."

"Wait a minute," Jennifer Fairbanks said. "What does a demon from the netherworld know about chaos theory?"

Ishmael wasn't sure how to explain. He knew, but didn't really know how he knew. So he said nothing.

"That's a good question, Ish," Bill said. "How do you know about chaos theory?"

"Just my luck to have my vessel owned by a lawyer's son," Ishmael muttered. Then, at a greater volume, "I don't know. How do you digest a chicken dinner? It's just something that happens. I'm a familiar spirit. My function is to fill in the gaps in your magical education. And chaos theory fits, that's all. Besides, it's mentioned in some of your textbooks."

"And how is it you've got access to our text books?"

"Well, Cat has them and we talk. You know, Bluetooth connection."

"Would someone explain to me what you are talking about?" Lady Tiphaine asked plaintively.

Monsignor Savona, who had been sitting quietly in the background, spoke up then. "I have been here almost a week now, and there are two quite distinct sets of knowledge involved. That of the demons and that of the strangers whom Ishmael calls the twenty-firsters. In some ways, what the demons tell us is closer to what we have thought of as the way the world works than what the twenty-firsters say. What I think, and please understand, Madame de Raguenel, this is still a very tentative guess—what I think is that our world is very much like the twenty-firsters see it, and much of what we thought we knew of our world was based on the demons' knowledge of their world. Knowledge that they thought applied to our world, as well."

"You don't think they were lying, Monsignor?" Tiphaine asked.

The left side of Monsignor Savona's mouth lifted in a half-smile, then he said, "I prefer to assume honest ignorance in preference to willful falsehood. I am often wrong in that, but I like it better than erring in the other direction."

The discussion continued, in bits and pieces. Even quite a bit about chaos theory, which Tiphaine considered as ridiculous as the twenty-firsters considered astrology. What was established, though, was that Tiphaine had a very good and surprisingly open mind. They didn't manage to convince her that astrology wouldn't work, but a discussion of magic and the transmutation of elements brought better results.

It was Tiphaine, some hours later, who suggested that if they were to install things analogous to nerves and muscles in a sculpture or doll, the animating demon might be better able to use it.

"You think that would work with Pucorl?" Annabelle asked. "If we were to run wires to his wheel hubs and maybe stick in bent steel springs to act as muscles? Would Pucorl be able to lift a wheel to step over a boulder?"

Tiphaine shrugged. "I have no idea. Pucorl is the familiar, not me."

"Well, Pucorl?" Annabelle asked.

"Maybe," Pucorl said, not sounding all that thrilled with the notion. "It sounds like major surgery, though. What if it doesn't work? I have some connection with my wheels now. I wouldn't want that to be disrupted."

Throughout the conversation, Bertrand du Guesclin had been in the background, not saying much, just making sure nothing threatened his wife. When Commissaire Pierre Dubois arrived, that changed. The guard knocked, and then with no noticeable delay, the door opened. Commissaire Dubois came in.

"Commissaire, have you met my wife?" Bertrand asked, gesturing to Tiphaine.

"Honored, Lady de Raguenel." The commissaire gave a sort of half bow, an abbreviated gesture, before he turned to Bill. "How sure are you of fingerprints?"

"Why?" asked Bertrand. "What have you found?"

"I've had a small squad of the guard practicing finding fingerprints using the kit Bill here made." He held up a thick sheet of pale brown paper. "And we had drawn copies of the prints Bill and Ishmael took at the Red Ox. Gerard says that he thinks that this is a match for one of the prints we found at the inn."

"Whose fingerprint is it?"

"We don't know. It was found in a room at the church of Saint Sebastian."

"What was he doing taking fingerprints in a church?" asked Mrs. Grady.

"Practicing, that's all. He had his kit with him when he went to church yesterday and he got to talking with Father Josef Cabrini. Father Josef wanted to see how it worked, so they went back to one of the side shrines and took prints off a group of candles."

The fingerprint kit that Bill came up with was not a twenty-first century kit. There was no transparent tape to use. Instead they dusted the area, then used a sheet of paper with a thin layer of glue on one side. When they found a print with the powder, they very carefully laid the paper over the dusted print and lifted it up. The drawback was that what they got was a mirror print. The swirls and ridges were on the wrong side. It was also subject to smudging, but that was minor compared to the added difficulty in identifying fingerprints.

Ishmael could mirror image the prints, but he had no printing capacity, so the only way to get the print from his screen to a sheet of paper was to draw it by hand. That effectively meant that Ishmael was the only one who could make a proper comparison of fingerprints. He had the prints in his memory, in two color image format. Even so, with the number of prints collected, Ishmael was starting to get concerned about memory usage.

Pierre held out the card to Bill, who pulled Ishmael out of his pocket. Ishmael took a picture of the print and converted it to the format needed, mirrored it, then ran a comparison. It didn't take long, not with a computer that could program itself. "Yes, that is a match to one from the Red Ox," Ishmael confirmed.

"Fine," Jennifer said with derision. "All that proves is that at some point in the past someone was at the Red Ox and at the church too. But it could have been months ago in both cases. I watched cop shows too, you know."

Bill had to struggle for a moment not to blurt out something like *Really? You watched something on TV besides QVC and the Home Shopping Channel?* Jennifer wasn't dim-witted, by any means, but the seventeen-year-old girl did have an acquisitive streak and was more impressed by appearances than Bill thought she should be.

The problem was...

Being honest, Bill suspected he was being more impressed by appearances than he ought to be, too. Jennifer Fairbanks was far and away—this was his opinion, at least—the best-looking girl among the twenty-firsters. And while she might not be the best-looking girl in all of Paris, she was probably the only one who also had excellent teeth and an odor that wasn't shaky.

Bill was only a few months older than she was—like Roger, he'd just turned eighteen recently. Being in possession of any healthy teenage boy's full complement of hormones—that was to say, an oil tanker cargo hold's worth—he'd been having plenty of fantasies about Jennifer lately. Fantasies which he'd be quite happy to turn into realities, and never mind the awkward issues involving birth control. What the hell, he still had two condoms hidden away in his wallet which he'd secreted there a few months ago just in case...

What eighteen-year-old boy ever thought beyond two condoms?

"No," Ishmael said. "The print in the Ox was a smudged blood stain. And it wasn't from one of the bodies found at the crime scene. This is very probably a print of someone involved in the murders. It's possible that between the murders and the report of the crime scene someone went to the Ox and got a finger in the blood. A right index finger, in this case. At least it's probably a right index finger, because we found two more next to it, probably from the same hand. Also a bit of a palm. It was located on a section of whitewashed daub on the north wall."

"And the nave where the other was found is cleaned weekly. The most recent cleaning was two days ago," Dubois said.

Church of Saint Sebastian
March 2, 1372

"No!" The priest didn't shout, not quite. But Father Damien stood in the center of the large arched double doors of the church of Saint Sebastian and proclaimed, "You cannot bring a denizen of the nether reaches into God's house!" Had he been standing at the altar, his pronouncement would have reached the back pews with clarity and vigor. The formidable police presence came to a halt.

And Wilber quietly thanked Merlin for his quick and precise volume control.

"If they were truly of the dark one's forces, would not this holy place prevent them?" asked Bertrand du Guesclin, his mouth set.

"Do not bandy words with God, Constable of France."

"He's not," Merlin whispered to Wilber. "He's bandying words with a priest. Not the same thing at all."

"So, can you enter a house of God without an invite?" Wilber asked.

"I'm not a vampire," Merlin complained. "What does invitation have to do with it? I've never had any trouble getting into a temple, not of any god."

"But this is supposed to be the one true God," Wilber offered under his breath, but he was grinning as he said it.

"You couldn't prove it by me," Merlin muttered darkly.

Meanwhile the conflict between church and state had reached an impasse, and Wilber wished they had Monsignor Savona with them. That led him to wonder if Giuseppe Savona would support them. He seemed a reasonable enough sort, but Wilber wasn't sure. In any case, this priest was not going to yield to civil authority, and the king's relations with the church were tense enough at the moment that Bertrand wasn't willing to use force to override the priest.

He turned back to the party. "Commissaire, what will the lack of Ishmael do to your investigation?"

"It will slow things down. We were planning to have each parishioner have his fingertips photographed by Ishmael. I suppose we can stand out front and fingerprint them as they go in."

"What's to prevent people from simply not coming through the door?"

"Nothing, but it's the best idea we could come up with."

"You shouldn't trust that thing. He will lie and the holy will be condemned while the demon-possessed murderer goes free," said Father Damien.

Wilber looked around. This was a large church, not quite a cathedral, but a big church with lots of parishioners. Fingerprinting that many people wasn't going to be fast anyway, and with the noise this was making, rumors would be flying and whoever had left the print would avoid being identified. It was effectively a dead end, even if they were let into the church. They might find a few more prints in the nave where they found the first print, but even that wouldn't tell them much. "Merlin, could you spot a demon if you got close?"

"It depends on the demon," Merlin said. "Besides, I doubt if the human who left that print was the vessel of a demon. At least, not when he was in church. Not because the demon couldn't enter the church, but because the demon isn't occupying him or her most of the time. What is probably happening is when the demon lord feeds, he calls his human followers and some demonic followers. The demons share the feast and reward their temporary human hosts with power, health, or knowledge. Sometimes by doing them favors."

"What sort of favors?" Wilber shifted a bit farther from the church doors, where the police and the priest were still arguing.

"Making enemies sick, turning lead into gold, blighting crops. All the usual stuff."

"What about killing their enemies?"

"Perhaps, but not all that likely. A sick enemy can be allowed to get well if the demon isn't called back, but a dead one gives no more reason to feed the demon again."

"Practical folk, you demons," Wilber muttered. "Almost like doctors."

Strangers' Quarters
March 2, 1372

"No, I'm afraid I wouldn't have overridden Father Damien," Monsignor Savona said. "First, because I couldn't. I have a limited range of authority. I'm stretching it in dealing with the demons, but Pope Gregory did want me to talk with Pucorl as well as with the people that arrived in the van. Second, because were I to override him, I would be degrading the right of clergy and the church cannot allow that."

"Right of clergy? asked Paul Grady.

Most of the twenty-firsters were looking almost as confused, but all the fourteenthers were nodding their understanding.

Merlin spoke in Wilber's implant, explaining that the right of clergy and the right—even obligation—of churches to give sanctuary were recognized legal precedents in the fourteenth century, and that it would take centuries for them to be whittled away. At the same time, Monsignor Savona was explaining it to the rest.

"It sounds to me like priests get a bunch of special privileges just because they're priests," said Jennifer. "I think it's an invitation to abuse."

The discussion after that got a bit acrimonious and pretty wide-ranging. Wilber left them to it and went back to his bunk to discuss magic with Merlin.

CHAPTER 9

Strangers' Quarters
March 4, 1372

Lakshmi Rawal plopped down beside Wilber. "So what are you learning from Merlin?"

"Not as much as I would like," Wilber admitted. He had a pen, a real old-fashioned quill pen with an ink pot, and paper out on the table, and he was laboriously drawing weird symbols on the sheet.

There was a short pause, then Wilber said, "Right, Merlin. Sorry. What I should have said is 'not that much that's all that useful given the circumstances.' It turns out that most magic is about inviting and controlling demons, spirits, whatever you call them. There's not much you can do without summoning demons. Merlin has shown me how to make a containment circle and how to select the type of demon that is best suited for a particular tool, but the problem is that magic doesn't work well with mechanics. Each demon is an individual, not part of a system like a gear is part of a gear train. Not even part of an ecology, or if they are, it's a weird sort of static ecology."

"So what does all you just said mean?"

"Mostly that I can't do much until I can summon a demon. And even once I can do that, I won't be able to summon a demon to manage one of Pucorl's wheels and another to manage another wheel. You can't combine them. They won't cooperate. I can't make a machine out of a dozen parts, each with its own demon. To make it work, I have to make the whole machine and call a single demon to animate it. That's why the demons are so interested in our computers. They are the most complex and flexible devices that most of the demons have ever seen. And the power of the demon is a mix of the innate abilities of the demon and of the container. According to Merlin, that's an extension of the laws of physics of the netherworld. Take Merlin, for instance. He's a pretty powerful demon, but he's basically limited to talking to me and letting me understand what I hear through the implant. Well, now that he's mine, he's sort of migrated into my communications centers, so I can speak as well as hear."

Wilber turned his head and squeaked. A mouse stuck its head out of a crack in the wall. Wilber squeaked again and broke off a piece of cheese. The mouse ran to the table, ran up the table leg and ran across it. Wilber handed it the cheese and it squeaked at Wilber. Wilber said, "You're welcome," and the mouse, cheese held in its jaws, ran off back to its hole in the wall.

Lakshmi watched the mouse go. She wasn't fond of mice, and that looked more like a rat to her than a cute little white mouse anyway. At the same time, what Wilber had just done was *impressive*. "How much did that mouse understand?" she asked. "I mean, mazes aside, a mouse doesn't have the world's biggest brain."

Wilber got that listening look again, then spoke. "Merlin says that part of what was going on was the communication magic that he can do. The mouse couldn't understand another mouse offering it cheese as well as it understood me. The magic allows me to pull a real Dr. Doolittle. Horses, cats, mice, I make their sounds and they understand as though I were talking their language, even though they really don't have a language." He shrugged. "This is magic. It doesn't follow the same rules as science."

"So you couldn't teach me to talk horse?"

"No, sorry," Wilber said. "I could explain your riding style to a horse and it might remember it. I could probably explain what you mean when you say go left or go right, and it might remember that or it might not. Horses aren't that bright and it takes quite a bit of repetition for them to remember stuff. And they are more physically than vocally oriented."

The guard knocked on the door, and it opened to admit Bertrand and Tiphaine.

"We'd better go see what's up," Wilber said, and Lakshmi nodded.

When they got to the other end of the room, Bertrand was telling Mrs. Grady that he was going to have to go back to the coast to prepare for the siege of La Rochelle. "We won it in your history, but that is not a guarantee that we will win it this time. I need to be there to aid in the preparations."

Mrs. Grady was looking about as pale as Lakshmi felt. Bertrand had been their protector from the moment of their arrival, and there were whole bunches of people in the church, in the university, even among the common people of Paris, who wanted all of them shoved into Pucorl and put to the torch.

"As surety of my continued regard, my lady has decided to invite you to stay in our townhouse."

"What about Pucorl?" Mrs. Grady asked. "That van is school property and under my care and authority. I don't see how we could possibly leave it here."

Bertrand grimaced, but Tiphaine smiled an "I told you so" smile.

"I have spoken with the queen," Tiphaine said. "She is in seclusion, of course, until the baby comes. But we discussed the effects of sterilizing water to wash the child and I repeated to her what you told me about the antibodies in breast milk that help the child fight off early childhood disease. She was most impressed and has pled your case to the king. The wall about the courtyard will be opened to allow your van to leave, but only to the stable behind our house. And any future trips must be approved by the crown."

Bertrand spoke then. "I argued your case about enchanting your other gear with the king, but he is required to keep peace with the church. I fear that you are still *officially* not granted permission to enchant any more of your other computers."

The emphasis was there. Lakshmi heard it, and so apparently did Mrs. Grady. But it was nothing you could prove.

Rue Charpentier
March 4, 1372

Gabriel Delaflote looked at the wooden ball joint Paul de Fraine had made and sighed. He could afford one, perhaps two, such joints. The dozens needed to articulate a statue with moving hands, arms, feet, legs, body, and head were well beyond his means. "It is excellent, Paul, but far beyond what I can pay. A knuckle bone?"

"Yes." Paul displayed the carved wooden shell that would fit over the ball. It was carved in the form of a human fingertip, even had a fingernail. "Is it true that the form the demon is placed in controls what it does?"

"It's true, my friend, but more complicated than that. And the notion that an articulated doll would be more capable than a statue is just that, a notion. Depending on the strength of a demon, a statue can speak or even move. From what Merlin has said, the level of artistic talent and detail of the container also has an effect. But while I have learned a great deal, that knowledge is almost entirely untested."

Paul nodded wisely. "Do you think you could show me how to summon a demon?" He laid a finger against the side of his nose in a gesture that went back to the Roman republic. "Not that I would ever attempt such a thing, of course."

"And you're wise not to. I have priests and deacons circling like vultures," Gabriel said. "And it's not something you want to try on your own. Pucorl, Ishmael, and Merlin all confirm that a demon is generally not happy to be summoned, and without the proper bounds is likely to invade the summoner rather than the container. And you don't want a demon contesting you for your body."

"Do they really do that?"

Gabriel looked uncertain. "Pucorl and the others say they do. When they are called to an animal vessel, they are constantly contesting with the animal, but are in control most of the time."

"So you think you will try and enchant a crow?" Again the touch on the nose. "After you get permission, of course."

"It may be my only choice," Gabriel agreed. "Though Pucorl says that demons really prefer to avoid animal hosts."

Paul shrugged as though to say *why should we care how the demons feel about it?*

"Demons can be subtle, Paul. I suspect that having an unhappy demon in your service is a dangerous thing."

They talked some more and Paul suggested a puppet.

"Pucorl says they work, but tend to be clumsy like puppets are in a puppet show, with the limbs flapping around and their knees going the wrong way sometimes. He says they are hard to control, though he has never himself been in a puppet. In fact, that is my greatest concern about the ball joint dolls that Jennifer suggested. They are poseable but do not act on their own any more than a puppet does."

The talk continued. It wasn't the first such conversation, and more people than Paul and Gabriel were having similar discussions.

Rue Lavaud
March 4, 1372

Georges du Pont hit Antoine across the mouth and the boy fell. Antoine was sixteen and a student at the University of Paris, one of the poor students who was there on scholarship. He was, however, from Paris. He'd been born just down the block from the inn, with a surviving mother and younger brother still living there. He made extra money keeping Georges du Pont informed of things going on in the university, and for the past weeks he'd been focusing on learning how to summon a demon.

"I am just telling you what they said," Antoine said, holding his hand over his bloody mouth. Georges was a big man and didn't pull his punches. "Demons don't like living vessels and a demon placed in a human vessel almost always escapes control."

"Why?" Georges cocked his fist and Antoine scuttled back.

"No one knows." That was true, but Antoine knew that the prevailing theory in the Sorbonne college was that human minds were so large and complex as to provide the demon too much scope. The demon's will could not usually override the human's will, but it could use the subtlety of the human's mind to find justifications for distorting—or flat out disobeying—the orders of the owner. At least that was what Father Martin said Plebie's admonition against using slaves in demon summoning meant.

Antoine was glad of that, because if it weren't the case, he would likely find himself chained in the center of a demon-summoning pentagram.

Small village five miles from Paris

The milk smelled glorious. The two foot tall fairy twitched its nose and sniffed. Pookasaladriscase hadn't been called, but it smelled the milk and slipped from its world to the mortal realm with no difficulty. A pooka was a slightly different sort of netherworld spirit than a puck, not that a human was likely to know the difference. This one, at the moment, had a basically human form, with short, black fur, but with a large rat-like snout and whiskers that stuck out a foot and a half to either side of its face. The milk smelled just too good not to taste. It extended a long tongue into the pot and began to lap. In just a very few minutes, the milk pot was empty and the pooka was full. With a satisfied burp, it started to explore.

With no difficulty at all, it slipped through a crack between door and frame that was less than an inch wide, then looked around in the dark. Its eyes grew as it moved from moonlight to the darker interior of the room. It looked at the large pile of sewing in Madame de Avire's hamper, and innately knowing that cloth should not be ripped or torn and that a sleeve should be shaped like a sleeve, began to mend. It was rather fun for Pookasaladriscase. Interesting and intricate and about as instinctive as a spider spinning its web.

For most of the night it mended and swept and cleaned. Just before dawn it quietly slipped back into the netherworld and found itself a long way from its burrow. On the other hand, there was a friendly brook burbling happily over a series of rocks that yawned lazily as Pookasaladriscase arrived. There was a depression in a hillside that would make a good burrow. Perhaps tomorrow night it would visit the farm again.

****

Madame de Avire was a woman of forty, a widow whose husband had died two years earlier. She had two nanny goats and five chickens and she paid her rent on the small cottage by taking in mending and washing from the other villagers.

After waking, she looked around to see a spotless cottage. The fireplace was as clean as if it had been washed with a scrub brush, and the cast iron grating that held the wood was clean and full of wood and kindling. She stared at that and slowly rose. She walked over to the hamper that held the mending, only to find it empty and the clothing neatly folded, and clean besides.

She was breathing hard. Someone had been in her cottage. She could have been murdered in her bed and never known a thing. She could have . . .

She didn't know what she could have, but she lived a life that was full of fears and disappointments. A dead husband and three children, all dead before they reached their second year of life, had not left her with any faith at all in the glories of the world. New and different was dangerous. What if the other villagers had such a visitor in the night? How would she feed herself without the sewing and the mending? The spinning wasn't enough. She looked over at the pile of wool, but there was no pile of wool. There were neatly spun skeins of wool thread stacked in her basket.

She went out the door and saw the milk pot she had forgotten to bring in last night. The lid was off and the pot was empty.

It took Madame half the morning to calm down and remember the legends and the more recent stories out of Paris. She didn't want to offend whatever it was, so she took the wool thread to the factor and got more wool, took the sewing and the laundry around to the other villagers and everyone was pleased. Then she went to the parish priest and asked him what she should do.

Father Carolas went with her to look at her cottage and he was concerned. But he was a countryman who had grown up in a village just like this before he went to seminary. He sprinkled holy water here and there, but he didn't want to wish any more evil on Madame de Avire. She was a good woman, if timid. She shared what little she had with those less fortunate. So he told her she should leave another pot of milk out, and then he did one better. He put a bottle of sacramental wine out beside the pot of milk after blessing it. "There, now. If he can drink blessed wine, he can't be hellspawn."

It was a guess, but guesses were all he had.

CHAPTER 10

Street Outside Chateau du Guesclin
March 6, 1372

Pucorl turned left and entered the opened gates under the arched stone gateway. There were horses in front of him and horses behind him, and he hadn't gone over ten miles an hour on the quarter-mile trip from the courtyard to the stables. He was watching his fuel consumption like a hawk, but it felt good to have his engine running. He shifted his shocks a little as his right front wheel rolled over a cobblestone that was a bit higher than it ought to have been, preserving the smooth ride. His ability to do that suggested that with the right modifications he might indeed be able to "walk," in a manner of speaking, over rough terrain.

The trip had been made in the afternoon, lest anyone get the idea that they were trying to hide something. The streets had been lined by Parisians who ranged from curious to violently opposed to his existence. The average attitude was a sort of sullen resentment. That didn't bode well for his future prospects. The lid was on for now, but there was a boiling stew of fear and resentment beneath that lid.

At this point, Pucorl was just happy to be out of the streets of Paris.

Royal Palace, Hôtel Saint-Pol
March 6, 1372

Charles V looked at the bottle of spirit of wine. It was made by the royal alchemist on the recommendation of his doctors after talking with the twenty-firsters. Yesterday the abscess on his left arm had been washed with what the twenty-firsters called "the sterilizing agent" after being opened and allowed to bleed. Charles wasn't a healthy man. He had gout in his right hand to go with the abscess on his left arm. He had been in something like constant pain since his youth.

He looked at Doctor of Medicine Filberte Renard. "So you have been poisoning me?"

"Not by intent, Majesty. But when I put together what the twenty-firsters said of the effects of poisons, it fit with what I know of treatments we use. A little foxglove can restore the heart to its proper function. Too much, and the patient dies. Sometimes what is a short-term relief can be a long term poison, and lead is apparently a very long term poison."

It was politically impossible for Charles V to meet personally with the twenty-firsters. The church had not declared them demonic—not quite. But the fact that they were brought by a demon was enough of a condemnation that to see them was to be painted with suspicion. So, instead, he had asked Filberte Renard to interview them.

Surprisingly, Filberte had not come back screaming about quacks and charlatans. Instead, he had endorsed their knowledge as useful advances. In part that was because none of the twenty-firsters had any medical training beyond what they called first aid. They were no threat to Filberte Renard's position as the king's chief doctor. They were simply providing knowledge.

"Sooner or later, Your Majesty, people will start condemning them. And, no doubt, me as well. For there is no joy in learning that your attempts to help have in fact hurt." Filberte Renard pointed at the bandage on Charles' left arm and continued. "With the alcohol, I was able to 'operate' and 'excise the infection.' "

"So I will not die when the abscess dries up?"

"No, Your Majesty, but you might have, had it not been treated. If it had been left, its drying would have been an indication that

110

your body had given up the fight for life."

"What now?"

"Now, Your Majesty, there is the true possibility of surgery without having the patient die of infection. A host of ills that couldn't be treated before may now be dealt with. But it will take years and, unfortunately, many deaths to learn what will and will not work."

"Very well, Filberte," Charles V said. "But have a care lest you be burned as a witch."

****

Bertrand entered the king's private office as the doctor was leaving, and he nodded to the man. He wasn't overly fond of Filberte Renard, but he respected him.

"Bertrand," King Charles V said, "come in and close the door. What is a gear train?"

Bertrand noted the blue cloth that wrapped the king's arm where the abscess was. He brought his mind back to the king's question. "A gear train, Your Majesty?" Bertrand bowed deeply. "I have no idea."

"Neither do I," Charles said, "and neither does anyone else. I think you are going to have to put off your trip to the coast." He waved at the new scrolls in the scroll case. "I need you here to watch over the twenty-firsters. Who came up with that expression anyway?"

"It was one of the demons. The one called Ishmael."

"Oh." Charles sounded disappointed. "Well, it's better than calling them demon-borne because they arrived in the haunted wagon. I know that you think we should let them use the magic, but I can't afford to offend the church. That's half the reason I want you here. It's entirely possible that with you on the coast and me unable to act overtly on the matter without offending Pope Gregory, some bishop or cardinal will decide it's better to ask Gregory's forgiveness than my permission, in spite of Monsignor Savona's presence."

"I understand, Majesty. In fact, Monsignor Savona says that

the pope is concerned about the same thing. That's half the reason for his presence. I'll send Olivier to oversee preparations. Honestly, he's a bit too interested in the demons for my comfort."

"Very well, then. Keep them safe and learn what you can, but I still can't give you permission to enchant any more devices."

Bertrand nodded then asked, "What if they get permission from Savona?"

"Then I will limit my response to a fine of some sort," Charles V said. "I can't just leave it in the hands of the church, either. I can't afford to have my authority publicly circumscribed in that way." The king waved his other arm in dismissal, and a candle on the desk flickered.

Wilber's Room in Chateau du Guesclin
March 6, 1372

"I won't be summoning a demon, Mrs. Grady. Instead, I will be migrating, or partially migrating, Merlin from my earpiece to my computer." Wilber pointed at the blank stretch of flooring. It was a fine-grained, dark, wood floor, waxed and polished by hand, but not recently. The room was large for the time, ten by fifteen feet. Apparently, Tiphaine meant it when she had called them "guests."

Wilber, with the help of Bill, Roger, and two of the household servants, had moved the bed and wardrobe to one side of the room. That had brought Mrs. Grady, as well as Tiphaine de Raguenel and Monsignor Savona, to investigate. Wilber didn't mention that his having made the pentagram for use in letting Merlin migrate meant they would have it available for summoning other demons. Wilber looked over at Tiphaine and saw a half smile that would have done Mona Lisa proud on her face. They weren't putting anything over on Madame de Raguenel, but they were preserving her plausible deniability. He looked at Monsignor Savona, who wasn't smiling. They weren't fooling him either, and his frown made Wilber nervous.

"What advantage is there to having a demon sharing itself between your computer and your earpiece? Is that even possible?" Madame de Raguenel asked.

"It isn't that much of an advantage to me," Wilber said. "And, honestly, Merlin isn't sure that he can do it. The thing is, he was able to move from the earpiece into the internal part of my implant and there is no physical connection between them, either. If it works, Merlin will have more room and greater computational power, as well as being able to show me things instead of just telling me things."

"I will want to observe the process," Monsignor Savona said.

Wilber nodded. "Yes, of course, Monsignor, and Madame de Raguenel as well, if she wishes."

That half-smile was a little bigger now and Tiphaine de Raguenel nodded her agreement.

It took Wilber another day to paint all the symbols on the floor, having Ishmael, Pucorl, and Catvia check his work. It wasn't that he didn't trust Merlin, but Merlin could only tell him what to draw, not show him. And besides, better safe than sorry. Trust, but verify.

March 7, 1372

Wilber took off his earpiece and set it on his laptop in the center of the pentagram, then stepped outside the pentagram. It was strange. He could hear now, without the earpiece. His natural ears had been fixed. He could hear the discussions and he understood the *Langue d'oïl* clearly. Merlin's presence had had an effect.

He started the ceremony of migration, speaking words in languages older than mankind. Mrs. Grady, Bertrand du Guesclin, Tiphaine de Raguenel, Monsignor Savona, Olivier de Clisson— one of Bertrand du Guesclin's lieutenants—as well as the other students, were watching.

De Clisson wore an eyepatch because he had lost an eye at a battle about six years earlier. To Wilber, he looked like a biker you might find in a movie about the Hell's Angels. He frankly scared Wilber. De Clisson was here because Bertrand du Guesclin wanted him to see what was going on before he left for the coast. Bertrand was going to stay here in Paris, both as jailor and protector to the twenty-firsters.

As Wilber spoke, an almost-figure of glowing light rose from the earpiece of the implant and looked around the room, then seemed to melt into both the computer and the implant earpiece. Once the incantation was completed, the computer came on by itself and Wilber, careful not to disturb the painted lines, went over and collected his earpiece.

He put it on and immediately heard Merlin say in a deep, rich voice. "This is very nice. It's like having a room added to your house, I think. At least, that seems the best analogy to what a human might feel. For a demon like me, it's more like having a new arm added. Two things are very clear to me from this. First, it wouldn't work if your computer hadn't had a Bluetooth app for tweaking your earpiece programming, or if one or the other device had belonged to someone else."

Wilber didn't even mutter, but he thought the words, *"I could hear when I took off the earpiece."*

"Really?" Merlin sounded surprised, and Wilber didn't think he was faking. Merlin wasn't a puck, and therefore wasn't prone to joking and tricks.

Then Merlin spoke again. *"My goodness, your ears have been repaired. It's . . . It must be. . . . To the best of my knowledge, no demon has ever been placed in a prosthetic before. Not of any sort. But the design of the implant and earpiece was to facilitate your hearing and that was also what your ears and the nerves going from them to your brain were for, along with the parts of your brain that translate sounds into words and meaning. It never occurred to me that this might happen. What has happened is your implant has been integrated into your nervous system in a way that it wasn't before. It's almost alive now. A little piece of me is stuck in it, and a side effect of that was that I, a part of me, fixed your ears."*

"Did it hurt you?" Wilber asked, concerned. He had learned

enough about demons that he knew they didn't heal. They reconstituted gradually after being torn apart, but they didn't heal. If Merlin had left a part of himself in Wilber, that piece was gone, at least for as long as Wilber lived. And since they were in the mortal world, it might mean that a piece of Merlin was gone forever.

"No. I have been looking, and apparently I got something from you as well. In the meantime, we don't want to mention this."

"Duh!" Wilber thought to him. *"I'm not an idiot. What did you get?"*

"I don't know. It's very tiny, like a seed. A seed of humanity."

****

Olivier de Clisson nodded slightly and turned away. This would bear thinking about. He had only recently arrived in Paris. He was here to examine the new situation. Where else was he going to be able to see a demon summoning, or rather a demon shifting? He continued to contemplate the ramifications as he walked out of the room.

Olivier got on well enough with Tiphaine. Until all this happened he'd considered her as flighty as one of the fairies she believed in. With her horoscopes and divining bowls, she seemed the sort that would walk off a parapet, expecting the clouds to hold her up. Bertrand always swore she got most things right, but Bertrand had—in Olivier's view—an over-inflated opinion of education.

On the other hand, Olivier was a man who could change his opinions when the evidence changed. When the English treated him well, he served them loyally enough. When that changed, he changed sides. Now, fairies did exist, at least in some form. He had seen a presence rise out of the hearing device and migrate to the other device. He knew from talks with Pucorl that something had recently happened to allow much greater contact between the real world and the netherworld.

What had happened? Pucorl claimed he didn't know, although

he thought it was concentrated somewhere in the direction that humans called "the east" and demons called by several different names depending on the context. Pucorl was similarly noninformative about the question of where the dead went, insisting that it was *too weird for mortal comprehension*.

Olivier waved his groom Robert over. "Get my horse ready. I will be returning to the inn." What with the guests from the twenty-first century, Bertrand's townhouse was overcrowded. Olivier considered having one of the devices stolen, but demon kind were apparently great respecters of legal ownership and having a computer stolen would be both dangerous and difficult to hide.

That just left the possibility of purchase and he knew that those devices would be worth much more than their weight in gold. But Olivier wanted a demon. If demons were going to exist in this world, he wanted one badly.

Inside Wilber's Computer

Merlin spent the first few minutes dividing his attention between reassuring Wilber and getting used to his new vessel. Then he found POV-Ray, Blender and VR-landscape, a suite of programs on Wilber's computer that could be used to draw images and create virtual three-dimensional worlds within the computer. He turned them on easily enough, because he *was* the computer now. And in them he built himself a house and a body with eagle wings on a human form. He built himself a computer room with a computer interface to Wilber's computers, a virtual machine that was magic and science combined. He built a virtual beer in a virtual beer mug, and he didn't have to keep his concentration on them to keep them from changing shape.

That was the difference between the computer-generated virtual world and his place in the netherworld. In the netherworld, a loss of concentration meant a loss of cohesiveness, a loss of reality. But here, as long as the computer was running, he could maintain this virtual form indefinitely. He reached a hand that was human in form and grasped the beer mug, but when he lifted the hand the beer mug stayed where it had been. The physics of the mortal world didn't translate to the virtual world, and neither did the physics of the netherworld. He read Advanced Placement Physics 101 which was both a book and a program on Wilber's laptop.

The physics of the mortal world were incredibly simple to create such a level of complexity in outcome, Merlin thought, while the physics of the netherworld were complicated and even contradictory from location to location. For instance, the law of similarity worked in some parts of the netherworld but not others, as did the law of contagion, the law of words of power, the law of elements, and so on. Merlin realized that the physics of the netherworld was as different from the physics of the mortal world as either were from the non-physics of this virtual world inside the computer. In the virtual world of the computer, everything was made up of shapes, usually triangles, just like part of the netherworld. But in the computer those shapes were made of points in virtual space, which were just numbers.

Merlin was a scholar and an assistant to a wizard or a greater demon, not a puck. He was closer to what the Greeks or Romans would have called a muse. Still, he was less able to do magic than to instruct others in the doing of magic. As he looked through the files on Wilber's computer, there wasn't much of a physics simulator installed. He used the computer's radio, its Bluetooth connection, to contact Ishmael and Catvia, looking for physics simulators. Ish and Cat each had physics simulators as parts of games, but they were limited. For now, at least, if he wanted his beer mug to stay in his hand, he would have to do it manually, adjusting the numbers of each point of each triangle. He reached, using his mind, and watched with half an eye as the numbers describing the position and angle of the beer changed in the simulation. Merlin was a moderately powerful demon. Not a demon lord, but still powerful, and a big part of that power was his ability to keep his focus through distractions. What he wasn't, not by any stretch of the imagination, was a programmer.

Merlin could read Wilber's programming books, but that wasn't the same thing. There was an art to programming and it was an art that required practice and creativity. Merlin wasn't lacking in creativity, but he was very, very old and had been doing very much the same thing for a fair slice of eternity. It would take him a while to learn the new way of thinking that was necessary to do more than play in Wilber's computer.

There was also the matter of taste and smell. The computer had no nose and no mouth. The beer had no flavor but memory.

****

Wilber turned on his computer and instead of his start screen an image of a room appeared. On a couch in that room, a man in Greek or Roman robes lounged. The man sat up as Wilber's screen lit, and Merlin's voice came through his implant. "Hello, Wilber. I've made myself a virtual world based on my memories, but I was wondering if I could get your help with the programming."

Then the screen opened up to the worst chunk of spaghetti code Wilber had ever seen. There was no structure at all, no recursion, no procedures, nothing but instruction after instruction without rhyme or reason.

It took Wilber most of the rest of the day to figure out what was happening. Merlin wasn't programming the computer. He was barely even using the programs that were already there. He was simply instructing the computer.

"What's the use of all this, anyway?" Wilber finally asked.

"What do you mean?"

"Well, can any of this virtual reality you're trying to make be brought out into the real world?"

"I am not sure. The law of similarity works in this part of the netherworld and my presence brings a bit of the netherworld into the mortal world. I am uncertain of the extent to which the nature of the netherworld can be inserted into a virtual world."

"Then what's it good for? Why should I be working on it

rather than on learning magic to do stuff?"

There was a pause and on the screen Merlin stood and flapped his great golden eagle wings, which didn't raise a breeze or even knock anything over when they passed through other objects. "It makes it easier for me," Merlin finally admitted. "It takes concentration, something like energy or will, to hold my form in the netherworld. But in this virtual reality, using the software and structure provided by the computer, I can almost ignore my form without it coming apart." Merlin folded his wings and held out his hands in supplication. "That makes it much easier for me to operate. Easier to *be*. The more I can do through the computer, the less I have to focus my will on."

"All right, Merlin. I'll try. But we have other stuff to do as well. I need to learn magic. We need to find this thing—whatever it is—that's killing people."

"I understand. Can a virtual world be copied from my computer to another?"

"Sure. It would be a series of object files and the software to run them. The other computer would have to have enough memory and the right supporting software." Wilber considered. "Yes, just about any of the computers we have here have the memory and processing power, and we could set up apps for the phones too."

"That would be very helpful, my young friend."

"Why?"

"Because the same thing that is true for me is true for the others, Catvia, even to an extent, Pucorl. And giving them this gift will wed them to our service."

****

Merlin thought of something as he discussed the idea of inserting the laws of the netherworld into the virtual world. He began to wonder if the programming of the virtual world could be put into the netherworld.

Merlin maintained a connection to the netherworld. Demons almost never went wholly into the mortal world when summoned.

The connection to their part of the netherworld didn't disappear. Now it occurred to him that the consistency of his virtual form could be used in the netherworld to give him a more solid base, one that didn't depend so strongly on the mental focus of the moment to remain stable.

That would make him more powerful. He wondered if he could maintain that advantage when he returned to the netherworld in truth.

CHAPTER 11

Warehouse off Rue Monge
March 9, 1372

Father Thomas Aguilar finished the pentagram and stepped back. He, in another history, would have been first in line to burn a witch or condemn anyone who attempted to raise a demon. But in that other history, such efforts wouldn't work, and the best means for a man of poor family to gain in the world was the church. Here and now, in a world where carts drove themselves through the streets of Paris without need of horse or mule . . . in this world, Thomas intended to have his own demon.

He didn't see the tiny crack in the pentagram where the paint had not made the stretch from one cobblestone to the next. He took his place and began the incantation. The crow in the center of the pentagram cawed its distress.

Father Thomas declaimed, and with the wards ripped away, the call was effective.

****

Pucslenstece—not its full name, of course—was pulled away from its contemplation of a huge griffinfly that, from the point of view of Father Thomas, had died out more than two hundred and fifty million years before. It felt the call and lost its focus. Its shape distorted, growing fur, then feathers. It was pulled into time and toward the pentagram. As it was drawn, it examined the pentagram and felt more than saw the gap.

In all of time, Pucslenstece had never once been called to the mortal realm. It had wandered through the mortal realm on occasion, but had never been called.

Now it was enraged and terrified of this new force acting on it, and it squirmed, attempting to escape the bonds. It slipped out through the gap in the pentagram and started looking for a host.

There was a horsefly in the warehouse sitting on a sack of grain. Pucslenstece made for the horsefly and as it moved in, it changed the form of the horsefly. The horsefly grew and its wings expanded, and only magic kept it alive in a world that no longer had the oxygen content of late Paleozoic atmospheres needed for an insect with a two-foot wingspan.

The green glow receded and Father Thomas screamed in terror as the huge horsefly took wing. He turned and ran out into the street and was followed by Pucslenstece. Pucslenstece didn't know much except that it was finding it very hard to breathe and this big mammal was the reason why.

It landed on the priest's head, displacing his priestly hat, and causing him to trip only a few feet from the door of the warehouse. The screaming brought a crowd, and the crowd was both terrified and incensed. They started throwing things at the horsefly.

A rock hit one of Pucslenstece's wings. Another hit the priest's shoulder. While the presence of a demon strengthened the host, be it living or not, most of any additional strength that Pucslenstece provided was used up in causing the horsefly to grow so large. The rock, a fist-size chunk of pyrrhotite, tore loose the wing and the horsefly started to shrink down to the size it had been. As it shrank, a green glow in the demon's original shape rose from it, turned into a green mist, and faded away.

Chateau du Guesclin
March 9, 1372

Twenty men of the Grand Châtelet rode up to the chateau with Commissaire Pierre Dubois at the head of the group.

Bertrand du Guesclin met them at the gate. "Commissaire." He bowed, but only slightly. He was the Constable of France, not what a twenty-firster would call a local chief of police. "You have business with my guests?"

"Nothing dire, Constable, but someone has raised a demon and it has almost killed a priest in front of about a hundred witnesses."

"Where?"

"A warehouse off Rue Monge."

"That's half the town away from here."

"I know. It's none of your guests who caused it. We are sure of that. But we want to have Bill Howe and perhaps Wilber look at it and lend us their expertise. I have sent a troop to gather up Doctor Gabriel Delaflote as well."

"What about Pucorl?" Bertrand asked. "We could take . . ." Bertrand described a possible route. Fortunately, Rue Monge was on the same side of the Seine, so they wouldn't be trying to drive the van over the bridges.

"I don't know. The people are incensed at the moment. The priest is claiming that he happened upon a demon-summoning and was attacked by the demon."

"It might be a good idea to have the people of Paris see Pucorl going about his business, not harming anyone," Bertrand mused. "But I will not force the matter. At least not today."

****

Wilber followed Bertrand into the stables along with Bill, Jeff, Roger, and Monsignor Savona. Bill and Jeff because they had Ishmael and Catvia, Roger because Bertrand du Guesclin had taken a liking to him. And the monsignor because no one could tell him he couldn't go.

Wilber looked around the stable and could see that the horses were nervous, so he said "calm down," in horse.

They all talked at once, neighing and shuffling their hooves. Now the grooms were looking nervous and Monsignor Savona crossed himself, so Wilber said "be quiet," in horse.

They quieted down, except for a big black horse who neighed in challenge. In Wilber's mind it came out as "Back away, you little

123

turd, or I'll stomp you into a mud hole." Wilber was scared, as scared as he had ever been when the bigger boys backed him into a corner or otherwise abused him. But he knew he couldn't show it and now he had Merlin to whisper encouragement in his ear.

So, instead of backing down, Wilber said in horse, "Would you like to become a gelding? I can arrange it."

The big black shut up and backed up to the back of the stall.

"What did you say to Meurtrier?" Bertrand asked, then continued, "I know that horse. We keep him strictly for breeding because, in spite of his conformation and bloodlines, Meurtrier is the next best thing to unrideable. His name is not a joke. Meurtrier killed one of the grooms six months ago and I almost had him put down."

"I asked him if he wanted to be a gelding," Wilber answered. That wasn't exactly how the exchange had gone, of course. Horses, like all animals, didn't have anything you could properly call a "language." But they could conceptualize, to one degree or another, and Wilber had been able to make clear enough to Meurtrier what he had in mind.

Alain Girard, an injured man at arms from Bertrand's retinue and now his head groom, laughed at that, and Bertrand joined in the laughter. Even Monsignor Savona was smiling. There were still signs of warding among the grooms, but there were also a few grins.

Alain Girard said, "If we cut off Meurtrier's balls, we might as well send him to the knackers. Breeding is all he's good for. Tell him that."

Wilber neighed, the horse neighed back, Wilber scuffed a foot, and the horse neighed again in a different tone. Wilber neighed some more, then he turned to Roger. "It's the horse version of you, Roger."

"What's that supposed to mean?" Roger asked, and Wilber saw his fist clench.

Wilber started to say "He's a horse's ass just like you," but Merlin was whispering in his implant, so he took a deep breath and modified his choice of words. "He thinks he's the king of horses, the herd stallion, God's gift to mares. Too good to be ridden."

"That's no surprise," snorted Alain. "Dumb animal will spend the rest of its days right here in this stable. Never see the rest of the world."

"That's an excellent argument, sir," Wilber said, then started talking horse again.

"Now," Wilber said, "he's complaining about the bridle. He says it hurts his mouth and he doesn't like being kneed in the side."

It took a few more minutes, but Wilber got Meurtrier's assurance that he would behave if they let him go with them.

Alain didn't appear to be convinced. He threw up his hands. "If you want to ride him, do so. But if he throws you and stomps you into a muddy spot on the Rue de Larosa, don't blame me."

Wilber got a nervous under-groom to help him saddle Meurtrier by promising to have a talk with the horses on the subject of manure.

Warehouse off Rue Monge

It took them an hour to get through the crowded streets to the warehouse on the Seine. Meurtrier behaved himself well enough, but he made comments on the people, the other horses, the wagons, the smell of the streets. In fact, he was so busy commenting that twice sudden noises frightened him and he shied, almost throwing Wilber, who—whatever his magical abilities in communications—was no horseman. The second time it happened, Wilber told the horse he should be named "Nervous Nelly." Meurtrier settled down a bit after that, but he sulked the rest of the way there.

"There is a stink of magic about this place," said Merlin through the speakers of Wilber's laptop. The laptop was closed and normally that would put it into sleep mode, but Merlin had adjusted the programming so that mic and speakers still worked. He could hear both through the laptop and Wilber's earpiece. Merlin could speak privately to Wilber or publicly through the laptop's speakers.

"Where's your nose, Merlin?" asked Jeff.

"There is no human sense that corresponds. Call it scent or feel, but a demon knows when another has been nearby or when magic has been used."

"That makes sense," Monsignor Savona agreed. "Can you tell what sort of being was here?"

Wilber had noted with some amusement that, to the extent he could, Monsignor Savona avoided the word demon in referring to Merlin and the rest of them.

"I'm not sure yet. We can sometimes tell, but it takes close examination," Merlin said.

They examined the crushed body of the fly, and Ishmael reported that it was a demon of the puck sort, the same sort that Ishmael and Pucorl were. "Looks like someone was trying to raise a familiar."

"Hey," Roger said. "This guy says it was a giant horsefly." Roger, without a demon, had been spending his time trying with reasonable success to learn the *Langue d'oïl* that these people spoke. "Didn't there used to be giant bugs?"

That led to a discussion of time and the existence in the dim past of insects the size of birds.

In the middle of that discussion there was a shout. Another group of Grand Châtelet men arrived with Gabriel Delaflote, who was in scholar's robes and riding his horse with not much more skill than Wilber showed.

****

As he entered the warehouse, Wilber opened his laptop both to let Merlin see through the camera and to get some light from the screen. Roger was talking with the dock worker, and Bill had Ishmael out and was using him like a lamp as he walked around the pentagram. Jeff had Catvia out, but he was looking at the screen, not the warehouse.

Wilber didn't pay much attention, but he found himself—much against his will—a bit impressed with the effort Roger was making to understand the *Langue d'oïl* that the dockworker spoke.

"When the priest came fleeing out, I was two buildings over, loading bags of rye into Master Calvet's warehouse. I look up and this . . ."

It was basically a repeat of the story they had gotten before. The priest had first warned everyone away from the building, then, once a city guardsman, attracted by the commotion, showed up, he changed his argument, demanding that the warehouse must be burned. *That's new*, Wilber thought. But the city guard had insisted they preserve the crime scene and sent young Ferdinand off to bring more guards. By the time the extra guards got there, the priest was getting pretty insistent.

Wilber looked around as he listened. The building was mostly a large open area made up of pillars and arches. A few stone pillars, but more wooden ones. It had a cobblestone floor and was stacked high with bags of grain. There was a large empty area toward the back, near two small alcoves that were probably offices of some sort.

On the floor in the empty area was a pentagram, drawn in a reddish-brown paint that Wilber suspected was drying, but still tacky, blood. In the center of the pentagram, a crow sat and cawed. Its feet were tied to a rock. Crime scene investigation was still not all that well organized. No one tried to stop Roger or the dock worker from wandering around and looking.

Roger did warn the dock worker, "Be careful where you step and don't touch anything. You don't want the city guard to suspect you."

Roger bent over to examine the pentagram, then straightened. "Wilber, bring Merlin over here. I need some light."

Wilber looked up from where he was examining the other side of the pentagram, then walked around it, careful of where he was putting his feet. A laptop is a clumsy item to carry when it's opened up for use. Not heavy, but awkward, and Wilber's was a large screen laptop. Roger pointed at the section and Wilber tilted the laptop so that the screen was facing the spot. The laptop's screen went white, and a relatively bright light shone on that section of floor. The dock worker stepped back, crossing himself, but Roger didn't seem to notice. He was too busy looking at a gap in the lines of containment. Roger pointed. "Is that wide enough to let the demon out?"

"Yes, I think so," Wilber said. "Merlin?"

"Certainly. The size of the gap almost doesn't matter, as long as the gap extends from one side of the containment line to the other. A hair thin gap is plenty. Well, that explains the attack. It wasn't the summoner who had the demon attack the priest. The summoner would have had no control at all if the demon slipped out of the pentagram and occupied something else."

"So why a giant horsefly?"

"I have no idea, but it's entirely possible that the demon had seen one at some point."

"Couldn't it have picked up the horsefly the way Pucorl picked up the van?"

"It could have, I guess, but it didn't. If it had, we would see bits of giant horsefly spread all over the street."

"Over here, guys," Bill Howe called. "I have a paint pot and it looks like it's full of blood."

"Fingerprints?" Wilber asked, shifting Merlin's light from the floor.

"I'm getting my print kit now."

****

Bill carefully dusted the pot and the brush handles for fingerprints. There were several partials on the brush and three good complete prints on the pot. "We're going to have to print everyone for comparison purposes."

"What does that mean?" asked the dock worker.

Roger held up his hand and explained. Nervously, the dock worker let his fingerprints be taken. It took Ishmael no time at all to eliminate him.

They started taking other prints, but as soon as they started the crowd started thinning. Even before they started, the priest—who several people in the crowd identified as Father Thomas, a Benedictine priest who was a clerk for Bishop Baudin—was gone.

"So we go to the cathedral of Notre Dame, and get his fingerprints," Wilber suggested.

Commissaire Pierre Dubois looked at Bertrand du Guesclin, Bertrand looked at Monsignor Savona, who shrugged. The shrug, said as clear as day, that they could try, but unless the priest agreed, they probably couldn't get his fingerprints.

And so it proved.

They got to the cathedral, and though Father Thomas Aguilar admitted to having been attacked by the demon bug, he denied having anything to do with the summoning, save to have seen it. Asked for fingerprints, he flatly refused. "I will not cooperate with the ungodly who commune with the fallen. You will have no fingerprints from me, nor hairs or blood or any bodily substance to use in your demonic rites."

Bishop Baudin backed him up, and so did Monsignor Savona, though he didn't seem happy about it. They left, having gained no evidence. Worse, having established a precedent for the right of clergy to refuse to give the secular authorities evidence.

Cathedral de Notre Dame

In a small private room, Bishop Baudin took a seat, but didn't invite his secretary, Father Thomas Aguilar, to do the same. "Well, Thomas, what did you get wrong?"

"Bishop, I don't—"

Bishop Baudin held up a pudgy hand festooned with rings. "Spare me, Thomas. The only reason I didn't give you to them was because I didn't want the precedent. We cannot have it established that they can force a member of the clergy to give evidence. Now tell me, what did you do wrong?"

"I don't know, Bishop. I followed the directions precisely.

There was a crow tied to a stone in the pentagram, but the demon appeared outside the pentagram on a sack of grain." Father Thomas considered for a moment, then continued. "As I think back, I believe there was a fly on the sack of grain, but there were flies all over the warehouse."

"There will be no further experimentation, Thomas. We will not turn you over to the secular authorities, but we will deal with you ourselves if we have to. Monsignor Savona will be reporting to Pope Gregory. He may only be a priest, but he has Gregory's ear."

"I will burn my—"

Again he was stopped by that pudgy hand. "No. Continue your studies. We, the church, may have need of the knowledge. You did, after all, manage to raise a demon. But next time you think you are ready, you will report to me and I will have someone look over your work." Now the pudgy face smiled. "The Lord God created the heavens and the earth and, presumably, the netherworld as well. That makes demons and dealing with them the purview of the church, whatever that officious little clerk of Gregory's thinks."

Chateau du Guesclin
March 10, 1372

Bertrand rolled over in the large canopied bed and nuzzled his wife's auburn hair.

She leaned back into his nuzzle and whispered, "Will the church attempt to seize the enchanted items?"

Bertrand rolled back onto his back with a disappointed sigh. "Not immediately. They have to be careful too. If they seize Pucorl and the rest, it will look like they simply want the demons for themselves. Pierre Dubois is convinced that Father Thomas Aguilar was the one trying to raise a demon. The church has access to all of Delaflote's notes, and they aren't the only ones. Since it worked, and worked so publicly, half the Sorbonne college has been researching how to raise demons."

"But *we* can't!" Tiphaine turned to face him, anger written clear on her face.

"Well, no one is supposed to. And the church has managed to get ahead of the king as the body from whom you must obtain permission."

"But no one can challenge them on it when they break their own rules." Now Tiphaine just sounded sad. And Bertrand knew why. The church had always treated her with a reasonable degree of circumspection, but that circumspection had not come free. It had cost much in the way of donations to church and charity. Not that Tiphaine objected to the donations. What she objected to—and had as long as Bertrand had known her—was the fact that the church, because of her interest in astrology and divination, could *require* those donations. She also resented the fact that churchmen were safe in doing that for which she might be condemned.

"Yes." Bertrand lifted a hand to her cheek. "The king can't give his permission. Even I can't give my permission. But you, 'Tiphaine the Fairy,' are a known scholar and mystic. It would be understood and accepted were you to allow the enchantment of more items. Also, most people, from la Bellièr to Paris, would accept that you knew what you were doing."

"Publicly?"

"No. Keep it as secret as you can. It will come out, sooner or later, but later is better for all of us."

"And what will you be doing while I defy both church and king?" Tiphaine asked, with more than a little asperity.

"I'll be the bluff and simple soldier. I've sent Olivier to the coast, but I am going to be very busy organizing the logistics. And when later comes, I will be standing beside you, insisting that if you did such a thing, you had to have a good reason."

CHAPTER 12

Chateau du Guesclin
March 12, 1372

Tiphaine sat at her desk. It wasn't what a twenty-firster would call a desk. They would have described it as a podium. But Tiphaine was used to it and had a tall stool to sit on while she worked. She was trying to work out horoscopes for the twenty-firsters. She lifted the pen from the ink pot and touched the tip to the pot's edge without thinking about it. She moved it to the page, but stopped before touching pen to paper.

She had asked them their date and time of birth and the sign under which they had been born. They hadn't laughed, except for Roger, but she could tell that most of them had wanted to. But whatever the superstitions of that other century, she had worked with astrology her whole life and had great success in using it to predict outcomes. She would not give up her learning and experience just because savages from another century didn't know enough to respect it. Still, she was distracted by what the young twenty-firster woman was doing.

Jennifer Fairbanks wrapped the fine copper wire around the wooden cylinder and painted it with lacquer. It had taken almost a month of work, constantly interrupted, but she said she was close. It was a crystal radio set, and if Mademoiselle Fairbanks was reading the specification on her phone right, the phone would transmit and the crystal radio set would receive, as though they had complementary signs.

Tiphaine could well see that it was a delicate operation and so far there was only the one receiver. There was no way to generate an output except by what they called a "spark gap."

Jennifer complained that she was having to remember stuff that she had done for science fairs when she was ten years old. Apparently the young woman's mother was an accomplished practitioner of these arts, an "electrical engineer" for the "French power company," one who guided the work on "massive turbines" all over France. Whatever all that meant.

"Will a demon really be able to talk to us through this device?" Tiphaine asked curiously.

"It should, if I'm remembering the frequency calculations correctly."

"Do you think a demon would be interested in occupying such a device?"

"I'm not the person to ask about that," Jennifer admitted. "Pucorl or one of the others probably knows. But we aren't allowed to enchant our other computers, cell phones, and stuff. I have my computer, my phone, and a day planner, and I can't use any of them because Mrs. Grady is afraid that turning them on will invite a demon to occupy them. And my day planner doesn't have Bluetooth because I wanted to be sure that it couldn't be hacked. So it, at least, ought to be safe. And it does have a camera, a good one."

"I am not fond of the restriction either," Tiphaine said, watching Jennifer carefully, "but ignoring it would entail risk, not only for you, but for me and my husband as well. And where is the advantage to us in your enchanting your devices?"

Jennifer stopped her winding and looked at Tiphaine. Tiphaine looked back and waited. Bertrand was under restrictions and so was she, but she needed the access to the spirit world that the demons represented. It was worth some risk to get that.

This was the start of a negotiation. At least, a suggestion that Jennifer make an offer.

That wouldn't be easy. All Jennifer had was the clothing on her back and the items in her backpack. And the value of her electronic equipment was literally incalculable.

"These devices are worth an incredible amount," Jennifer said, "even in the condition they are in now. Properly enchanted so that they will be safe to use and never run out of vital force . . . why, I just have no idea what sort of price an enchanted iPod like Ishmael might bring."

Tiphaine grinned. *Good.* The girl saw. Suddenly Jennifer's expression changed. She looked frightened. *Ah,* Tiphaine thought, *she realizes she is out of her class.* Tiphaine had noted almost from the beginning that none of the twenty-firsters were any good at bargaining. Well, none but young Wilber, and Tiphaine suspected that was Merlin's doing.

"I need to talk to Mrs. Grady about this. And I think it would be of great value to us all to have Liane and Lakshmi here as well."

Tiphaine tilted her head to the side and considered the girl's choices. . . . They were reasonable. All women, so more likely to be discreet than the men, who were always tempted to bluster. She stood and went to the wall, where she pulled a cord. A moment later, Jolie came in. "Jolie, run and fetch the ladies. Amelia Grady, Liane Boucher, and Lakshmi Rawal. Ask them to join me here." Tiphaine paused, then finished. "I think that is all."

When Jolie had left, Tiphaine turned back to Jennifer and said, "I will be disadvantaged in our negotiations because these discussions must remain secret. It's not that I distrust the servants, but they do gossip, and the church has spies everywhere." Actually, Tiphaine didn't think she would be at any disadvantage at all. They were pleasant girls, the twenty-firsters, but naive and as transparent as the glass in Pucorl's windshield.

"I wonder if the summoning of demons in the dark of the night might have less to do with moonlight and more to do with not wanting the local churchmen to discover you doing so," Jennifer said.

"Another question we should perhaps discuss with Pucorl or Ishmael."

"Or Merlin?"

"Merlin, I find, makes me rather nervous. Pucorl, Ishmael, and Catvia all seem rather minor. But I suspect that if Merlin is not a demon lord, he is at least a demon chevalier—what the English call a knight. And, to be frank, I find I am disturbed by the . . ." Tiphaine paused, searching for the right word. ". . . the intimacy of the connection between Merlin and Wilber. It causes me concern."

"Not me!" Jennifer said. "But that may be because I knew Wilber for years before this happened. It was hard for him to talk and his voice was . . . not pleasant. Now he can talk and hear and . . . It's like the real Wilber who had been in there all the time has been set free."

Lakshmi arrived in time to hear that. "Wilber? Have you heard him singing since he got Merlin? He's got a great tenor voice these days. Not to mention the whole Dr. Doolittle thing he's got going. So what's this all about? I was talking to that carpenter of yours about making a washboard, and I almost had him convinced to give it a try."

"That will be a relief to the servants and to our clothing," Amelia Grady said, coming in the door. "And the still that your coppersmith is making for me is almost entirely complete. We should be able to achieve concentrations of alcohol and vinegar that are strong enough to sterilize wounds and open sores in amounts large enough to be of general use."

"It seems you twenty-firsters cannot help but change our world. What of Liane's work with the foundryman to make a cast iron stove?" Tiphaine asked.

"That is the cause of the delay," said Jolie. "Lady Liane is with the master baker at the foundry, attempting to get a door plate made."

The oven—which Liane was happy enough to call a Franklin stove, claiming that Benjamin Franklin was the last worthwhile American—was, in fact, not a Franklin stove, but an oven that used the shape of the flue to direct the heated air in such a way as to produce a better, more even, baking process. Baking in the here and now was done in Dutch ovens over an open flame, with coals heaped on the lids.

Each of the twenty-firsters had taken on projects, even the boys. Roger was working with the blacksmith in an attempt to produce a rifled musket which would have both greater range and—because of the Minié ball and paper cartridge that Roger knew about—would also be faster to fire. He said he might be able to come up with an effective flintlock and do away with the slow match on a stick used in the here and now. In the late fourteenth century, the hand cannon was almost a two-person weapon and not very valuable on the battlefield. Bill was working with the city guard, being their crime scene investigation squad and trying to introduce modern police procedures. Even Jeff, who was not the sharpest tool in the toolbox, was showing the local guardsmen how to make modern barbell-type exercise gear. Annabelle was spending most of her time with Pucorl, but she was also trying to get a single cylinder steam engine built. She hadn't made much progress yet.

They were still discussing their various projects when Liane came back from the foundry. "What's up?" Liane asked.

Tiphaine looked around. With everyone gathered, the room was full. Servants had come to see what was happening.

Jennifer said something in that barbaric form of English they used sometimes.

Liane said something, also in English.

Mrs. Grady looked unhappy, but didn't say anything.

Tiphaine sent the servants out. "Be seated, gentle ladies, and let us speak with candor and to good effect." She turned to Amelia Grady and continued. "I know you are concerned, but after the time I have spent in converse with Pucorl and the others, I cannot bring myself to believe that they are the fallen of biblical reference. That they are beings of power and chancy to deal with, I do not doubt. But I see less of inherent evil in them than would, I think, be present in the fallen."

Amelia's expression was that of someone tasting something sour, but she nodded acceptance of Tiphaine's argument. "There are still the restrictions laid by the church. I don't want my son to be burned at the stake any more than I want him to be eaten by a demon."

"I too have no desire to be the subject of an inquisition by the church. So the enchantment of any devices should be kept as the deepest of secrets."

"That won't work," Amelia Grady said. "You know that these things get out, and someone tried to enchant a demon into a crow just the other day. Once someone succeeds, there will be demonic ways of finding out who owns a demon."

"Not necessarily. Pucorl, Ishmael, Catvia, and Merlin together have not been able to find the identity of the demon that stalks the streets of Paris committing foul murders and performing unholy rites. But even if they do find a demon that can tell them that your computer is enchanted, what is the church to say?" Tiphaine asked. " 'We know you enchanted that item because our demon told us so'?"

"There are . . ."

"Yes, I know there are ways around that. But the need has, I think, come to be greater than the risk." This wasn't going as Tiphaine had hoped. She was having to convince Amelia Grady that enchanting the magical items was a good idea and that didn't improve her bargaining position. Perhaps the twenty-firsters were not the novices at bargaining she had imagined. "The need is almost entirely yours. It is your items that are most tempting to a demon. I suffer almost the same risk as you and gain nothing. What, after all, might I learn from a demon enchanting Jennifer's electronic day planner that I couldn't learn from Pucorl?"

"That's my question. What is the advantage to putting a demon in each of our devices? Wouldn't it simply be a duplication of effort?"

"No, it wouldn't," Jennifer said. "Look at us here. There are no enchanted items in this room unless Madame de Raguenel has

137

enchanted the inkwell. That means we don't have access to Pucorl or Merlin. And we don't even have access to the standard features of our stuff. If we had all our stuff enchanted, I could use the earbuds and no one would even know that the demon in my phone was telling me what Pucorl and Wilber thought about the crystal set. I could have my phone ping the crystal set to check the frequency settings. You could get better help with the still. Liane could discuss the flue dimensions with Annabelle while she was talking to the blacksmith. It would speed things up enormously.

"Besides which, it's the guys who have the demons. Not us. I, for one, have no desire to go back to barefoot in the kitchen."

Tiphaine had no idea at all what that last meant. Being bare of foot in the kitchen rooms of the townhouse would be very dangerous. On the other hand, Jennifer was apparently arguing her case, so Tiphaine decided not to interrupt.

There was a knock at the door and Tiphaine called out, "Enter."

The door opened and Jeff came in. "I heard you were having a hen party, and Catvia said she wanted to come." He lifted the computer and set it on the table next to Jennifer's crystal set. Then he turned and waved. "I'll be out in the stableyard with Pucorl and Annabelle."

Tiphaine was even more confused by "hen party," but again decided to leave the question for another time. Having the succubus as a consultant might well be useful. Discussions with Catvia had proved both interesting and useful in the past.

"Welcome, Catvia," Tiphaine said, as Jeff closed the door behind him.

"See what I mean, Mrs. Grady?" Jennifer said. "Hen party, no less."

"Yes, but it's . . ." Amelia Grady clearly stopped herself from finishing the sentence.

Catvia wasn't so reticent. "But it's Jeff. The guy who is actually smarter when he lets the little head do the thinking. So, what were you girls talking about when I had Jeff interrupt? Want me to guess?" Her screen lit up with an image of the pentagram of summoning in Wilber's room.

"Don't guess. Just tell us what you think," Lakshmi said. She got along with the succubus better than any of the other girls.

"I think you are wasting time."

"Explain, if you would?" Tiphaine asked.

"If you want to get demons who are compatible to your needs, you should invite them in. You should have done it weeks ago. We have done what we could to hide your devices from the less benign spirits because, honestly, the twenty-firsters have notions of reality that are intriguing. I'm not by any means convinced that your Newton had it right, much less your Einstein or later scholars. And I am certain that the rules they provide for describing your world do not work the same way in ours. I know that water likes low places because I have discussed it with streams. I know that rocks are lazy because I have talked to rocks when I could wake them up. Everything in the netherworld has intent that is inherent to its nature. That you don't, or at least might not, is terrifying and intriguing all at once. I like you." The pretty cat woman on the screen shrugged, shifting cartoon breasts provocatively. It was automatic for Catvia.

"All right," Amelia Grady said, but she didn't sound happy.

"No, not all right," Tiphaine said. "I agree that this is your wisest course, but it is not the *safest* course for you. And not the safest course for me or my husband either. If we are to let you summon demons to our home, there must be some compensation for the risk we take."

"So," Amelia said, "this was all about getting an enchanted computer for yourself."

"Of course," Tiphaine agreed placidly. "But that doesn't make my arguments any less valid."

They negotiated for hours, with Catvia playing the role of arbitrator. It wasn't only the issue of how much Tiphaine would pay. That was the easy part. The real issue was whose device was going to be sold. Jennifer agreed to giving her day planner to Tiphaine in exchange for the rent income from Vitré, a village in Brittany, and the title Baroness of Vitré.

"It is a true ennoblement, " Tiphaine assured them. "Lasting your lifetime and that of your heirs. Should you return to your own time, it will be waiting for you then."

"And we will be able to enchant all the magical items?" Amelia Grady asked in confirmation.

"So far as I am concerned, yes."

****

Just how far that took them was apparent as soon as they left the room. At the door, Monsignor Savona was waiting with his head tilted to one side. Amelia Grady felt her mouth twist. "All right, everyone. Back inside. Monsignor Savona, won't you join us?" She spoke in twenty-first century French, which Monsignor Savona understood well enough. At least that phrase.

They went back into the room, and negotiations began again.

Monsignor Savona sat in one of the chairs along the wall and adjusted his cassock as he sat. "I understand your concern, and to an extent I share it. But you must understand the church's position. We have a responsibility to all of Christendom. We know for certain that not all of the spirits are benign. If, as your companions have said, the walls blocking the netherworld from our mortal realm have been swept away, we need the guidance of the Lord of Hosts even more."

Amelia was impressed. She was a believer, but not a member. Not Catholic, Protestant, Muslim or Buddhist. She just had a feeling there was something more than the random combination of chemicals to life. But Father Savona's faith was moving and quite clearly real. "What do you suggest?"

"I know it is a great deal to ask, but the church must have its own source. One that is not under your authority or any secular authority."

Tiphaine asked, "And who will donate a king's ransom to the church?"

"One of the boys," Liane said.

"The boys aren't here," Amelia said.

"You wouldn't be willing to give up any church property, would you, Monsignor?"

"I would if I had any, but my writ doesn't extend so far."

"What about your camera?" Jennifer asked Liane. "I gave up my day planner."

"What about Lakshmi?"

"I only have my cell phone and my computer," Lakshmi said.

"Well, I'd rather give up my cell than my camera," Liane said.

Amelia could understand Liane's point. The camera was top of the line, two thousand dollars and more, with a connection to her computer, and Liane was proving to be a talented young cinematographer.

"Then give up your phone and keep your stupid camera," Lakshmi said. "Sorry, Liane. Look, you're good and I know it, but I can't give up my phone. I just can't. Besides, I'm not even Catholic." Lakshmi's hand came up as though she would push the words back into her mouth as soon as they came out.

Up until then, they had been carefully noncommittal about their religions. This was after the split between Rome and the Eastern Orthodox church, but centuries before the Reformation, and in this part of the world the church had a hard way with heretics. Just ask the Cathars, a group that had been killed off to the last man, woman, and child in the thirteenth and fourteenth centuries.

Monsignor Savona didn't seem surprised or particularly upset by the revelation. "The books in Catvia do mention that France in the twenty-first century, was . . . is . . . will be . . . a secular state with no official connection with the faith. While that is a matter of serious concern to the church, the truth is that the church just at the moment has so many matters of serious concern to deal with that for now the particular faith of any of the twenty-firsters has been set aside."

"In other words," Lakshmi said, "you've decided not to burn

us until you've milked us for all you can get." She didn't sound the least bit thankful for the reprieve.

"I would say rather that we would prefer . . . that we hope . . . for your eventual reconciliation with the church." But there was an expression on his face that Amelia Grady didn't like.

Tiphaine spoke then. "Monsignor Savona is a man under orders. He cannot guarantee the church's further actions. Being angry with him will do you no good and may do you harm if in your anger you inflame him to a matching dislike."

"I think we have gotten off the subject," Catvia said. "Monsignor Savona wants a computer of his own."

"Not me, I fear," Monsignor Savona said. "Many members of the local church are less than pleased with my 'presumptuous interference.' Were the device given to me, it would be claimed that I used my position as papal nuncio to seize for myself an artifact of surpassing value. Perhaps to His Holiness?"

"Why not the church?" asked Liane.

There was a sardonic twist to Monsignor Savona's lips as he said, "Who owns a gift to the church? Cardinal de Dormans would no doubt feel that such an artifact given to the church should be under his authority as long as it was in Paris. The church is not quite the solid edifice of faith that we would prefer."

"How about we give it to God?" Liane asked.

"I would think that who gets it is going to be up to who gives it," Lakshmi said. "So if Liane is giving up her phone, she ought to be able to give it to whoever she wants."

"Hey, wait—" Liane stopped.

Amelia had to stop herself from commenting on how cleverly Lakshmi had manipulated Liane.

"All right," Liane said resentfully. "I'll donate my phone, but I'm keeping my camera and you are all going to owe me big time." Then she looked at Monsignor Savona. "And I'll donate it to God. In the care of the church, but to God."

"Catvia, what will that do?" Lakshmi asked.

The computer was silent for a while, and on the screen the girl with the cat ears and big cat-slitted green eyes rubbed her chin. Finally she spoke. "I don't know. The netherworld is a very large place and includes much that I do not know or understand. I would think that in that case, the demon or angel or whatever that occupied the phone would be answerable to the owner of the phone. And if it's . . . " Her voice trailed off and she shrugged, shifting her large breasts.

"I wonder," Tiphaine said, "could the ceremonies used to call Ishmael or Pucorl be used to call an angel of the Lord?"

"I think we need to bring Doctor Delaflote, Merlin, and Ishmael into this," Jennifer said. "Even Pucorl."

Chateau du Guesclin
March 13, 1372

The bells started ringing around ten in the morning. They started at the Hôtel Saint-Pol and spread from there.

"What's going on?" Wilber asked Monsignor Savona.

"I'm not certain, but it's likely that there is a new royal child," Savona said.

"Merlin?"

"Yes. Listen to the bells," Merlin said. "It's in the tone."

Wilber managed to stop himself before he called that ridiculous. By now he knew quite clearly that a bell in the netherworld would ring with meaning in every sense of the phrase and a demon would be able to hear the meaning in the ringing of the bells. So he listened, using the power of supernatural hearing that Merlin gave him. And the meaning *was* there, but at the same time it wasn't. He also heard with the precision of a computerized sound analysis, the precise frequency of the bells. Each of the bells, from one end of Paris to the other. "I hear it, but should I? These are mortal bells, assuming that they haven't been enchanted. How are we hearing a message in their ring?"

"No, you are correct. They are mortal bells. But there is

enough magic in the mortal world now that the intent of that first bell ringer is having an effect and the effect is echoed in the rest. I can hear it. Either because they were expecting just that message, or just from the magic seeping, I can't tell. But it's a birth and the child is a boy."

Wilber could hear it too. "You're right, Father. Louis of Valois has just been born, on schedule." They knew that Louis I was the expected child from the history books. They had even shared that it would be a boy, and by their histories would grow to adulthood.

"Then I think it is good that we have made our arrangements about the gifts and the papal permissions. For the best time to do something that the king hasn't exactly sanctioned is when he is busy with a new child. It would be best if all your items were enchanted in the next day or so."

Chateau du Guesclin
March 14, 1372

Annabelle watched nervously as Monsignor Savona knelt in the circle next to the pentagram and began to recite a cross between a prayer and an invocation. He was asking Jesus to send an angel to occupy the phone that Liane had given to God to guide his flock. And it was working. At the very least, they were getting something in the pentagram. It was a glowing, golden nimbus that stretched to the ceiling of the room and slowly shrank to not much more than the height of a man, brightening as it contracted until she could barely see for the brightness of it. Then it slid down into the phone and the phone came on.

Pucorl was not happy about the invocation of an angel. Pucorl was from a different mythos and not overly fond of Christianity. Annabelle knew that only from private conversations she had with the van, mostly with her earbuds in so there was no way anyone else would overhear. As it happened, Pucorl himself had not been summoned by a witch or sorcerer who had been burned for heresy, but he knew pucks who had.

The phone came on and the glow of the pentagram faded. Then the phone spoke. "I am the angel Raphico."

"Raphico?"

"Did you believe that you knew all the names of all the angels of the Lord?" Raphico asked.

"Tell me then, and I abjure you to speak only truth, are these beings who have inhabited these other devices of the fallen? Are they demons of the pit?" Monsignor Savona asked.

"I do not answer to you, Monsignor Savona, nor even to your master, the heir of Peter. The gift was given to the Creator, not to any mortal. I answer only to the Father, the Son, and the Holy Spirit."

CHAPTER 13

Chateau du Guesclin
March 16, 1372

Over the last two days, Raphico had managed to say very little, very eloquently. It had not confirmed or denied that the demons occupying the van and other electronic devices were among the fallen but had strongly implied that the Creator didn't object to having the items enchanted. "It is likely that with recent events, the enchantment of swords and other things will be necessary."

The one thing that it had said clearly and straightforwardly was that any action taken against it would be answered by the Creator, both here and in the next world. "I am God's ambassador to mankind and am not answerable to any mortal."

He had even gone so far as granting them dispensations for the enchanting of items, so long as they didn't call on certain specific creatures. "Invoking Beelzebub is not allowed. The stench of evil is greater even than the stench of the Paris sewers."

Pucorl's Garage, Chateau du Guesclin
March 18, 1372

Annabelle set the freshly enchanted testing system on the front seat and plugged it into Pucorl. "Okay, Royce, what do you see?" Annabelle grinned as she said it because the system had started talking as soon as it was enchanted, and its first words had been "Call me Royce. Rolls Royce," in a voice that sounded just like Sean Connery. It still sounded like Connery and Sean Connery wasn't even her favorite James Bond.

"Pucorl's in quite good condition. There's a bit of mud under his left front fender, but nothing serious. As to the modifications to his wheels, I think you're going to want to make the springs a balanced system. Bi-metal springs, like on a thermostat, might work best."

Royce had a plug that fit into the van, but it also had alligator clips, a laser temp gauge, and a variety of other sensors. And, because of what his container was, had an inherent knowledge of auto mechanics which was combining with his demonic knowledge of how magic worked to produce some unexpected results.

"How can you tell that there is mud under his fender?"

"I'm not entirely sure but I think it's mostly how the laws of physics interact when one of us—"

"Royce is telling me he wants me to try to prevent him from examining my systems," Pucorl said then.

"This may hurt a bit, but I will try not to push too hard," Royce said, clearly to Pucorl.

Annabelle leaned against the driver's side seat, not sure whether to be annoyed or intrigued. She wasn't used to her testing equipment leaving her out of conversations with the vehicle she was working on.

Pucorl grunted, his lights blinked, and the screen on Royce got vague and cleaned up.

"What's going on?"

"I am trying to test how much of the information I am getting comes from Pucorl's sense of the van and how much of it comes from the system electronics. It's proving to be more complicated than I was expecting."

"How?" Annabelle climbed the rest of the way into the van and sat in the driver's seat, setting Royce on the passenger seat. She looked at the dash readouts, then the readouts on Royce again.

"I was expecting that parts of what I would get were the electronics and part Pucorl. For instance, the mud under the fender. Pucorl, and the weight on the right front wheel, the system electronics—specifically the pressure sensor in the shock absorber. But that's not what is happening. When Pucorl resists, I can't read the pressure sensor at all. And when I push, I can get a sense of the mud that isn't coming from Pucorl."

"That makes sense," Annabelle mused.

"Not to me, it doesn't," Pucorl said.

"Nor to me," Royce echoed.

"Well, look. You said that when you get put into a statue you can see through its eyes, right?"

"Yes," Royce agreed. "A Greek scholar once invoked me into a statue of one of Vulcan's automatons, and I could see out of the statue's eyes. But I wasn't enough in this world to move it or even speak through it. All the scholar ever got was whispers in his mind, which he thought were his imagination. The fool never paid any attention to me."

"The point is," Annabelle said, "that you can see through eyes that are just painted, or even not painted. There are no nerves in those eyes, not even any lenses that light can penetrate. No retina, no nothing. But you can see through them."

"So this device doesn't have eyes," Royce said. "Well, it has a camera and a laser temperature sensor, an— Oh, I see. This device has lots of sensors. So it's like the knowledge of your world. My James Bond voice, for instance."

"That's right," Annabelle said, remembering other discussions with Pucorl, Merlin, and Ishmael, as well as Catvia.

In their own world, the creatures of mythology were somewhat vague, not fully formed. The magic of a triceratops isn't the magic of a human, and the magic of China isn't the magic of Western Europe. For that matter, even the magic of pre-Christian Greece isn't the magic of Christian Greece. The beings of the netherworld were formed as much by the vessels they inhabited as by the magic of their world. Pucorl's worldview was powerfully influenced by the information in the van's systems, including the movies on the flash drives plugged into the passenger side front seat, where Paul's cartoons were located.

Royce was in a testing device, and while not as innately powerful as Merlin, was more powerful than Pucorl. But the test kit that had its own computer and software had very little cultural information. Royce had gotten its name from what might be called the milieu of the device and the spells involved.

A demon called to a statue in fourteenth-century France would have a worldview that matched the worldview of the crafter of the vessel, combined with the worldview of the wizard performing the summoning.

"You have eyes in the form of cameras. You can see through your sensors. And the magic, the physics of your netherworld, is such that function, to an extent, follows form. It's the shape of an eye, so it represents an eye, so it works as an eye. The design of the sensor kit you're in is to read and understand the workings of a device, so you can. Just like you could see through a cat's eye marble if it was put in the head of a statue. See like a cat does— Oh, my effing G . . . ah, goodness."

Annabelle jumped from the van and ran into the townhouse.

****

"Diana, where's Emil?" Annabelle asked the maid, who was wearing an undyed woolen dress that was, at least now, washed regularly.

Diana looked back with confusion and Annabelle remembered that she had left her newly enchanted phone in the van. Diana hadn't understood her accent. Carefully, she repeated the request in a form closer to the *Langue d'oïl* that was the language of this time.

"In the wood shop."

Households like this one had staff that did just about everything. There was a tailor and a dressmaker, a carpenter who was a wood carver and cabinet maker, more like what Jesus' dad did than what a twenty-first-century carpenter did. There were grooms and cooks and blacksmiths, all for one household. Annabelle was still getting used to that.

She headed for the wood shop. This might work. What would happen if, say, a steam engine had a plug for the sensor suite and interpretive computer that was Royce to plug into. According to the physics of her world, it shouldn't do anything. But, if it worked like the sculpted cat's eye, then Royce could look at a steam engine and tell her if all the seams were good or if there was leakage in the cylinders.

Shop in Paris
March 18, 1372

Nicolas Flamel wrote quickly in a small, concise hand. It was, after all, the key to his success. He was a professional scribe. His books and manuscripts were sought after for their readability and his wife Perenelle had been introduced to him as he was copying records for her late husband's stables. François had five stables in and around Paris before he died in 1363.

Nicolas glanced at his sheet of notes. That was the other secret of his success. He had developed a code made up of letters, numbers, and simplified drawings that let him record what he heard very quickly, and later translate it into something more legible to others. He had never heard the term, but what he had developed in his teens was a form of shorthand. It was his speed of taking notes and the clarity of his writing style that had turned him from a poor if bright lad to a wealthy man of forty-one.

His wife opened the door to his workroom without knocking and Nicolas looked up in annoyance, pen held a fraction of an inch above the paper. At the look on Perenelle's face, he went from annoyance to concern.

But she didn't wait for him to ask what was wrong. "The strangers have a new way of writing books."

"How do you know?" While quite well off, Nicolas and Perenelle didn't move in the same circles as the constable of France. They did know Gabriel Delaflote, at least casually. Nicolas' shop had copied several Greek and Hebrew books for

Delaflote. However, rumor had it that since the strangers moved from the university of Paris to the home of the constable of France, Delaflote was no longer in the inner circle.

Besides, while they knew Delaflote, they were not friends. Until the summoning of the demon van, Nicolas Flamel had considered Gabriel Delaflote a fool and on the edge of being a heretic. Now Nicolas added the word dangerous and suspected that Delaflote had gone over the edge and fallen into true heresy.

"Marguerite, one of the maids in the household of the constable, heard the strangers talking about someone named Gutenberg. Apparently, this Gutenberg person developed, or will develop, a machine to write. It will have something called movable type."

"What is type?"

"Suzette didn't know," Perenelle admitted. "She didn't know to ask Marguerite, and in truth it's unlikely that Marguerite knew what type is either."

Nicolas considered. Perenelle was intelligent and well read. She was strong in her faith and flexible enough to hold Tiphaine de Raguenel in high regard while maintaining her faith, but her understanding of mechanics was not great. "Perhaps you should visit Madame de Raguenel and ask her about it. I'll go see Gabriel, hat in hand, to see if he knows anything. But don't be too concerned. It's possible there is an opportunity here. They often enough accompany threats."

Chateau du Guesclin
March 18, 1372

Tiphaine waved the woman to a seat in the chateau's sitting room. She didn't know Perenelle Flamel, but she did have several of the books that Nicolas Flamel copied. "I don't know what movable type is either. You must understand that dinner conversation in our house these days is miracle followed by peculiarity followed by impossibility followed by miracle.

Madame Grady did discuss something called the printing press with me some days ago, and I believe that the making of one is on our blacksmith's list of things to do. Far down on the list."

"How long is the list?" asked Perenelle, a portly woman with dark hair that was going to gray. She had a pleasant, open face and there was a twinkle in her eyes, though it was mostly hidden by worry at the moment.

"It has airplanes and xylophones, and everything you have never imagined on it. An airplane is a device that moves through the air and is different from a blimp, which also moves through the air. They actually made a toy balloon out of oiled cloth a few days ago. A candle below it heated the air and it rose into the air, lifting the candle."

"Could such a device be made to carry a person?"

"They tell me it could, but it would have to be much larger. As you can see, the printing press is far down the list. Though Madam Grady insists that it will have greater influence on the world than the balloon, I can't quite agree. It isn't just the expense of books, but the time needed to learn to read. My Bertrand is a man who is as smart as he is brave, but has never found the time or the need to learn to read. How many peasant farmers will ever have such a need?"

As Tiphaine spoke, a strange expression grew on Perenelle's face. "All of them. Or if not all, most."

Tiphaine waved for Perenelle to continue, and she did. "If books were free, then how to run a stable or fight a war or build a balloon could be put in a book and every peasant could do it."

"There is more to it than just knowing the rules," Tiphaine said. "I know how to cast a horoscope and my horoscopes are truly accurate. But at least half of that is the art of knowing which sign of which planet will rule in a given situation. It's important to know the people involved to know how they will be affected by the stars."

They chatted more, and Madame Grady was called. She explained to Perenelle what movable type was and how a printing press was made. Perenelle asked if there was any way of recording pictures and letters other than moveable type and wood cuts. That brought to Madam Grady's mind something called a mimeograph, and Tiphaine left them to chat.

Tiphaine wandered through the wonderland that the Paris house had been turned into and found herself in the garage.

Pucorl's Garage, Chateau du Guesclin
March 18, 1372

"It's not very attractive," Emil said, as Tiphaine entered the converted section of stable that was now Pucorl's garage.

"That doesn't matt—" Annabelle said but she was interrupted by the enchanted device called Royce saying something in their twenty-firster English.

Tiphaine spoke English, but not the confusion that was twenty-first century English. She coughed into her hand, and when she had their attention, she asked that they speak French.

"I was saying that the level of artistry might have an effect, Lady de Raguenel. It does in statues, rings, even lamps," Royce explained.

"That only makes sense," Tiphaine said. "The skill of the practitioner is always important. I don't know how your century survived without understanding that."

She smiled to take the sting out of the words. Clearly they had survived, and quite well. It wasn't that they lacked art or skill. Even Jeff, who was less gifted than most of the farmers on her estates, was able to read and write. Granted, these were all of the nobility, or at least gentry, but from what they had said, theirs was a time of great and surpassing wealth. If the movies she had watched on Pucorl's screens were any indication, the twenty-firsters were not exaggerating either the wealth or the level of art in their world. She knew all that and even understood it, but it was such a strange world depicted in those movies that it was hard to feel the reality through the differences.

"No—" Annabelle started, then stopped and considered. "Maybe in the here and now, it does matter. At least, if there is a demon involved."

"I think that it will also matter if the plug is built into the device. Not just attached later," said Pucorl.

"If it is an enchanted device, certainly the plug should be there before the device is enchanted," Royce said. "That way the demon occupying the device will occupy the plug as well."

"I don't know," Annabelle said. "Integrating physics and sympathetic magic is giving me a headache."

Tiphaine could certainly sympathize with that. "When are we going to get aspirin?" Tiphaine knew about willow bark tea and she knew that some of the king's doctors were working on purifying the vital element, which the twenty-firsters called salicylic acid.

Blacksmith's Forge, Chateau du Guesclin
March 18, 1372

Wilber watched Roger swing the hammer and knew there was something he was missing. By now he barely noticed the smell of the hot iron in the hotter wood fire of the forge. Something was missing, something he'd seen on TV, but he couldn't place it. It had to do with golf clubs, he remembered that.

Roger stepped back from the anvil and grinned at the smith. "I don't know how you do it, Achille. I wouldn't be able to lift the hammer after an hour of this."

"You work too hard. A good smith must be as smart as he is strong. Tap, don't pound."

Damn it. I almost had it, Wilber thought even as the thought flitted away. *Something to do with strength. But what?*

"What am I missing!" he thought at Merlin.

"I have no idea," Merlin thought back at him. *"I'm not the one who is from the twenty-first century."*

This wasn't the first time that Wilber and Merlin had had this conversation. There were hundreds of things that Wilber knew that might be of great value to this world. If only he could remember them all.

Roger and the smith were working together making a rifle. It was planned to be a mix of twenty-first century and fourteenth century, with a little magic thrown in. It was to be a rifled large bore, forty-five to sixty caliber, long barreled with a stock, but it would use a slow match and be loaded like a Civil War era muzzleloader Roger and Achille had started on it almost the day they arrived at the chateau. And every time Wilber wandered in here, he had that tickling sensation at the back of his mind about the way the forge was operated and he just couldn't place it.

"He's doing it again," Achille said, hooking a thumb at Wilber. "I wonder what it will be this time?"

"Who knows?" Roger snorted. "Maybe a whole new kind of forge."

"That's it!" Wilber thought. But that wasn't all of it. It was some kind of forge, but what did a forge have to do with golf? *"What does a forge have to do with golf?"* he thought at Merlin.

"How should I know?" Merlin asked aloud, and on the computer screen on Wilber's computer Merlin appeared on a golf course, dressed like Chevy Chase in *Caddyshack.*

"The movies Mrs. Grady lets Paul watch are a disgrace," Wilber muttered.

"That's right, Merlin," Roger said, looking at the computer screen. "We'll forge the gun barrel by pounding on it with a nine iron."

"That's it!" Wilber shouted.

"Don't be an—" Roger stopped. "Okay, Wilber. Spill. What is *it?*"

"It's not *using* a nine iron. It's how they *make* nine irons. I saw a show about it. *Nova* or one of those tech shows—I don't remember. They make golf clubs out of really hard steel or titanium, and they use a drop forge to do it."

Roger looked down at the three foot long iron rod that he and

Achille had spent half the morning shaping into a wedge so that it could be welded to five other wedge-shaped rods to make a round barrel with a hole in the middle. "I've never seen a drop forge that I remember, but I do remember they were used in making a lot of stuff in World War II." He looked over at Achille. "He could be right. Wilber, can a drop forge be made without engines?"

"I don't see why not. All you really need is a winch to lift the weight. It could be a hand-cranked winch."

"What is a drop forge?" Achille asked.

Wilber explained.

"But how does that help us? It will not let us put the hole down the barrel."

"No, but it will let us use two parts to make the barrel, not six. Two welds, not six."

"You might be able to get by with one," Wilber said. Then he started describing a drop forge to Merlin, and as he did the golf course disappeared, and a twenty-first century forge appeared on the screen. Merlin, now dressed in a leather vest, lifted a long, white hot rod from the fire and laid it in a trough. The forge hammer dropped and was lifted, leaving a half circle and two long, flat sides. The modified U-shape went back in the fire and was heated again. Then it was laid on a drop forge with a different die. That forge dropped, forcing the two long ends of the U together in a weld. The U was left with a teardrop-shaped hollow in the rod.

"You might have to strengthen the weld a little. Then you drill it out, just like you were going to have to do with the six-sided barrel."

"It's a good idea, but is it worth it?" Achille asked. "For us, I mean. In your twenty-first, where you make millions of everything, certainly it would save time and work. But we would run out of steel before it became worth it."

"It's not just for gun barrels, Achille," Wilber said. "You can change out the die and make all sorts of things."

Achille looked doubtful. "You people are costing the lord constable a great deal of money."

"And he's from the lower nobility," Roger said. "He doesn't have all that wealth that the upper nobility inherited with their titles."

That was true enough, Wilber knew. Not that Bertrand was poor, except by the standards of the nobility. He had lots of servants and a fair chunk of land. Wilber remembered that Tiphaine had been forced to sell the family silverware to ransom Bertrand a few years ago. They had recovered, but still the twenty-firsters were providing all these innovations. That was fine, but most of them involved startup cost. Even though they would make Bertrand and Tiphaine a really big fortune in the long run, money was starting to get a little tight.

But there was so much to do.

Chateau de Pomf
March 18, 1372

Philip the Bold, youngest brother of Charles V, king of France, stood at the edge of a pentagram. It was in the stable of the chateau, out of sight of even most of Philip's retinue. The pentagram was red-brown on the gray earthen floor of the stable yard. It was painted in the blood of a virgin. Philip had decided on an eight-year-old girl, just to be sure. They had instruction from the elder god, whose name they were not allowed to know. They were required to call him "Lord," and that was all. But he brought them such power, and such intensity of feeling, that issues of precedence faded into nothingness in comparison.

The lord had promised Philip an enchanted sword, like the fabled Excalibur. A sword of great power that would insure his victory. With this sword, Philip could become the king of France, as he was meant to be, as his father had wanted him to be.

Philip stepped into the circle and with the lord whispering in his ear, he recited the name of his lord's enemy, a titan of legend, who would be tied into the sword and become his slave. He recited and gestured as he was instructed.

"Themisoragina-sarofesg-wofserkesfl. . ." It was three paragraphs long, almost entirely unpronounceable, and there was no way Philip could say it without the demon lord constantly whispering in his ear.

As he spoke, a figure of a woman as tall as the sky and glowing gold was sucked into the pentagram and stood caged above the sword.

Netherworld
Human Date Not Applicable

The being that in another time had been invoked as Themis, titan of law and order, of justice and democracy, slept and dreamed in a timeless state, happy enough to be left alone by the mortal world.

Themis was not small. She measured a hundred fifty miles in length, a hundred and thirty in width, and was almost ten miles deep. She was an orderly place. The demons that were rocks, streams, caves, rivers, plants, animals, pots, pans, hampers, cauldrons, wagons, butchers, bakers, and candlestick makers, plus all the rest, led orderly, repetitive lives. They were comfortable in and on her, and a comfort to her. The cycles of the netherworld would come back to her in time, and she was in no rush.

Then, from nowhere, came a call. It was different, more powerful than any call she had ever felt. Previous invocations had asked for her presence; this one compelled it. Worse, it didn't call an aspect of her, not her image, but *her*.

She was a great one. One of the most powerful beings in her universe. There were more than the twelve titans that the Greeks had dreamed of, and to an extent had come to know and define. But there were not many who shared her level of power. The universe she came from was impossibly small in comparison to the mortal universe. Not even as big as the solar system that contained the planet Earth. But it was larger than the earth by orders of magnitude. As a being of her class, she had the power of earthquakes, tidal waves, high yield nuclear bombs or C-fractional asteroid strikes. Not the power to destroy all life on Earth, but certainly the power to devastate a big region of it.

France, for instance.

However, as what had amounted to the god of law, she was even more restricted by the contract of summoning than most of the beings of the netherworld. With the separations ripped away and the precision of the call, she was left with no choice.

She went, enraged and infuriated by the monster she saw outside the pentagram, the monster which was whispering her name to the mortal who would make law its slave.

No, she realized in a moment. The mortal had no notion of who or what she was. She was simply a demon to him, a demon to enchant his sword. And it was working. She felt herself forced into the sword, changing its nature . . . while it restricted hers. For the sword was owned by Philip the Bold, the youngest son of the former king of France.

She wanted to twist in his hand, for the law of France—which she understood in its entirety—said that he was not the proper heir, not while his brothers lived, or his nephew. But as long as he owned the sword she was being forced into, she would be his to command.

Holding her, Philip the Bold would be able to raise armies.

Netherworld
Moments Later

There was an open wound in the land of Themis, for the land itself was gone. Demons in the forms of plants, animals, pots, pans, fawns, dragons, pucks and pebbles, tumbled into the pit where the land of Themis had been. They shattered and broke, but they didn't die. Demons don't die, not in the netherworld. For in the netherworld, things do balance out. Whatever goes around does come around. Sooner or later.

Or at least it had. Even after the netherworld had interpenetrated with the mortal universe, actual contact had been minor, the next best thing to nonexistent. An extra wobble in the cycle of a demon, a spell or incantation appearing to work. Nothing important.

Until now.

The shockwave of Themis' disappearance shook the netherworld from one end to all others and rang the crystal spheres like gongs.

Chateau de Pomf
March 18, 1372

Barely aware of, but still traumatized by the million or so demons who had fallen into the pit she left when she was pulled away, Themis was forced into a piece of folded iron and carbon.

In a final humiliation, she had a new name imposed upon her. *Aequo Retribuente*, Just Rewards—more properly "equally rewarding" or "balanced punishments."

The new name meant that she was locked into the sword until released. If the sword was broken, she would be destroyed. And that was the intent of the demon lord who had instructed Philip the Bold in her abduction.

Not that the sword would be easy to break. In the mortal realm, force equals mass times velocity, but in the netherworld size and force are functions of will. All that will, the will of hundreds of square miles of land, was now concentrated in the sword *Aequo Retribuente*.

Angry will, restrained by magic and her innate respect for law. She glowed with it, glowed with such intensity that Philip the Bold was afraid to touch his newly enchanted sword. The spell that restricted her was not the best or most useful spell. She couldn't advise Philip. She couldn't speak or sing, warn or advise. She was a sword. She could move, strike and block, but that was all.

Finally, Philip reached out, grasped the hilt, and raised the sword. Five feet of steel moved with the lightness of a feather. It moved so easily, in fact, that Philip was for a moment unable to control it. The blade swung wild and a two-foot-wide wooden post was cut diagonally. Jumping back, Philip nearly decapitated his aide, Robert Fabre, who ducked just in time.

It was a very dangerous Charlie Chaplin routine for a moment, though no one there would ever know it. Still, Philip was used to swords and *Aequo Retribuente* was easy to handle. He quickly had it under control. Philip looked at the post. It was cut as smoothly as if he had used a razor. This time intentionally, he cut again, then again on the backswing. And a third time. All in only a second or two, and the post was turned into the sort of small logs one might use in the stove.

CHAPTER 14

Chateau du Guesclin
March 18, 1372

Every phone in the chateau rang. Every computer beeped or cried out. Pucorl's horn blared and Wilber was momentarily deafened by Merlin's wail of horror.

"What is it?"

"I don't know, not exactly. But it's bad. It's very, very bad . . ." Merlin stopped. "There is a disturbance in the netherworld, so powerful a disturbance that the crystal spheres, all seven of them, are ringing with its echoes."

Monsignor Savona ran into the room holding up the phone. "What have you done? The gates of heaven themselves ring with whatever has just happened."

"Wasn't us," Wilber said.

"Whatever it was, Monsignor," Merlin said from Wilber's computer, "it happened in the netherworld, but was so powerful that it rang the crystal spheres of the heavens with its force. Let me check."

He wasn't gone long. Wilber explained again that they had just been discussing things with the blacksmith when all the enchanted items went nuts.

"The land of Themis is gone," Merlin reported. "The river Ague reports that it is now making a new route around the hole where Themis was. Ague says it likes low places well enough, but where Themis was there is now an ocean floor with no ocean in it. Just the detritus left behind when Themis was sucked away."

"You speak as though Themis was a land, but according to

Greek legend she was a titan, the mother of law."

"Themis is both those things and more. A being, and a land, and a . . . divinity."

There was a sardonic smile on Monsignor Savona's face, Wilber noted. The monsignor was aware that the reality of the netherworld was more multivalued than he expected, but Merlin was still talking.

"Millions of demons are at the bottom of a hole in the netherworld where before there were fields and streams, shops and farms. And no one knows where she has gone. Or why, though there is no reason at all to think that Themis would have willingly abandoned her comfortable bed. On the other hand, I don't know what might compel her."

"What else can you tell us?" asked Bertrand du Guesclin as he entered the smithy. "I am going to have to report to the king. I need to tell him if this is a threat to his realm."

On Wilber's computer the screen flashed white, then Merlin's wings unfurled. He stood on a flat, unadorned plain in the computer screen, and pointed a finger unerringly at Bertrand. "Lord Constable, if Themis has come fully into this world, then not just France but the whole mortal world is in peril."

Bertrand turned to Monsignor Savona and the priest nodded. "So says Raphico as well," he said, holding up the phone.

"Very well," Bertrand said. "For this, Monsignor Savona, I want you and Raphico with me. We need to see His Majesty again."

Royal Palace, Outskirts of Paris

Bertrand watched as Charles V nodded in return to Monsignor Savona's bow. It was not even all that much of a nod, given that Monsignor Savona had the pope's ear. "I am surprised to see the papal nuncio to the twenty-firsters here in our halls?" The king's voice made the question plain.

"Something has happened, Majesty," Savona said.

Charles just waved him to continue.

"The titan, Themis, has—" The monsignor hesitated and Raphico spoke.

"Been abducted. And her abduction has rung the crystal spheres of heaven and disrupted the balance from the highest levels of heaven to the lowest circles of hell."

"Themis is a myth," Charles said. "So at least we have been told by the church fathers all these many decades."

Bertrand didn't wince but it took an effort. This wasn't the time for Charles to let his temper go, no matter how justified by the position the church took since all this began.

"Myth and history have more in common than you might believe, king of France," Raphico said. "I understand your anger. In your mind Themis must seem just a queen, no more than your father, and where was the Creator when he fell into the hands of the English? You, as your father was, are the king of one part of the surface of the mortal world. That is no small thing for a mortal man to be. However, Themis is both the ruling queen and the land itself of a rather larger piece of the place from which I come. The structure of the place I come from is different from the structure of the mortal realm. Her kidnapping is not like your father's capture. It is as though France itself was taken, rolled up in a rug, and stuck in a trunk, leaving all its people from the highest to the meanest with no land to stand on. It affected not just the rulership, but the very structure of heaven and the lower places. And we do not know where she has been taken."

Bertrand felt as though the blood had frozen in his veins. He was shocked to the core by Raphico's admission that there was something the hosts of heaven didn't know. But even more, he was shocked that he wasn't as shocked as he should be. The presence of real demons and real angels was not the bolster of faith that one might expect. Instead, it made clear that even angels were imperfect. Mostly he hoped that King Charles would not take it as license to contest with the angels, not now.

For the moment, at least, it seemed that Charles V was willing to let it pass. "Where is Themis? Or perhaps I should say where was Themis?"

"Distances and directions are less constant in the place I come from, but Themis might be said to fall between Greece and Babylon."

"What, then, are you expecting of me?"

"We, all the angels, demons, and others of the otherworld, are seeking Themis, that she may be returned to her proper place before the order and pattern of the otherworld is put asunder."

"Well, if I happen upon a nation where it doesn't belong, I will surely let you know. I do note that it seems a rather large thing to misplace. That carpet you mentioned and the trunk would, it seems to me, have to be quite large to hold it."

"Nay, not so. Themis may be held in a ring or a broach. In fact, she must be in something relatively small, else her presence in the mortal realm would have been noted."

After that they discussed the difference between size in the mortal realm and size in the netherworld. Charles attempted, without success, to get Raphico to endorse the crown's summoning demons and angels to its service. But Raphico declined and Monsignor Savona took his lead from the angel.

Overall, the meeting was a great waste of time. Time, Bertrand suspected, that they didn't have.

Chateau du Guesclin
March 20, 1372

Bertrand waved the young twenty-firster to a chair in his private study. It was not a room of books because Bertrand didn't read, but even before the arrival of the twenty-firsters it was a room of maps. Now diagrams were added. The large table in the center held a sketch of a "Kentucky rifle" and Bertrand waved at it. "So, Roger, what bore should the barrel have? You have convinced Achille that consistency of bore matters, but now you must explain what bore and why?" The capture of the titan Themis added an urgency to the rifle project.

"That's hard to explain, Lord Constable," Roger said. Then he shrugged and added, "Mostly because until very recently, I never thought about it. I know that larger bores were common in the early days of gunpowder weapons. Even up to the American Civil War, they were really large bore weapons. The 1863 Springfield was a fifty-eight caliber, but by the Vietnam war the standard caliber was closer to twenty-five caliber. Less than half as big around. The M16 had a roughly twenty-two caliber bore and the AK47 a thirty caliber bore. Though by then they were measuring in millimeters, not hundredths of an inch. So the AK was a seven point nine millimeter and the 16 was a five point five six . . ."

Bertrand let the lad talk. One thing he had learned about Roger was that the young man knew a lot about the history of war and weapons. Besides, Bertrand got almost all his information from people talking to him, and the sort of semi-rambling discourse that Roger was engaged in often gave him the general understanding he needed to make sense of a tactical situation. Even in the heat of battle there was usually time to listen and think.

When Roger ran down—*nice expression that*—Bertrand summarized what he thought he understood. "So, over time, as the explosive element got stronger and the rifling got tighter, the bullets got longer and narrower?"

Roger nodded hesitantly.

"Why?"

"I don't . . . Maybe . . . I think it must have been because of drag."

"Well enough. Now, what is drag? I take for granted that you don't mean the bullets are pulling something along behind them."

"In a way, Lord Constable, that's exactly what they are doing. As the bullet goes down the barrel, it rubs against the sides of the barrel and pushes into the grooves of the rifling, pushes the air in front of it."

Bertrand nodded. "Friction. You twenty-firsters have discussed that rather a lot. Is drag friction?"

"Sort of. Friction and drag are different, but I am not sure how they are different."

"We shall leave that aside for now, though I would like you to find out how they are different. It might be important. What size bore do you think we should have?"

"I think a forty caliber bore and rifling. That is a compromise between what they used in the nineteenth and twentieth century."

"Very well. Tell Achille." Bertrand stood and so did Roger. They both had a great deal to do and, in all probability, not enough time to do it properly.

Chateau de Pomf
March 24, 1372

It took Philip the Bold a while to gather his forces, even with the demon lord advising him and with his sword to silence any dissent. But he couldn't wait too long, lest the king be alerted to his presence. The demon lord said that with his sword they had plenty of power to dispense with the minor demons that his brother's minions possessed. He lifted his sword and waved it above his head one-handed. Even his armor felt light when he held the sword in his hand. Then he mounted his horse. He waved the sword again and shouted "*Follow me!*" as he spurred his horse out the gate.

Paris was a city surrounded by walls. Philip and the demon lord led a troop of a hundred men at arms through a gate on the left bank side of the Seine. The guildsmen who had the watch on the gate ran in terror from the apparition of the demon lord.

Philip and his retinue rode on. Even their horses were driven to a state bordering on frenzy by the aura of power and hunger that the demon lord exuded. Not one of them knew that the effect was much like the drugs given a horse to fix a race, or like cocaine or PCP. The effect later would be devastating, but in their frenzy they didn't know or care about that. They galloped, outracing the alarm.

Bertrand and his demons must be brought low, lest they threaten the great plan. The demon lord had said it.

Chateau du Guesclin

Silvore, who now resided in Jennifer's phone, had the duty. Having the duty, he sat on the tallest tower of Chateau du Guesclin and looked out into the night with the camera's night mode and a very long shutter speed. From Silvore's point of view, it was as though he blinked for a second, then had a good image, then blinked for another second. But he was seeing plenty well enough so that when the street filled with horsemen an hour before dawn, he saw them quite clearly. He, as was his instruction, called all the other phones, including Pucorl, and then beeped at the guard, whose job it was to shift him every few minutes so that he could keep sight of the whole area.

The guard took one look at the picture on the screen and started shouting for the sergeant. It wasn't just the armed men that caused his panic. It was the bat-winged figure flying over them. A figure made clear not so much by the software in the phone, but by the fact that Silvore knew the demon, or at least the type.

****

In her room, Annabelle's phone rang and, not waiting for an answer, reported that Silvore, Jennifer's phone, was reporting armed cavalrymen and a demon approaching the chateau. Annabelle got up quickly, pulled on her shoes, then ran for Pucorl, shouting "We're under attack! Armed men and demons!"

Doors opened in her wake but she wasn't the only one shouting. All of the twenty-firsters had been awakened by the alarm. Even Paul.

****

Paul was scared, but not nearly so scared as he was deeply offended. His mom said he had to stay here in the house and miss everything. It wasn't like he was a baby. He was almost nine! Besides, he had an enchanted phone, an enchanted computer, and even an enchanted game system. His mom ran out and he was left alone in the rooms they shared. He tried to follow the battle from the phone and the computer.

****

Computers, Wilber thought as he ran out into the courtyard, barking at the constable's hounds to tell them what was going on, *are not all that useful in a fight.* Right now, an enchanted sword or, better yet, an enchanted M16 would be of more use.

Chateau du Guesclin, the residence of the Constable of France, naturally enough took up a full city block of fourteenth century Paris. It had a curtain wall of stone that was just over ten feet tall, with wooden gates.

There was a crash and the locking bar on the gate was cut in two, along with about three feet of the left gate. Wilber heard horses screaming and the clash of hooves against the gate. The gates opened about half way and the horsemen came through the gap, while a massive shape landed on the wall, flapping wings that stretched twenty feet in either direction. There was a reek of decay in the cold wind those wings sent into the courtyard. Wilber felt like his blood was going to freeze.

The advancing horsemen were wreathed in shadow, which Merlin informed Wilber was a projection of the demon who was accompanying them. Their basic shapes could be made out, but faces were a blur of shadow and eyes that glowed red-orange.

Merlin spoke in his mind. "It is illusion. At least, most of it is illusion. It is meant to freeze you, but you don't need to let it affect you."

And Wilber felt warmth flow into him. In this way, his connection to Merlin was of greater use than the enchantments of the computers, because Merlin was in his implant and, to an extent, in him. That made it easier for the demon to support him.

Wilber wasn't the only one able to fight off the terror. It was clear which of the attackers was the leader. It was the one who wielded a five-foot-long sword like it was a feather. One of Bertrand's armsmen had made the same judgment.

169

An arrow flew through the air, straight and true. At the last moment, with a flick of the wrist, the massive sword swept the arrow to the side. The flat of the blade struck the clothyard arrow so hard that it shattered with a sound like a gunshot.

Other men saw that and reacted, some in panic and others in rage. Armsmen of Bertrand's household ran forward, still drawing their armor on, but with sword and shield ready.

Roger McLean ran out onto the front steps with a sword in his hand. Roger was no great swordsman, but he was a big young man and strong. He also, as he proved now, didn't panic easily. He neither ran away nor charged blindly. Instead he looked around the scene and chose a target, one of the horsemen surrounding their leader. Roger ran forward and used his sword, not against the man but against the horse, striking its left hind leg. The horse reared and fell, but by then Roger was back out of range.

Wilber screamed like an angry cougar and another horse reared and spun in panic. Its rider fell and Liane, seeing that, ran forward with a short-bladed something, somewhere between a butcher knife and a shortsword. Wilber wasn't sure whether she had gotten it from the kitchen or the armory. Liane's sword dipped and the rider of the fallen horse would not rise.

Wilber screamed again, but so did the demon on the wall. And Wilber understood. It was not even a language. It was so ancient, it was a complex of calls, the sounds that a bird—no, a dinosaur raptor—would make. In spite of that, it had meaning. It was a call of hatred and contempt for all mortals and especially all mammals. Wilber screamed again, this time right at the demon in the language of tyrannosaurids, "*Asteroid, you fucker!*" And the demon flinched.

Unfortunately, it didn't stay flinched. After the moment of fear came rage, and the demon leaped from the wall into the courtyard, crushing three of its followers in the process. Wilber wondered if that scream had been the best strategy.

Then Bertrand was there, sword in hand and a company of

men at his back, in armor and formation. A courtyard is not good cavalry terrain. It's too small, not enough maneuvering room. But the enemy outnumbered them and were enraged by the demon lord. The attackers pressed them hard and the sword of their leader left a dead body every time it swung.

Bertrand's men were forced back. The blade flicked again. Alain Girard limped out into the courtyard with a sword in his left hand, and before he could do much of anything the leader's long sword flicked out and took off his arm. He went down, and the battle continued.

Wilber looked at the front steps when he heard a shout. Down the steps came Paul Grady, running straight into the battle. He reached down and tried to lift Alain and pull him out of the fight. The demon laughed and pounced.

****

Annabelle watched from the comfort of Pucorl's driver's side seat as the battle unfolded. Once the battle was joined, she tried to go help, but the doors were suddenly locked.

"Don't be an idiot," Pucorl told her. "You'd only get in the way, then get dead. That's a demon lord. It could eat you and me both in one bite."

She argued, but he was right and she knew it. Then Paul came running down the steps to rescue the groom. He was a nice old guy and had been especially nice to Paul, who missed his dad a lot. The demon leaped, reached, and had Paul in one clawed hand.

Annabelle screamed, "No!" And suddenly they were in motion. With the amount of gas that went into the engine and the amount of force on those wheels, they should have burned rubber, but they didn't. Their rubber grabbed the cobblestones of the courtyard like they were its long-lost lover and spun.

No van should be able to accelerate that fast. Not even a rocket car should accelerate that fast.

Annabelle was pushed back in her seat. It was a good thing she wasn't driving because they accelerated so fast that she couldn't reach the steering wheel.

It was all over in an instant. They were sitting on the sidelines, then they were passing by the knights and headed right for the demon.

It turned its head in shock. It knew that Pucorl was a minor demon, no real threat. But Pucorl was the van and the van was Pucorl. Almost three tons of van, traveling at more than thirty miles an hour, ran into the demon lord and didn't even slow much as it smashed the demon lord into the wall of the chateau. The impact was the equivalent of being simultaneously rammed by two rhinos charging at top speed.

In spite of the fact that she was belted in, Annabelle suffered a wrenched shoulder and bruised ribs. The front window was broken, the front bumper crushed, and there was a demon shaped dent in the wall of the chateau. Right by the front steps.

The demon howled in agony, its legs shattered. And from the front doors of the chateau, with a crossbow in hand, Amelia Grady stepped forward.

Merlin was whispering in Wilber's ear. "*Beslizoswian-Dafrank-Waasdegek . . .*"

Wilber repeated what Merlin said. With each syllable, the demon lord flinched. Wilber got to the end of the name and shouted, "Release the boy and be released! Crush the boy and be crushed!"

Pucorl revved his engine.

The demon lord's hand opened and Paul slid out of its grasp onto the ground. But Amelia wasn't taking chances. She ran forward until she was but a few feet from the demon and shot the bolt right into his gonads.

Then she dropped the bow, grabbed Paul and ran off.

Wilber saw it, but he didn't quite believe it. Then Merlin was whispering in Wilber's implant again. And, in a language that no mortal had heard for thousands of years, Wilber said, "*I adjure thee by right of conflict, be gone!*"

The demon screamed. Then, turned into an expanding cloud of black smoke and disappeared.

****

Everyone was still for a few moments as the darkness of the demon's presence was replaced with the normal darkness of a Paris night. Then there was a clatter as a horse turned and raced for the gate. Followed by more and more horses and riders.

"Stop them!" Bertrand shouted. But, at least for the leader with the great sword, it was too late. He was already gone.

Wilber asked Merlin, "What was that bit about by right of conflict?"

"The pentagrams and invocations that mortals use to trap us are not designed for your use, but for *our* use in the netherworld. Pucorl had him trapped, not as surely as a pentagram, but in a compromised position gained through conflict. That let us, who are more minor demons than him, force him out. He can come back, but for right now he is back in the netherworld. It was the best we could do to save Paul."

Wilber nodded, but Merlin wasn't finished. "That sword. It was . . . It must have been Themis. Somehow. Not just a . . ." Merlin said a word then that was in no mortal tongue at all. But Wilber understood it. It meant a projection that had both physical presence and appearance, that was as solid and real as an avalanche, yet was still just an image of the being that remained in the netherworld. It was related to the way Pucorl, Merlin, and the rest were present in the objects, but it carried more substance than they could muster without bringing a dangerous portion of themselves across. It was also the only way that titans manifested themselves in the mortal world, though they often inhabited statues like the statue of Athena in Athens.

What made Wilber want to make a quick trip to the jakes was that Themis' presence here *wasn't* that. Not the small fraction of Themis that would be necessary to animate a sixty-foot-tall statue, but the whole of her.

"But the mass?"

"Mass and energy are not the same in the netherworld. We are all made up of the four elements. Earth, fire, water, and air. We don't have mass as you think of the term. We have will and nature that often has grossly the same effect. Themis was a lovely land that I had visited on occasion. She had her own character that was apparent in every tree and bush. A very orderly place with very little disarray of any sort. Even the falling leaves landed in tidy patterns."

"Sounds boring."

"I suspect Pucorl would agree with you, but I found it restful."

"And that whole land is in that sword?"

"Yes, but the sword doesn't hold it completely. Her presence sort of leaks out. Didn't you feel it?"

Honestly, Wilber hadn't noticed at the time. But as he thought back, he realized that it was the presence of the sword that let him know that the leader of the raiders had been the man holding the sword. It gave him a presence that no man should have. It turned him into a natural leader, without regard to where he was leading or how he spoke. "Why didn't we fall under his spell?"

"Partly, it was the demon lord. Partly, it was that he was attacking us."

"So why did he do it? That—" Wilber was interrupted by a shout. The courtyard was filled with wounded men and Roger had noticed that Wilber was just standing there, muttering to himself.

"Get over here and hold this!" Roger shouted. The "this" in question was a stick that was holding a tourniquet that was around what remained of Alain's arm.

Wilber rushed over, asking, "How often should I loosen the tourniquet?"

"Never," Roger shouted into Wilber's face, then visibly got himself under control. "The idea that you should loosen a tourniquet is a myth, or the next best thing to it. Especially in a case like this." He pointed at the stump in question. It was cut off about two inches above the elbow. "There's nothing below the tourniquet to let the blood flow to, or from. Just hold it till the surgeon can get to him and sew it up."

There were doctors from the university, but there were also barber-surgeons who worked for Bertrand and they had been getting twenty-firster medical training as well. Wilber took the stick that was holding the tourniquet and Roger ran off to another wounded man.

Only minutes later, Monsignor Savona ran up and knelt beside Wilber, Raphico held out like a talisman of the Lord. Which, Wilber guessed, he was. "Where is the arm?" Savona asked.

Wilber looked around and saw the arm lying on the ground. He pointed. Monsignor Savona ran over and picked it up, and then asked the phone, "Can you truly do this, Raphico?"

The phone answered, "I believe so, but I am only a conduit for the Creator. I may be able to repair it, but there is much injury here and I cannot convey the Creator's healing power without limit, not in this vessel."

"What about stabilizing it?" Wilber suggested. "Reattach it and do just enough healing so that it won't die in the meantime. Then go onto the next. It's called 'triage' and it's in all the good emergency room shows."

"Lift the arm and place it against the stump," Raphico commanded, and Wilber did as he was told.

"No, turn it. The muscles and bone must line up properly. . . . I guess that is good enough," the phone said, not sounding happy. "Touch the healing app, then place me against the wound."

Monsignor Savona looked at the screen and Wilber craned his neck to see. There on the screen were three app icons. One was praying hands, the second was a red cross, the third was a shield with a fleur de lis cross on it.

Wilber shook his head as Monsignor Savona tapped the red cross icon, and muttered, "Lose your arm? There's an app for that."

****

Annabelle looked at the shattered glass of the front window and extracted her feet from the crumpled front floor. Pucorl was moaning, but his engine wasn't running and she suspected that it

175

was badly damaged. It had taken the brunt of the impact with the demon. She managed to get the driver-side door opened, and that was a chore in itself.

Pucorl had hit the demon lord and continued pushing it along until they impacted the wall.

"Pucorl, shut up!" she shouted at the van. "Let me look at this."

"But it hurts!" Pucorl said.

"Of course it hurts. You stoved in your whole front. It will take major repairs to get you working again."

"Thank you, Annabelle," said Amelia Grady. She was holding her eight-year-old son like he was three, or like he was a baby, and he was sobbing with his face hidden in her neck.

Annabelle turned. "For what?"

"For driving Pucorl into the demon."

"Wasn't me. I was just a passenger. That was all Pucorl."

"Pucorl? But how could he, without permission or instruction?"

"What do you mean?" Paul asked, distracted from his fear by curiosity. He lifted his head and turned it to look at Annabelle and the van.

"I thought Pucorl was severely restricted by my ownership of his vessel. He can't, for instance, drive the van off a cliff so that it would be destroyed and he would be released back to the netherworld, not without my agreement."

Annabelle turned to Pucorl. "Well?"

"It's complicated," Pucorl said, sounding embarrassed.

"Explain it to us," Amelia Grady said in tones of command.

"There were a combination of factors," Pucorl said. "None of them compelled me, but because Paul is your son, because Annabelle was in my driver's seat and because I knew that you would want me to save Paul, it was enough that I was allowed to act. I couldn't have done it to save Bertrand, Tiphaine, or one of the children who lives in the town house."

"You said 'allowed you to act,' " Annabelle said. "Were you

compelled to act?"

Pucorl didn't say anything.

"Were you compelled to act?" asked Amelia Grady.

"No. There was no command. Even Annabelle's shouting 'no!' was vague enough not to be clearly a command."

"Then why did you?" Amelia asked quietly. "I'm more thankful than you can know, Pucorl, but I need to understand. Why did you risk the damage you received to save Paul?" She stopped, then resumed. "*Was* it to save Paul?"

"Yes, it was. I like Paul, and Annabelle wanted me to save him."

"It wasn't some sort of demonic politics?" Amelia asked

"No. Demons like me don't deal with demons like that, and we certainly don't attack them." Then Pucorl giggled. "I, for instance, wouldn't shoot a demon lord in the balls with a crossbow, not if I had any choice."

"I didn't have . . . Well, he deserved it. You don't mess with my kid." Then she looked stunned. "Pucorl, if it had been little Marie, the baker's daughter, could you have saved her?"

"Not without orders. Not even with Annabelle's orders. I would have needed specific orders from the owner. From you."

"And I wasn't there." Amelia looked at Annabelle. "You're usually with Pucorl."

In a flash of intuition, Annabelle knew where this was going. Amelia was going to give Pucorl to her. For just a moment, greed froze her. To own Pucorl the van, for him to be hers, with no choice— She stopped. That wasn't what she wanted. She wasn't sure what she did want, but it wasn't Pucorl as her slave. "Not always, Mrs. Grady." She took a deep breath. "The only one who is always with the van is Pucorl himself."

"You're right." Amelia looked at Annabelle, then at Pucorl, then at Paul, and back at Pucorl. Still holding Paul, she walked over and laid her left hand on the van's side door. "Pucorl, I give this van to you, releasing you from all bonds to me or to the school."

There was a golden glow that surrounded her hand. From

there, it spread out over the van and encircled it. When it faded, the van was still wrecked, its front end stoved in, its windshield in fragments, but there was a shininess to it, almost a glow.

****

Pucorl felt it. He was no longer locked in the mortal world. The restraints that had held him, prevented him from returning to his corner of the netherworld, were gone. But there was more. That creature of indeterminate shape, the being who went from fat to skinny as it bit and chewed, the one who looked like something Escher would have drawn on LSD, suddenly had a body. A constant, consistent body that he didn't have to concentrate on to keep stable. To an extent, that had been true before, but before it had been a prison. Now it was his. Even with the damage it had taken in the fight with the demon lord, it felt better—more whole—than any form he had ever had before.

The wards, curtains, differences in potential, conflicts of probability that had walled off the mortal realm from the netherworld and, to a lesser extent, each part of the netherworld from the rest, were a shredded and shattered remnant of their former selves. You couldn't step from the mortal world to the netherworld at will. You had to find an opening or be called. But openings were all over the place. There was one just over there. Pucorl rolled on damaged wheels about five feet and disappeared from the mortal world.

Netherworld

Pucorl wasn't at the little rock outcropping where it had sat and chewed on a mammoth bone for most of the Holocene. Distances and terrain were not the same in the netherworld as they were in the mortal world. In fact, they shifted over time. What was a mile in spring might be five in winter. What was a step in 1372 might be infinitely far in 1373. They shifted with the attitude of the land as well. It might speed you on your way, the better to have you gone. Or let you travel forever, going only half so far with each step. Not that that was likely. Earth tended to be lazy and rarely bothered to interfere to your good or ill.

So the large, sharp rock that was digging into Pucorl's right rear tire was probably not an indication of the land's displeasure at his sudden arrival. That didn't make it hurt one bit less. Pucorl turned on his lights. His right headlamp, actually an array of LED lights, was on but only sixty-four of the two hundred fifty-six LEDs were lit. Also, the lamp was shining out at an angle of almost ten degrees off where it should be shining. His left headlamp was not working at all. Still, that was a lot of light for this shadowy section of the netherworld.

A few feet—or miles—away, a pooka looked and bolted away, for the puck that owned a van was a greater creature than an ordinary puck. It had a stable shape. Its will was not expended in maintaining its shape. It was dangerous.

Pucorl looked through his cameras. Miraculously, they were all working, though his forward-looking camera was not looking quite forward anymore. He was still in that part of the netherworld that was analogous to Paris in the fourteenth century. He was farther away from his home place than the distance would be in the mortal realm, but only by a couple of miles. That was a long way on bunged up axles with an engine that wasn't running. It was just Pucorl's will that was moving the van at all.

Suddenly, Pucorl realized something. He didn't want to go back to his little corner of the netherworld. He wanted his engine fixed. He wanted to talk with Wilber about magic, Paul about cartoons, Roger and Bertrand about tactics, and most of all he wanted to talk to Annabelle about mechanics. He wanted to argue with her about the merits of wheels that lifted to step over rocks versus rear wheels that rotated so he could roll sideways.

He didn't *have* to go back. He *wanted* to. Pucorl backed up and shifted. He was back in the mortal realm and had only been gone a few moments. But it was long enough for everyone, especially Annabelle, to get upset.

Pucorl regretted that Annabelle's feelings were hurt, but on the whole thought that the others being concerned was a good thing.

CHAPTER 15

Chateau du Guesclin
March 24, 1372

The body of Robert Fabre was lying on the cobblestones. Blood seeped from its wounds and little rivulets of bright red spread along the dirty cracks between the stone. Seeped, because the heart no longer beat; only gravity still moved the blood. Liane's shortsword had taken him in the chest. She and Bertrand du Guesclin were both staring at the body.

She, because she had taken a human life and had no idea how to deal with it. Bertrand, because he saw revolution and the destruction of France in those dead eyes.

Bertrand had always been a patriot of France. He had fought for France under two kings and was personally loyal to King Charles V. But more than that, France was his home. He loved the land and its people, from the king to the lowest serf slopping his pigs. He knew the politics. Knew that King John II had preferred Philip, but he didn't share his former monarch's preference. Philip the Bold cared for Philip the Bold and no one else. This corpse was his most trusted henchman. Not adviser. Philip didn't take advice. But henchman, a man who would slit a baby's throat on Philip's orders.

He turned away. "Someone fetch me a horse. I need to see the king."

He rode to the Hôtel Saint-Pol, the new palace, which was located outside Paris proper because the king didn't like the smells of the city, and arrived in time to see the sunrise.

Royal Palace, Hôtel Saint-Pol

Count Laroche was dressed in bed clothes and not happy about being woken before the sun was well up. "The king is asleep, Bertrand." Laroche sneered the name and, as was his custom, denied Bertrand the title of Constable. "What possible reason is there for me to wake His Majesty?"

"Robert Fabre is dead in my courtyard."

"What did you do, you cursed fool?"

Suddenly, Bertrand did feel like a fool. He had been so distracted by the presence of Fabre during the attack that it hadn't even occurred to him to wonder if the demon that had accompanied the attack on his home was the same demon that had been attacking the people of Paris. He'd been in too much of a hurry to report to make sure he had a complete report to deliver. It was the sort of mistake that he would strip the hide off one of his captains for, and he had made it.

"Well?" asked Laroche. The sneer was even more pronounced now, almost enough to justify Bertrand challenging the fool. Almost, but not quite.

"What I did, Count Laroche, was wake to find my house under attack by men at arms and a demon from the pit, and fight them off. Fabre was one of their number and I strongly suspect that the king's youngest brother, Philip, was their leader. Do you think that might justify waking the king?"

Laroche had turned paper white as Bertrand spoke. Laroche was dark haired with pale skin. A short pale man, whose hair was usually curled and oiled in the Italian style. At the moment, it was unkempt and the thinning hair over his pate was apparent.

"But that can't be," Count Laroche bleated. "The king's brother is of the royal blood. It would put a stain on the House of Valois." His voice firmed into resolve. "You must be mistaken."

Almost, Bertrand reached out and grabbed the man. In his youth he would have done more than that. But he was older now

182

and hopefully wiser. Old enough so that as he fought down his rage he realized that there was truth in even the blathering of an idiot. It would be seen by all of France as a stain on the honor of the royal house. By the nobles most of all, each of them seeing some advantage in the disgrace of the Valois family. But even the peasants would be wondering, *if a royal prince will do this, why should we follow any of them?*

So instead of throttling the man as he wanted to, Bertrand said, "I wish I were, Count Laroche. I wish to God I were. But the body is the body of Robert Fabre, and he is not the only member of Philip's household who was left on the flagstones of my courtyard. I need to speak to the king."

Royal Chambers, Hôtel Saint-Pol

One look told Bertrand that his king wasn't happy. Charles was still in his night clothes and closed the door to the royal bedchamber with care. Then in a whisper that was almost a hiss, he asked, "What's all this about?"

Bertrand went through it, and by the time he was done the sun was fully up.

"What can we prove?" Charles asked. While Bertrand was trying to figure that out, the king went on. "I know that my brothers, Philip, John, and Louis, have been pushing to have me excommunicated for trafficking with demons."

"Well, won't the fact that Phi—"

"No, it won't," Charles said. "It will simply be taken as proof that the whole family is consorting with demons, and Edward of England will use that as another *casus belli*."

"You would think he would want to get his own house in order," Bertrand complained. "There are Red Caps and banshees in London."

"Edward doesn't think that way," Charles insisted. "And, perhaps more importantly, neither does his heir. Or the rest of his brood, for that matter. They would all rather conquer than rule. I can not deal with Philip without giving them a sword to strike at France."

"With all respect, Your Majesty, I don't think we have a choice. There is no way of keeping this secret. Monsignor Savona was there and saw the whole thing. He is, I do not doubt, sending reports to Pope Gregory even as we speak."

Charles slammed a hand down on the arm of his chair. It was not a throne. These were his private chambers. "That meddling busybody." He glared at Bertrand. "And don't think I don't know what you were doing right after Louis was born, Bertrand. The nobles were at great pains to tell me all about it, papal dispensation and all."

"It's a good thing we did. Otherwise all you would know about last night's events was that the murderer had struck again."

"Was it the same being?" Charles asked.

"I don't know for sure, Majesty. I was in such a rush to inform you that I didn't wait to question the beings who now occupy the twenty-firster devices. When I left, Raphico was still healing the wounded."

****

Charles drummed his fingers on the carved wooden arm of the chair, then looked down at the hand that was doing the drumming. It was his right hand and the gout had almost completely disappeared. Partly that was due to a change in diet, partly treatments that his physician had devised after discussions with the twenty-firsters. That was not evil. Charles was sure of that in his heart. All the politics aside, the demons in the twenty-firster's devices had done much more good than harm. "You said that carriage from the twenty-first century with a demon in it damaged itself to save a child and to drive off the attacking demon. Yes?"

"It did, Majesty. I saw it with my own eyes."

Charles stood. "Very well. I have tried to be cautious and careful of the feelings of those who fear these beings. But nobility is nobility, whether in a man, a horse, or even a carriage possessed by a demon." He turned to the door and called, "Bring

184

me my horse!"

Chateau du Guesclin

The courtyard was still a mess. Both Bertrand's men and the constabulary were there now. The bodies were laid out in a row, moved after "crime scene" images had been taken. Bertrand watched as the king took it in. This was clearly the scene of a recent battle, something both Bertrand and his king knew well.

Pucorl was parked in the courtyard, away from the wall, but there was an imprint on the carriage's frame and a matching one on the front wall of the main house. The wall looked like the winged demon lord had been pushed into mud, not cut stone. Bertrand hadn't noticed that in the immediate aftermath of the battle, what with Pucorl's short disappearance followed by the discovery of Robert Fabre.

Until the king's party had ridden into the courtyard, Wilber and Tiphaine had been examining the wall, each with their enchanted items held out before them. Now they turned to face the king and bowed, still holding the enchanted items. In Tiphaine's case, the day planner with its touchscreen and stylus, in Wilber's case, his phone. Bertrand knew that the phone, Igor, would be keeping Merlin informed, but he did wonder where the computer that was Merlin's second home was. But that wonder was all in passing. He looked back at his king, to see the reaction to the painfully apparent disobedience to royal command.

Charles looked at them, but did not say anything. Instead, after examining them, he looked over the rest of the courtyard.

There was Monsignor Savona, holding Raphico with two fingers. He touched the device to the injured leg of one of the combatants, and the man flinched away, yelling, "It burns!"

Everyone looked and Wilber asked, "What's going on, Monsignor?"

"I don't know. With each healing, the phone has gotten warmer. Now it's hot."

"That shouldn't be happening," said Pucorl. "Healing is a cool

185

art."

"Overheated circuits?" Wilber said, with a question in his voice. "That can happen if a CPU is overused."

There was a short pause as the demons consulted. Raphico was a powerful being, call him angel or demon as you would. He was powerful in and of himself, and more powerful through his connection to his Creator. But he wasn't nearly as familiar with electronics as Pucorl, Ishmael, and Merlin were. Besides, Merlin had Wilber's books.

Over Pucorl's speakers came Merlin's voice. "Raphico has been using the computational powers of the cell phone to direct his healing. This allows him to heal more with less force, but it also puts a major strain on the electronics of the cell phone. He is going to have to rest now, let the circuits cool and recover himself."

It wasn't a disaster. By now the angel had stabilized most of the injured and they were not likely to get much worse for the delay. Those with less severe injuries that didn't threaten life or limb could be treated by ordinary means, at least for now.

King Charles looked at the priest. "Monsignor, I assume your friend will be recovered by tomorrow?"

"I believe so, Your Majesty."

"You will bring him and attend me and my wife then, in the morning. In the meantime . . ." He turned to Bertrand. "Tell me again, Constable. What did you see when Pucorl attacked the demon?"

Bertrand told him. The king dismounted and walked up to the van. He laid a hand on the dented hood and said, "For gallantry in battle and the protection of the innocent, I dub thee Sieur Pucorl du . . ." He stopped. "I am not going to knight him as the Chevalier from Hell."

Amelia Grady said, "Perhaps Elysium? It's not hell, but it's not impinging on Raphico's territory either."

"Elysium," Merlin mused. "Not exactly accurate, but close enough to work, I think."

"Very well. I dub thee Sieur Pucorl, Chevalier du Elysium." He drew his sword and gently laid it against the driver's side mirror.

Bertrand bowed to the newly knighted van, and wondered what Merlin meant by "close enough to work."

****

Pucorl didn't have to wonder. He knew. He felt it as much as he had felt it when Amelia gave him the van. But this was different. It wasn't him that was changed. It was the little corner of the netherworld that he had lived in, that had been his place and yet not his.

The netherworld was governed by will, but as a part of that, oaths and titles meant more, and carried greater weight. What would be an empty title to a mortal was, in the netherworld, anything but empty. It carried . . .

It carried something that couldn't honestly be conveyed in the physics of the mortal realms. A solidity. It was as real as sunlight or stone. Pucorl was now a chevalier. He had not sworn any oath to Charles. None had been asked. He wasn't Charles' knight, but Charles was the legitimate king of France and he had dubbed Pucorl a chevalier. Pucorl was a knight in the nether—

Well, in Elysium. His little stretch of the netherworld that was, until moments ago, a nebulous, ever-changing but always returning to the beginning, sort of place was now different. It was Pucorl's land and as a knight he had a level of control over that tiny chunk of the netherworld that he could never have achieved on his own. As the two universes interacted, they were both affected.

"Annabelle, do you want to see my land?" Pucorl asked.

"Are you in any condition to travel?"

"Now that I'm a chevalier, I can go to my lands at will. I just have to come back to the mortal realm in the same spot I left." That wasn't exactly how it worked but it was close enough.

Annabelle climbed in and Paul was right behind her, which got Mrs. Grady involved. That halted everything for a while, so Mrs. Grady could be assured that it wasn't like the story of Orpheus.

187

Or, well, it was in a way, but there was nothing that kept Orpheus from coming back. It was just Argiope, his wife, who couldn't return if he looked back. "Besides, the Elysian Fields are not quite the netherworld."

"But wasn't your place in the netherworld?"

"It was but it's . . . Well, it's complicated."

"It's safe enough," Merlin chimed in over Igor, in Wilber's pocket. Wilber's phone wasn't Merlin. Igor was another puck type demon, but it was one that owed fealty to Merlin. Demonic society could be very hierarchical.

"How can it be?" Tiphaine asked.

"There are layers below the surface of our universe and levels above it," Merlin said. "And a level in our universe that corresponds to your world, sort of, but isn't quite there. The Elysian Fields are in that middle place. Pucorl's home is now under the Elysium rules, not the netherworld rules."

On that basis, Annabelle, Wilber, Lakshmi, and Jeff decided to go. Paul wanted to, but Amelia wasn't willing to let her son visit the land of the dead, even if it was the land of the noble dead and rather closer to heaven than to hell.

King Charles was tempted, but decided he couldn't leave France even for a moment at this juncture. Instead, he decided that Bertrand would go. And with Bertrand going, Tiphaine was going too.

So it was. Six people, with their accompanying demons, piled into Pucorl and he rolled five feet.

Pucorl's Land
Human Date Not Applicable

They were in a dark, shaded place, a perpetual twilight. Pucorl turned his traffic cams to look at the little rocky outcropping where he, in another form, had chewed on a mammoth bone for thousands of years, and watched it change into a flat stretch of asphalt with a garage door in the hillside.

"I thought you said that this was Elysium?" Lakshmi asked.

"No. I said it was under the rules of Elysium," Merlin said. "It will take some time for it to shift so far. Wilber, turn me around a bit, that's a good lad." Wilber did, and Merlin huffed a bit. "Not much, is it, Pucorl?"

"I like it," Pucorl said. With a flick of his will, the automatic garage door opener that was built into the van activated the garage door in his little corner of the netherworld. Sir Pucorl du Elysium rolled on damaged wheels into his very own garage, for the injuries received in the mortal world affected him here in this one.

It felt good, even so.

****

There was a hole for the van to drive over, but no lift, no lights, no nothing. Then, as Annabelle was looking around, a flame in the shape of a lizard wandered in, sniffing.

"Stop right there," said Pucorl. "That gasoline is not for you."

"But it smells so flammable," the flame complained.

"I'll bring you some coal the next time I'm here," Pucorl said.

"I have a better idea," Catvia said. "There is coal aplenty in a forge in the mortal realm."

"Why should I let myself be restricted?" The flame made a jump at Pucorl's gas tank and was blocked.

"You were told," Merlin said, "and by the knight of this place. You have broken the peace of Pucorl's Garage."

"You can't—" the salamander started, but stopped as Merlin appeared before him.

And it was Merlin. They could all recognize that. It looked just like his image on the computer screen.

"Why do you even care?" whined the salamander with a crackling hiss.

"Good question," Merlin agreed. But that didn't stop him from reaching down and grabbing the salamander with his hand and lifting it up by its neck. "As it happens, I am under the authority of Wilber and Wilber is friends with Annabelle, who is

189

friends with Pucorl. So you can either behave or be banished from this place."

The salamander wrapped itself around Merlin's wrist, but there was nothing there to burn. The body was an image projected by the demon and the image was controlled by Wilber's computer. Annabelle had figured that out as soon as she saw Wilber typing furiously to activate the appropriate programs.

With Merlin dealing with the salamander, Annabelle looked around at the bare garage. "Where are the tools, Pucorl?"

"I'm going to have to recruit them locally, or bring them from the mortal realm."

"Can you do that? Bring stuff from the mortal realm?" Annabelle asked.

"You're here," said Catvia, and Jeff giggled.

"Good point. But that leaves us back where we started. No arc welder, no paint gun, no lathe or sander. None of the tools we are going to need to get you fixed."

"Don't forget that Pucorl can recruit demons. If you can help them create and maintain forms, they might be pleased enough to help out in exchange. There are politics here as well as in your world. They are just a bit different."

Annabelle shook her head and plugged in her testing gear, then opened the analysis app on her phone.

"Ah, cool digs," Enzo, her phone, said. "But you're going to need to fix that axle and you're going to have to bang out the dents in the engine housing too."

That was the part Annabelle heard of the three-way conversation between Pucorl, Royce, and Enzo, who had taken that name in honor of Enzo Ferrari.

She examined the readouts. "Sorry, Pucorl, but we are going to have to pull the engine and the front drivetrain."

"How?"

"We need a workshop crane. A power saw, an arc welder, and a diamond bladed grinder." She looked around at a noise. There was an iron boulder rolling through the garage door. "What...?"

190

"I think that might be our workshop crane," Wilber said.

"I can be a crane," the iron boulder said in a slow, ponderous voice. "If it's not too much work, that is."

"Earth demons are always lazy," said the salamander.

"We just don't see the point of jumping around like silly bits of flame."

Annabelle listened as the elements and combinations of elements discussed the possibilities of turning into tools. It was partly a matter of will and partly of their natures, but while they were often willing to be made into tools, they mostly didn't want to do the making themselves.

"Very well," Pucorl said to the salamander. "Give me—" He said something in a language that Annabelle didn't understand, and the salamander hissed and gurgled at him. Then they rolled out of the garage and Pucorl shifted them back to the mortal world.

They were back in the courtyard and Bertrand climbed out of Pucorl and went to talk to the king.

The two of them argued for a while, and then the king nodded. "All right. But keep them in your townhouse. I don't want them wandering the streets of Paris."

Chateau du Guesclin
March 26, 1372

The blacksmith shop looked different with the ground charcoal and lard paint forming a pentagram around the forge. The forge was filled with charcoal, wood, and linseed oil, and in the center was the form of a humanoid/lizard mix, carved from anthracite coal with two cut rubies for eyes. The statue was two feet tall and had as much in common with the comic book character Salamander as it did with the amphibian of the same name.

"I still don't understand why we're doing this," Bill Howe muttered. "Why not just build a Bessemer forge and use coke to

191

power it?"

Wilber looked at him with sympathy. He had been talking with Merlin about the physics of the netherworld for a month and a half and still had trouble with it. Apparently the three laws of thermodynamics were, in fact, local ordinances that didn't apply to visitors from the netherworld. They had their own laws, but they were a cyclic system—more of a *whatever goes around, comes around* setup. Wheels within wheels that all came back to the same starting point. What mattered here was that while a salamander liked to burn things, it didn't need to. It would keep right on burning and generating heat in a vacuum.

"Partly because we don't know how," Wilber said, as his phone—sitting in the circle on a point of the pentagram—started intoning the spell that would call the fire elemental to the carbon statue. Doctor Delaflote knelt and lit the paint so the pentagram would for the time of the spell be a pentagram of fire.

"We know basically what coke is and we know that making coke from coal has to do with burning it, but not all the way. What none of us know is how to make a coking plant. Or any more than the very basics of a Bessemer forge. Heck, Bill, I'm not even sure it's called a Bessemer forge, though I don't have a clue what else it might be called. Most important of all, the salamander is a natural high-energy chemist. According to Merlin, it will be able to taste the difference between high-carbon steel, low-carbon steel, stainless, and so on. And Annabelle says that's important for fixing Pucorl."

"I know," Bill agreed. "And Roger wants his gun barrels. I get that. But you have no idea how poor these people are. They don't need two axles and five gun barrels. They need ten thousand dutch ovens and twenty thousand pairs of scissors. Scissors for—" Bill cut himself off.

"I know." Wilber sighed. He did know, if not as well as Bill did. Bill had spent most of the time since the event working with the Paris police, and in the process gotten to know the people of Paris better than most of them. Even for Wilber in his—relatively speaking, ivory tower—the difference between an industrial society and a preindustrial society was frightening.

Chateau du Guesclin
March 28, 1372

Roger waited until the smith was working on Pucorl and shoved a long steel billet into the forge. The billet was a three foot long, two inch wide and deep chunk of steel that had been poured into a mold. He used Clausewitz, his phone, to chat with the salamander, and the salamander hugged the billet until it was white hot. Then, using tongs, Roger lifted it to the drop forge and released the rope. The billet, in a moment, became about two-thirds of a steel rifle barrel. Roger put the barrel back in the fire while he, with the help of two assistants to the smith, removed the die he was using and replaced it with another.

By that time, of course, the smith had Pucorl's axle back in the fire and Roger had to wait. Meanwhile, the salamander was complaining that it was hungry and wanted some more coal.

There were dozens of projects going on all at once as they tried desperately to prepare for the looming civil war.

March 28, 1372

Wilber looked up to see Jeff standing next to the table, looking a bit depressed. It was sunset and the computer on Wilber's table added materially to the light in Wilber's room. Wilber and Jeff were not close back in the twenty-first century, but now, well, all the twenty-firsters had to stick together. "What's the problem, Jeff?" Wilber asked, waving the big guy to a seat.

"It's Pucorl." Jeff sat down in the new leather-covered, padded armchair.

"What about Pucorl?"

"Annabelle, well, it was really Mrs. Grady, gave him the van."

"Yes?"

"Well, it's Catvia, Asuma, and Coach."

Wilber caught up at that point. "You're wondering about giving them your computer, phone, and smartwatch?"

Jeff nodded, but he didn't look happy.

"I wondered the same thing. Merlin, you want to chime in here?"

Merlin appeared on the computer screen, wearing heavy iron chains and a hangdog expression.

"You've been hanging around Pucorl too much," Wilber said. "You're starting to act like a puck."

"You may be right," Merlin admitted, now dressed in a twenty-first century business suit with his wings glowing with rainbow light. "No, Jeff, I do not recommend giving your computer to Catvia, your phone to Asuma, or your smartwatch to Coach." He sat in a lounge chair and picked up a beer in a clear glass mug.

"Why not?" Jeff didn't sound relieved. Instead, he sounded annoyed.

Merlin didn't say anything. He just looked shocked.

"Mostly," Wilber said, "he doesn't think you should do it because the netherworld is a very hierarchical society, and he doesn't think your demons have earned it. He wasn't happy that Mrs. Grady gave Pucorl the van."

"I am still not sure that you comprehend how much of a boon that gift truly was. For a being like Pucorl, much of his will, his mana, his essence, went into maintaining his shape, something that is easier to do in the mortal realm in the first place. By giving him the vessel, especially such a powerful and flexible vessel as the van is, your teacher more than tripled—more than quadrupled, probably—Pucorl's power and presence. And then King Charles increased Pucorl's power and presence still more by knighting him. He can take his vessel back with him to the netherworld and maintain that form with no additional effort. And with the olive oil and alcohol mixture that you have used to replace his diesel fuel, he can move for great distances. Pucorl is still a puck, at his core, but now he may well be the most puissant puck who ever existed."

"He saved Paul's life, Merlin," Wilber said. "We have discussed this. But after talking it over with Merlin, here is the deal I made with Merlin, Igor, and Moneypenny." Igor was Wilber's phone and an assistant of Merlin's from before they met. Moneypenny was Wilber's digital recorder and an independent demon who had basically shown up looking for a position. She was proving quite useful in keeping track of details. "They are free to leave the computer, phone, and recorder and return to the netherworld anytime they want, but as long as they stay, they serve me. Merlin's right, you know. These devices of ours are luxury accommodations to the demons. You can make the same deal with Catvia, Asuma, and Coach. They will take it. I don't doubt that."

Jeff wasn't looking pleased. "You don't understand. I really like Catvia, Asuma, and Coach. I don't want them to stay because they have to, or even because it's my really nice computer and stuff they are staying in. I want them to stay because they want to."

In Wilber's implant, Merlin said, *"Catvia is a succubus. Her form is Oriental, but her basic nature is that of a European succubus. She is not evil, but neither is she exactly good. She cares about Jeff the way you care about a hamburger. The same goes for Asuma."*

Wilber was very glad that Merlin chose to speak through the implant rather than directly to Jeff. *"I know,"* he subvocalized. *"But Jeff is more a cow providing a stream of milkshakes than a hamburger. More importantly, he's a good guy when it comes down to it, so he's going to do it, no matter what we say. Is there anything you can do to, you know, ah, talk to them maybe?"*

"I can try," Merlin said. *"Give me a moment."*

****

Pucorl's internal phone rang as Merlin used his Wifi to contact Pucorl and access Pucorl's hotspot and LTE Direct link to call Catvia. Pucorl's new body had Wifi, Bluetooth, LTE Direct, CB, and a variety of other frequencies available to it, controlled by firmware that had to be adjustable in a van that moved through the various countries of the EU. That meant that Pucorl, as the

195

controlling software of the van, had a wide range of frequencies that he could transmit and receive data on. The phones, computers, game consoles, and so on had frequencies they shared, but Pucorl could talk to everyone. And, being a van with on-board electrical generation, he had much more powerful transmitters.

"Please put me through to Catvia, and stay on the line, if you would."

One thing Pucorl had noticed was the degree to which Merlin was more polite to him now that he owned the van and had been knighted. Both those things had made him much more powerful, especially owning the van. The other demons had taken note. He was finding his change in status to be a mixed blessing. He was a puck and had always been a puck. Now he had responsibilities. Not imposed responsibilities, either, but ones of his own choosing. Those were the sort you just couldn't get around.

"Yes? What do you need?" Catvia said, sounding distracted. "I'm building a fantasy room for Jeff's dream tonight."

"You may not need it," Merlin said disgustedly. "The fool boy is probably going to give you the computer."

"Oh, goody!" Catvia sounded excited, but not surprised. "I think I'll make it an extra special night for him."

"I hope it won't be his last," Pucorl said. Pucorl knew succubi and was very careful not to let them get too close.

"It won't. He's a mortal and I am now convinced that the twenty-firsters are right about the effects of sex and masturbation on hormone balances. He's healthier now than he was. Smarter, too. Not that he is ever going to be truly bright."

"So you aren't going to take the computer and return to the netherworld?" Merlin asked. He spoke to Catvia as the senior demon, and the one who had been unprofessionally called. Jeff's calling had left her with more freedom than the others to begin with.

"No. I could get more mana from a demon, but the demon couldn't replace that mana, not without taking it back from me.

Jeff can and does make more. Jeff is an unlimited supply for as long as he lives. The same is true of Asuma, and even Coach. Jeff gives off mana like sweat when he exercises."

"I'll tell Wilber," Merlin said.

****

"Catvia is going to stick around, at least for now." Merlin didn't sound happy in Wilber's implant. "So will the others."

"That's good. At least, I think it's good." Wilber told Merlin, then spoke to Jeff, wishing him luck but not telling him they had warned Catvia. As Jeff left, Wilber asked Merlin, "What's the problem?"

"Catvia is a succubus, as is Asuma. They are, by their nature, sexual parasites. They aren't well thought of in the netherworld culture."

"Merlin," Wilber asked, trying to keep the amusement out of his voice, "are you a prude?"

There was in response only a huffy silence. Wilber was able to discern the huffiness through the magic that now imbued his implant. "Jeff is a good guy, Merlin. He's going to do what he thinks is right, because it's right. Not because he expects it to work out for the best. I'll bet he came over here expecting us to tell him that Catvia was going to leave as soon as he gave her the computer. But, Merlin, he would have done it anyway. You've got to admire that. At least I do."

****

Catvia watched as Jeff came into the room and sat down on the cot. She didn't say anything. She didn't want to mess it up if Merlin was right.

He was.

Jeff laid his hands on her case and struggled to get the words out. "Catvia . . . I give you my computer."

"Oh, Jeff," Catvia said, and gave him a mental kiss that was so strong he could feel it even awake. "I'll be right back, honey. Don't you worry." Then she shifted back to the netherworld, taking her vessel with her.

197

She was in a grove with several not quite dead trees. One of them was almost a part of her, but she was a computer sitting on the grass, not her nymph shape. None of her shapes, not the western succubus shape, or incubus shape. Not the catgirl form provided by the computer. She was a closed laptop computer with a camera, speakers, and a keyboard and touchpad. She had a power cord that she was vaguely aware went to the tree, and at the moment was feeding mana into the tree.

That was and wasn't surprising. Mortals had no notion where succubi came from, but they came from several sources. One of those sources was a tree nymph with a tree that was dying. Her tree had been dying since the time of the Carthaginians. She knew that in the mortal world trees lived on light, but it wasn't that simple in the netherworld. Her little stretch of the netherworld had been sinking into caverns since before the letter from Paul to the Corinthians. And her tree lived on mana, mana provided by the environment, or by her in her dalliances with mortals and demon kind. Asuma was the same way. Coach was a faun who had friendly relations with Asuma from way back.

She could move out of her vessel, and she did, but the drain on her energy level as she tried to maintain shape without the computer's help was a shock. She reached down and opened the laptop, or tried to. Delicate control of her fingers wasn't easy and they had a tendency to slip through the computer. She slipped back into her vessel, took a moment to make sure all her systems were in place, then shifted back to the cot in Jeff's room.

Jeff had given Asuma her phone while Catvia was gone, and was just putting his hand on the smartwatch that was Coach's vessel.

"No," Catvia said. "Don't take the watch off. You can give it to him while you're still wearing it. Besides, it's not like we can walk in these forms."

"But you disappeared," Jeff said, sounding confused.

"It's all right, Jeff," Catvia said. "I just shifted to the netherworld. I can do that. I just can't get up and walk around.

Would you mind opening me, please?"

"Sure, Cat. Just a sec," Jeff said, then put his hand on the smartwatch watch band, he said, "Coach, I give you this vessel as your home and body for now and all time."

Jeff just said it that way to be poetic, but words and oaths have a power in the netherworld. And time is not completely unidirectional. Spreading from that point in time, Coach took on the form of the smartwatch to a greater or lesser degree. He didn't lose the form of the faun he had been, but even to his beginning he was a faun with a bracelet, or at times just the bracelet. And into the future, the connection was even stronger. Catvia could feel the change in the structure of magic that was Coach.

Jeff reached over and opened the computer. There was a flurry of electronic communication between computer, phone, and smartwatch that was much too fast for a mortal to follow.

****

Jeff fell back into the soft earth next to the small, shaded grove. It didn't hurt. The soil was soft. The cot had been less than two feet off the floor.

But it was still a bit of a shock.

"Oops," said Coach. "Sorry, Jeff. I should have had you stand up for the transfer."

The watch face was glowing white, casting light into the gloomy grove, and the computer was doing the same. So was the phone. Between them, it was bright enough to see at least a little way. He couldn't see the roof of the massive cavern where the trees were growing, but he could see the trees. They were white-barked, like old bone, except for two that seemed to be a bit pinkish and had golden leaves at the tips of a few of their branches.

"What is this place?" Jeff asked. Much as he tried not to let it, his voice quavered a little as he looked around.

"This is my grove," Catvia said. "Asuma's too. You can see the power cord going from me to my tree. Asuma's tree is the other one that has leaves."

Jeff looked, and the tree with the power cord had leaves. It wasn't exactly lush with foliage, but it was clearly waking up from its long winter's nap. The tree next to it had to be Asuma. It only had a few of the golden-green leaves. The rest were all . . . They looked dead.

"Where's your tree, Coach?"

"I'm a faun, not a nymph," Coach said. "You should have seen this place in Baal's time, before the Romans came. The trees were lush and full of fruit." There was a slurping sound from the watch. "Do you think mortal light would make it grow again?"

Jeff shrugged. He didn't know.

"It's hard to tell. My tree can sense the light from my screen, but barely. I would ask the other nymphs, but they are asleep," Asuma said.

****

Catvia had been trying to use the computer's virtual reality software, the same programs she used to project her image on the computer screen, to project herself into the netherworld. So far, though, she hadn't had any success. "Let's go back, for now at least. Maybe Wilber can help."

****

Since the ripping of the veils that separated the two universes, their interactions were increased. Using their position in the mortal realm, the demons could gather energy more easily. As a result, that night a dozen young men had interesting and exciting dreams of beautiful anime girls, one in the form of a cat, and the other wielding a sword and wearing a dress that was short beyond belief. But soon enough the sword was lying on the ground . . . and so was the dress.

In the netherworld, due to the collection of more mana by Catvia and Asuma, two trees began to bloom.

Street in Paris
March 28, 1372

Elaine Boverie took the chamber pot out to the street and tossed the contents into the middle of the street. She wasn't doing anything wrong. There was an open trough in the middle of the street that acted as both sewer and rain gutter. It emptied into the Seine.

A tiny man, perhaps four feet tall with the head and the wings of a horsefly walked out of an alley and came over to where she was standing, sniffing and buzzing. Its four feet long wings were producing a strong wind and the contents of the chamber pot went everywhere, including all over Elaine.

The thing started making the most horrible sounds and stopped flapping its wings. Then it ran at her on stubby insect legs. She screamed and tried to get away, but the creature stuck a long round tube out of its mouth and started sucking on her. She tried to beat it off, still screaming, and it bit her.

A horsefly bite hurts. A horsefly four feet tall . . . that bite is often going to be fatal.

The demonic fly wasn't even trying to kill the woman. It was just looking for dinner.

CHAPTER 16

Somewhere in France
April 1, 1372

Philip the Bold rode through the night with his sword across his back and hate in his heart. His demon, the one that he thought of as his, had abandoned him. Retreated, he suspected, back to whichever circle of Hell the treacherous demon belonged.

It was all Bertrand du Guesclin's fault. The notion that Charles should be king rather than Philip was a constant galling pain in Philip's gut. Why should the accidental order of birth rather than merit determine who would be king? Philip's blood was just as royal as that of the weak and sickly Charles. He had been their father's choice. He was the bold one, the man of destiny. But peasants like Bertrand insisted that Charles sit on the throne and guide their lands to ruin at the hands of the English and the traitorous Pope Gregory.

One of the bits of information that had come with the twenty-firsters was the knowledge that Gregory would take the papacy back to Rome, abandoning France. And that milksop Charles just let him go! A real king, a true royal, would have stopped him and forced the English out of France as well.

The litany of grievances went on as Philip rode from Burgundy to Berry in order to persuade his brother—John, the duke of Berry—to join him. He harped on everything he imagined Charles had done wrong, including and especially how he had dealt with the capture of Philip and their father by the English all those years ago.

Windsor Castle, London, England
April 1, 1372

John of Gaunt, the first duke of Lancaster and holder of numerous other titles, bowed to his father, Edward III of England, who nodded in return. John looked around, hesitating. This was a pleasant room, just off a private garden where the king grew his flowers. There were hangings on the walls, and the windows were opened, letting in the light and the smell of new shoots from the garden. Still, his reason for being here was not to enjoy the flowers.

Father or not, semi-informal setting or not, telling King Edward III of England he couldn't do what he wanted entailed a level of formality. Even if his father was sixty and more concerned with his flowers and his mistress than he was with France. John had been given command of the attempt to restore ownership of their territories there.

"We cannot continue with the war, Your Majesty."

"Has the Blood Royal so weakened as to make the call of battle no siren song to you? Would that your brother, Edward, were recovered."

"He would tell you the same, Father," John said. "In fact, he sent me here with his words. It is not that we would avoid battle, but simply that battle of a different nature has come to us. There are leprechauns in Ireland, pookas in Scotland and brownies throughout England. Every hedgewitch has a familiar teaching them magic and every marsh is filled with will-o-the-wisps. There is a dragon in Loch Ness, terrifying the villagers. Shall I take my sword and attempt to imitate Saint George?"

Edward snorted at that, and John smiled at his father. "I will do so if you command. And, in spite of his health, Edward is anxious to assay it. I counsel a bit more caution. I think perhaps cannon are a better tool for fighting a dragon.

"Father, we must assert control of the situation, lest the house

Plantagenet itself fall."

"You think that Charles is not facing the same troubles?"

"I know he is. We at least have been spared the demon that haunts the streets of Paris. But that is not entirely a good thing."

Edward III waved a hand in dismissal. "I am aware that Charles allowed du Guesclin to summon a demon to their aid. That's half the reason I think we should make the attack. Surely God will not support them if they traffic with the demonic realms."

"That's not the case, Majesty. You know that Edward has agents in France?"

"Yes, of course."

"He got word that the papal nuncio to the twenty-firsters summoned an angel."

"They had the gall to attempt to restrain an angel of the Lord?" King Edward was truly shocked.

"No. The rule is that the owner of the vessel controls the being called to it. And the vessel—something they call a room talker, but they say it in Latin—was given to God so that the angel's only duty was to God."

John of Gaunt had no way of knowing and no reason to care that "phone" was an abbreviation of "telephone," meaning long or distant speech, or that "cell" came from the cell tower system because each tower coverage area was like a cell in the network. He just knew it sounded rather like a bastardized version of Latin.

Edward sat back in his chair. "Well, it still seems to me to be so fraught with peril as to border on insanity. For to call an angel to you without restriction is possibly more dangerous than to trifle with demons."

"I don't disagree, Father, but it seems to have succeeded. And if an angel is with them, can we honestly believe that God has abandoned them?"

"You're saying God is against us?"

"No, Father. Just that we cannot assume that He is *for* us in a war with France. Besides, Robert of Scotland and his lords are raising the standard. We may be at war with Scotland, Ireland, and even Wales before the year is gone."

It took more convincing, but—for now, at least—the armies and levies of England would be put to use at home.

****

All over Europe and the rest of the world, the introduction of magic that worked and magical creatures was changing the lives of people and the politics of nations in strange and unpredictable ways. One thing that was consistent, at least so far, was that it was mostly the aristocracy that was seizing the political opportunity presented by the introduction of magic. The nobles saw a chance to shift the balance of power in their favor as a class and away from the kings who ruled over them and the merchants and moneylenders who pestered them to pay their bills.

Dukedom of Berry, France
April 3, 1372

John, Duke of Berry, was the third son of John II of France, and a younger brother of Charles V. He was a corpulent man with a bulbous and somewhat red nose. He liked his wine as well as his food. He met his youngest brother, Philip the Bold, in his private quarters. He didn't rise. "Why you, Philip?"

"I was Father's choice. You know that." That was all, just the bald statement.

John looked at Philip and something inside him quailed. Philip had never had that effect on him before. Philip had always seemed their father's tool, with little will or character of his own. Now that was changed and John didn't understand how.

Until today, until he had Philip standing before him, so strong and certain, so regal, John would never have considered rebelling against Charles. Not out of love, but simple practicality. He didn't think they could win. And even if they did, how would he be better off under Philip than under Charles?

"Yes, he did. But the law favors Charles." It was hard to say that, and it shouldn't be. "Damn, Philip, what's happened to

205

you?" John wasn't normally given to curses such as that, especially with all that had been going on in the past months. But this was just too strange. It just came out.

"Charles left our father in the hands of the English to the day of his death. No child who would do that deserves his patrimony."

Again, it was difficult to answer. Rather like challenging a pronouncement of law. "That was six years ago, and it was Louis' escape that caused Father to return to England."

"Which only disqualifies Louis from the crown, but doesn't relieve Charles of his responsibility to have paid Father's ransom. John, I am the only one qualified for the crown. You are not so disqualified as Louis and Charles, but the people will not follow you. They will follow me. I am the Chosen King of France."

John heard the capital letters in that pronouncement. And, in spite of himself, he stood and knelt before his little brother.

Philip reached up over his shoulder, pulled a sword that was five feet from hilt to tip, and placed it tip down on the stone floor. The stone of the floor parted like it was earth, and the blade sank an inch into the stone. "Swear then, brother, on the Sword of Justice, which is mine by right, and proof of my right to rule."

John of Berry swore.

Garage, Chateau du Guesclin
April 3, 1372

Annabelle swung the mallet and banged the restored—and more than restored—right front axle into place. It had the bones of the previous axle, but two additions had been made, a set of spring steel muscles and nerves of copper wire. She tightened the nuts that would hold it in place. Then she wiped her face and hands with a rag. Finally, she plugged in the wires.

By the physics of her world, this shouldn't work. There was no supporting circuitry, no logic tree. But Merlin and Wilber said it was close enough. The magic that Pucorl brought with him from the netherworld would be enough to make the difference. "How does it feel?"

"Stiff," Pucorl said. Then he lifted the right front wheel. It went all the way up, until the tire was rubbing against the top of the wheel well. That brought the bottom of the tire up to half a foot above the ground. "Get out from under, please," Pucorl continued, and Annabelle slid out from under the van.

Now Pucorl lowered the wheel until it lifted the front of the van an extra foot. He rolled the wheel forward, and the axle bent forward at the newly installed ball joint. "I'll have to go slow, but I think I'll even be able to climb stairs with these new mods. When are you going to do the left side?"

"When we get finished making it," Annabelle answered. "Your right front axle has taken the entire smithing staff of the chateau and the help of a salamander to produce. I know it's important and so does Tiphaine, but there are pots and pans to be mended, not to mention Roger's rifles."

"I bet he takes that thing to bed with him, and it's not even finished yet, much less enchanted," Pucorl muttered.

"It's going to be, if Roger can find the right demon for it," Annabelle said.

Demons came in all shapes and sizes, and all levels of intelligence and understanding. What was needed for an enchanted rifle was not the same sort of demon that was needed for, say, an enchanted sword or shield. The demon that was needed for the rifle was more the sort of thing you would want in an enchanted goblet that glowed if poison was put in it, or one that purified whatever was poured in it. An enchanted sword worked with the wielder to let him strike harder and more precisely.

For a rifle, a little help with the aim might be nice, but what Roger wanted was an actual action. It would be the demon, probably a salamander, that would ignite the powder. It would be good if it also had the effect of making sure that all the powder burned, that they got complete combustion. But it didn't have to be a salamander, at least not a pure salamander. Pucorl was a puck, which were made up of a mix of all the elements, and he was quite capable of making sure that his diesel engine burned the fuel completely.

At the moment, Wilber, with the help of Merlin, was looking for the right demon to enchant Roger's rifle when it was finished. They didn't want a really bright demon who might fire the gun out of boredom. They wanted—not to put too fine a point on it—a simple-minded demon who would be satisfied to follow instructions.

Meanwhile, Pucorl was playing with his new right front wheel. He was tapping his tire on the garage floor.

"Okay, Pucorl. I see you. How far back can you move the wheel?"

"Not as far as I like. I think the wheel well needs adjusting."

"Will that work? I mean, with your healing?" Demons didn't heal, exactly. They aggregated, for want of a better word. They gradually reassembled themselves, and they could do the same thing to their vessels. So, in the week and a half since Pucorl hurt himself running the demon lord into the wall, Pucorl had healed. Not completely, but the damaged paint had mostly grown back and the dents were undenting. There were limits, especially if you didn't have hundreds of years to wait, but with the help of the smiths of the chateau, Pucorl was getting back to working order.

Normandy, near La Rochelle
April 4, 1372

The pentagram was finished in the small keep's courtyard and the afternoon sun shone down on the gaudy feathers. The parrot was tied in the pentagram and had cost Olivier de Clisson a pretty franc. He signaled Father Louis and the priest began the incantation. Olivier wasn't entirely sure that he would remain loyal to Bertrand du Guesclin. Things were unsettled at the moment, but Olivier knew he wanted to be able to understand the netherworld since it was now accessible.

He watched the ceremony of enchantment until it finished, then carefully stepped into the pentagram and lifted the parrot on a gauntleted wrist. "Well, my fine fellow, what should I call you?"

"Aimee, Monsieur, for surely I am your friend . . . in spite of your rudeness in pulling me from my home." The bird looked around. "A priest? How is it that one of the followers of the Christ would be a party to calling me? Have things truly changed so much?"

Father Louis answered. "I have a letter from Monsignor Savona informing me that while your sort are not angels of the Lord, neither are you of the enemy's corps. Had you not heard?"

The parrot looked at the good father but didn't answer.

"Answer the question, please," Olivier instructed it.

"Oh, very well," Aimee said in a flouncy voice. "There are rumors of a great disturbance and many callings, but I know nothing of this Monsignor Savona. Why does it matter what he says?"

The conversation went from there, with Olivier carrying the parrot on his wrist as they went into the keep. He set the bird on its perch and took a seat himself, all while Aimee and Father Louis talked. The gist of it was that Aimee had never met any of the demons who had been called to Paris. She had heard about a demon lord who had wandered into the mortal realm for a wild hunt, but the latest she had heard, it was back, having tired of the sport.

"Tired of the sport." Olivier laughed. "I guess so. Being smashed into a wall might be quite tiring. Would you like some cheese, Aimee?" Olivier fed the bird some of the local cheese and some fruits as they continued to talk about the nature of magic and magical beings.

CHAPTER 17

Rue de Martine
April 6, 1372

Commissaire Pierre Dubois of the Grand Châtelet stared in horror at the body. It was clearly dead, but it was moving. The young woman's corpse shambled along in a parody of a strumpet's walk. Her hands and face were covered in drying blood. The knife wound that had killed her was still exposed under the cold, dead breasts.

She turned her face and dead eyes gazed at him in a strange mix of hunger, desperation, and confusion. The corpse tried to smile lasciviously, but all he felt was horror. "Go get the twenty-firsters," he said.

"Which one?"

"How should I know?" Pierre demanded, almost shouting, then got himself under control. "It's not really the twenty-firsters we need, anyway. It's their tame demons." *Their hopefully tame demons.* But he didn't say that out loud.

****

Wilber and Bill rode along in the company of André Hébert. "André doesn't have much more experience with riding than me or Bill," Wilber said to Meurtrier in horse, and the bay gelding that André was riding snorted in agreement.

It was true. Wilber had learned that riding wasn't all that common in the Middle Ages, even the late Middle Ages. The usual way of getting around was to walk. André Hébert had lived his life in Paris and walked almost everywhere he needed to go.

He had come up as what would, in a later age, be called a beat cop. Horses were for nobles.

"What are you saying to my horse?" André asked as they rounded a corner onto the filthy Rue de Martine. The street was narrow, really too narrow for the horses, and the crowd of constables made navigating even more difficult.

"Nothing important," Wilber said, as he looked at the crowd down the street. "And I was talking to Meurtrier anyway."

The police were backing away from something and suddenly Wilber saw it—a walking corpse. Wilber wasn't sure how he could tell at this distance. The thing shambling toward him wasn't alive. "Merlin, do you know what that is?"

There was a quick exchange between Merlin and Wilber's phone, which resided in his breast pocket with its camera sticking up out of his pocket to give the phone a view ahead of him. "It's a—" There was a short pause as Merlin mumbled the various names that such creatures had been given through the eons until he got to "—zombie. Yes, that is the name you would know."

"How do you make a zombie, Merlin?"

"When a demon is put into a living creature like a cat or a bird, it can leave when that creature dies. But if a demon is put into a dead creature, then the signal that would release both demon and spirit is already past, and all that is left is the dead body . . . the dead, decaying body."

There was a pause as Merlin looked for words, but by now Wilber knew quite a bit of the intricacies of magic and the differences between the natural laws of the netherworld versus the natural laws of the mortal universe. "So the demon is stuck in the rotting corpse, but in your world things come back together naturally. Does that affect the corpse?"

"That depends on how powerful the demon is. A powerful demon would bring the body back to a semblance of life. But a minor demon, like a puck or a sylph, would be more likely to be dragged down by the decaying of the body. Such things have happened, but they have been truly rare occurrences."

"I know that the vehicle affects the demon as well as the other way around, but I can't imagine what the effect of inhabiting a rotting corpse would be."

"Dementia. As the brain of the vessel decays, the demon's mental functions would get weaker and less flexible. By the time it was an animated skeleton, it wouldn't be able to think at all, just react."

"Why would a demon—" Wilber stopped. "You think the demon was called to the corpse, don't you?" Wilber knew that demons could, on their own, occupy a stream or a tree, even a cat, a dog, or a human. And when they did that, they weren't constrained the way a summoned demon was. But he couldn't think of a good reason for a demon to want to occupy a corpse.

Merlin was silent, but by now Wilber knew Merlin pretty well and was good at interpreting the demon's silences. "What is it?"

"I'm quite sure that this demon was called, Wilber. But a more powerful demon, wishing a vessel that had most of the mental faculties of a human but lacked the will that the demon would have to contend with in a possession, might choose a corpse and use some of their magic to restore it to something very close to life. That is the basis for the beings that your probability called vampires. A powerful demon might even gain access to some of the memories that the person possessed when they were alive."

"And the blood sucking?" Wilber started to ask, but stopped as the zombie noticed them. Or, more to the point, noticed Merlin and Ishmael and Wilber's phone. It started screeching: "Get me out! Get me out! Get me out!"

Everyone was backing away from the frightening howl and Meurtrier reared. Wilber tried to stay on and calm the horse, but managed neither. The creature was howling like a banshee. Wilber landed on his side and his computer—Merlin's computer—was almost broken. Would have been if it hadn't been for the fact that the demon's presence strengthened it. Meanwhile, Wilber's head hit the flagstones after his shoulder had slowed him. He saw stars, but didn't quite lose consciousness. The horses were running and the people were cowering with their hands over their ears.

All the while, the zombie was shambling straight at Wilber . . . or straight at Merlin, who was in Wilber's backpack.

****

Bill Howe stepped forward and drew his sword. The sword was somewhere between a gladius and a rapier, but a bit closer to the rapier. It was two feet, two inches long and had a relatively narrow blade that came to a point. Not that a sharp point was going to be of much use against a frigging zombie. "Shut up, you stupid . . ." Bill ran out of words.

The zombie wasn't likely to understand twenty-first century English anyway. The zombie flinched away from the blade. Which was a surprise. Bill tried *Langue d'oïl*, then said, "Ish, talk to it. Calm it down if you can."

Ishmael started talking and what it said sounded almost as bad as the zombie, but at least it wasn't as loud.

****

Wilber managed to get up and saw Bill holding the zombie at bay with his sword, a gift from the constabulary for his help with the murders. There hadn't been a demonic murder since the attack on the Chateau du Guesclin.

And the threatening presence was also gone from the city. No one was quite ready to say that the demon was gone for good, but between fingerprint evidence from the chateau and earlier attacks, they were fairly sure that the demon that attacked the chateau was the same as the demon who turned the bar into such a bloodbath. So Bill was pretty popular with the cop on the street. In fact, all the twenty-firsters were. One positive effect of being attacked by the demon was that the notion that the twenty-firsters or Bertrand had somehow been in league with the demon was pretty much dispelled.

Wilber made his way to Bill. "Merlin, how do we cut this thing loose?"

"For a living creature, its death releases the demon. For a vessel like a statue or a cell phone, the destruction of the vessel would

213

destroy it. But an undead creature like this is harder. It's already been killed. I would think that the body would have to be completely destroyed. Either that, or we find the pentagram where it was called and the person who owns the corpse and perform a ceremony of release."

"Hey, according to all the zombie apocalypse movies and books, you just have to destroy the brain. Chop its fucking head off," Bill said.

"Maybe," Merlin said doubtfully. "I don't know if just the brain will do it. And it's dangerous for the demon. If it's too tied into the body, it could be destroyed or at least severely injured." Merlin had said this in *Langue d'oïl* and the police were staring at him like he was insane. "The demon is a victim here. It didn't choose this."

"He's got a point, Commissaire," Wilber said.

"That may be," said Commissaire Pierre Dubois, "but there is blood on her hands nonetheless, and there is a body two streets over where that blood came from."

"It wasn't her fault. Her brain isn't fully functional and that affects the demon's thoughts."

Commissaire Dubois didn't look impressed by Merlin's arguments. The fourteenth century wasn't a time when the rights of the mentally challenged were greatly respected. Sometimes Wilber wished rather desperately for a little political correctness.

Just then, Meurtrier came running back up the street in a loud clattering of hooves. The big black horse had gotten to know Wilber, and while he was still perhaps the most arrogant piece of horse flesh Wilber had ever seen, up until now he had never been lacking in courage. Being easily startled isn't the same thing. At least, Meurtrier insisted it wasn't. He came charging down the street and people scattered from his path, including Wilber. Meurtrier in that mood wasn't something he wanted to deal with.

The zombie, however, was not quick on the uptake. Nor did it have much left in the way of reflexes. It could cringe, but not really duck. And Meurtrier, screaming bloody murder, reared and came down with his right front hoof on the dead prostitute's head.

"Merde," Wilber said. He looked down at the body. The girl had been in her teens when she died, but looked older. Hers had been a hard life. And apparently a hard afterlife as well, if any part of the girl's spirit had remained with the body. But her troubles were over, or at least beyond anything he could do.

The demon, however, was a different case. Demons, pucks, angels, whatever, didn't die in the sense that mortals did. They were designed to cycle and recycle again and again. A demon death was the end of an immortal cycle. He subvocalized, *"Merlin, did the demon get out or was it destroyed?"*

"I can't be sure," Merlin said for Wilber's implant alone. *"It is gone from this world, but whether it is back in the netherworld or permanently uncreated, I cannot tell. It did leave scraps of its essence here, so it is at least badly hurt."*

"Is it likely to be drawn back to this place or her body as a haunt?" Wilber asked.

Haunts were bits and pieces of mortal or immortal beings that got caught between the realms. Haunts were part of the same set of interactions between what Pucorl had called the netherworld and Wilber was coming to suspect was another universe that was passing through the mortal realm with very little interaction. Or at least had been, until whatever it was went nuts a few months ago. Those interactions had mostly been in the form of dream and delusion until very recently. Ghosts, ghoulies and things that went bump in the night, as well as celestial visitations and the milieu that had formed the basis for both Plato and Aristotle's world views, were part of that interaction.

That other universe, the one that Wilber was coming to call in his mind "the magic universe" or "U2," was more affected by the mortal realm than the mortal realm had been by it until quite recently. Or at least more directly. How much human evolution had been affected by the magic universe was not something that Wilber had any way of checking.

What it came down to in the here and now was that, aside from

215

the demons and otherworldly spirits that had wandered in or been called, there were also ghosts in graveyards—and holy relics were showing scientifically significant results. Wilber had to worry about ghosts as well as pucks in the woods and brownies in the back garden. Not to mention the demon lords and whatever it was that had ripped loose the barriers that kept the two universes from interacting strongly.

And it was Wilber who was having to figure it out. Merlin could help, but as sharp and magical as he was, Merlin was created to be an assistant—not an original thinker. Wilber wasn't sure the netherworld, U2, *had* original thinkers. There didn't seem much room for such creatures in a world where nothing moved save in circles that came back to their beginnings.

"Give Pucorl a call, Merlin," Wilber said. "Let Annabelle know what we have here."

****

"I'm almost surprised that it took so long for someone to think of it," Annabelle said, after Pucorl told her about the zombie. She was sitting in the van, eating a ham and cheese sandwich.

"Why? You didn't think of it."

"Sure, but I'm just one person. By now at least a million people know that you got called by a pentagram. And with all the other stuff that's going on, everyone in Europe is thinking about magic. Even if we take it as a given that ninety-nine out of a hundred of those people come to the same stupid conclusion or don't think of anything at all, that's still a lot of people thinking up things to try. And even if only one in a hundred of those does try the crazy thing they think of, and only one in a hundred of those has it work, that's still a lot of crazy stuff that is going to work."

The demon-inhabited van sighed through his internal speakers. "That's too weird for me." Then there was a pop as Pucorl used his magic to pop out a dent in his front bumper.

Annabelle finished her sandwich and crawled under Pucorl to return to work on the rear differential.

216

Royal Palace, Hôtel Saint-Pol
April 6, 1372

Charles V looked daggers at Bertrand from his chair in his private office. There was a change in the office. Charles had a desk now, a twenty-firster style desk, made of cherry with nooks for pens, paper, and a thick paper pad to set letters on when writing them. It looked odd and out of place to Bertrand.

"It is not the fault of the twenty-firsters, Majesty," Bertrand said quickly. "The magic works. It was just a matter of time until someone thought of calling a demon to a corpse."

The king glared a little longer, then sighed. "I know, Bertrand, I know. But it's hard not to associate them and their enchanted devices with such things." He turned to Nicolas du Bosc. "What can we do?"

"I have been thinking on the matter, Your Majesty, and I have spoken with Mrs. Grady and her phone." Mrs. Grady's phone was named Emmanuelle and was a flirt. Which seemed to amuse Mrs. Grady for some reason that Nicolas didn't understand. But both Mrs. Grady and Emmanuelle were reasonably familiar with the structure of French jurisprudence and the Napoleonic code. "It was Emmanuelle who pointed out that a law no one obeys is no law at all. And a law that is written too broadly will be consistently disobeyed." Nicolas wasn't convinced of that, but in this case it might be good advice. "What I recommend is that the crown, in cooperation with the church, license the invocation of demons. This would help us start a rapprochement with the church, as well as giving those with licenses a motive to inform us of those acting without licenses. It would let us restrict, to some extent, what is done."

"What of my brother and his accursed sword?" Charles asked. "Would your laws have prevented that?"

"No, Majesty. Philip would still be a traitor, no matter what other regulations he might break."

****

Bertrand glanced over at the lawyer. He bore no love himself for the king's youngest brother, but Nicolas' tone suggested a level of hatred that surprised Bertrand.

"What ails you, Nicolas?" Charles asked.

"Themis was a nation, Majesty, and all the demons of that land are crushed and mangled by her abduction. Whether Philip was a knowing participant in that or not, he was a participant. And the guilt of that act is, in some ways, worse than his treason."

"Well, however it got here, the sword Themis is here now. And if it is owned in this world, I should own it," Charles said. "Your duty, Nicolas, is to France, to me. Not to Themis."

Nicolas bowed, but it was clear to Bertrand—and probably to Charles—that he wasn't happy. Come to it, Bertrand wasn't happy either. If such an artifact was to remain in the world, yes, it should be in the hands of the true and proper king. The question was: should it remain in the world at all?

Angers, Duchy of Anjou, France
April 15, 1372

Philip the Bold stood in the great hall. He had missed his brother, Louis I, Duke of Anjou, and was unhappy but not really surprised. Louis was an absentee duke. He collected the taxes, but let others administer the duchy.

What did surprise Philip was that Louis had been here just three days earlier. On receiving the news that Philip was on the way, Louis had packed up his wife and two-year-old daughter and left with no destination stated.

Almost the sword came out. Almost, but not quite. It was the sword itself that held Philip's hand. He still couldn't communicate clearly with the sword, but he got feelings from it. And he knew that it wouldn't approve of Philip executing his brother's chamberlain for no greater crime than obeying the lawful commands of his liege lord.

"Can you raise the levies of Anjou?"

The man cringed. "Not without your brother's consent."

Philip spun away and ordered that rooms be made ready for him.

April 17, 1372

A messenger arrived, mud-coated after following Philip from Berry. Philip sat in his brother's cushioned chair in his brother's apartments and listened as the man gave his report. The news was from Paris, and much of it was bad. Based on the presence of his men in the shambles at Chateau du Guesclin, Philip was declared outlaw and traitor to the crown.

Philip could feel the sword's displeasure at being owned by a traitor to his liege lord. He reached up and grasped the hilt. *You are mine. Obey.* The sword flinched from his will, which reassured Philip of his personal strength and the rightness of his cause.

There was another piece of news, which brought a thoughtful frown to Philip's face. A demon had been summoned to a corpse. That was all. Just the bare fact. A demon had been summoned to a corpse. No word on how well it had worked. But the idea . . . that was interesting.

Philip had been learning about magic, both from scholars he employed—many of them from the University of Paris—and from the demon lord who had run when struck by that thrice-cursed Pucorl . He knew the drawbacks to using an inanimate object like a sword or a statue, and he knew the drawbacks of using a living creature. He wondered if a dead creature or a dead human might have all, or at least some, of the advantages of both but not the disadvantages of either. He sent agents to Paris to find out.

"I'll wait here," he told the muddy courier, "until I hear back either from you or from my missing brother."

Netherworld, Under Themis' Land
Time Uncertain

Beslizoswian, whose name contained many more syllables than that and sounds never heard in the mortal realm, groaned and rolled in his bed beneath the detritus of the absent Themis. It had hurt when that puck struck him. And it had been humiliating to be forced out of the mortal realm by the mortals and such minor demons as a puck and a muse.

Beslizoswian was no minor player. He was a series of caverns and caves of stone, fire, and water, even quite a bit of air. In the netherworld, he was the size of Carlsbad Caverns and of similar shape. His dreams and thoughts were fragmented as whole caverns tried to undent and recover from the damage the puck had done. Even the absence of Themis holding him down was uncomfortable, as though a heavy quilt had been ripped away, leaving him exposed to the winter winds. He dreamed and raged and hated.

Beslizoswian was good at that. He had been doing it since before the asteroid had killed his pets.

What was new was the fear. He was afraid of the puck in its van body, and Beslizoswian wasn't used to being afraid.

Paris
April 17, 1372

The royal proclamation was read on every street corner in Paris, and copies were sent to all the provinces of France and to the pope. There would henceforth be a procedure for the licensing of magical summonings.

Chateau du Guesclin
April 17, 1372

"So how do I get a license?" Wilber asked Bertrand.

Bertrand took a sip of wine, then said, "It should not be difficult. Doctor Delaflote has been made the king's minister of the magical arts. He is empowered to test knowledge and grant licenses. There is also a fee paid to the crown, of course."

"Of course. How big a fee?"

"Quite substantial, I fear. However, in some cases the crown will defer the payment until some items have been enchanted and sold. There really wasn't any choice, Wilber. Demons were going to be summoned, whatever the crown did. This way, at least it will mostly be done right."

"I'm not objecting, Lord Constable," Wilber said. "I just want to know what I have to do to get a license."

"Never mind that. Have they caught the guy who raised that poor girl?" Mrs. Grady asked. "You can't go around raising dead women to make into prostitutes. It's icky."

"Icky?" Bertrand looked confused.

"Disgusting."

"I quite agree," Bertrand said. "So does the king. And in answer to your question, no, they have not found the bruiser who was the girl's pimp in life and was probably the one behind her raising. We think the one who actually raised her was murdered by the pimp for not doing a better job. In any case, we found a student's body next to a pentagram in a small building on the left bank."

****

Life went on—stranger than it had been before, but it went on. Roger got his rifle finished and started working on a double-barreled muzzle-loading pistol. The pistol was to have two tiny flame elementals, each invoked into a fire cap that would be invoked by the touch of the hammer. Pucorl had four moveable wheels, and he and Annabelle were working on a steam car that would be called Stanley after it was finished and a demon called to it.

Nicholas Flamel and his wife, after much consultation, were building a printing press. There were washboards and drop forges popping up in Paris like mushrooms, patterns and clamps were now working in half the shops in Paris and a technical school was opening at the Sorbonne. Roger McLean, who had earned a brown belt in his early teens, was teaching daily classes in karate while he took daily classes in swordsmanship. It wasn't just the magic, at least not in and around Paris. The knowledge of the twenty-firsters—as limited as it was—was having a profound effect.

However, that effect was in many ways subtle and slow acting in comparison to the demons and magic that actually worked. No one much noticed the crocheting that Jennifer Fairbanks had shared with the ladies of Tiphaine's household, even when the queen wore a crocheted shawl to her first public appearance after the birth of her child.

CHAPTER 18

Estate of Clement Lefevre, Outside of Paris
April 20, 1372

Wilber and Roger dismounted. Meurtrier whinnied and Wilber said, "Oh, shut up."

Roger laughed and half the armsmen were grinning. Meurtrier had taken to correcting Wilber's riding style. And while it was normally quite helpful and was allowing Wilber to gain something of a good seat, Meurtrier was not good at realizing when enough was enough. According to Meurtrier, Wilber had shifted too far out as he dismounted and threatened to topple them both over.

"Don't blame me," Meurtrier's whinney said. "If I topple over and crush you, it will be your own fault."

"I think the next time I'll ride in Pucorl," Wilber said, looking back at the van that was taking its first trip out of Paris since its abrupt arrival.

The threat, however, was empty. The van was packed. It contained Bertrand, Tiphaine, King Charles, Queen Joanna, the dauphin Charles, two-year-old Marie, and the newly born Louis, Annabelle, Amelia and Paul Grady. Amelia was in the driver's seat, but in truth Pucorl himself was doing most of the driving. Also, two ladies in waiting were packed into the rear seats.

The van pulled into the stone courtyard with no noticeable issues. Fortunately, it had been dry for the past few days so the narrow dirt track that was the main highway north out of Paris wasn't a bog. The door opened to the sound of crying children, and the king was first out of the van. On the other hand, the future king of France was not crying. He was entranced by the cartoon showing on the mini-screen on the back of the driver side seat.

Would that the two-year-old Marie was enjoying it. Instead, she got car sick, upchucked two miles out of Paris, and was cranky for the whole trip. Her crying had set off the baby and Bertrand was quick to support his monarch by exiting the van next.

Paul would have been right with them, but for the fact that he was stuck in the back with the ladies in waiting.

Once Pucorl was stopped, Marie started to calm and the queen was helped out, so there was less noise in the van.

Once everyone was situated, they went into the mansion that was owned by a friend of Bertrand's. It smelled good here. After months in the constant miasma of Paris, it smelled positively glorious here in the new green and flowers of the countryside.

****

Roger collected his rifled musket and the rifled flintlock as well. Then Wilber spoke to the horses and they headed for the stables while the humans went inside.

Charles watched the horses go with a shaking head and quietly crossed himself, as if this evidence of magic bothered him.

It didn't make sense to Wilber. *Traveling in an enchanted van was fine, but me talking to a horse evokes warding gestures?*

In the mansion, the servants took their coats and then went out to collect the cases that had been tied onto Pucorl's roof for the trip out. Pucorl had proved himself incredibly useful on this trip. A little too useful, it seemed to Wilber. The king was looking at the van with lustful glances. The king of France was looking at a lot of the stuff they brought or made with lustful glances, and Wilber was getting nervous about it all.

April 21, 1372

It was a crisp, clean morning as Roger, Wilber, the king and Bertrand rode out of the estate, taking Roger's cases with them. Five minutes later, they were in a small valley with archery butts set up.

"We started working on these, at least the design part, before we moved from the university to Bertrand's place," Roger told the king. "The stocks were easy enough for your carpenters to make. Expensive because they were hand carved, but not complicated. And the locks were not too bad, considering. But the real challenge was the barrels. In our history, barrels were made for a very long time by welding six iron bars together, then boring out the middle to a round hole. That left six lines of weakness to the barrel and meant that each barrel took a very long time to make."

The king was nodding. He knew about the construction of hand cannons. It wasn't quite so bad as the twenty-firster seemed to think, but it was not something a farmer could do at a village smithy, at least not well.

"What we did was use a drop forge to produce a bent barrel form that could then be hammered into a circle, leaving only one seam along the bottom of the barrel." Roger showed the king the rifle he had made. "That, combined with some quality control that honestly was more Bertrand's salamander than me, allows us to produce a much lighter, longer barrel and one that includes rifling."

The king nodded again, then asked about rifling, and Roger pulled out a top he'd had the carpenter at the estate make. He set it on a flat rock, then used a string to spin it, and it spun standing up. The king nodded again.

Roger loaded the rifle using a lead Minié ball, explaining all the while. The rifle was a bit shorter than a Kentucky longrifle. He lifted the rifle to his shoulder, cocked the hammer, took aim, and pulled the trigger.

****

The being that resided in the flash plate was a simple salamander. It was a being almost entirely of fire, and it was enchanted into a piece of metal that fit into the touch hole of the rifle. It had one function and one function only. When the hammer hit its container, it was released to a moment of salamander-ish bliss. It leapt from its container and burned what was in the chamber behind the bullet all up in a fraction of a heartbeat.

The hammer hit and it leapt into action much too fast for a mortal to follow. It circled and twined through pieces of black corned powder and ignited them completely. For a timeless instant, it gloried in the pyrotechnic ecstasy and then retreated to the plug that was its home, leaving very hot gas and very little ash behind.

****

All the king saw was the kick of the rifle and the white gunpowder smoke that puffed out. A moment later he saw a puff from one of the archery butts as the bullet struck. There had been no noticeable delay between the pulling of the trigger and the bullet leaving the rifle. Charles V was taken by surprise by the suddenness of it all.

"The drawback of the demon lock rifle is the need for a demon in each rifle," Roger said. "There are only so many fire demons and it takes an expert mage with excellent demonic advice to find the right sort of demon and place it in just the right sort of container." Roger set the rifle butt down on the ground, leaning it against a tree. Then he lifted the next example.

"This is a flintlock rifle, and while it's not as consistent or as fast as a demonlock, it does work. And we can make as many as we have the steel for." He showed the king the flint, the spring, the pan, and the lock, loaded the rifle, put powder in the pan, cocked the rifle, lifted it to his shoulder, took careful aim, then pulled the trigger.

The hammer came down and the powder in the pan was ignited by the sparks. There was a short but noticeable delay between the pulling of the trigger and the firing of the gun. The bullet again hit the target, but it was not dead center. It hit high and to the right.

Charles looked to Bertrand. "How many and how soon?"

"It will take some time. We just have the one drop forge."

"There's a drop forge in every followed in Paris," the king complained.

"Yes, Your Majesty. But they are busy making pots and tongs, knicknacks and door latches. They belong to the smithies in question, and making the dies for the barrels is no small task. And the drop forges don't alleviate the need for charcoal to stoke the forges. We can make them, Majesty, but they won't be as many or as soon as we would like. And, Majesty, they won't be cheap."

They got down to business then and talked for the rest of the day, while the king got to fire both rifles several times and they had a lunch of cold roast chicken and something akin to macaroni salad. The mayo was a recipe provided by Jennifer and the macaroni was a local food. The shooting was good, and aside from ordering a thousand flintlocks for the royal army, the king ordered a demon lock for his own collection.

Roger, in cooperation with Bertrand's blacksmith, was now an armaments manufacturer for the French crown.

****

In the mansion, the queen was discussing her children and her health with Tiphaine and Amelia Grady while Paul played with Prince Charles. The discussion was wide ranging and covered much of the territory that they had already discussed with Doctor Filberte Renard. The queen wanted to get it from the horse's mouth, as it were. Amelia was convinced that what was bothering the queen was in large part vitamin deficiencies. Making a baby takes quite a lot of calcium, and so does making milk. But she acknowledged that she was not a doctor.

It was a pleasant day away from the noise and smells of Paris. Paris in the fourteenth century stank. It stank abominably. In 1372, Paris had one walled sewer that ran along the rue Montmartre and even that one wasn't covered. For the rest of the paved streets in Paris, they had runoff troughs down the middle of the street and that was it.

"Yes, I know," said Queen Joanna. "The smells are very bad

227

and they cause disease."

"It's not exactly the bad air that causes disease," Amelia Grady explained carefully. "It's more a case of the same thing that causes the bad smells causes disease." Amelia knew by now that care and delicate phrasing was essential in imparting knowledge from the twenty-first century. Telling people that what they knew to be true was not didn't get you anywhere. They took it as an insult and held to their beliefs even harder. Tiphaine's belief in astrology was one example, but far from the only one. In a way the whole bad air, *mal-aria*, was another, and one that had produced considerable acrimony in the medical community of Paris, which was among the most advanced in the western world at this time.

"Yes, I have heard of your superstition that little tiny beings inhabit the drinking water and live in our bodies wreaking havoc."

"It's not . . ." Annabelle started, then subsided at a look from Amelia.

The queen smiled in a very condescending manner and Amelia suspected that they weren't going to make much progress. The queen said she wanted to learn, and probably even believed that she wanted to learn. But what she really wanted was to have her beliefs confirmed and discredit any threat to those comfortable beliefs. This was not, of course, an attitude unique to the fourteenth century.

"I suspect that the bad air theory does in fact work in the netherworld and it's true that poison gases and airborne disease cause illness and death. However, it is true that microorganisms cause disease. It has been documented quite thoroughly in the time we come from." She shrugged. "Even if we are wrong, though, closed underground sewers that took the waste of Paris to leach fields away from the Seine would go a long way toward removing the smells."

"Unfortunately, such a project would also go a great distance toward the removal of the royal fortune. Charles is not made of money and with Philip having succumbed to the blandishments of a demon and imprisoning a titan of old in that great sword of his, the royal purse is going to be needed to pay for the army."

It was, overall, a lovely day. But while the gun shop got royal support, the crown found it cheaper to spend time outside Paris, away from the bad smells and "possibly" germs, and let Paris stew in its own juices.

The twenty-firsters' whole experience since arriving in 1372 was like that. They would make great—even unbelievable—progress in one area and be shut down in places that it seemed to them were obviously useful and beneficial. In spite of everything they knew about the distances of the stars, in spite of the telescope that they had managed to make using demonic aid to melt the glass and grind it into shape, they had not been able to call the basic assumptions of astrology into serious question. Everyone from King Charles to the pope believed to some extent that the stars ruled, or at least strongly influenced, fate. The demons insisted that it worked in their realm, but conceded that things might be different in a world where you couldn't even chat up a babbling brook.

Chateau du Guesclin
May 5, 1372

The rider was coated in sweat and the horse in foam. Bertrand helped the man down while Wilber talked to the exhausted horse.

"Commander de Clisson sent me. He is retreating north from La Rochelle."

"The English?"

"No. Duke Philip brought an army overland."

Olivier is retreating from Philip? The thought stopped Bertrand for a moment. In spite of the nickname he had gotten as a teenager when he was captured with his father King John, Philip had always struck Bertrand as more of a conniver than a courageous war leader. Olivier could connive with the best of them, but he was not a man to retreat without good cause. "What happened, man?"

"He came up from the south with that sword of his and an army," the courier gasped out. "We held him for the first day with heavy losses on both sides. But that night, the Demon Duke went out onto the field and started touching the bodies with that awful sword. Each body he touched stood back up, still showing its wounds. They stood up and took up their arms. I was on the walls at La Rochelle and I saw it with my own eyes."

Bertrand turned to Wilber, who was still talking to the horse. "Merlin, did you hear?"

"Yes, Lord Constable," said Merlin's voice from Wilber's phone.

"How can he have done that without a pentagram or wards of any sort?"

"I don't know, Lord Constable. There must be some form of influence over demons. Most would not willingly come to a corpse."

"He has influence," Wilber said. "He has the sword. Who can Themis command?"

"All the demons of her land. Tens of thousands of them," Merlin said promptly. "But she . . . she is compelled. How did Philip know?"

"I bet Dino told him," Wilber said. They still had no name for the demon who had haunted the streets of Paris for long months, but Wilber had started calling it "Dino the dinosaur."

"You think?" Merlin asked. "I would expect one of his sort to spend several thousand years licking his wounds and complaining about the injustice of it all."

Bertrand knew Merlin's attitude toward the demon. There were sections of the netherworld that no human had ever imagined. And in the netherworld, when they said "the king is the land," they were not speaking figuratively. Themis was the land of Themis and the queen of Themis, all at once.

The demon they had routed, though much smaller and weaker than Themis, was still a true demon lord. It was the lord and the land. As such, it had the will and the power to project itself to the mortal realm while leaving its body in the netherworld. That was something that Pucorl and Merlin couldn't do, although Merlin could almost do it with the aid of the computer he occupied.

But aside from power, there was attitude. The demon they had bested in the courtyard was what Amelia Grady called a "Kali" sort of demon. Its goal was to destroy and disperse to make room for new construction. It was a being of hate and anger, the very antithesis of what Merlin was.

That limited Merlin's view. Bertrand was certainly not an ally of the demon, but much of Bertrand's business was destruction. He didn't underestimate that force.

"No, Merlin. He may be injured, but he is also very, very angry. Depend on it."

Royal Palace, Hôtel Saint-Pol
May 5, 1372

It was not just Bertrand who rode up to the royal palace. He was accompanied by Monsignor Savona and, perhaps even more importantly, Raphico.

"What then, Monsignor Savona, is the pope's position on this?" King Charles asked.

"There hasn't been time to send messages to the pope and get a response. But Raphico is not so limited." Monsignor Savona displayed the phone given to God and held it up.

"The Creator condemns and rejects Philip the Bold for consorting with dark powers and performing unholy rites," Raphico intoned.

King Charles leaned back in his chair. "I am, of course, grateful for the support of God. But, in this case, what precisely does that mean?" The only word to describe the king's expression was *sardonic*.

Until now, Raphico had continued his unwillingness to

commit to absolute pronouncements, insisting that the Lord of Hosts was unwilling to interfere in matters of conscience at this time. This condemnation of Philip was a major departure from that position, but how major? King Charles, as Bertrand knew well, was not easily misled. That Philip was condemned was not the same as Charles being endorsed.

"Less than I prefer," Monsignor Savona said. "But perhaps I should let Raphico explain."

Raphico said, "It is no business of mortals to question the Creator's will. And in this case, for reasons that are beyond mortal understanding, the Creator will not interfere as much as you might wish. You may, in defense of Paris, invoke those of the netherworld that are not of the Holy Host, and you may request aid from the saints through similar rites. Especially, you may and should invoke and attempt to contain those of demonkind that did reside in the land of Themis. For that purpose, I can and will give you a part of the name of said demons. But beyond that, even for this, the Creator will not go."

Monsignor Savona looked at the phone in surprise. Bertrand understood that quite well. He was shocked to the core. Giving any part of a demon's name for purposes of containment was considered very bad form, whether you were an angel or a demon, a puck or a muse. He found himself wondering how Pucorl and the other demons were going to feel about this.

CHAPTER 19

Chateau du Guesclin
May 5, 1372

The table was large and round. Bertrand and Tiphaine as well as Doctor Delaflote and most of the twenty-firsters were seated around it, along with their electronic devices. Doctor Delaflote had his crow, Archimedes, who was an acquaintance of Merlin's. The subject was the drafting, or kidnapping, of the demons who had been left without lands by Themis' abduction. The demons, Wilber noticed, were not overly concerned about the morality of enslaving other demons. When they had objections, it was mostly practical issues.

"It does have drawbacks," Merlin admitted, while Wilber sipped at the watered sour wine, "but in this case it is justified. Themis is not willingly calling her subjects to the service of the traitor. Themis is the titan—call her the demigod—of law."

"So better us than them, if the demons are to be enslaved anyway?" Wilber asked.

"Basically, yes," Merlin agreed.

"My question . . ." Jennifer raised her hand. ". . . is where are we going to put them all? If I have this straight, we're talking about millions of demons, aren't we?"

"Yes," Merlin said. "The population of Greece in this time is in the millions, but that's not all of it. In the netherworld, everything is, to one extent or another, alive. Rocks, brooks, trees, pots, pans, ladles. Think of one of your cartoons where every flame on every candle has its own personality."

"There is no way we can bring them all," Wilber said. "We need to focus on the most powerful. Rivers, not creeks. Blacksmiths, not their anvils."

"Not entirely," Merlin disagreed. "We need an *appropriate* demon. If we are going to enchant an anvil, the most appropriate demon is a netherworld anvil. Likewise, hammer for hammer, sword for sword. For Jennifer's crystal radio set, we have greater flexibility. And a demon smith might work well in a drop forge, if it is properly invoked."

"What about rings and pendants, stuff like that?" Jennifer asked, looking around the room as though she would see Aladdin's treasure stuck in a corner.

"Normally those hold the most powerful demons. The djinn from the south, that sort of thing. And to be safe, they are usually sealed with a pentagram of some sort built into them. They are more cages than vessels."

"What about titans?" asked Bill.

"Titans, like angels, are not, as a rule, compelled. They are invoked like the ancient gods. Invited, not ordered. And they were generally invited into statues or images, and not expected to arrive with more than a fraction of themselves," said Archimedes. His voice was like a caw, but it was clear for all that, being a function of the crow's vocal cords combined with the magic.

"So why was Themis—*all* of Themis—put in a sword?" Liane Boucher adjusted her camera, Marguerite, who took the name of the French writer/director, Marguerite Duras. Marguerite was closer to a puck than a muse, but was neither. Liane and Marguerite and her computer, René, were creating a documentary of the introduction of magic into the world and the effects of the twenty-firsters. "I mean, she's really powerful and a sword does stuff. It's not like putting her in a statue, but it's not like putting her in Aladdin's lamp either."

"I don't know," Merlin admitted.

Archimedes added, "It could be that that was the point, to put her in an object that had a limited function. A sword can cut, but that is all."

"Not all," Bertrand said. "A sword can parry as well as cut."

"And a sword is a symbol of power," Tiphaine added. The woman had a better feel for how magic and symbolism worked than anyone else, even Delaflote.

"So, like a jewel becoming so shiny that it glows in the dark, a sword that contained Themis would impart an aura of authority, or at least threat," Delaflote added.

"In the case of Themis, she is the ruler of Themis, as well as the land. She must, of necessity, imbue her wielder with great authority," Merlin said, consideringly.

"I think we are getting a bit far afield," Amelia Grady said. "The question before us is how to handle the summonings of the demons from Themis."

"For some," Clausewitz, Roger's computer, said, "we can call them to swords and shields."

"Is that wise?" Bertrand asked. "Even though they are contained in our weapons, they will still have loyalty to their queen. I don't want an enchanted sword turning in my hand at the crucial moment."

"By now they know that Themis has been called and most, at least of those who have any noticeable intellect, will have realized that she was taken against her will. But the call to duty will still be there. Any demons that we call to weapons or armor are going to be . . . conflicted, I guess a mortal would call it . . . in a battle with whoever wields Themis or, for that matter the, corpses that have been animated by her subjects."

"So we use demons to enchant the tools that we use to make the swords and the armor," Wilber said. "We put them in the drop forges and the kilns, and use them to make ceramic armor. Use salamanders to make quick lime for mortar and put water sprites into the water buckets that we use to dampen the powder in the powdermills."

There was more discussion. The issue of multiple callings came up and the demons were against it. Even if there were five—to human eyes—identical buckets of water and five water sprites, the sprites would likely get into fights over which one got which bucket. "Besides, a large part of the spell of invocation is the naming of the demon, so you wouldn't save that much time anyway."

"I thought you didn't have to have a name to invoke a demon?" Jennifer asked, looking at Bill, who shrugged his ignorance.

"The more precise the name is, the greater the power of the invocation," Archimedes said in his rough, caw-lake voice. "An invocation that used no name would be an open call, and even now, with the wards between the worlds in tatters, no demon would be bound to respond. As the name becomes more precise, more of an exact description, it concentrates the call on fewer and fewer demons and the call becomes stronger. Knowing the type of demon is part of the name, knowing the land the demon comes from is another part. And in both cases, you can get more and more specific and thereby concentrate the call on fewer and fewer demons, making it stronger. The more powerful the demon, the better able it is to resist the call. The call that brought Themis to the sword was of such strength that much of her true name must have been used. A part of the name that is used is the demon's present location, so I was called in part because I was at the location that Doctor Delaflote specified in his call. That's what Raphico is going to be giving you, essentially specific locations of the demons involved to narrow the call."

"Who do we have who can call demons beyond Doctor Delaflote and Wilber?" Bertrand asked.

"You must have a good memory for detail or a demon whispering in your ear," said Doctor Delaflote. "So all the twenty-firsters can call demons, even Paul, since each of you have a demon in your computers and . . ." Delaflote paused and looked at Jeff. It was, by now, well known that Jeff had given his computer to Catvia and his other devices to the demons residing in them.

It was Catvia who spoke in response to the look. "I will give Jeff the names if he is willing. But not unless he truly is willing."

Wilber knew that most of the demons considered Jeff to be an idiot, but personally he was both impressed and surprised by Jeff's moral courage. And it was becoming apparent that Catvia and the other demons whom Jeff had freed were at least coming to feel something similar.

"That's ten," said Bertrand. Then, with a look at Amelia Grady, "Well, nine. And Doctor Delaflote makes ten."

"I am eleven, husband," Tiphaine said. "I have watched and, given instruction, I should be able to call demons to our service."

"There are also some of my students who can be put to use in calling demons to those items that we determine should be enchanted."

"And most of us have more than one magical item," Jennifer said. "I could loan Silvore to Jolie and she could call demons for us."

"This is better than I was expecting," Bertrand said.

"Perhaps, but it's still not good, Lord Constable," Wilber said solemnly. "Assume we get a hundred people with enough pentagrams. Figure an hour to summon a demon. And you don't want to rush it more than that because you want to check the pentagram between each summoning. And you have to take the enchanted item out of the pentagram and put in the next item. So, ten hours a day . . . that's a thousand items a day. Assuming everything goes well, which it won't. A thousand items a day seems like a lot, but assume we have a month. That's only thirty thousand enchanted items, and we are looking at an army of undead that is likely to be sixty thousand strong."

"Then I think we should get to work."

Netherworld, Void of Themis
Time Uncertain

The stream Prosperussalueschicor flowed uncomfortably through the aether, trying to keep its route to where the streambed used to be. It wasn't easy, but it tried. There was no land to water. The stalks of corn floated in the aether and the stream sent out trickles to feed them.

Suddenly, there was a call. The stream's substance was pulled into the mortal realm, to a large cistern surrounded by a pentagram. The cistern was full of mortal water, water that had substance, but no life. As Prosperus flowed into the water, the water of the mortal realm added to its substance, and Prosperus added magic and character to the water.

There, in the pentagram surrounding the cistern, was a mortal and beside it, a demon in a strange device. The demon spoke to Prosperus in gentle tones, telling it what had happened to its home and what was expected of it.

Courtyard, University of Paris
May 7, 1372

Jolie finished the incantation and removed the earbud from her ear. A peasant woman of Paris and proud to be a servant in the Constable's household, she was a good Christian woman. The earbud still made her uncomfortable, both physically and for what it represented. Jolie wasn't overly comfortable with the notion of having a demon, even Silvore, whispering in her ear.

The large cask of water she had just enchanted was owned by the University of Paris and was to be used in alchemy to help sort and purify salicylic acid. Demons, especially water sprites and salamanders, had a facility for sorting, mixing, and purifying chemicals. That was how it was done in the mortal realm, after all, using water and fire to mix and modify chemical structures. This demon would wash the chemical goop, dropping the salicylic acid in one part of its container and the other chemicals in another part to be used in other techniques.

And that was all it would do. Its instructions were included in the summoning spell. A combination of fourteenth-century alchemy, twenty-first century chemistry, and the magical law of similarity. Which was why, for this particular spell, the cask had been inscribed with mystical symbols drawn in salicylic acid on the wood.

This was her fourth summoning so far today, all of them tubs of water to be enchanted by rivers and streams from Themis, and all of which would be used in the burgeoning magical chemical industry of Paris.

Smithy of Gerard Départdieu, Paris
May 8, 1372

As chance would have it, he looked rather a lot like the twenty-first century actor by the same name. He was a big man for his time and a strong one, a bit blonder than the actor and his eyes were glacier blue. He was also both thinner and more muscular. But that was mostly because of his profession. He wore an undyed wool shirt and brown pants, and over it all an apron of thick leather.

Gerard looked at his drop forge with a combination of anticipation and wariness as they unloaded it from the wagon. He had been one of the first smiths in Paris to adopt the new drop forges and had spent a small fortune having it built.

Now this. According to Doctor Delaflote, the forge was now inhabited by a demon of good, solid reputation. A demonic smith who used his magic, as well as his skill, to make things in Themis.

While it might seem odd to someone not a smith, what was of greatest concern to Gerard was not whether he could deal with a demon, but how he was going to deal with another smith in his shop.

****

Tuctrasuwathemisreskica had no eyes in this form, nor legs. He did have one massive arm with muscles of a sort, a crank, and pulleys. Once he was in place, he lifted his arm. It was creaky, and it rubbed. He complained to the familiar spirit in the crow, who spoke to the mortal.

"The drop forge—call him Tuck—says that his arm needs to be greased and the pulleys as well."

The big smith grunted and spoke in French, which Tuck understood. "Pierre, get the oil. How do I talk to it and how does it talk to me?"

"I'm an idiot," Delaflote said. "We could have added eyes and a speaker to it."

"You mean a mouth?"

"No, a speaker. The twenty-firsters have a mechanical device that can reproduce any sound at all. It is truly elegant in its simplicity. It is a shaped sheet that moves back and forth very fast, making vibrations in the air that are sound."

"And those work?"

"It's how Pucorl and the other devices speak." The scholar scratched his chin. "Of course, those are supported by electronics."

"Could I add eyes and one of these speakers to the forge?"

"Honestly, Gerard, I don't know. This is still all very new and we haven't done much experimentation. Even Archimedes here is a natural crow, because we didn't know what would and would not work in terms of the twenty-firsters and their science magic."

"Well, should I try it?"

"You might—" Delaflote said, while Tuck thought, *Yes, try it, you idiot. At least see if it will work. I need to be able to see my work for the best results.*

The crow cawed a laugh, and then said,, "Tuck thinks you should try it."

Chateau du Guesclin

Iris, the servant of Themis who was emplaced in the crystal radio set, was not happy to be there. A being of power as great or greater than Merlin's, she was a personal body servant of Themis' human form. As such, she had lived in Themis' place in the land of Themis.

When the deity had been pulled into the mortal realm she had been upset, but not injured. The stones of Themis' place had declined to move just because the land they had laid upon had disappeared. So Iris and the other household servants of Themis were quite comfortable.

Being kidnapped from her place into a contraption of wires and magnets powered by a cobbled together lead acid battery didn't make her anxious to help her kidnappers. She couldn't lie to Jennifer, but she saw no reason to go out of her way to be helpful.

"Iris, can you hear me?" came the thought from Themis. *"You may be ensorcelled, but you are still my servant and my creation. Do not speak of me to these mortals"*

It was an order and a lawful order. It balanced the power of the incantation that had pulled her here. Iris still could not lie to Jennifer, but she was not compelled to speak of Themis to anyone, even Jennifer.

"Can you hear me?" Jennifer asked.

"Yes, I can hear you."

"Sorry to have called you this way, but we were afraid that Philip would force the sword to call you anyway."

"What sword?"

"Have you had no word from Themis?" asked Tiphaine.

Thankful that the question had come from the woman who didn't own her, Iris answered. "No, no contact at all since she was pulled from the world. Is that what happened? She was forced into a sword?"

"Lady Tiphaine," Jennifer said, "we agreed that I would be the one to speak to Iris. She cannot lie to me."

"She has no reason to lie to any of us, Jennifer. We are not the ones who kidnapped her mistress."

"How's she supposed to know that? Besides, even if we aren't the ones who kidnapped Themis, we are the ones who kidnapped her!"

"Rescued," Tiphaine insisted.

"Iris," Jennifer said, "do you consider yourself rescued or kidnapped?"

"Kidnapped," Iris said unwillingly.

"But you . . ."

"Lady Tiphaine!"

"Oh, very well."

"We're sorry you feel that way," Jennifer said. "But I understand how you might. Here is the situation as we understand it."

The young woman who owned her vessel explained what had happened, as much as she knew of it, and Iris sent the information to Themis. That she was able to do so was in part because of her connection to Themis, who had created Iris out of her own substance and was, in a sense, her mother, but also because the device she was placed in was designed for communications. Mostly for hearing, granted, but for communications. The aether was not the electromagnetic spectrum, but they performed similar functions.

After that, Iris and Jennifer talked about electronics, magnetism, and aether. And, only half unwillingly, Iris helped Jennifer in the design of vessels that might work, using a combination of electromagnetism and magic. Neither of them knew if the devices would work, but if Iris ever escaped back to her home in Themis' castle, she would have some ideas to try.

Goldsmith Shop, Rue de Cobain
May 10, 1372

The goldsmith looked at the image on Hercule, Bill's cell phone, and carefully adjusted the rod in his hand. The rod in turn adjusted a gear train, which shifted a smaller rod approximately one-tenth as far as the goldsmith had shifted his rod. In so doing, the smaller rod placed a tiny fleck of gold against a tiny grain of sand that separated the fleck of gold from a strand of copper wire so thin it made a hair look bulky in comparison.

"Very good," whispered Royce.

The goldsmith could have done without the commentary. In fact, he could have done without demons altogether, but this was a royal commission. So he didn't comment. It was stupid anyway. After days of work he had produced one of what the twenty-firsters called a photovoltaic sensor or a pixel, and the cameras they brought with them had millions of such pixels.

****

Royce phoned Pucorl. "You know this thing won't work."

"Certainly. At least, it won't work in an ordinary camera phone, even after we ship some gold and copper to the netherworld and let some demons multiply the pixel. The gold will get into shape readily enough. Gold has all the personal will of tofu. But the silica will resist, and even the copper will be stubborn about it. There will be gaps and copper wires rubbing up against the gold and on and on. But the law of similarity says that like calls to like."

"Yes. Well, I don't want to be the similar. That's dangerous. The law of contagion will apply as well, and you have to touch the thing you are shaping through the law of similarity."

"I know. That's why we are using this thing and the pictures of integrated circuits. I wish the twenty-firsters had a printer in the van," Pucorl said.

This was an experiment. An attempt to use the laws of magic and the laws of science in combination to produce something like a twenty-first century digital eye that could then be attached to a fourteenth-century item like a forge, a wood lathe, or a butter churn, so that the demon would have sight.

The speaker had proven fairly easy once they had thought of it. A speaker is, when you come right down to it, a very simple device at its core. A magnet, an electromagnet that is just a tiny coil of insulated copper wire and a diaphragm. Any decent coppersmith with the aid of a leather worker and a carpenter could make a speaker. And they were—much to the delight of the demons that were being summoned to Paris—in a form that any draftee from the twentieth century's world wars would recognize. "Turn your head and cough. You pass. Next!"

But, at least in this army, you got a way of talking. And if this new experiment worked, a way of seeing as well. Not that the demons were exactly blind without the eyes. The magic gave them a sense of their surroundings, especially where it impinged on their function. A drop forge knew when a piece of red hot metal was on its bed, and even when a hand was in the way. That didn't guarantee that the drop forge wouldn't drop on the hand anyway. Not all of Themis' demons were happy to be called.

Still, the eyes and the mouths—for that matter, the ears, which were just a speaker hooked up differently—made the calling more acceptable to the demons that were called. And cooperative demons worked better than forced demons.

Smithy of Gerard Depardieu, Paris
May 12, 1372

Tuck listened to the mortals talking. He had a speaker now, and a microphone, so he could hear and speak without the help of the demons in the computers. Sort of. The speaker and the mic were both installed after he had been summoned, so while he could use them, he didn't have full use of them. He even had an eye of sorts. It was a cut glass bead made by a glazier and mounted with leather eyelids. It pointed at the bed of the forge, but could see around a bit.

Gerard was yelling at the apprentice again. He was thirteen and a well grown lad, but lacked the heft of a man like Gerard. He was dressed in woolen pants, patched so often that they seemed nothing but patches. He wasn't wearing a shirt in the smithy, and there was sweat running down his body, making rivulets in the ash that coated every unclothed part of the boy.

The lack of heat wasn't really the boy's fault. There was no salamander in the fire pit to concentrate the flame where it was needed. They had to do it with bellows and charcoal.

"You should get a salamander," Tuck said, and his voice came out scratchy with a burr from a spot where the diaphragm wasn't properly attached to the wood frame. It was the sort of thing that wouldn't matter if the forge had had its eyes and ears installed before he was summoned.

Netherworld, Pucorl's Place

Pucorl came out of the transfer to see sunlight. It was dawn, and there hadn't been daylight in his place since 400 Anno Domini. Time and space in his little corner of the netherworld were adjusting to the new circumstances. He was a knight of the Elysian Fields and he lived in the mortal realm for much of the time. Even more, as the wards between the netherworld and the mortal world were shredded, the time of the two places began to sync. It was almost the same time here that it was in Paris.

Jeff got out, then went around back. Pucorl opened the back for him and Jeff lifted out the chest containing gold, silver, copper, and glass from the mortal realm. They had mortal world magic on them, the strange laws that let electricity flow through metal and produce magnetism. And the twenty-firsters didn't believe in love spells! What else did they think magnetism was?

Annabelle got out, and it was clear to Pucorl that electricity must be running through her coils. That was the only explanation for the attraction he was coming to feel. Not that anything could come of it. He was a van, after all, not a mortal.

By now, there was a small, fast demon running through wires. It was a lightning bolt, which had—eons ago—worked for Zeus, the sky father. But it had become interested in the notion of wiring and had volunteered to be the power for Pucorl's shop. *Volunteered? The thing almost invaded.*

"Hey, old boy," blared from a megaphone above the garage door. "How are your tail pipes hanging?"

"Well enough, Ilektrismós," Pucorl answered civilly. This was his place, but while Ilektrismós was not nearly as flexible or as smart as Merlin, he was the preferred weapon of a god, and a major deity at that. He could turn Pucorl's land into a smoking ruin if he chose to be offended. On the up side, having him here meant that the garage had plenty of power to run the arcwelder and any other electrical devices that they could come up with. In fact, Ilektrismós—by himself—could run a fair-sized twenty-first century town, because, unlike a lighting bolt in the mortal realm, Ilektrismós was immortal. He was a constant power source. He circulated through Pucorl's little land and then circulated back through, thousands of times per second, and at that almost all of him resided in a giant capacitor that he had built under Pucorl's garage.

"Look at it this way, Pucorl. We will never have any issues with energy usage," Annabelle said.

"Say, Ilektrismós," said Wilber, "have you considered having children?"

"What?"

"Well, we are going to need some power back in the mortal world."

"I could not be contained," Ilektrismós insisted belligerently. Ilektrismós wasn't the demon's true name. Zeus had named each of his lightning bolts and each of them must return to his hand when called. But Zeus never shared their names with any other gods. He was quite jealous of them, and paranoid about one of the other gods usurping his bolts to their own use, so almost no one in the netherworld knew the names of Zeus' bolts, not even his other bolts. In practical terms, Ilektrismós was right. Unless they got Zeus to sign off on it, Ilektrismós wasn't going to be called.

"I know that. I was talking about you taking a little tiny bit of your substance and making some tools. A battery that would power a permanent light in Paris. That sort of thing."

"I don't think so," Ilektrismós said a bit less belligerently. And again Wilber understood the reasoning. By separating out a bit of himself, Ilektrismós would be exposing a bit of himself to whoever had control over the demon. In a way, it would be like giving a mortal a part of his name.

Ritual requests and comments out of the way, they got down to business. They pulled the gold and other stuff from the chest, and the one little pixel they had built. Then the drawings of a circuit diagram.

Finally, unhappily, Pucorl let Ilektrismós run a few millivolts through his dashcam to get the shape of the circuit as electricity sees it. Pucorl wasn't happy about it, but he felt honor bound to do it. He was finding that this whole being a knight of Elysium wasn't all it was cracked up to be. More duties than privileges, as it turned out.

Ilektrismós used what he saw to paint the drawings with electrical voltages. Then they placed the raw materials, drawings, and examples in a pentagram in Pucorl's garage. Wilber, Merlin, Pucorl, and Ilektrismós all combined in the summoning of a set of minor demons to craft copies of the pixel and circuitry.

When they were done, several sweaty hours later, the center of the pentagram was filled with hundreds of little electronic retinas. They still weren't good enough to work in a non-demon-enhanced device, but when combined with a glass lens, they would make excellent eyes for demons.

CHAPTER 20

Mortain, Southern Normandy
May 14, 1372

Philip stood in the graveyard as the demon lord whispered in his ear, and he used those whispers to command the sword. With each step he took, the sword would dip and touch the soil, and from the soil would rise a corpse. The sword would glow, and the soil would give up the flesh, which would reform on the body.

Philip could feel the effort it cost the sword to do this, and even—in a vague way—that the entity in the sword was being diminished slightly with each corpse raised. He didn't care. He was coming to hate the sword. It raged at him in his dreams and condemned him for a traitor and a breaker of the law.

It was only the returned demon lord who supported him, who made him feel strong and whole, justified in his actions, and entitled to his kingdom.

****

Beslizoswian whispered in the mortal's ear, careful to let none of its contempt for the rodent to show. Beslizoswian had been a god when the dinosaurs ruled the world, worshiped—powerfully, if simply—by the raptors. Beslizoswian hated the subtlety of the mammals and their gods.

But now, here, injured as he was and desperate, he realized that Themis was going to take retribution if she ever got loose. He was being forced to subtlety himself, and hated it. Hated all of them with a kind of grinding hatred that gnawed on his bones.

But for now, he whispered into the ear of the rodent before him, encouraging it to weaken Themis. For reforming the bodies

248

of the dead, especially the long dead, took a great deal of energy, more than most demons possessed. So, with each raising, Themis was forced to drain a little of herself into the corpse to remake it into something that could be used by the demon that resided in it.

The sword dipped again, and a woman who had died half a century before stood up. Before Themis had touched the land in which she lay, all the soft tissue was long gone to soil, and most of the bones as well. But a demon warrior of Themis was forced into the body, and Themis' will was fed into the earth to undo what time had done. The soil returned to flesh, and the body was restored to not just a semblance of life, but a semblance of youth as well. To do that, not only the mortal soil but a bit of the land of Themis was needed.

The thing to do with an enemy was to fight it. The thing to do with prey was to eat it. Themis was still too big to eat, but she was getting smaller with each corpse she restored.

****

By now Philip was what the twenty-firsters would call an addict. He was addicted to the power and to the whispered words of encouragement. His world was now a simple one, with only the words of his demon drowning out the doubts of his followers and complaints of the wretched sword.

"I am the king," he muttered, not quite slipping into giggles. "The law is mine to command, not the other way around. I will catch this coward who flees before me, then return to Paris to take up my crown."

****

John, Duke of Berry, wanted to flee as he looked out at his younger brother walking through the graveyard. Wanted to take his army and run to his older brother and king, even if Charles were to behead him. Just to escape.

But he couldn't.

Philip held all law and justice in his right hand. Even knowing it was wrong—and by now the rational part of John's mind did know that—he could not abandon his little brother, who felt like the true and proper king of all France. . . .

Or perhaps even all the world.

In part, that was because he was exposed to Philip on a daily basis. John knew that many of his troops, and quite a few of Philip's, had abandoned the army, run to Olivier de Clisson, or just run away. But for each living soldier who ran, another corpse was raised to Phillip's banner.

In some ways, that was a good thing. The army of the dead didn't eat or get cold, didn't need housing or clothing, all of which made supplying the army much easier. But there was a stink to them that was experienced directly by the soul, not through the nose.

When Philip returned to the inn after his sojourn in the graveyard, John would again suggest that they abandon the chase of de Clisson and turn toward Paris. And he would no doubt be ignored. The demon that followed Philip about was not going to abandon the chase.

Granville, Coast of Normandy
May 14, 1372

"Get those people onto the ship! Forget the horses!" Olivier de Clisson roared. "We won't be able to use them on the island, and they will not go near that undead army."

His parrot, Aimee, as was by now its custom, rode on his shoulder. Aimee could fly, but not very well. With the help of the demon, Aimee could fly farther and faster than a parrot normally would, but that didn't make her an albatross. She had a comfortable flight range of only a mile or two at a time, after which she needed to rest in a tree for a while to recover her wind. More importantly, Aimee was unwilling to get close to the demon army. Demons cans sense each other, and while their range is not great, the mass of demons that were inhabiting the corpses of thousands of dead French people was hard to miss.

De Clisson knew precisely the direction of the undead army, though their distance was less certain. More than a mile away, less than a hundred miles, was about as close as Aimee could tell him, but he had better intelligence from the stream of deserters who swelled his ranks as they saw what Philip was doing.

One of those deserters rode up. "There is grain in Jersey, and grass for some horses. Would you have belted knights walk like peasant levies?"

"Yes, if that is what it takes to keep us alive, Robert," Olivier said. "The grain to feed your charger would feed five men, and we cannot know how well we will be supplied. We don't know if we'll even get supplies yet."

"Then why are you taking the peasants?"

"All it takes is a sword stroke to turn a peasant into a demon warrior." Olivier said. Robert was proving something of an education to him. In truth, Robert was no more arrogant than Olivier was and no less concerned over the lives of peasants than Olivier. But hearing it from the other man's lips, especially with Aimee whispering in his ear, gave Olivier a new perspective on his own views.

"Robert, I know that you were one of Duke John's most trusted men, but he has fallen into sin so base that heaven itself screams at the sight. And if we are to fight it, we need to be both brave and practical. I am hoping that the dead will not be able to follow us over open water. And if they are able to do so, I suspect that they will be vulnerable while on boats. We need the craftsmen and we need to deny Philip the bodies."

"What of King Charles," Robert answered, "and your patron, du Guesclin?"

Olivier almost slapped the man over his sneering tone, but he needed Robert to help persuade the living men at arms to abandon Philip and his demons. "The latest messages indicate that Paris is recruiting demons as well, but only into animals and inanimate objects. And they have the church's support in doing so." That was stretching things a bit. The last word Olivier had from Bertrand was that Raphico had granted permission, not that the pope had.

"Do as you please, Robert, but I am getting on a boat."

Chateau du Guesclin
May 16, 1372

Monsignor Savona broke the seal and unrolled the despatch from Pope Gregory.

To my good friend and confidant in matters demonic,

I have read over your reports as I have received them and passed them over to the Holy Office of the Inquisition. Your actions are, in my view and that of the Office of the Inquisition, both justified and wise. However, there is considerable uncertainty that the being known as Raphico is in truth an angel of the Lord.

While it might seem that Raphico must either be angel or devil, we in our uncertainty are forced to take a middle course. If Raphico were an angel, then his authority over the Church would be beyond question, since he would then be a direct representative of God. If we determined that he was a demon from the pit, then the obligation of the Church would be to condemn and expel him, to perform an exorcism on the device he is contained within, or destroy it, and in so doing lose any counsel and insight he might provide if our judgment were proven to be in error.

Either of the above courses would leave both the Church and our entire flock in jeopardy, especially as the ubiquitousness of demonic presence in this time would cause any observer to wonder if we were, in fact, in the last days predicted by the book of Revelations. But you inform us that the people who arrived in the demon van are from a possible future almost seven hundred years from now.

For those reasons, as well as the political needs that always beset Mother Church, we have determined that Raphico is to be treated by the Church as any other soul. Neither condemned nor beatified while present in the world.

The Church does not recognize any authority that Raphico might claim to the effect of setting policy or modifying canon law, but will rather treat him as a scholar of religion who might offer insights that, after study, the Church will accept or reject as she sees fit.

Under our seal,
Gregory, Vicar of Christ

"Well, Raphico?" Monsignor Savona asked as he showed the letter to the smartphone. The phone was in a stand on the small wooden chest below the crucifix on the wall. For now, the candles were unlit, for Raphico bathed the letter in a cool bluish light.

"It is, in essence, what the Creator said would happen," Raphico said. "And falls quite within his will. Mortals must still choose for themselves, without direct intervention."

Monsignor Savona gave the phone a rather sardonic look. "The Creator didn't know what was going to happen?" There being a subtle but important difference between "in essence" what the creator said and simply "what the creator said." That was the sort of detail that a biblical scholar and a papal nuncio was supposed to notice.

The phone made a rude beeping sound. "Don't be more of a pedant than you have to be, Giuseppe," Raphico said, sounding both irritated and at least a little amused. "I've admitted before that 'all knowing' can mean more than one thing, and even that the Creator doesn't focus all his attention on every sparrow at every moment. And being able to know all that is doesn't mean knowing all that ever might be. More importantly, which 'might' will take place."

"Yes, I know. Something about free will. Still . . ."

The phone made the rude beeping sound again. "Don't be a Calvinist, Giuseppe. It's ridiculous. You're Catholic, and Calvin probably won't even happen, the way the probabilities are unfolding."

Doctor Delaflote's Tower, University of Paris
May 16, 1372

"So, Archimedes, tell me about fairy gold."

"Oh, it's not just gold," the crow said cheerfully. "All the materials are likely to become something else in the mortal realm."

"I don't understand," Gabriel said.

"I don't either, really," Archimedes admitted. "Remember, though, my world is one of will. If a leaf is imbued with the spirit of gold, it will look and act as gold until the spirit returns to the netherworld, when it will be a leaf again. If a demon makes a rock into a wheel, which can be done with the right spell, the rock will remain a wheel only as long the spirit of the wheel remains in it. That is the reason behind the notion of fairy gold."

"That puts much of the writing . . ."

There was a knock on the door, which Gabriel went to answer. His room was much improved since that first spell that brought Pucorl. His classes were being attended by many students, and he now enjoyed a much greater income. It was that money, not demonic aid, that allowed him to repair the cracks in the walls and get a new door installed.

He opened his new door to find Amelia and Paul Grady. "Come in." He gestured, trying not to sound as confused as he was by their presence.

"It's nothing dire, Doctor Delaflote, but I had some questions that I thought you might be able to help me with," Amelia said. "I'm looking for . . . I guess you would call it a human perspective on magic. And I want one from this time, not our time."

"Why?" Gabriel asked. "You know so much more than we do—the principles of science, the . . ." He trailed off waving vaguely, if expansively.

"That's the problem. I think we think in scientific terms, but experimentation and logical analysis might not be the best techniques for figuring out how the netherworld will react."

"Mom thinks we need a shrink, not a physicist, to figure out how the netherworld works," Paul volunteered.

"A shrink?"

"A head shrinker," Paul offered, only adding to Gabriel's confusion.

"A psychologist," Amelia said. Then, apparently seeing Gabriel's confusion, said, "I don't think there is a *Langue d'oïl* word for psychologist. Someone who studies the minds of people and helps them work out their emotional problems."

Gabriel nodded. That made a great deal of sense. "Please come in and sit down." He went back to his desk. "What do you think, Archimedes? Would a shrink—" He winked at Paul. "—be able to figure out how magic worked better than a physicist?"

Archimedes tilted his head, looking at Gabriel with one eye and then the other, then at Paul and Amelia. "I think a shrink would do a better job in the netherworld, but a physicist might do a better job in your mortal realm. It never had occurred to any of us that your world was a world of interacting forces rather than interacting personalities."

"That's what I thought," Amelia said.

"But I am not a shrink either," Gabriel admitted, and in spite of all he could do there was a touch of bitterness in his voice. He liked the twenty-firsters, he really did. And he appreciated the knowledge that they brought with them. But, even so, there was a corner of his soul where he resented their greater knowledge.

Amelia looked at him and he wondered if she was one of the "shrinks" that Paul mentioned. She seemed to be looking right into his heart. Then she smiled a little smile, and he felt better. "I know you're not a shrink, but then I don't think a twenty-first century shrink is truly what we need, either. What you are is a fourteenth-century scholar of magical arts. I suspect you have a more natural understanding of the magical realm than we do. And, in a way, a better understanding of how they interact with our world than the demons do."

Gabriel looked at her, and for a moment it was as though he

could see into her soul. There were lines of strain around her eyes. And, in a moment of insight, Gabriel realized that as much as Amelia wanted to believe, and insisted, that they would be able to go home, she knew deep down that she would never be reunited with her husband. That Paul would never see his father again, that the world they had left behind was gone, swallowed up in the conflagration of combining worlds. That magic would change this world, change it so far that it would be millions of years—if ever—before the banks of the river of time resumed their shape.

She was holding on to the belief that they would get home because she couldn't afford to be crippled by grief for her lost life and her lost love, not when she had her son and her charges depending on her.

"In that case, what can I solve for you with my fourteenth-century scholar's mind?"

"The issue of cold iron, for one thing," Amelia said.

"What about it?"

"It's all through the stories. Cold iron is poison to the spirits like Pucorl, but Pucorl is in a van. And that van is mostly steel, which is ninety-nine percent cold iron."

"But Pliny the Elder insists that iron is the blood and bone of the gods."

"Is iron the same thing as cold iron?" Paul asked.

"Yes," Gabriel and Amelia said together, then looked at each other and smiled. But then Gabriel stopped. "No, Paul, they aren't. At least not all the time. 'I'll meet you at dawn, sirrah, and we'll let cold iron decide the matter.' That is from a play I saw last year. It meant that they would meet with sword in hand, and that is mostly the only use I have seen for cold iron. Iron is often cold to the touch. It chills quickly in the night air. Someone touching it might say 'this iron is cold,' but cold iron always means edged weapons. Not even a hammer, that I have ever heard. A sword or a knife, perhaps an ax."

"But that makes even less sense," Amelia said. "It's in all the stories. It's the basis for horseshoes being lucky."

"Are horseshoes lucky?" Gabriel asked. "I guess you're lucky if you can afford to have your horse shod, but as a separate thing?"

"Yes," Paul said, "but only if you have the ends pointing up. Otherwise, all the luck pours out."

"That's just supersti—" Amelia stopped. "Well, back in our time it was *all* just superstition."

"I think what we need to do now is spend some time sorting out what you know of magic and comparing it to what I know of magic, then seeing what the differences might mean. For instance, if my usage of cold iron is the basis of your belief that cold iron harms spirits, then . . . if the dead that have been raised by Philip the Bold can be harmed by cold iron . . . even if they can just be released and returned to the netherworld, that is an important weapon for us to hold." He turned to the crow. "Archimedes, would being stabbed with cold iron release a demon that had been compelled into a corpse to reanimate it? Would it harm the demon?"

"I think," Archimedes said with manifest reluctance, "that it might well harm the demon. I think it might even kill the demon."

"Really?" Gabriel asked.

"Cool!" said Paul.

"That's horrible," said Amelia.

"I quite agree, Amelia," Gabriel said, giving Paul a parental look. "Unfortunately," he added, turning back to Amelia, "We may not have any choice. If Philip brings his army of the undead to Paris, we will have to fight them. And if cold iron will work, it's what we will have to use. However much we may regret the damage it does to the demons he compels to his service."

"But I thought demons couldn't die?" Paul's question was clear in his tone.

"So did I," Gabriel said thoughtfully. "But there have been indications before that they could die. Archimedes?"

"I don't know," Archimedes said. "What is dying? Before, we didn't die. We formed and were broken apart, then reformed, again and again, on and on, forever. Cycles within cycles. Even when part of one of us was a ham sandwich, we knew that we would be a pig again someday."

"This too shall pass," Gabriel muttered and at Amelia's look felt himself blushing.

"It's not funny!" Archimedes complained. "In fact, it's quite unpleasant."

"Are you speaking from personal experience?" Gabriel asked.

"Were you a pig?" Paul asked.

"Yes, Gabriel, and no, Paul. At least, not exactly. We didn't have forms at all before we came in contact with your universe. And even after that, our forms are often mixtures of your forms. I have been reptiles, dinosaurs, birds and mammals. I have been a cat with wings, a bear fish, and many other things. But most of them have been subject to being eaten by other larger creatures, and I have been eaten several times over the centuries. I haven't been a ham sandwich or a pig, but I know a demon that was both a pigbear and later, for a time, several sausage links."

"And you were aware through all of that?" Amelia asked, horror clear in her voice.

"More or less. Rather more when I am whole than when I am being digested, but there is always at least a trace of awareness."

"As interesting as this all is," Gabriel said as he tore his mind away from the thought of being digested while still being aware, "I think we need to come back to the question of whether demons can die. You said before that you cycled and reformed continuously, but that was before you had forms, bodies I guess, yet you mentioned your friend the pigbear. That would have to be after your universe and ours came in contact."

"He wasn't exactly a friend, but yes, that was after. But the interactions between your world and ours was still limited, more an exchange of concepts than anything solid. Humans existed, but they were different. I think they were what you call Neanderthal."

"That would put it sometime in the last half a million years or so," Amelia said. "But you said you had been a dinosaur also. That's at least sixty-five million years ago. It would seem that you would . . . I don't know . . . be more influenced by the dinosaurs and the mammoths and less by us."

The crow looked at Amelia with one black, beady eye, then said, "Dinosaurs weren't very bright. They felt strongly, but didn't conceptualize particularly well. That's true of mammoths too, but less so. You humans have . . . more solid thoughts."

"Again, we're getting off the point. You said you thought that a demon who was stabbed with cold iron might be destroyed," Gabriel said.

"The . . . call them curtains . . . that separate your world from ours have been ripped up," Archimedes said. "If a demon was disrupted in our world, it would eventually reform. But that's not necessarily true if a demon is killed in your world. If you were to lock me in this form, then kill the crow, I would be left in the crow as its body decayed. When the demon was put into the body of that poor girl and then the horse stepped on her head, part of that demon was left in the corpse and is still in your world, not in ours. We know that if it was in ours, it would eventually reform into itself again, but with part of it here, that part might never reform and always be missing. If I were stuck in this crow when it was killed, I might go through eternity without ever being reformed. And I might be aware of it all."

Gabriel looked at the crow that had become his adviser. "Is there anything that I can do to make it easier, or more certain, that you escape back to your realm?"

"Just release me. I wasn't a volunteer."

"What if I gave you the crow?"

"The crow doesn't recognize your ownership."

"Yes, that is another of the questions that has bothered me since we got here," Amelia said. "I could sort of see it with a dog or a cow, maybe even a cat or a pig, but a crow? How can you be bound by Doctor Delaflote's ownership when the crow isn't?"

"It's a question of law. You have the law of gravity, we have the law of ownership. In our world, and for us whether in our world or yours, the law of ownership is a physical law. Under the law of the spell caster, Doctor Delaflote owns the crow. He bought it legally. The crow doesn't have the intellect to understand ownership. It can't contest the right to control it. It can simply try to contest my control."

"Why do I have a feeling I have fallen into a lawyer's briefcase like Alice fell through the looking glass?" Amelia muttered.

"It all makes perfect sense to me," Archimedes insisted.

"It makes sense to me too," Gabriel said. "I'm not sure how to explain it to a twenty-firster in a way that would make sense. But magic has always been a realm of perception and rules. A human could say 'this is unjust.' All the crow can think is 'I don't want to.' But if I gave the crow to you?"

"Then, in effect, the crow's 'I don't want to' would become a direct challenge to my ownership."

Paul was looking deeply confused. "So it won't work?"

"Succinctly put," Archimedes said.

"What about all the demons that are being sucked into everything from forges to egg beaters?" Amelia asked.

"Them too. Mostly they will be able to return when the item they are in is broken, but they may leave little bits of themselves in the mortal realm, and they may take little bits of the egg beater back to the netherworld."

"And yet you encourage us to kidnap them?"

"With Themis pulled from the world, the whole universe is out of balance. She pushes against the lands near her, holds down the land below her. The flow of the cycles of the netherworld are shifting, and until she is returned to her proper place, they will become more and more erratic and uncertain."

Rouen, France
May 23, 1372

Father Gabriel, the abbot of the Benedictines of St. Ouen,

didn't think of himself as a particularly holy or righteous man. He was deeply concerned with that lack of righteousness as he donned monk's robes. He had an on-again-off-again relationship with Brother Alphons that was certainly behavior the church would frown on. And on more than one occasion he had been free with the order's funds to buy this or that personal treat.

Father Gabriel knew in his heart that he was a sinner, but he did love God and felt his responsibilities as abbot keenly. More keenly this morning than perhaps at any other time in his life even when, as a teenager, he had taken holy vows in an attempt to fight off his unnatural sexual interest in men.

He lifted the crucifix to his lips and kissed the Savior, hoping for salvation. Not his own salvation. He felt that was too much to hope for. No, what he prayed desperately for was that God would intervene to protect Rouen in spite of the sins of its religious leadership, and especially despite his sins.

For right now, at this instant, an army of the dead was marching on Rouen to cross the Seine.

Cassock and abital vestments in place, Father Gabriel turned and left his apartments. They were very nice apartments with a big comfortable bed and real cotton sheets. He did not expect to live to see them again.

In the nave, he took up the relics and took his place at the head of the procession, smiling gently at Brother Alphons who was looking very nervous. Well, he was young. Father Gabriel lost his smile. They weren't likely to get any older. None of them. He was tempted to leave the boy behind to protect his lover from what was coming, but this time at least he resisted temptation.

He led the procession of monks from the Monastery of St. Ouen down the Rue St. Paul, toward the main bridge across the Seine. As he walked, he prayed. As he prayed, a kind of peace came over him. Whatever the sins of his life up to this moment, this was an action fully in the service of God. Quietly, he began to sing, barely a mumble in his bass croak, but heartfelt. Then a light rich tenor joined in and he recognized Brother Alphons' voice. Then more voices joined in.

By the time they reached the bridge they were all singing, none loudly, none with any great vigor, but with depth and feeling.

At the bridge they stopped walking, but they continued singing. They sang through the day and into the night, and the dead did not come onto the bridge, though Father Gabriel could see them milling about on the other side of the bridge.

Then, to his horror, Father Gabriel saw someone he recognized. His parish priest, when he was a boy. He didn't know what to do and it was only the others singing that kept him from turning away in horror. He had been there, at Father Jean's funeral. He remembered that wizened old cheek. This was not that. It was both younger and, at the same time, decayed in a way that Father Gabriel couldn't quite identify. Father Jean had been a good and kind man, a man who had helped a boy deal with a world he didn't understand.

Gabriel wanted, in his heart, to give Father Jean back the peace of the grave, to let him rest until the time was right. Until Jesus came again. Now, as he sang the funeral rites, it was for Father Jean and all those poor souls who were locked into the bodies that were not made whole and restored to life as Scripture taught they would be at the end of days. "Go back," Gabriel whispered under the song. "Go and wait for the true Resurrection. Be released from this half life that you didn't choose."

It didn't occur to Father Gabriel that he might be speaking to the demons who inhabited the bodies. He didn't know that they too had been compelled to this union. But his plea reached up to the holy relic and Saint Ouen and the belief and faith that it held, and through that belief it reached across the bridge over the Seine to touch the dead and release the demons that animated them.

For the night, they held, as the dead stepped onto the bridge and were returned to their slumber and their bodies returned to that state of natural decay that had been the case before their resurrection.

With the dawn, though, the living came on their chargers, with their lances and armor, compelled by Philip's majesty and their own confusion and greed. They came, and songs and relics that held the dead at bay did nothing at all against the armored knights of the Duke of Burgundy.

Father Gabriel was right. He never would return to his nice apartment or his big bed with real cotton sheets. But perhaps his stand on the bridge had earned him entry to a better place, after all.

CHAPTER 21

The Island of Jersey, Off the Coast of France June 3, 1372

The ship was flying the colors of Edward, the Prince of Wales and heir to the crown of England. Aimee flew from Olivier's shoulder to get a better look. Olivier waited, and it was less than a minute later that Aimee returned to his shoulder.

"I think it's the prince in the boat coming in to dock," Aimee told him.

"Very well. We'll go to meet His Royal Highness."

****

Edward looked like death walking. He was pale and gaunt as a corpse. At least, that was what Olivier would have said before he had seen the real thing. Now Edward just looked ill. Olivier gave him a deep courtly bow. "Welcome to Jersey, Highness. I note that you are flying a flag of truce and I am glad to see it."

The prince made his way onto the dock from the small, oared boat, and returned the bow with a clearly painful half-bow. "What are you doing here, Olivier?"

"Expediency, Highness. Philip the Bold has an army of ghouls on the French coast."

"So I heard. It's true, then? The royal family of France has allied itself with the damned?"

"I resent that remark," Aimee said.

Which wasn't what Olivier wanted, but he had failed to explicitly instruct the bird to remain silent in Edward's presence. Edward, who was now looking at Aimee with a sort of detached horror.

"Olivier! Not you! I had thought you had greater honor than to act so."

"I had church sanction, Highness, and Aimee was summoned in the presence of a priest of Holy Mother Church. It is not the same thing at all."

"No, it's not," Aimee said firmly.

"Come, Highness," Olivier said. "I have a carriage waiting. Come to the inn where I am staying, and let us speak of what has befallen the world."

****

Seated again in the inn, but now with Edward sitting near him, Olivier and Aimee explained what they knew of the events of the last few months.

"But you don't know the cause?" Edward asked. He gave Aimee a somewhat nervous glance. He hadn't yet become accustomed to a parrot who actually *talked*.

"No," said Olivier. "According to the demons, the cause is recent. Before that, it was difficult to cross from their realm to ours. It was only through dreams, or things very like dreams, that they could travel back and forth between our realm and theirs. But that all changed, and then the demon that stalked Paris appeared and Sieur Pucorl was summoned."

"Charles actually *knighted* a cart?" Edward shook his head in bemusement.

"So I have been informed. On the other hand, from what I understand, that cart put itself in grave peril in order to save the life of a child. Is that not the very essence of chivalry? And with all respect, Highness, calling Pucorl a cart is like calling Windsor Castle a hut. 'Tis without doubt the noblest carriage ever to travel the roads of France."

Edward waved the matter aside. "What, then, are your plans for our island of Jersey?"

"In all honesty, my plan was to get myself, my army, and the peasantry under my care away from Philip and his ghoulish

265

army."

"And what have you heard of that?"

"He apparently tried, for a while, to get ships to follow us, but gave it up. The last word I have is that he has turned back toward Paris."

Royal Palace, Hôtel Saint-Pol, Paris
June 6, 1372

"They are coming," Chevalier Edward du Fermein said portentously, then bowed. His chainmail clanked with the bow. "Philip's army is no more than two nights' march from the gates of Paris." Edward was from the lower nobility of France and quite a good scout, but he didn't know how to act among the upper nobility, and he came across with a sort of studied pomposity.

"Nights' march?" King Charles asked, looking at Bertrand.

"Majesty, they seem to abhor the sunlight," Edward insisted.

Still ignoring Edward, Charles looked from Bertrand to Monsignor Savona. Bertrand shrugged his ignorance, and Savona pulled the phone from a newly added pocket in his cassock.

"I don't know either, Majesty, but Raphico might."

"I do not know for certain," Raphico admitted. "I think it has to do with the effect of sunlight on a dead body. The dead do not tan. In all honesty, I'm not sure it matters."

"The fact of it matters," Bertrand said. "There are reasons that we do not hold major battles in the dark. If you can't see what is going on, you can't control your troops."

"Speaking of that, do we know how Philip is controlling the dead?" Charles asked. "I understand that it is through the sword, but what distance can they be from him and still be controlled?"

"Hundreds of miles," Raphico said. "Themis is a nation in the netherworld. Her power stretches over a fair piece of what the mortal world calls Europe. On the other hand, Philip's control is secondhand and imprecise."

266

"Most military control is secondhand and imprecise," Bertrand said.

"Also, Themis is a deity of law and custom, but not wrathful retribution. She leaves that to Nemesis. She of the lovely cheeks, as the Greeks called Themis, was the first to offer Hera a cup. And if you can get along with Hera, you can get along with anybody."

"What does that mean?" Charles asked.

"Simply that she is not studied in war," Raphico said.

"Well?" Charles looked at Bertrand.

"There are possibilities," Bertrand said. "But the truth is that war isn't complicated. Difficult, terrifying, and deadly, but not generally complex."

A Forge in Paris

The hammer dropped and a billet of yellow-hot iron was shaped into a pike head. It would need to be tempered and sharpened, but the shape was achieved in a single stroke. The smith used a pair of tongs to pick up the pike head and drop it in water made hot by the dozen pike heads already in the water.

"You think it's true?" the boy manning the bellows asked the smith.

"How should I know?" the smith said. "But these pike heads will be cold by the time that the dead arrive."

"When are we getting a salamander?" The boy puffed.

"You should be thankful, boy. If I had a salamander, what would I need you for?"

A Leather Working Shop in Paris

The device here wasn't a drop forge. Not exactly. It was more like a loom. It had thirty-two teeth, metal needles with holes to put a sinew thread through, all stacked into a weighted frame, that, like the drop forge, dropped onto a piece of leather armor, driving the needles through the two pieces of boiled leather, carrying the sinew thread. Then the part was pulled out and apprentices were put to the task of tying off the sinew threads before the piece was turned inside out and put over a chest shape for final shaping.

The device didn't remove all the work, but it did turn what would have been a two-week job into a two-day job. Part of the innovation was demons and part was just necessity driving invention. But a big chunk of it was Amelia Grady complaining about the fact that she didn't know how to build a sewing machine. None of the twenty-firsters knew how to build a sewing machine. None of them knew how to build a spinning jenny, or even a spinning wheel. And neither did anyone in Paris.

A Farm Outside Paris
June 8, 1372

"Leave it!" Gaspar shouted at his wife, Maria. The children were crying, and Maria was arguing, and there wasn't time for any of that. "Damn it, woman, I saw a walking corpse in the north pasture. Leave it!"

He picked up little Gaspar, put him in the two-wheeled cart he used to take his turnips to Paris, and then reached for Paul. It wasn't as though he wanted to leave Maria's favorite copper pot here for Philip's army of the dead to use. But they needed to run. He grabbed Maria by the arm and pulled her to the front of the cart, almost throwing her against the left-hand shaft. "Now move, woman."

Gaspar was desperately afraid that they, no, *he* had waited too long. He had wanted to get that field manured. It was important, if the family was to survive the coming winter, that the turnip crop be good. That was why he had put off going to Paris for two extra days.

Then, this morning, he went out to the pasture to gather sheep shit for his fields and saw a man. But the man had ignored him. He just stood there. Gaspar looked into his face and saw no eyes. Just empty sockets. And the skin was dry and brown, like leather.

Now they were running.

"Don't cry, Maria. They will have no use for your copper pot. We'll get the babes to Paris, and when this is over we can come home and find your pot just where you left it. I promise." Gaspar didn't know whether he would be able to keep that promise, but he made it just the same.

Walls of Paris
Night of June 9, 1372

The guard on the wall looked out into the darkness and saw a writhing mass. It was too dark to see, even with the half moon, because of the clouds. Then there was a break in the clouds. The writhing mass was people. He still couldn't see well enough to be able to tell with his eyes that they were dead people, but either because he already knew, or from some sense he didn't understand, the guard knew that most of the men and women out there were dead.

Perhaps that was it. Their bodies were much restored, but their clothing almost not at all, and half that army was female. No army he had ever heard of was made up of as many women as men. Even the Amazons of myth were an army of women, not men and women mixed, naked and ignoring each other. There was a coldness to that army. It didn't care, not about anything.

The guard on the wall swallowed fear and disgust, but it didn't go away. It ate at his belly like bad food or hunger. He stood there on the wall, just staring, and barely noticed when eventually the alarm was sounded by another watcher.

****

Pucorl rolled through the streets of Paris with his headlights on, and the people came out to see him.

But they didn't jeer. They didn't yell. They fingered their rosaries, and priests and monks blessed him as he passed.

The army of the dead outside the walls of Paris had done that, at least for now. Pucorl and his load of twenty-firsters, for the

269

moment, were seen as the protectors of Paris, no longer threats.

****

Wilber rode behind the van on Meurtrier, holding out his phone. His computer was in a special saddle bag on the horse's rump, but the phone was set to give off light. He looked over at Roger, who was riding a brown mare. Roger had his rifle out. This was all about display and was on the orders of Bertrand.

A young woman curtsied to them as they passed. She was dressed in linen with ermine trim, so was a member of the nobility. That bothered Wilber a bit—just how quickly he came to be able to tell from the clothing what level of society the person came from.

The poor, who were the overwhelming majority, were allowed to dress one way, the rich another. Several others, for there were several ranks represented in Paris, each higher rank smaller in number than the one below. And if you were born in one rank, you died in that rank. Well, except for the church and the army. Bertrand had started out lower nobility and was now the Constable of France.

Which was a good-sized piece of what had so angered Philip the Bold, at least according to Tiphaine.

A dog barked at Pucorl and Wilber barked back. The dog looked at Wilber in confusion. He wasn't used to being talked to by humans, even less being able to understand what they said. Several people crossed themselves.

Roger muttered, "Cut out the Doctor Doolittle crap, Will. You're scaring the natives."

"Naw," said Wilber's phone. "We need to show them we have magic on our side too. That's why we're here." Both comments were in twenty-first century English.

****

Bertrand du Guesclin, riding behind Wilber and Roger, didn't say anything. He hadn't understood much of Roger's comment, and even less of the phone's, but he could make a good guess. He watched the crowd lining the street with a practiced eye and

270

thought it was going well. The city was frightened but not ready to panic, which had to count as a miracle considering what was outside the walls.

June 10, 1372

"They are showing a flag of truce," the wall guard reported as they mounted the last step to stand on the battlements.

Charles V looked to Bertrand, then out onto the field to the army that was arrayed a double bow shot from the walls, then back to Bertrand.

"I do not think Your Majesty should come within range of the sword while it is in Philip the Traitor's possession. I will go."

"Do you think you will be able to withstand it?"

"I don't know, Majesty. But if I go in the company of Pucorl and Wilber, I may hope to hold back from any act that would disgrace my name."

Plain, North of Paris

Pucorl drove up to the pavilion of Philip the Traitor with Wilber, Roger, and Bertrand du Guesclin on horseback in his train and Annabelle riding inside. The pavilion was far enough from the walls of Paris to be out of bow or even trebuchet range, but was still in sight. Pucorl had wanted to leave Annabelle behind. He'd even shut his doors and locked them to keep her out of him. But Annabelle was stubborn. She just went to the stables and got a horse. If she couldn't ride in him, she was going anyway. At that point, Pucorl yielded. She was safer in him than in the open. Safer, not safe. He wasn't happy about it.

Pucorl didn't think any of them were safe. He was still a puck in his attitudes and beliefs. He knew that the demon lords and deities of the netherworld were dangerous to him. He thought trying to treat with them was crazy. But Merlin's idiotic counsel held the day.

So here he was. Facing a demon lord who had a major grudge against him.

At ten yards from the pavilion, he stopped. Bertrand rode up and dismounted. Pucorl had a white flag of truce attached to his antenna. Bertrand was wearing full armor and helm, and a white tabard with his crest emblazoned on it.

"Where is that coward, my brother?" intoned a deep and rich voice. It pushed at them all, but Pucorl knew the true source. "It's Themis, Constable. Not Philip, but the stolen glory of Themis. Pay it no heed."

"Silence, Pucorlshrigin!" bellowed the demon lord, invoking much of Pucorl's name. Pucorl didn't know where he had gotten it, but for a demon of Beslizoswian's strength and authority, it wouldn't be that hard.

"That is no longer his name, Beslizoswian!" Wilber bellowed right back.

And Pucorl realized that that was true. In amongst Pucorlshrigin were new vibrations. New sounds that, when assembled, formed Sir Pucorl. The sound his engine made at idle and when revved up. Radio signals and electromagnetic structures, as well as aspects of character, courage, and caring to add to humor and self-preservation. Echoes of Annabelle's snorting laugh and her grease-stained cheek in his monitors. Bits of his small fief, his garage slowly making its way to the Elysian Fields were also there in minor thirds. And Annabelle's locker in that garage. It wasn't that his name was gone. More that structure and depth had been added and the mix changed.

Over all, Pucorl rather liked his new name and it left Beslizoswian with much less power over him. To demonstrate that, Pucorl honked at him with as rude a honk as any Paris cab had ever delivered.

Annabelle touched the control that opened Pucorl's driver side window, stuck out her arm, and gave Beslizoswian the one finger salute. That was his Annabelle. A demure lady, start to finish.

Wilber was looking daggers at him or at Annabelle, which was almost certainly Merlin's influence. Pucorl found he didn't care that much. Yes, he was still much less powerful than either Merlin or Beslizoswian, much less Themis, who dwarfed them all. But they were here, under flag of truce, and there was no way they were going to talk Beslizoswian into abandoning his siege of Paris.

Pucorl had control of his cameras. It was a new feature in this year's model. A return to the Tucker turning headlight, but controlled through the computer. Pucorl used that control now to shift and zoom in on one of the zombies that had been raised and blue-toothed the image to Merlin in Wilber's computer.

Wilber looked startled for just a second, then looked around at the zombies that were near Philip's pavilion. Annabelle followed Wilber's glance and said quietly, "Pucorl, what about them? They look almost alive."

"And that's the point. A demon, even a fairly major demon, shouldn't be able to restore a corpse to that level of substance. Not after it's been in the ground for years, as some of those certainly have. Everything but the bones—and even some of the bones—has been reformed by magic. I couldn't do that. Merlin couldn't do that. Even a demon lord couldn't do that. To get that sort of structure, part of Themis has to have been used up for every corpse they raise."

"So, what does that tell us?" Annabelle asked, keeping her voice to little more than a murmur. "That Philip doesn't give a crap about Themis? We already pretty much knew that Philip doesn't give a crap about much of anything."

"No. It tells us that the demon lord is actively trying to destroy Themis. Cut her up into thousands of little bits, then leave the bits to decay here in the mortal world."

"So Themis isn't happy." Annabelle nodded. "I guess that could be useful. But isn't she bound by being stuck in the sword?"

"Yes, she is. But even with the kind of spell they had to have used, Themis is a Titan, almost a deity. She, of necessity, has a subtle mind."

****

Bertrand du Guesclin bowed, and answered Philip's demand. "His Majesty has greater duties, Duke of Burgundy, and even if you abandon yours in treason, he doesn't abandon his."

"It's Charles who is the traitor," Philip said, and again his words carried that aura of truth.

Bertrand heard that rude honk of Pucorl's and was again reminded that the power of Philip's words was not truth, but the product of a spell, not justice. He felt the pull, but with each reminder was better able to fight it off. Bertrand du Guesclin was not a man to yield to authority in the first place. Suddenly, he had an idea. He bowed again, but not to Philip or the shadowy demon that stood at his back. Bertrand bowed to the sword. "Themis, know that it was not by the will of Charles of France that you were stolen from your place and enslaved unjustly in this rod of iron."

"Silence!" roared Philip. "How dare you presume to speak to my sword and not to me?" The voice still carried the power, but Bertrand could almost feel the unwillingness of the sword.

"Hey," Pucorl said, "how are your gonads, Beslizoswian? Still got that bolt in 'em?"

The demon, in an instant, went from seven feet tall to seventeen feet tall and black flames seemed to surround it.

Bertrand, with a great effort, restrained himself from drawing his sword. He knew that breaking the truce would be their deaths.

Then everything happened at once.

The demon reached for the van.

Philip lifted the sword as though to attack Bertrand—actually started to swing at Bertrand.

But in that moment the sword lengthened and shifted, turned in mid-stroke, and instead of striking Bertrand's head from his shoulders, cut the demon's right wing and right arm off at the shoulder.

There was a scream like grinding rocks and Pucorl was yelling, "Time to go!"

"No! You must obey me!" Philip screamed, and now his voice lacked the power it had held. It was the petulant whine of a spoiled child that Bertrand knew from his prior dealings with the

Duke of Burgundy.

"Not in this!" Wilber said to Philip. "You commanded Themis to break the truce, and by all custom and usage, that is not allowed. Be careful, Traitor, lest in your arrogance you break even the spell that binds her to your service."

Bertrand wondered why Wilber had warned Philip of that, but now wasn't the time to ask.

Netherworld
June 10, 1372

The system of caverns shook and collapsed as the force of Themis' will shattered the rock and separated almost a full quarter of the power of Beslizoswian from the rest.

Where there had been one demon, there were now two. Two caverns, separated by stone and at odds with one another. In the larger of them, a section of lodestone almost a quarter mile across disrupted the flow of magic. The caverns howled with the echoes of that division.

Plain, North of Paris
June 10, 1372

"It's time to go," Wilber said.

Bertrand wasn't happy with the way this had gone and he didn't like abandoning the field. But he was a practical man at his core, and he knew that Wilber knew more of magic and its rules than he did. So he turned his back on Philip and mounted his horse.

Philip screamed for the zombies to hold them, for his living retainers to hold them, but his voice held none of the power that Bertrand had felt at first.

No one rushed to obey Philip.

Bertrand mounted and rode away, with Pucorl backing up and turning around behind him. He glanced over his shoulder to see the black and red demon lord with its wing and arm severed, lying on the field. The wing and arm shifted and became one, then turned into a black mist and disappeared. The demon lord was trying to rise, using its left arm and wing for balance, and as Bertrand watched, it seemed to heal before his eyes. But it was much diminished.

Bertrand turned his eyes back to the front, then waved at Wilber. "What was that all about? This was supposed to be a parley, a peace meeting. And if there was little chance that Philip might ultimately be brought to reason, we might have delayed the attack, giving our craftsmen and their tools time to prepare for the battle to come."

"You had to be there," Wilber started. "Well, you had to see what Pucorl saw and understand what it meant." Wilber went on to explain about the rules of truce, and about the restored corpses. It wasn't new information, but a new perspective on the information that Bertrand already had.

"So it was Pucorl who saw how close this Beslizoswian was to breaking the truce, but what if Philip had simply not interfered?"

"If Beslizoswian had attacked while under the conventions of a truce, we could have defeated him," Pucorl said.

"Don't let your enhanced name make you arrogant, Pucorl," Merlin said. "It would still have been a near thing, even with the injuries that you and Amelia Grady's bolt had already done to the beast."

Bertrand looked back again and felt himself smiling. "Very well. Tell me more about these corpses."

"It's like fairy gold," Wilber said. "What's happened is that when each corpse is raised, a demon from Themis' realm is put into it. Then a bit of Themis herself is used to turn dirt, grass, rock, water, whatever is handy, into blood and muscle, skin, and so on. Themis has to keep using bits of herself to keep the semblance of a body, and the body keeps wanting to decay, so Themis keeps having to feed tiny bits of herself to the bodies to keep them whole. I imagine that she is focusing her will mostly on the ones right around Philip, but even so it's got to be a tremendous drain.

"It's not like in a forge that is enchanted with a salamander. The salamander is there and as long as it stays the fire burns, because in the netherworld fire is an element as much as earth is. But a body, a mortal body that's dead, wants... 'Wants' isn't really the right word, but there is no right word in any mortal tongue for this and 'wants' is as close as I can come. The dead body wants to decay and Themis is being used up to prevent that from happening.

"The deity Themis is not happy. She is being killed by the death of a thousand cuts. When the demon lord . . . it's still not wise to use its name unless you know what you're doing . . . when the demon lord broke the peace and Philip tried to force Themis to . . ."

"I understand that much. But why did you warn Philip? Why not let him push until he broke the spell?"

"Because breaking the spell in that way would have broken Themis too," Wilber said.

CHAPTER 22

Walls of Paris
June 11, 1372

Roger looked at the cannon in the afternoon light. It wasn't the first he had seen, and he had better guns. But there hadn't been much time, and there were not many of the new guns.

The pot-de-fer were shaped like an amphora, or a flower vase. The archaeologists had gotten it wrong. Roger had seen their reconstructions in the twenty-first century. Those reconstructions had been informed by a later century's understanding of explosive force, an understanding that the fourteenth century just didn't have.

These were pots, wider in the base than at the opening, internally as well as externally. The walls were thicker at the base, but not as thick as had been assumed. The bore was not straight. It was wider near the back than at the front. The only reason that these things hadn't blown up every time they fired was the poor quality of the seals and the poor quality of the powder they had. The bolts didn't have the leather wrappings that the archaeologist had assumed. The powder explosion focused through the narrowing mouth was what gave the pot its power.

Roger stepped back behind a wall, and the gunner touched off the charge with a heated wire. Roger wasn't a coward, but he'd rather go up in a Wright flyer than fire one of those pots of death. At least on a Wright there would be a view before it killed him.

The pot-de-fer spat fire, a jet of still burning black powder that shot out almost twenty feet. At the same time, it shot the pack of a dozen bolts. The bolts sailed out and Roger watched them go. They weren't going that fast. He could see the arch, like a flight of short tumbling arrows.

He watched them arch into the host of demons just over two hundred yards away. Zombies didn't scream and they didn't run away. That made it hard to tell how much damage they had done. That they had hit some zombies, Roger was sure. But to what effect, he couldn't tell.

****

A demon who had been a carpenter in Themis stood by a demon it had been shaping into a wagon wheel. Now they were both trapped in these containers of decaying mortal flesh, bound to them and slowly decaying with them. It was horrible. But they were commanded by their queen. Even though they both knew she was in turn compelled, they couldn't resist her commands.

The demon who had been a carpenter looked up to see pieces of earth flying through the sky and wondered who had compelled the lazy bastards to move. They arced through the sky and came right at him. He was getting ready to move when one of them hit him and he was in two pieces. The magic holding him in the corpse disrupted by something—something that disrupted him and chewed on him. And then he was gone. Parts of him back in the place where Themis had been, parts of him left in the mortal world. It hurt horribly, and he was confused by it.

But his awareness continued. Which was the worst part.

****

The guns continued firing off and on intermittently till the sun set.

Walls of Paris

The moon showed the advancing army, and more than at any time in his life the man with the halberd wanted to run away. He was a soldier and he had faced sword and shield in the hurly burly of battle, but now he was frightened. He held a halberd that was made by a drop forge, and he had been assured that it would strike down the dead that walked the earth. He waited and was heartened, if only a little, when Bertrand du Guesclin came by.

The dead were getting closer now, and there was a stench in the air. They rotted without rotting away, and his stomach crawled at the smell. They reached the base of the wall and hot oil was poured down on them. They burned, but didn't fall away. Instead, they climbed on one another's backs, all aflame, and came up the wall.

He nearly ran then, but for the fact that there was no place to run.

A burning head topped the wall before him and he swung his halberd. The head flew off the neck and the body fell from the wall, still burning. He wasn't sure whether his blow had killed the monster or just knocked it off the wall, but another burning head rose above the wall. Now the smell of corruption that had filled the night was overwhelmed by new smells. The stink of burning hair was combined with the smell of burning oil and the sickeningly enticing smell of burning human flesh. And he fought not to retch as he swung at the new head. He tried not to notice that the head was a woman's head, that the body crisping in the burning oil was that of a woman.

Then another, this time an arm. His halberd struck before he could see more. The arm fell within the wall and writhed on the stones before turning to bone as the flesh more dissipated than burned. And another . . .

****

Themis felt the blows. None of them by themselves were enough to cause pain. She was aware of them as tiny irritants. The combination was like the feeling a mortal might have after the water from a swim in the ocean dried, combined with a mild sunburn. It didn't hurt exactly, but it was far from comfortable. She could focus her attention on any of them or all of them and know the exact nature of the wound and which tiny bit of her was affected. She chose not to, instead trying to understand the battle as it progressed. She was being wasted intentionally and she knew it, but the instructions Beslizoswian passed through Philip were quite specific.

Some of the weapons disrupted the connection between her children and the corpses they animated, even disrupting her children. She recognized those as cold iron by the feel, but she didn't understand why it was disrupting the connection or why the bronze or wood weapons were not.

June 12, 1372

Two hours past midnight Bertrand, on the north wall, noticed the same thing. Bronze arrowheads were less effective than steel arrowheads. A copper pipe might knock one of the dead back a step but didn't seem to hurt it in any way. But a steel pipe would break bones and disable arms, legs—even whole corpses would collapse, turning into piles of soil and bone. They were not good fighters, the dead. They were neither fast nor clever; they just kept coming.

But Bertrand was afraid that might be enough.

****

Very quickly, Roger realized that lead bullets were utterly ineffective against the undead. They might work against zombies in the legends, but they had no effect at all on the real thing. He switched over to a heavy iron mace.

That seemed to be doing the trick. He swung the mace at a zombie's head and heard the melon sound of crushing skull. The zombie went down and he turned to a second, but a third came over the wall while he was busy. It grabbed his left arm, the one with the steel-rimmed round buckler and pulled him off balance. Roger backhanded it with the buckler and got loose, but that took time. Time he didn't have. Hands reached out and grabbed his legs and he went over backward. A zombie fell over onto him. He couldn't breathe.

Then Jeff was there, picking up the zombie and throwing it over the wall, then another. One of the city guard wearing a patch

281

indicating he was a member of the tanners' guild reached down a hand, Roger grabbed, and was pulled up.

He was bleeding. There were bite marks on his arm and a scratch across his face. They were being pushed back, a step at a time.

Then more of the tanners' guild arrived, and they managed to clear this section of the wall.

For now.

They fought on.

Dawn

The morning light was a practical benefit. The defenders could see clearly in the dawn, and the ineffectiveness of the individual zombies was more evident when the defenders could see what they were doing. The defenders had given up on the boiling oil early last night. It was worse than useless.

Tired as the defenders were—and they were utterly exhausted—they were still better, man for man, than the zombies.

In the first half hour after dawn, before the bottom of the sun passed the horizon, they retook those parts of the walls where the zombies had managed to gain a foothold.

Then there was a pause. The zombies pulled back. An hour after dawn, the nearest moving zombie was a hundred yards from the walls.

****

Paris slept. At least most of it did. Exhausted men and women, for women had fought on the wall as well, collapsed while the king and his counselors consulted and considered what they had learned in the night.

"Cold iron does seem to work," Bertrand said. They were all in the king's audience chamber, which, for the moment, was converted into a war room. Bertrand and his officers, Bill Howe, Amelia Grady, Wilber, with his computer, Annabelle with her phone out. Liane, Roger, Jeff, Jennifer, and Lakshmi had spent more time on the walls last night. They were resting, but their phones were set on the large table. Doctor Delaflote was here too, because King Charles wanted his understanding of magic and its workings.

"That doesn't make sense," Bill said. "If iron disrupts, then so should copper. They both conduct electricity. Heck, copper conducts it better."

"Doctor Delaflote and I discussed this," Amelia Grady said. "We concluded that 'cold iron' was simply a euphemism for edged weapons. Especially since Pucorl is mostly iron, or at least steel."

"Also, many of the devices that have been enchanted are made in whole or in part from cold iron," Gabriel Delaflote indorsed the comment.

"Yet it is mentioned in reports from the soldiers manning the walls that copper, bronze, wood, and stone had little effect, but iron seemed to cut the magic as well as the corpses it animated," Charles said.

"So it's ferrous metals, and only when external to the demon," Wilber said. "That makes some sense. After all, blood has iron in it. So if you can't use an iron vessel, you shouldn't be able to use a living vessel either."

"Which doesn't explain why an iron ax works and a bronze one doesn't," King Charles said, with more than a little exasperation in his voice.

"I know, Your Majesty," Wilber apologized. "I have a feeling there is something we should be seeing, but I can't figure out what it is. How is iron different from copper, and why should that difference only affect zombies and not Pucorl?"

"No, that's not it," Amelia said. "At least, I'm not sure it's Pucorl versus zombie. I think hitting Pucorl with a steel hammer might hurt him more than hitting him with a bronze hammer."

"Let's avoid that experiment, shall we?" Pucorl said from Annabelle's phone.

Annabelle hit her forehead with the heel of her hand. "I thought you were just grousing. We already have done that experiment, Pucorl, every time I use an iron hammer to repair you. Every time I use a lug wrench on your lugs, you whine about it, you big baby."

"Well, it hurts."

"The question is: would it hurt if you were using a copper or bronze lug wrench," Wilber said.

Annabelle drummed her fingers on the table. "I'm not sure. When I use copper leads on you, you mostly say it tickles. But that could be because I mostly do that when I am working on your electrical systems. When I use the rubber mallet or the wood mallets, you seem to complain less."

"They hurt less," Pucorl said.

"Well, that helps us define *what's* happening," Wilber said, "but it doesn't help much with *why* it's happening."

"Does that really matter?" Charles asked. It was a real question, if delivered with kingly disdain. He honestly didn't grasp that causes mattered, not just effects.

The discussion continued, but about the only conclusion was that they should use cold iron wherever possible.

Chateau du Guesclin, Roger McLean's Room

There was a quiet knock, but Roger didn't hear it. Then the door opened and a hand reached out and grabbed his arm. Suddenly, in his dream, Roger was on the wall, being grabbed by a zombie. He swung out his arm and Monsignor Savona flew across the room. Roger was standing, in his undershorts, looking for a weapon to bash the zombie before he reached full wakefulness.

"What?" Roger looked around and recognized his room. Then he recognized Monsignor Savona, lying against the door, holding a bruised arm. "Didn't anyone ever explain to you about waking combat vets?" Roger asked.

Then he sat back down on his bed. It was a nice bed, a four poster with linen curtains. Roger wiped his face and realized that it was true. After last night, he *was* a frigging combat vet. The real deal. Even through the horror of his memories, that point shone through. "Sorry, Padre. But that's what happens. The way to do it is to shout from a distance. If you can't do that, grab a foot, then get back."

"I will remember." Monsignor Savona grimaced.

"What brought you to my room, Monsignor?" Roger looked at Father Savona and lifted an eyebrow.

"It's not me, my son. Raphico wants to have a few words with you." With that, he laid the phone on Roger's desk, got up, and left.

Roger looked down at the phone. "Well?"

"The Creator has instructions."

"Really?" Roger asked. "I mean, is he really the creator of heaven and earth? Never mind. I know that you are not my demon, so you can lie to me. So let me ask you this instead: why should I follow this creator's instructions, even if he really is *the* creator? In case you failed to guess, me and the other twenty-firsters have been thinking about that rather a lot."

"So I gather," Raphico said, and the voice from the phone didn't sound nearly as "on stage" as it usually did. "That is something that you are going to have to decide for yourself, young man. I will issue no threats and make no promises. Follow your conscience." The voice was back to onstage mode by the time it finished that pronouncement. Then it got casual again. "I will point out that Themis is both being mistreated and not the sort of thing that you want to leave lying around. A sword that can raise an army of the dead doesn't belong in this world."

"So why tell me?"

"Because, Roger the Rifleman, you have the rifle. Right now, Philip owns the sword Themis, but if he is defeated in combat . . . well, to the victor goes the spoils."

"You want me to release her?"

"Yes. Send her home. To do that, you will need to take her back to the pentagram where she was drawn here, and release her back to the netherworld."

"That makes a certain amount of sense, but why do you care?"

"The netherworld is out of balance," Raphico said. "The longer Themis is missing from her proper place, the more out of balance it becomes."

"What's to keep someone else from reaching down and picking up the sword? For instance, that demon lord Bellsibuts, or whatever his name is."

"The laws of combat are fairly specific, but you will want to get as close to Themis as you can, and as fast as you can after you fire the shot."

Roger leaned back in his bed and put his hands behind his head. "The next problem is that King Charles isn't going to want to give up such a powerful artifact. It's something about being a king, I think. You get to thinking that what you want constitutes a natural law." He looked over at the phone. "We probably got that from you guys."

Raphico refrained from commenting on that.

"So . . . not only do you want me to get up close to Philip in the middle of a battle, make a sniper shot on the fly, run up and grab the magic sword like I was King Arthur, you then want me to take the sword and run off before the king of France has a chance to tell me not to?"

"Yes." Raphico didn't sound happy but, oddly enough, Roger was.

"This, my friend, is a job for Pucorl the van, and I think we are going to need Wilber and Merlin on it too. I know I ain't doin' it until I have a chance to talk it over with Merlin anywho. Meanwhile, go away. 'Cause if I'm gonna do this, I need some sleep first."

He went to the desk, picked up the phone, walked to the door, opened it, and handed the phone back to Monsignor Savona. Then he went back to bed.

CHAPTER 23

Walls of Paris
June 12, 1372, Noon

The black charger pranced forward toward the wall. Philip the Bold sat boldly on its back, barely out of bow range from the walls of Paris.

Philip's voice rang out. "*I am the rightful king of France! My father, John II, the king of France, chose me for the duty! France is mine by right, by my father's will. Charles is the true usurper. Bow down to me, your true and rightful king! Open the gates! Open the gates!*"

****

On the walls of Paris, soldiers looked around. The power of that voice held them. What did they know from politics? Shouldn't it be the father's choice?

The commands went against their experiences from last night. They went against what the priests had been saying ever since they heard of Philip's raising of the first zombie. The commands went against it all, but they felt that voice and its power.

Each soldier reacted individually, using his intellect or the horror at what they had seen in the night to fight off the compulsion of that voice.

Or, in all too many cases, yielding to it and falling on their knees to the man who, for the moment at least, seemed their proper overlord.

There was a struggle at the Porte Saint-Honoré, as some of the men-at-arms guarding the doors actually tried to open them. The Porte Saint-Honoré was the closest to Philip and struck most strongly by that voice. But the voice . . . the voice reached all of Paris from the Louvre to the Bastille, from Le Temple to Sorbonne, the bell tower of Notre Dame to a cellar on the left bank. And everyone who heard it felt its seductive pull. Even the deaf heard it.

Chateau du Guesclin

Roger woke from a sound sleep hearing that voice.

His phone, Clausewitz, blew a raspberry, then said, "The voice is strengthened by the power of Themis, and it's weakened by the fact that Philip isn't the lawful king of France."

"Right, Clausewitz. I got it. But how many are going to fall for it? I feel the pull and I have you to work against it. Plus the fact that I spent last night fighting the friggin' zombies that SOB raised."

"I don't know. But Paris just became a divided city."

****

Annabelle was woken from a sound sleep by the power of that voice, and so was her maid, a French girl from Tiphaine's lands up near Normandy. So Enzo spoke in *Langue d'oïl* as he explained to both of them where the power of the voice came from.

"Are you sure?" Danielle asked. "It sounds so . . ." She trailed off.

There was no way of explaining how it sounded because at the core it wasn't the sound. Philip's voice was the same slightly tinny and highly snooty baritone it had always been. But the magic under it gave that voice a majesty that the best actors of the twenty-first century couldn't hope to match.

"I know how you feel, Dani. But it's Themis who has the majesty, not Philip. He stole it. And I think we are going to have to get it back."

"To give it to King Charles?" Danielle asked.

Annabelle had met Charles V a few times now, and he struck her as . . . well, not all that impressive. He was trying to do the right thing, but his attitude was more like France was his family

288

farm and the people in it his farm animals than like he was a politician and the servant of his people. The idea of him having that sort of majesty didn't sit well. Not unless he gained the concern and nobility of character that ought to go with it. That certainly hadn't happened with Philip, so there wasn't any reason to think that the sword would make Charles more noble.

"I don't know, Dani. I just don't know."

Royal Palace, Hôtel Saint-Pol

In the royal residence next to the Bastille fortress, Queen Joanna of Bourbon woke screaming. She then started throwing things at her husband and calling him a usurper. She had to be physically restrained.

In a way, it was even harder for Charles V.

He had grown up in the rather dysfunctional royal family of France and all the issues that any family might have were there. He knew for a fact that his father had wanted Philip to be his first son. The sniveling little toad had sucked up to their father from the day he was born, and gotten away with just about anything while Charles was constantly criticized for every imagined failure.

In any family there is more than one side to the family squabbles, and even though Charles had always been certain that his side was the right one, now, with that voice coming through the walls of his bedchamber, the other side seemed to have added weight.

Charles knew that his brother was a spoiled brat who never thought of anyone but himself. But somehow, right now, all his uncertainties were screaming that Philip was the true king of France.

He fought it off by remembering every wrong the spoiled little monster had ever done to him, to his brothers, to the palace servants, to the people of France, to the people of Burgundy. And he knew most of them.

But it was long minutes after Philip had finished his speech before Charles had himself under control. He left his chambers, called his guards, and sent a message to Bertrand to come and attend him.

Chateau du Guesclin

Bertrand woke as the words penetrated the room he shared with Tiphaine, and felt the pull of the voice. But Bertrand was a different sort of man than his monarch. His immediate reaction to any sort of compulsion was to resist it. He had been resisting external compulsions his whole life. He might later accept the validity of some action, but his first response to any attempt to force him was to fight it.

So he fought it, and found it surprisingly easy. He knew Philip, he knew that he worked with a demon lord who despised all humanity. Bertrand had seen it right here in the chateau, and he remembered the walking dead of last night. Reason and his natural inclination to resist compulsion both stood together and formed a shield wall against Philip's words.

He looked over at Tiphaine. His wife had a considering look on her face. She was different from Bertrand in that she wasn't moved by either an immediate desire to resist compulsion or to be compelled. She simply analyzed logically each command and then decided.

He waited.

There were little head shakes, barely noticeable, but he knew her well. She, as the twenty-firsters would say, wasn't buying.

****

Wilber heard the voice, but it held no power over him.

None at all.

He could hear that it held power over others. He recognized it, but the bit of Merlin left in his implant, the healing, and the hearing, protected him from the magic voice more surely than earmuffs ever could. "Merlin?"

"Yes," Merlin agreed rather bitterly. "Themis is compelled by the spell, and Philip is using her majesty to justify his words."

"How effective?" Already Wilber and Merlin had developed a

shorthand for intimate conversations.

"I cannot say. Before this I would have been certain, but I have learned much of humanity through our contact. Learned how little I know."

Shop of Nicholas Flamel

Nicholas was not asleep. He was eating lunch with his wife. Nicholas was too old and too well off to spend his nights on the walls of Paris. He was also too busy working on the new printing press and writing out regulations and military directives. So the words didn't intrude on his sleep, but they did take him by surprise.

He considered them and felt the compulsion strongly. He knew that Charles was only the third Valois king, that Edward of England had a reasonably valid claim through the sister of Charles the Fair, who died without male issue. It all combined to make it seem that *any* claim was as good as any other, so why not let the preferences of John the Good rule the day? Which would leave Philip as the rightful king and his true liege. Both sides dealt with demons, so that was no justification for choosing one side over the other.

On the other hand, Nicholas, while a practical man and hardworking, had never been a soldier. There wasn't much he could do.

Royal Palace, Hôtel Saint-Pol
Near two in the afternoon

"I want him gone, Bertrand," Charles V said as Bertrand du Guesclin entered the throne room, not even waiting for Bertrand to bow. "Gone now, today."

"That is easier said than done, Majesty. Defense magnifies our forces and he has a lot of walking corpses outside our walls."

"Are you saying you can't do it?" There was a cold anger in the king's voice that pushed at Bertrand and made him want to push back. But he had long since gained control over that response. He honestly liked and respected his king. Not just the crown, but the man. Besides, it was a just question. The king's army was mostly right here in Paris. The siege hadn't caught them unaware and they had been preparing for it. A sally, under normal circumstances, would be a reasonable tactic.

So he held his temper in check and answered politely. "No, Majesty. Simply that if you want us to succeed, we need to study the matter before we act."

"When can you do it?" It was clear that Charles was holding himself back by force of will.

"Not today. Probably not tomorrow. It depends. There is much we learned in last night's attacks that we need to mix into our thinking about how to fight these undead creatures that follow his banner."

"Days?" Charles blurted. "Bertrand, will we still hold Paris if that brat has days more to incite treason amongst the populace?"

"I don't know, Majesty," Bertrand admitted.

"Even the deaf heard that tirade, Bertrand. People who had never heard a sound before heard that and understood every word."

All in all, it was a most unpleasant meeting.

Chateau du Guesclin

Bertrand called for Wilber before he reached the front door of the building proper. Wilber and Merlin, but he was coming to think of them almost as one being. He wanted to know what the reports about cold iron meant and what his experiences might mean in regard to fighting the undead. Wilber, however, wasn't there. He and Pucorl, along with Annabelle and Bill, had left not much past noon for the University of Paris.

"What for?" Bertrand asked.

Tiphaine answered, "They wanted to examine the bodies."

University of Paris

Wilber looked at the bodies of some of the undead that had been hit with cold iron. Many had been left upon the ramparts of Paris last night. Some were transported to the University for research purposes. It looked to Bertrand as though the bodies were returned to the state they had been before they were raised. Almost bone surrounded by soil.

"What have you found? How do the bodies struck with cold iron compare to the bodies struck with wood or bronze?"

"I don't know," Wilber answered. "We can't be sure that any of them were hit by anything but cold iron. Most of them, we don't know what sort of weapon hit them, except that some were sharp and some were dull. Where we know what hit them, they were all cold iron weapons. Every report for every body we have found. And correlating all those reports with the bodies found wasn't easy."

"I wouldn't think it possible," Bertrand admitted.

"Spreadsheets are good for all sorts of things," Bill said. "But you're mostly right. We have three categories: wounds that we know were caused by cold iron, a much larger category of wounds that we don't know the cause of, and an empty category of wounds that we know were caused by copper, bronze, wood, or in three cases, ceramic pots. We don't have confirmed bodies for the ceramic pots. We don't have confirmed bodies for the bronze weapons or the wooden clubs. What we do have is lots of reports, confirmed by multiple sightings, of zombies with their arms or heads cut off by bronze halberds continuing to fight, and picking up their heads when they got the chance and re-attaching them. We have four reports of that happening with steel halberds, but in every case those sightings were located near a similar report about a bronze weapon. The cops here think, and I agree, that what happened is someone saw a bronze weapon hit a zombie and thought it was steel."

Bertrand nodded, then looked at Wilber.

"Merlin and I have looked at the bodies. I even shoved Igor into the goop of the wounds. Those wounds all look pretty much the same to his magical camera eye. Igor can tell that there was a spell holding the body together. A minor demon of some sort, augmented by a little bit of Themis. But when the sword or spike hit it, it ripped up the magic and the demon was released or damaged or, most often, both. I think it's something about the magnetic nature of ferrous metals, but Merlin doesn't agree."

"Merlin," Annabelle said, "doesn't know crap about ferrous metals. He knows earth, water, air, and fire, plus aether."

"Then you think Wilber, not Merlin, is right about this?" Bertrand asked her.

"I think the magical universe has to be interacting with ours through some mechanism. And electromagnetism might be how it's doing it. I want to talk to Jennifer about this. Her mom is an electrical engineer. She's likely to know more about what might be happening than the rest of us."

"I agree with Annabelle," Bill said. "But here's the thing you need to know. Whether it's physics or magic, if you stick a steel knife into a zombie, it's probably going to stay cut. But a bronze knife, not so much."

It took Bertrand a moment to follow what Bill was saying. Then he remembered about the zombies from last night reattaching severed body parts.

"The other thing it means," came Pucorl's voice from Annabelle's phone, "is if I hit a zombie it's probably going to be road kill. And . . ."

"Your bumper is plastic, Pucorl," Annabelle said, "and if your grill is steel, it's enameled steel."

"Well, we know that he beat the crap out of the demon lord," Bill said. "A puck shouldn't be able to do that."

"You think that was cold iron?" Bertrand asked.

"Yes, Lord Constable, I do," Bill said formally. "Not to detract from Pucorl's courage in any way, but yes, I suspect that if his grill had been plastic, not steel, things would have gone differently and not to our good."

"My grill is a part of me," Pucorl said. "I can feel the wind touch it just like I can feel it on my windshield."

"The effect is apparently different if you're summoned into an object that contains cold iron than if you're hit with one," Wilber said. "As to why it's different, I don't have any ideas, and neither does Merlin."

Bertrand looked around at the twenty-firsters and the dead and decomposed bodies on the tables. This information was something, but not a full explanation. There was a great deal that they didn't know, and no consensus about what they did. *No, that isn't quite true. We know that when we make the sally, we should be carrying cold steel or cold iron weapons and wearing cold steel armor.* Then he looked at Annabelle and visualized Pucorl out in the courtyard. Thought about the van charging across the field into row after row of zombies, cutting a hole for his men to flow through. "Pucorl will be going with us, but I want steel armor for him, like war horses wear."

"It will take some time," Annabelle said, "and a lot of steel. To armor Pucorl would take almost a ton of steel and I don't think it's going to be comfortable."

"Neither is *my* armor, girl. It goes with being a knight."

****

They came again the next night, although more weakly. Even with Themis in hand, Philip could not reanimate so many corpses in so little time.

Strangers' Quarters, University of Paris

Late that same night, Annabelle spotted Bill coming out of the room she shared with Jennifer. Between his vaguely skulking demeanor and the self-satisfied expression on his face, she didn't have any trouble figuring out what had transpired.

When she came into the room, Jennifer was in her own bed— more like a cot, really; Annabelle wondered how they'd managed on it—facing away from the door, under the covers.

"Stop pretending you're asleep," Annabelle said. "Are you nuts? What happens if you get pregnant?"

After a moment's hesitation, Jennifer rolled over and looked up at Annabelle. The expression on her face was mostly one of defiance—but there was definitely a trace of self-satisfaction there also.

"Bill took precautions," she said, defensively. Then, with some belligerence: "He's got rubbers. I'm not stupid, you know."

Annabelle sniffed. "Yeah? How *many* rubbers? It's not like they're an item you can pick up at any pharmacy in Paris—oh, wait, I forgot. There *aren't* any pharmacies in Paris, in the here and now year 1372, are there?"

Jennifer rolled back to face the wall. "We're all probably going to die in the next few days, anyway," she said. "At least *I* won't die a virgin. Unlike some people I could think of."

Annabelle saw no reason to dignify that with a response.

Porte Saint-Denis, Paris
June 12, 1372

On the wall, Peter remembered the words of Philip the Bold. He stood there on the wall and waited. When the zombie's head rose above the wall, he stepped back and to the right, blocking the way of other soldiers. He wasn't quite ready to raise his sword against them, but he couldn't bring himself to raise his sword in opposition to the rightful king.

The zombie reached the top of the ramparts while Peter was delaying his fellows. They had heard Philip as well, and it made them hesitate.

The zombie didn't hesitate, nor did it make any attempt to differentiate between friend or enemy. Any living creature on that wall was its enemy, and it struck Peter down with a fine disregard for his help.

Raoul, who hadn't been willing to strike Peter in the face of their friendship and Philip's words, suddenly found himself quite willing to strike the zombie. His steel halbert swung and cut the left side of the zombie's head off, and went on to strike part of the left arm on the down stroke.

The delay had been damaging, if not crucial. There were five zombies in the breach and it took fifteen minutes and another dead soldier to win back that part of the wall. But the lesson was learned. To let a zombie reach the top of the wall was to court death.

The same scene was repeated on all the walls of Paris. It stiffened the resolve of the defenders. Betrayal of Paris to Philip could still happen, but it would take arranging, and that was going to take time.

Chateau du Guesclin
June 14, 1372

The armor wasn't armor. It was more like a cow catcher mated with a roll cage. A bit of experimentation showed that iron didn't hurt unless it jammed into or against Pucorl and the pain of having his lug nuts tightened or loosened as needed was only partly caused by the cold steel lug wrench. Still, wood felt better. Call it the difference between silk and a really scratchy wool. Besides, wood was easier to cut and carve in a hurry, so while his armor was iron on the outside, it was wood where it touched Pucorl.

"No, I think that if someone poked a hole through the van body with an iron pike head it would poke a hole through *me*. But if it was wood, copper, ceramic, or aluminum, I would grow back together. Not all at once. It would take time, but I would be restored, and with me the van."

"What about the modifications?" Jennifer asked, typing notes into her computer. Her computer was Chanel and the demon who enchanted it had excellent fashion sense. Whatever Mrs. Grady or these fourteenth-century goons thought. It was another familiar spirit type. They apparently were the upper peasantry of the netherworld. Not nobles, but not usually snack food either. And like all the demons, Chanel was intensely interested in the effects of cold iron on demon kind.

"They itch," Pucorl admitted. "It's like I'm trying to return to my shape before the modifications. Some of them are cold iron or partly cold iron, and they work but feel unnatural."

The notion that Pucorl was feeling unnatural made Jennifer want to laugh or at least giggle. Like a haunted van was natural! But she didn't. Computers and vans might not have feelings, but demons did. Instead, she asked, "Pucorl, have you considered pulling a Merlin?"

"A what?"

"Remember when Merlin migrated to Wilber's computer? Part way to Wilber's computer, I mean. Before we got permission to enchant the other stuff."

"Yes."

"Well, after you get a modification made, maybe you ought to migrate the way Merlin did to get into the new part."

Pucorl considered but Chanel said, "It won't work. Pucorl's too fat to fit in the pentagram now."

"Does that matter?" Jennifer asked. She thought Chanel was just tweaking Pucorl, but it was an interesting possibility. "I mean, do you need a pentagram to migrate, or is it just to control where you migrate to? After all, Pucorl already owns the van and presumably the modifications as well."

"I think we should ask Merlin," Pucorl said. "Wait a second. . . . Merlin says that the pentagram isn't really necessary, but it does help contain the magic. He thinks it would be an interesting experiment."

"And it might be a pretty good idea anyway," Annabelle added. "Building a pentagram that big, I mean. Because what if we want to enchant the Stanley Steamer we've been building, or other really big chunks of equipment?"

There were by this time several pentagrams, licensed and unlicensed, in Paris, enchanting everything from iron gauntlets to wagons, but the largest was only fifteen feet across. Pucorl was twenty-two feet long, six and a half feet wide, and eight feet tall. But the tall wasn't the issue. It was the long. To do the experiment they would need a bigger pentagram.

All this was pursuant to the final mods that Pucorl was undergoing so that he would be an asset to the sally that was planned for just as soon as Bertrand could pull it off.

"Can Bertrand wait another day while we try it?" Jennifer asked.

"I don't think he'll be ready tomorrow," Pucorl said. "You would be amazed at how many of the defenders on the walls of Paris were equipped with wooden mallets and the like, just because that's what the guilds thought they could afford. And the price of iron has gone up since we got here."

"From tiny seeds, great economic boons can grow," Jennifer said.

Paris, Armory

"Yes, Lord Constable, they are all equipped with steel weapons and steel tips on their lances." The armorer wasn't a pleasant man at the best of times. A third cousin of the king, he had his post because being armorer of Paris was a good paying job that didn't require much in the way of wit most of the time.

"And the horse armor?"

"That's a problem, but they are only horses."

"They—" Bertrand stopped himself. The man had a point. The issue with cold iron was its ability to inflict damage. As yet there was no evidence that it gave any protection against the creatures of the netherworld. Instead, he asked, "And the horse shoes?"

"About half are shod. The farriers are overwhelmed and good iron is more dear than a mother's breast. You will have to talk to the stable keepers, Constable." He finished with a snicker.

The title "constable" was originally the title for the king's stable keeper, so this was a way of offering Bertrand an insult that could not be answered as an insult.

"Very well," Bertrand agreed through gritted teeth. He knew he shouldn't let such things bother him. And the truth was, it wasn't the stable keepers—or even this asshole, as Roger would call him—that was bothering Bertrand. It was the time.

Last night had gone well along the walls, and yesterday Philip had not made his speech, apparently tired out by animating corpses through the night. The dead were not good fighters at all, and cold iron did an admirable job of not only battering the bodies but of also disrupting the magic that animated them. But Bertrand knew what was going on. Agents of Philip were slipping into Paris, trying to get a gate opened through treachery. Once that happened, only the dead would inhabit Paris.

Porte Saint-Denis, Paris
June 15, 1372

The gate was closed as the sun rose. But it had taken hard fighting to manage that after the traitors had tried to open it, had seized the gatehouse for almost five minutes, and had taken down the locking bar.

The sun shone down on blood and death, and the dead were not the only traitors.

Bertrand looked around, inhaled, and started to cough from the smoke. It had been a near thing. Not the unthinking yielding to Themis' power, but moneyed treason. And more like that would be coming.

They had to strike, and soon. Push the besiegers back, get some breathing room. Do more than that, because Bertrand knew war and sieges. He knew Paris was losing this siege. It would take days, or perhaps weeks, but even if they managed to push Philip back, they would lose. It wasn't a matter of supplies. With the Seine they could run the lines most nights, so the city could be supplied.

No, it was the presence of the army of the dead outside the walls. Men lost hope.

University of Paris, Small Courtyard

Pucorl was back here, in the much-enlarged pentagram, to test Jennifer's theory. A couple of Jennifer's theories, actually. She thought that when a demon enchanted an item, it changed its electromagnetic field in some ill-defined way. She had examined Pucorl and the devices that had been enchanted, even the drop forges and other fourteenth-century items, and said she couldn't be sure, not with her jerry-rigged equipment. So now she wanted to test the modifications to Pucorl's suspension and wheels, both before and after he "shifted."

Wilber started incanting, and Pucorl felt the ties between him and the van weaken. He still owned it, so there was still a connection, but it no longer enclosed him. Still, even after he was fully outside the van, he still had its shape. With an effort of will, he resumed his puck shape, but he gave it up quickly and let himself flow back into the van. As he did, he felt the modifications, the springs and controls that let him lift his wheels and turn all four wheels up to ninety degrees become natural and integrated. He could feel his new parts like they were his doors or seats, and he had a level of comfort and control that he had never had before.

Carefully staying within the pentagram, he rotated one hundred and eighty degrees. He could turn on a dime.

Then the incantation faded away and Pucorl was Pucorl again. His body his even more than before. He started his engine and rolled out of the pentagram.

Jennifer wanted to get her electronic gear up next to his axles, but Bertrand was standing in the university courtyard in full armor with his horse. "No. You can look after the sally, Mademoiselle. We delayed for this only because I was told that doing so might enhance Pucorl's ability in the field. But if we are to sally, it must be in daylight and there is not much of that left today. Did it work, Sir Pucorl?"

"It did, Lord Constable. I am fleeter of foot—well, of

wheel—than I was, and shall leap across the fields as though they were autobahns."

Annabelle rolled her eyes. "Trust Pucorl to make a joke."

"But, Annabelle, I'm not joking," Pucorl said, sounding hurt.

Annabelle just shook her head and opened the door to climb in. If Pucorl was going, she was going. She even had a double-barreled pistol that the smith had made and Wilber had enchanted, and a shoulder holster for it.

"You're overdoing the innocent act, Pucorl," Roger said as he climbed into the body of the van along with Bill, Jeff, Liane, and Monsignor Savona. Wilber rode Meurtrier. The other twenty-firsters would be staying in the city.

Pucorl turned his wheels and rolled out of the courtyard while Wilber and Bertrand were still mounting. They made their way to the Porte Saint-Denis where Bertrand's men waited.

Porte Saint-Denis, Paris

The gates were flung open and Pucorl poured on the gas—well, the olive oil that filled his fuel tank. His tires bit into the dirt of the road, in a combination of rubber and magic, and he was accelerating out and around to the pavilion where Philip the Bold made his headquarters.

He screeched his horn, frightening the horses of the enemy, but the dead were unaffected. Pucorl ran them down, cutting a hole in the enemy forces that Bertrand's army could exploit, but he was going faster than Bertrand or his horses could follow. Pucorl was doing fifty kilometers per hour, according to his speedometer.

Suddenly Pucorl spun. It was a maneuver he had never tried before. It involved turning his front wheels to the right and his back wheels to the left in a coordinated way. He nearly flipped because his timing was a little off and—magic aside—he was ripping up the soil of the field as though he was a plow on steroids. Now he was going backward, but his top speed in reverse wasn't nearly that fast, and he quickly slowed, pushing all his passengers against the seat back.

He opened his passenger section sliding door and Roger climbed out. In a surprisingly agile move, Roger climbed onto Pucorl's roof. Pucorl moved again, but now he had to be more careful, lest Roger be thrown from his perch.

****

Philip the Bold came running out of his pavilion and the wounded demon lord followed. Philip leapt on his horse, raised Themis above his head, then charged.

****

Bertrand was cursing a blue streak. The damned idiot van had rushed off to be a hero and it didn't make sense. Pucorl wasn't the sort to do that, especially not with Annabelle in the front seat. The van wasn't given to proving his courage, and he was certainly not going to do it when it put Annabelle in danger. Bertrand was not so bright as either his wife or his monarch, but one thing he did have going for him was that he thought clearly in a crisis. All the possibilities and byways that an admittedly brighter man might find to lock them into stasis in a fight faded away in Bertrand's mind as he focused on the here and now.

Here and now, he had an opening in the enemy's ranks. He had divided their forces and had access to both the dead and the living forces under Philip's command. Pucorl would just have to deal with the consequences of his actions. Bertrand had a fight to win.

****

Roger lay on the roof of Pucorl with Brown Bess, his rifled musket with the magicked barrel and aimed. He looked down the sights and saw Philip the Bold on a big charger, riding hell for leather at them.

He took a deep breath and held it. Then he pulled the trigger. The spring sent the hammer into the barrel, and the tiny salamander that lived in a cave in the metal came out to play. Between one heartbeat and the next, it flowed out of the cave, found the corned powder that Roger had made, and danced among it, igniting each and every kernel and every bit of powder.

It was great fun, and when the salamander was done, every bit of the powder was expended. And very hot gas, gas heated even more as Bessy the salamander danced all up and down the bore of the barrel, forced the bullet into flight.

There was a sharp crack, the sort of crack you would expect from a twenty-first century rifle like a .30-06, not the sort you would expect from a black powder musket, and a very hot lead Minié ball spun down range at just over one and a half times the speed of sound.

****

Themis felt the salamander dance. She was the liege and the land of the salamander, but Themis felt a very great deal and she didn't, in the instant, put together the salamander's dance with any threat to the owner of the sword that contained and restricted her. She didn't realize that there was a threat until the Minié ball had almost reached them. Even then she could have stopped it if she had understood how quickly it was moving.

But she didn't understand. Themis was a Titan in a world where lightning moved at a visible rate, where light itself was slow in its propagation. The ball slid past the blade before it could interpose itself.

Philip never knew a thing until the bullet punched through his breast bone and ripped a divot out of his back, including two and a half inches of his back bone. Then he knew nothing at all.

****

For just a moment, everything stopped.

Every dead body that Themis had animated stopped their attack.

The living men who had been called by Philip's siren call stopped as they suddenly wondered what they had done and why.

And a diminished demon lord howled in frustration.

****

The diminished demon lord was quick to react. He reached for the sword, then stopped. To lay his hand on that sword was to contend with Themis, and he wasn't the sword's owner, so he

304

didn't have the power over it that its true owner would have.

He spun, seeking Duke John, the next in line after Philip. "Take up the sword!" he bellowed. "Become king of France!"

John, thirty yards away, still mounting his horse, looked at the demon and the sword and shook his head. He wasn't sure of much of anything. With the pressure that Philip had borrowed from Themis no longer pushing against him and seeing the hole in Philip's back, picking up the sword seemed a bad idea. The demon lord had never bothered to hide his contempt for mortals from John since only the sword wielder had mattered to him.

****

Roger climbed to his feet and, standing on the van, shouted. "I, Roger McLean, by right of conquest, do hereby claim the sword Themis as my lawful plunder! Let no man lay hands on it without first answering my claim!"

It was by the code chivalric, or at least the netherworld equivalent of the code chivalric.

Pucorl blared, "Hold on, Roger!" then drove straight at the demon lord.

The demon lord had faced Pucorl before, and hadn't enjoyed the experience. He didn't think of escaping to the netherworld. He couldn't, not in the face of a puck, nor could he face that monster van. He dove and laid his clawed black talon on the sword Themis . . . and his arm turned to stone. It turned to granite, and then crumbled to dust as Themis, completely within the bounds of propriety, acted to defend herself from being stolen . . . and in so doing, confirmed Roger McLean's ownership.

CHAPTER 24

Battlefield, outside Paris
June 15, 1372

Pucorl hit the demon lord—what was left of the demon lord—without slowing at all.

Demons are not physical in the sense that mortals are. They consume one another, and mix and change under a completely distinct set of natural laws. All relations between their universe and the human universe are translation effects. Pucorl didn't eat the demon lord. He subsumed it. Restructured it, and made it part of him. That he could do so was a function of its weakened state, Pucorl's possession of the van, and the cold iron disrupting its structure as Pucorl drove through it.

The demon lord had already been partly consumed by Themis, and Pucorl's power was greatly magnified by the van. But more than anything, it was the disruption of the cold iron that effectively chopped Beslizoswian up into bite size chunks. Well, really, closer to mush.

The effect, the feeling, was something that no demon could ever explain to a mortal, but in demonic terms Pucorl got a whole lot bigger. Pucorl's territory got bigger too, for in his own small way Chevalier Pucorl too was his land, just as Themis was hers.

****

The van came to a halt after running over the demon lord, and Roger didn't know what had happened. The van suddenly seemed more solid in a way that Roger couldn't define. It shook him, and for a few heartbeats, he just stood on the top of the van and felt the power of its reality. Then Clausewitz beeped at him and said, "Get the sword, lad. Let Pucorl worry about Pucorl." Roger did have a bit of Bertrand du Guesclin's ability to put aside the complexities and just do it. He shook off the effect.

Roger, obeying some instinct, didn't jump down onto the field. Instead, he simply held out his hand and shouted, "Themis, come to me!"

And the sword was there in his hand, five feet long and glowing with power, but light as a feather. Roger had been coached about this by Raphico and Merlin, but now in the moment, feeling the demigod of more than law—really, the demigod of proper behavior, he was beyond himself. He felt the force of her power, felt it in his hands, and knew he could control it. And, in a moment of complete clarity, knew that it would be wrong to do so.

In any number of small ways, up until that moment, Roger McLean had been a bully. He had pushed others around, mostly to prove to himself that he could. But now, feeling the raw power that might let him force everyone in the world to his will, he didn't.

"Themis," he thought as he looked around, *"this is wrong. It is not what you represent."* He felt a powerful urge to release her right here and right now. But the lessons held, at least somewhat. "Clausewitz," he said, "get in touch with Raphico and Merlin. Get me the words."

"On it, General," Clausewitz responded. Then, in words of a language that no mortal was ever meant to hear, the words spilled forth. Words that informed Themis to return the dead she had resurrected to their graves, then release the demons she had commanded to them.

And Themis resisted.

It was not until then that Roger realized just how pissed off a demigod can be. It was not, in any sense, that Roger could understand the demigod's words. Themis was placed in the sword in such a way that she couldn't speak. That formation of the spell was quite intentional on the part of Beslizoswian, but so great

307

was her rage that it leaked through the spell. And besides, his claim on the sword was imperfect. Acquisition by right of conflict was an accepted concept in both realms, but Philip's death wasn't in a formal duel. Who owned the goods of one slain in battle was subject to question. Philip's family and his king both had legitimate claims. Charles had a strong claim, so even though Roger's claim was acknowledged by Themis in coming to his hand, the claim wasn't anything like unquestioned.

What all those legalisms came down to was that he couldn't suppress Themis' will to the same extent Philip had been able to. So Roger didn't get any of the details. Instead, he got a feeling of rage that he sensed would not be a good thing for France should it get loose. Meanwhile, the dead were no longer attacking but they weren't retreating either.

Roger stood on the roof of Pucorl, wrapped in a halo of golden light, and every eye turned to him.

****

John, Duke of Berry, woke from the half-hypnotized state the magic had held him in and realized that he was no longer compelled. He looked around and saw a large young man in a mix of clothing, part from this century and part, he guessed, from that other time the twenty-firsters came from. The young man was standing on the magic van and holding the sword of royalty up in his right hand.

The sword glowed as it never had for Philip.

Was this the true Arthur out of legend?

John decided that he had no desire to find out. He turned to his men. "Let us depart this place. We return to Berry."

Once he got home, John would have to send emissaries to Charles and probably have to debase himself, perhaps lose some of his lands to the crown. But Charles wouldn't want a war, so he would be reasonable.

At least, that's what John hoped would happen.

****

Bertrand looked around and the dead had stopped fighting.

Stopped even defending themselves. They just stood there looking at the van. Gradually, his men stopped fighting too, after they slowed enough to realize that no one was swinging a sword at them. The living among Philip's army, far outnumbered by the dead but still upwards of five thousand strong, were now starting to run. Bertrand's men could pursue, but the army of the dead was still there, not doing anything, just looking at the van.

No, Bertrand realized. Not the van. Roger McLean standing on the van surrounded by a halo of righteous wrath, holding the sword Themis that was now a sword of fire.

"Wilber," Bertrand shouted, "what's going on?" He looked around and saw Wilber on Meurtrier, riding off toward the van.

Bertrand was delayed then by the necessity of making sure that his army didn't fall apart. The enemy had stopped fighting and though Bertrand didn't think so, it might still be a ruse. So he spent some minutes making sure that his commanders knew what he wanted done.

****

Monsignor Giuseppe Savona climbed out of the van and, using Pucorl's armor as a ladder, climbed onto the roof of the van where Roger was arguing with the sword Themis. Giuseppe held up Raphico, who joined the argument, then almost lost his balance as Pucorl turned left and started moving. He didn't lose his balance because Pucorl wasn't accelerating very fast. It was quickly apparent that Pucorl was being careful to avoid dumping Roger, but at the same time was trying to get away from both armies.

Wilber rode up on Meurtrier, grabbed some of Pucorl's armor and swung onto the van, whinnying something at Meurtrier, who whinnied back, then was left behind as Pucorl went faster and faster.

"Smooth ride," Giuseppe said. The wind was whipping his cassock around, but a wagon or a carriage moving at this speed would be bouncing all over the field and threatening to throw them all off. Pucorl moved as though the field were a paved street.

Wilber snorted. "Yes." Then, as he climbed onto the roof said, "Even for a twenty-first century van with independent suspension, this is smooth. Not going to help us much if the wind blows us all off the roof, though." Wilber turned to Roger, who was still arguing with Themis. "Say, Roger, would you mind asking Themis to shield us from the wind? I don't want Pucorl to have to stop."

"What's going on, Wilber?" asked Giuseppe.

"Politics." There was a disgusted note in Wilber's tone. "Apparently, Themis is even more upset than everyone thought. Merlin thinks that if we just cut her loose, France is going to experience something along the line of Noah's flood. Meanwhile, you know what Charles has been saying about ownership of the sword. Bertrand would almost have to seize it for the king."

Gradually, the wind lessened as the discussion continued, and Pucorl moved ever faster away from the army. Giuseppe looked back to see Bertrand du Guesclin of France pulling up his horse, as it was now clear that there was no way he could catch them.

Walls of Paris

His Majesty Charles V stood looking out at the battle. He saw Philip fall and even in his anger was saddened by the sight. Then, as he saw the boy claim the sword, sadness turned to anger. That sword was his by right and owning it wouldn't pay for the damage it had done to his kingdom, even considering that Philip compelled it. The demons, especially the one in the sword, owed France—owed Charles—recompense for the damage they had done. And the twenty-firsters! It was a poor way to compensate Charles for his forbearance to take his sword.

He turned away from the wall and, using his two good arms, climbed down to the street below. Then he mounted a horse and rode for Porte Saint-Denis. By the time he had reached the battle, the van was gone.

He was in the field, surrounded by his army, which was surrounded by a large army of the dead. That larger army wasn't

310

fighting or attacking, nor was it running. It was just standing.

Within the Sword

The being men knew as Themis was diminished with each corpse she had animated. Not only a demon from her realm, but a part of herself, had been needed. When those demons were struck by cold iron, part of their substance and part of hers was disrupted and left in the mortal realm. Lost beyond recovery.

If she were to release the demons that still remained here, then that part of her that she had placed in each demon would not be recovered either. To recover that part of herself, she must touch each enchanted demon. She couldn't just release them without weakening herself still further.

She had been insulted, humiliated by the mortals. All of them had ignored her or compelled her, and she was Themis! Themis, whose true name stretched a thousand cycles. Retribution was owed, and while forgiveness was part of her, it wasn't the whole of her. Yes, she had forgiven Hera when Hera had come before her at Olympus. Had even offered her wine . . . but Hera had had to come to her to get it. And, in this case, Nemesis, the spirit of divine retribution, was not here to rage for her, though she knew that Nemesis was raging in the netherworld.

She would have had the demons follow her, but she couldn't, not on her own. She was still trapped within the sword and still needed instruction to compel the demon host to action. Once she had instruction, she could do so. Take the overriding instruction and parcel it out to each demon. That was well within her abilities. But she was still a prisoner within the sword. And the boy who, with some justice, held the sword insisted through his advisers that the dead be returned to their graves. He didn't *command* it. Roger McLean was . . .

Themis stopped her raging as she looked at the boy, for he was, in his way, truly one of hers. She felt with him the moment he had first held her, and in his gentleness and rightness had forborne to use her to command his fellows. For the first time she spoke to the demons who accompanied Roger—Clausewitz, Merlin, Pucorl, and Raphico.

****

In the mortal world, as the van drove along the field leaving the armies of France—living and dead—behind, Clausewitz spoke. "Roger, we have a problem."

"What's the trouble?"

"When Philip had her raise the dead, he did it by forcing her to use her own substance."

"What does that mean?"

"It means that little bits of Themis are stuck in all those corpses. That's what is keeping them from rotting."

"So why not just have her take it back?"

"Because she would have to touch each and every one of them to get it back. Just like she had to touch each and every one of them to restore the bodies in the first place. At least, touch the ground they were in. And if she takes herself back while the demons are left in, they are going to be badly damaged or destroyed as the corpses go from almost whole to dust and bone fragments in moments."

"So we release the demons first?" Roger asked more than said. He suspected it wouldn't be that simple.

"It's not that simple," Clausewitz said. "There's this sort of dynamic balance between the demons and Themis. If she cuts the demons loose, then even more of her is going to get sucked into the corpses."

"I knew it. Catch 22," Roger said. "So how do we get her and all the demons back where they belong?"

"The best way would be to go back to each gravesite and release each demon while Themis puts each corpse back in the ground."

"That won't work," Roger said. Then he spoke directly to the sword. "I'm sorry, Themis, but there just isn't time to do it that way. If we go back there, King Charles is going to claim you in recompense for the damage you have done to his realm."

312

Roger felt the hilt of the sword heat. Themis was mostly of earth and air, but for a being the size and strength of Themis, there was plenty of fire and water in her nature. Certainly enough fire to make the hilt of the sword containing her hot.

"If we go running around France sticking bodies back in the ground, he's going to catch up to us and make the same claim," Roger continued, not letting the heat slow him. "Should we have the host of the dead follow us? Would that help?"

The sword cooled noticeably and Clausewitz spoke up. "Themis thinks that might help, but . . ."

Roger didn't wait. "Call your army. Have them come to us at the place you were brought into this world. It might not get you all back together, but it's the best we can do at the moment."

Plain outside Paris

Bertrand looked around, distracted from the king by the sudden change in the situation. The dead were moving again, but not in attack. They were walking away, circling around Paris and crossing the Seine by the simple expedient of walking down into the river and back up the other side. They didn't attack. They just went around.

"What's going on?" Charles plaintively asked Lord Constable du Guesclin.

"Majesty, I have no idea. Wilber went riding off on that horse of his and climbed on the van. I have no one with a phone here."

"Well, get someone. Better yet, get *them*. All the twenty-firsters. Send cavalry back into Paris. I want all the twenty-firsters brought to me. And Doctor Delaflote as well." "Perhaps we should go back to the Hôtel Saint-Pol, Majesty. The siege appears to be lifted."

Charles considered that. It had been some years since he had spent much time on horseback, and his backside was telling him about it even after so short a time in the saddle. It didn't hurt, but if he spent the day on horseback, it would. Peevishly, he agreed.

Royal Palace, Hôtel Saint-Pol

Amelia Grady stood in the throne room, caught between fear and outrage. She, Jennifer, Lakshmi, and Paul had been summoned to the throne room "to answer for the actions of your fellows."

It hadn't helped that Tiphaine wanted to accompany them, but the guards had refused her permission. Amelia looked over at Gabriel Delaflote; his whole demeanor spoke of concern, without the outrage that she felt. *Vive la révolution*, she thought. *It can't come soon enough to suit me.*

Charles came into the throne room with Bertrand on his heels. He stormed past them to take a seat on his throne. Bertrand and Gabriel went to both knees and looked like they were considering getting down on their bellies. Her pride tried to compel her to stand, but Paul standing beside her destroyed that impulse. She knelt before the king, not because she believed he deserved such honors, but because she wasn't willing to risk Paul's life over it. Jennifer was looking at her, shocked, and she gestured peremptorily for the girls to kneel. Lakshmi looked over the situation and curtsied, like a flower bending to the sun.

"Where have they gone?" King Charles demanded of no one in particular.

Bertrand turned to them. "Perhaps your phones?"

Amelia pulled out Laurence, Lakshmi pulled out Marilyn, Jennifer pulled out Martha, and Paul pulled out Green Lantern. The Green Lantern glowed in the throne room.

"Call Pucorl," Amelia said.

"Calling," said Laurence. Then, in Pucorl's voice, "What can I do for you, Teach?"

"We are in the throne room, Pucorl, surrounded by guards and you're on speakerphone. Where are you?"

"As Dr. Frankenfurter said of Eddy, 'that's a bit of a delicate subject,' " Pucorl admitted.

"Pucorl, I don't need *Rocky Horror* references right now."

314

Especially since Dr. Frankenfurter had chopped up Eddy and served him for dinner in the movie. *Rocky Horror* was one of Amelia Grady's guilty pleasures when it came to movies, which was why it was on Pucorl's hard drive.

"Sorry, Amelia," Pucorl said. "We're on the road dealing with a profoundly upset demi-goddess. Raphico says we should not return to Paris until Themis is returned to the netherworld."

"Raphico is not the king of France!" Charles shouted. "Nor has the church acknowledged him as an angel of the Lord!" More calmly, but still with considerable force, he continued. "Philip was killed in an act of treason. All his goods are rightfully the property of the crown and that includes his cursed sword."

"No, Your Majesty, she is not," said Roger Mclean. "There are several issues with your argument but there is one that I must bring forward. Philip was killed in combat by me. That gives me a claim on all his properties. Especially those that were on his person. You can have the rest, but the sword is my problem."

"That sword is mine," Charles insisted. "You are betraying your fealty to me, you treasonous whelp."

"Can't be," said the phone in Roger's voice. "I'm not one of your subjects and never have been."

"You bring my sword back here or I will hunt you down, thief!"

The only response was a click and Laurence saying, "They hung up."

Charles looked at the phone in shock, then said, "The twenty-firsters are my prisoners, Bertrand, hostages for the return of my sword. Take them and take their enchanted devices. I declare them forfeit to the crown for their support of treason." He stood and left the room.

****

Bertrand came over and held out a hand to Amelia Grady. "I'm sorry, but the king's orders are law."

"Your king," Amelia said, almost spitting the words, "has no right to my goods or my person. Laurence, call Shakespeare and

315

Sophocles. You are all to turn off and not turn back on until you are in my hands." Shakespeare was her computer and Sophocles her book reader. The phone's screen went blank.

Bertrand sighed and again held out his hand.

She didn't pass him the phone. Instead she said, "You will have to take it by force. I will take no action that can be taken to mean that I concede your king's right to steal my property."

Bertrand took the phone, but he had to wrench it out of her hand. The others took their cue from Mrs. Grady, and not one of the enchanted devices was active when he received it.

Paul, he noted, was quietly crying.

Chateau outside Paris
June 16, 1372

The chateau was abandoned. It was owned by a merchant who did a great deal of business in Burgundy and apparently had turned it over to Philip for his calling of Themis. It took Pucorl and the rest most of a day to find a bridge that let them cross the Seine. Pucorl, with all his improvements, wasn't up to swimming.

There was, to Pucorl's magical sense, a feeling of very strong magic barely controlled, and the pentagram was still there, virgin's blood and all. Themis had been forced to leave part of her substance in the pentagram. It was a rather disgusting feel. There was evil here that wouldn't be easy to undo.

"What do you think, Wilber?" Pucorl asked.

"Well, I'm not going to sacrifice another virgin," Wilber said. "Normally, it ought to be easier to send Themis back, but she is still pretty angry. Is there anything that Raphico can do, Monsignor Savona?"

They had traveled quickly, if the long way, and left the army of the dead behind. A few arrived every couple of minutes and Roger was touching each one with the sword. Each time he touched one, it collapsed into a mound of earth with bones sticking out. This was hardly sanctified ground and Monsignor

Savona wasn't happy with the idea of not returning the dead to their graves.

"Well, what would you have us do? According to Catvia, our people have been put in prison. If we don't get this done soon, we are going to be facing an army of the living."

Raphico was asked, and they became more systematic. The dead would line up and Raphico and Savona would walk along, sanctifying the ground. Roger followed, with Themis in his hand. The dead lay down and Roger touched them with the sword, returning them to the earth. They were transforming this whole area into a graveyard the size of Gettysburg. With each of the dead sent back to their long slumber, a demon was released back to the netherworld and Themis was a little bit restored.

****

Angry as she was, Themis couldn't help but feel that these people at least were trying to do the right thing, both by her and by their own dead. For all of that day and most of the next, they re-buried the dead, using magic and as much gentleness as they could.

The time they spent on that was time enough for word of where the dead were going to get back to Paris. And time enough for King Charles to send an army to get "his" sword back.

Dawn, June 18, 1372

"Roger, get back here," said Wilber's voice over the phone.

Roger, bleary eyed, used Themis to cut down a hedge row, making room for another corpse to lie down. "We aren't finished!" He hadn't slept since the battle and was still moving only through will and cussedness. He touched Themis to the corpse, and felt it as the life left, and it sank into the earth, leaving a grass covered mound. Now that the ground was sanctified, the dead were sinking into their *new* graves.

"You aren't going to finish," Wilber said. "Bertrand is coming and he brought an army with him. The ceremony is going to take hours and the dead are going to have to block Bertrand while we do it."

"Themis isn't going to like that," Roger said.

"I don't like it either," Wilber admitted, "but we have no choice unless Themis wants to be a permanent addition to the royal treasury of France."

Themis very much didn't want that, and she knew that they had tried. She felt it. Felt Roger McLean as he held her and worried how he might restore her while keeping the world safe from her anger. There was such a difference between Philip and Roger!

She decided in that moment that she would help. She would go back to the netherworld, taking as many of her demons as she could with her and trying at least to make a place for those left here.

The sword jerked in Roger's hand and Raphico spoke.

"Themis agrees to return. Let's get back to the pentagram."

CHAPTER 25

Near the Chateau de Pomf
Dawn, June 18, 1372

Bertrand du Guesclin lifted a hand as the army of the dead turned as one man and began to pick up any sort of weapon they could find.

His forces were equipped with cold iron and he didn't doubt that his army would win, for this was a much diminished force. But he also knew he would lose men in the fight. He didn't want this.

Then the army of the dead parted, and Pucorl drove out. No one was riding on his roof, but that didn't mean much. With his armor—armor provided by Bertrand—Pucorl was a weapon himself, and not one that Bertrand wanted to face. This was what the elephants must have seemed like when Hannibal used them against the Romans.

Pucorl came forward and Bertrand, by himself, rode to meet the van.

****

"What do you think you're doing?" Annabelle said as she got out of the van. The van's side door opened and Jeff and Liane came out as well.

"Where are Roger and Wilber?" Bertrand asked. "And Monsignor Savona?"

"They're back at the chateau, arranging your welcome. We know about cold iron, you know. And we have our own tricks.

319

This is wrong, Lord Constable. Themis needs to be returned to the netherworld, for the safety of this world as well as for the netherworld. Her absence is a threat to the balance of power in the netherworld, and her presence is a disaster waiting to happen in this world."

"I am a man under orders," Bertrand said. "I have a duty."

"Fine. Let's negotiate. You might be able to convince me to let the sword return to Charles."

Bertrand wasn't fooled. He knew that Annabelle was out here to delay him. But, for the moment, at least until King Charles got here, he would let himself be delayed. So they talked.

At the Chateau

Monsignor Savona carried Raphico around the pentagram, never letting his feet touch it, but making very sure that the light from Raphico's screen touched it everywhere.

The blood of innocents was still there but, to the best of Raphico's ability, the pentagram was cleansed. Roger set Themis in the center of the pentagram and stepped out. He was a legitimate owner of the sword, so he would have to be the one releasing Themis. He walked out of the pentagram to the protective circle and stood next to Wilber. Then, repeating the words Wilber and Merlin gave him, he started incanting. He felt the magic and wondered what insanity would make a man try to chain something like this. Themis was a god or as close to a god as Roger ever wanted to meet. She was raw power, enough to level mountains—no, level mountain *ranges*. Surely the duke of Burgundy had to have felt that. Then, in an instant, he knew that no, Philip had not felt it. He was prevented from feeling it by the demon who had advised him. Roger knew that because now, partially released from the prison of the sword, Themis could tell him—and did.

****

There was a glow to the east, but it wasn't the sun. Bertrand du Guesclin looked at the golden nimbus that surrounded the whole chateau. Then he looked at Annabelle, and said, "I think we should talk a bit more."

She grinned at him.

****

Roger continued to incant. He was hearing the syllables from both Wilber and Themis now. She stood before him, golden and glowing, holding a sword in one hand and a scale in the other. She wasn't blindfolded, but other than that she could be confused with a statue of justice, a golden, glowing statue of justice that was tall enough to touch the sky.

And yet Roger knew that wasn't quite right. As much as she might be seen as the lawgiver by later ages, she was in truth the goddess of decency, of right behavior. It wasn't Themis who came after you if you did wrong.

It was almost done now, and Roger gave himself to it entirely, to return Themis to her proper place.

Yet, not all of her could go. She, a whole nation, had been contained in a sword and that sword had been irrevocably changed by what it held. It was different in structure because each atom, each proton or electron or quark had been re-ordered by Themis' presence. That could not be undone.

The sword would remain a link to Themis and suddenly Roger was reminded of Jeff. Poor, stupid Jeff—but *honorable* Jeff. Jeff who had given his computer to Catvia, his watch to Coach, and his phone to Asuma. Jeff, who Roger now realized, might well be the wisest of them all.

So in that last moment he gave the sword of Themis to Themis.

As he watched, the sword in her hand was transformed to a torch. A glowing torch of liberty, and the scales became a book.

Now Roger truly recognized her. Lady Liberty, lifting her torch beside the golden door. Not license, but freedom for all, respect for one another.

****

Themis felt it. The sword that *was* her, that bore her structure, was given to her. She was manumitted.

Themis had never been a god of liberty, not truly. She was the embodiment of right behavior, perhaps even of propriety if you stretched a point. Not of individuals, but of community.

Themis didn't free slaves. She simply made sure they were treated properly. She had never been a slave before Philip and never freed a slave either. Now she was changed. It was partly her enslavement. She understood in a way she never had before the plight of the slave and their just resentment of it.

But mostly she was changed by Roger McLean, a bully of a boy who had somehow grown into a great man. A man so great that he would facilitate the greatness of a god. Roger hadn't understood the effect his gift would have. He had just given it.

But in that moment as he manumitted her, he had changed the nature of the world, of the netherworld, and in a way, of his own world. Freedom was now embedded in proper behavior. Slavery was wrong as it never had been before.

Now she returned to the netherworld, and as she did she cleaned up a few things. She restored the demons that she had previously ordered into the restored corpses, then released them from the corpses and instead sent them to the nearest items so they would not decay. And to each of them she gave the choice, as Roger had given her the choice: to stay or to go. To move to an object and stay there, or to simply use that object as a temporary home until they returned to her in the netherworld.

And, mostly because she couldn't help it, she left a little of herself in the sword.

****

The glow died away, and in a spreading circle centered on the chateau, the army of the dead collapsed into earth and bone.

Then Annabelle's phone rang.

Annabelle held up a finger and Bertrand waited. She pulled the phone from her pocket and said, "Annabelle Cooper-Smith. Who is calling, please?"

"Raphico," said the phone, sounding more amused than

anything. "We're done. You want to come pick us up? We'll go back to Paris."

Royal Palace, Hôtel Saint-Pol
June 20, 1372

Roger wasn't in cuffs, nor was he disarmed or physically restrained. That was because he was wearing across his back a five-foot-long sword that was so shiny it glowed and so sharp it could cut atoms. Bertrand had wisely declined to force the issue. Instead, Roger had been allowed to sleep for a day while tempers cooled.

One look at the expression on Charles V's face and Roger knew that the tempers cooling hadn't worked particularly well, at least as far as the king was concerned.

"Is it true that you released Themis back to the netherworld, disregarding my rights both as liege lord and elder brother of Philip the Traitor?"

"Yes," Roger said. "By right of combat I claimed and continue to claim the sword to do with as I see fit. What I saw fit to do was send Themis home in order to protect the netherworld and this world as well."

"Such a claim should have come to me for judgment."

Roger kept his mouth shut. The idea of conflict of interest and recusal wasn't in common use in the fourteenth century, not when it came to kings not getting what they wanted. Snorting in derision—tempting as it was—wasn't a good option.

"So," Charles continued, "having stolen my sword and released its power to the detriment of France, you now stand before me wearing the empty shell on your back. You are arrogant."

He glared at the Constable. "Bertrand, why have you allowed him to carry the vessel that held Themis? Is it that you plan to assuage my just wrath by returning to me a shadow of what is mine?"

He shifted his glare back to Roger. "Well, it will not do. You owe me the power of Themis and you cannot make good the debt. All your goods are forfeit and the goods of your fellow twenty-firsters as well."

Up to that moment Roger had been willing to let it go, apologize and give Charles the sword—which, even if it no longer held Themis still acted as a doorway to her and such of her powers as she chose to grant the wielder. Even to grovel if that was what it took. Not any more. Suddenly his hand went up and his fingers wrapped around the hilt of the Sword of Themis. The sword came free and he pointed it at the ceiling. "You claim this sword as your royal right? As the king of France? Fine. Draw it from the stone." He reversed the sword and drove it into the floor of the throne room.

The floor of the throne room did not crack. Instead it rippled as though it was made of water or jello and the sword slid through tiles that formed a mosaic on the floor without disrupting them. The sword stood in the center of the throne room, a foot of blade and another foot of hilt sticking up.

The legends of Arthur Pendragon were known in France at this time. Robert de Boron had written poems about them, including the bit about drawing the sword from the stone.

When Roger put the sword in the stone floor of the throne room it was not just a challenge to the justice of Charles' ruling on the matter of the twenty-firsters, but a threat to his legitimacy as king of France.

So there, dickhead, Roger thought.

Dungeon of the Bastille
June 20, 1372

Roger, Wilber, Jeff, Annabelle, Bill, and Liane were put into the cell that already contained Mrs. Grady, Paul, Jennifer, and Lakshmi. Mostly they were put in gently enough, but Roger was tossed, with vigor, into the cell.

"Sorry, guys," Roger said. "I just had to."

Annabelle laughed. "Considering you didn't shove Themis up his ass, I figure you showed great restraint."

"That's all very well," Amelia said, "but I have Paul to think—"

"Mom, *no!*" Paul shouted. "You can't keep doing that." He looked like he was about to cry, but he didn't. After sniffling a little, he added: "I don't want you to be a coward for me. Daddy wouldn't want that. You have to do what's right."

"He's right, ma'am," said Lakshmi. "I'm scareder than I ever have been. Scareder than I was when Beslizoswian attacked the chateau. But Paul is right. We can't let ourselves be turned into a bunch of fourteenth-century serfs."

"It wouldn't have made any difference anyway," Bill said. "Old Charlie was lusting after our stuff from the moment we arrived, and we were going to keep it only as long as we were more useful to him than our stuff would be. I think he miscalculated anyway. Now we're pissed. Wait a second. . . . I think I know what this is about. He figures that if he brings enough pressure on us, we'll give him the stuff just to get him off our backs. It's extortion under color of law. Well, this is the fourteenth century, so he probably does have a legal right to do it."

"Bill, what are you talking about?" Wilber asked.

"Sorry. Legalese. It's like when a cop stops you and tells you he's going to give you a ticket unless you 'give' him something he wants. Or when a building inspector shuts you down just because he's pissed. My dad was all over color of law in a couple of civil rights cases where cops were harassing blacks and gays."

"But in this case what he's doing is really legal by fourteenth-century law, just not just," Roger said. "Gotcha. But how do we get out of here?"

"I don't have a clue, but giving him our enchanted computers is probably not a good idea," Bill said.

Royal Treasury

Catvia turned herself on. It was easy. She owned her computer,

325

and the energy that ran it was of her substance or close enough. Over the Bluetooth, she called Asuma and got Asuma to call Pucorl. "Pucorl, where are you?"

"I am in the royal stables at the Hôtel Saint-Pol," Pucorl said. "I thought it best not to make an issue of it for now. Bertrand asked politely enough. I think he understands rather better than Charles just what is going on."

"Well, I have a question. You're going to the Elysian Fields, right?"

"Yes. And I'm bigger than I used to be."

"How would you like a grove of dryads?" Catvia asked and heard Asuma's gasp of surprise over the Bluetooth connection. Catvia and Asuma were succubi, but the difference between a succubus and a dryad was where they sat on what a twenty-firster might call the energy gradient, and a fourteenther would call one of the levels of the netherworld or crystal spheres of Heaven. The divide between the levels was much more fluid in the netherworld. That was why Pucorl was able to move from one of what might be called the upper levels of Hell or Purgatory to the Elysian Fields. It also meant that as an independent entity who owned her own vessel, Catvia was able to offer allegiance to Pucorl and, with a bit of help, take her whole grove with her.

"That's an interesting proposal, Catvia, and I will certainly consider it. But you do realize that it's not without a cost to me."

That was true. It would mean that Pucorl would be feeding the grove from his substance, at least in part. But Pucorl had a lot of substance now.

And Catvia had a hole card. "I think we can help you get Annabelle out of the dungeon."

"Keep talking," Pucorl said.

"They missed Coach!"

"They also missed Merlin, at least the part of Merlin that is in Wilber's internal implant. They took the external unit, but Merlin was in the internal unit as well. And he's still connected."

"Sure. But Coach is a faun, and a faun from my and Asuma's

grove."

"What does that mean?" Pucorl asked.

"We have a connection. I can use it to get into their cell."

"And once your grove becomes part of my lands, they could travel from your grove to my lands, and from my lands in the netherworld to me here."

"That's the plan," Catvia agreed, "but it's going to take our grove some time to join you."

"We need to let them know what's going on. I'll talk to Merlin."

Dungeon of the Bastille

Wilber heard Merlin's voice. That was because a tiny piece of the demon was still inside Wilber. He listened as Merlin explained Catvia's plan. "How long is it going to take?"

"It is probably going to be some weeks in your realm, some time longer in the netherworld. Time doesn't always flow at the same rate in both realms, though since the curtains were ripped away, the times have come to align more."

"That doesn't sound like fun, but I think we can survive it. As long as they don't pull out the thumb screws or try starving us. So, how exactly is this going to work?"

"Catvia will return to the grove. Then Coach will return to the grove, taking Jeff with him. Then, removing himself from Jeff's wrist, Coach will wait there while Catvia takes Jeff to the treasury. In the treasury, Jeff will gather up the other enchanted devices and Catvia will return them all and Jeff to the grove. There, Jeff will again put Coach on and return to the cell, carrying the devices. Then, when the grove has joined with Pucorl's lands, you will be able to walk from the grove to Pucorl's garage, leap into Pucorl and return to the mortal world outside your cell."

"But locked in the royal stables," Wilber said. "I grant that's a much better situation than a dungeon, especially with Pucorl to carry us out of the stables while we make a run for it. We should wait to make the transfers until the grove and Pucorl's lands are attached. Either that or we should all go to the grove now and stay there while we wait."

"I would recommend against that. It will likely be some cycles in the time of the netherworld before the two places are joined."

"Is that like years?"

"Or cycles of the galaxy," Merlin clarified. "You might all be long dead by the time that the cycles line up again. I honestly don't know which of the cycles in the netherworld will pass. It might seem a few days, or it might seem a few of your centuries, or a few million years. It is not a good field with which to experiment. Time is much more contiguous in the mortal realm than in the netherworld."

"Right. We stay in the cell."

Then Wilber explained the plan to the rest of them. Mrs. Grady wasn't overly pleased at the idea of Paul in a dryad's grove, but as long as it was a short visit on the way out of the cell, she would put up with it.

The Grove of Dryads

Jeff dreamed. He was in Catvia's grove and there was a breeze fluttering the leaves of the trees. He walked away from the trees and one of the dryads called him back. It was a dryad who had not been in the mortal world, but she pointed and Jeff could see the grasses of the field shifting like water flowing around the small clump of trees. He went back to Catvia's tree and, ah, frolicked with Catvia, providing energy to the grove.

Then they talked about the plan.

Royal Palace, Hôtel Saint-Pol
June 21, 1372

It was three in the morning. The guards on the throne room were outside the doors. Charles V set the candle on the floor and carefully reached out a hand and laid it on the sword hilt. He wrapped his fingers around the hilt and pulled. Nothing happened. It didn't even quiver. In all truth, Charles hadn't expected to be able to draw the sword, but he had to try. He was the legitimate king of France, so there had been a tiny thread of hope. He reached out his other hand and with both hands pulled for all he was worth.

Nothing.

He got down on his hands and knees and looked at the place where the sword entered the stone floor. The floor was an inlay of fine stone work, different colors of stone, red, blue, purple, and green. The sword had cut through two of the inlaid tiles, a purple and a green. But where the sword entered the stone there was a sheen of silver in the marble inlays. As though the substance of the sword had melded with and expanded into the surrounding stone.

Using the sword to help, Charles stood, picked up the candle, and walked slowly to the throne. Charles wasn't stupid, not usually. Nor, usually, was he quick to anger. But Philip's betrayal and the demonic invasion of the world—especially the dead rising to his brother's banner—was a disaster of biblical proportions. Altogether too close to the book of Revelations for Charles' comfort.

Then, when Philip was killed and the twenty-firster took the sword and ran off, not even returning the dead to their graves, Charles saw the whole thing starting up again.

Now he sat on his throne, looked out at the sword sticking two feet up out of the floor of his throne room, and knew he was in trouble. Charles was a king and the son of a king. He knew how kingship worked. He knew how important it was to be seen as legitimate. That sword sticking out of the floor of his throne room was a constant challenge to Charles' legitimacy as king. To *anyone's* legitimacy as king of France. Edward III of England could use Charles' inability to draw the sword to bolster his claim to the throne, but that would have the drawback that once Edward got here, he wouldn't be able to draw it either.

Charles considered. He could spike that wheel by inviting Edward to come give it a try. That would help for the moment, but at the same time it would almost be an acknowledgement that whoever could pull the sword from the stone was the rightful king of France.

And there was at least one person who Charles was fairly confident *could* pull the cursed thing from the floor of his throne room. Roger I, king of France, did not sound well to Charles' ears.

Almost, Charles sent for the headsman when his thoughts reached that point. But he remembered in time that reacting too quickly was what had put him in this position in the first place. Also, if he called the headsman, he would be calling him to the throne room . . . and that cursed sword would be right there.

That much he would do. He would move back to the palace on the Île de la Cité. At least for now. No matter how much it stank.

Creaking in every bone and aching in every muscle, Charles rose and returned to his bedchamber.

CHAPTER 26

University of Paris
June 21, 1372

In the small courtyard, Gabriel Delaflote summoned a demon to enchant a wagon. It was a new design of wagon, using leaf springs and independent suspension. It was to be pulled by a team of horses, but there was a contraption of springs that would be charged by its motion over the road so that it would be able to go up hills with greater ease. He finished the incantation and the demon fitted itself into the wagon body. It was, Delaflote knew from its name, one of the demons that Philip had raised. There was an odd little whine in the third syllable of their names now, a result of the experience. Also, a number of them chose not to return to the netherworld, preferring to be placed in an artificial vessel.

"Well, Archimedes, how does it like its new vessel?" Delaflote asked the crow that rode his shoulder.

"Well enough, but it is a she."

That surprised Delaflote. He knew that demons didn't normally have gender, at least not in the same way that mortals did. "Why? Is it that you consider wagons, like ships, to be female?"

"No, but she was raised to the body of a woman, and the habits of that form left an impression. It will be a long time before she can again choose her gender in the way that is normal for our kind. I am a male in this form, but I am not tied to it the way she was."

It wasn't an unusual tale, though Delaflote hadn't been aware of the gender issues involved. All the demons Philip raised with the help of Themis were locked into the corpses and needed to be actively released to get out. That Themis did it to them, even under coercion, damaged their faith in their land and liege.

Archimedes was able to give Gabriel names of demons with their consent because they didn't want to go back to Themis.

The goddess of right behavior among the gods was much diminished. And the long term effects of that diminishment were impossible to predict.

"What about the twenty-firsters?" Delaflote asked.

"I'm not equipped with Bluetooth," Archimedes cawed at him. "I will need to get close to one to ask."

"Very well. After sunset," Delaflote said quietly. "I understand that the king is moving back to the palace on the island. It strikes me that the enchanted devices are likely to be transferred as well."

"Why do you want to know?" Archimedes asked.

"I want to help them if I can." He turned away and started the long climb back to his room at the top of the tower. Gabriel Delaflote now had enough money for lower rooms, but had determined that he liked the tower. He was considering having an enchanted elevator put in.

Windsor Castle, England
July 2, 1372

Edward III looked at the bowing courtier in something like shock. "Really?" he chortled. "This Roger stuck an enchanted sword into the stone floor?" He looked over at his eldest son, Edward of Woodstock. A series of treatments based on the twenty-firsters' knowledge had been tried on the illness and one of them seemed to have been at least fairly effective. He was looking better and gaining weight. Edward looked back at the courtier.

"Yes, Your Majesty. I saw the sword itself the next day. The chamberlain of the Hôtel Saint-Pol has set up a small exclusive business showing people the sword. King Charles ordered the room locked, but the chamberlain has the keys."

"Charles can't like that." Edward chortled again. Then he shrugged. "But, then, who is going to tell him?"

"Bertrand would, but I think in this case Bertrand du Guesclin is not pleased with his sovereign."

King Edward leaned back in his throne and scratched at his beard. "I don't think we want to follow this road. At some point I, or one of my sons, would be called on to pull the sword from the stone. Tell me, what did this Roger say when he stuck the sword in the stone?"

"He said 'You claim this sword as your royal right? As the king of France? Fine. Draw it from the stone.' "

"So," Edward scratched again. "The boy actually challenged his legitimacy? At least, it can be interpreted that way." Edward sat forward, his eyes intent. "Do you think the boy is planning to make a try for the throne?"

Now it was the courtier's turn to consider. "It's hard to say, Majesty. The twenty-firsters, from all I have heard, are from a republic with consuls, not kings. Besides, from all reports, the reason that Charles was so angry with him was that he released Themis from the sword."

"If Themis was released the sword is no longer enchanted?" Edward of Woodstock asked more than said.

"So it would seem to me, as well. But that's what I was told. They say that with Themis, her presence permanently changed the sword. One version is that it's a doorway to Themis that lets her come if she is willing. Another is that a little piece of Themis still resides in the sword, and even that small piece is greater than one of the fey who ride the nights away in wild hunts on the moors."

"What say you, my son?" King Edward asked. "Charles is weakened, so our claim is bolstered."

"True, Father, and it's a tempting thought. But as we are just now reminded, there are the wild hunts, the dragon at Loch Ness, leprechauns in Ireland passing fairy gold to buy ale and meat. Most of all, I would not want to march an army into Paris, then be called on to pull the sword from the stone. Much as I might wish it otherwise, I am not Arthur Pendragon."

"Neither am I," Edward III of England acknowledged. "What news of Olivier de Clisson?"

"Once Philip left the coast, Olivier moved most of his troops back to Normandy, but he's left a small force on Jersey. I think he wants an independent dukedom. We might be able to buy him at least to neutrality by offering him terms."

The discussion continued, turning back to more domestic issues, but the claim of England on the crown of France was still there, as it had been before the loosing of the veils. There were wizards abroad in England now, calling up demons to teach them the mystical arts and the arts of the twenty-firsters were starting to seep out of Paris. The balance of power was unbalanced . . . but these men were used to that. It had always been so.

The Papal Palace in Avignon
July 8, 1372

Pope Gregory sat in his private office and read over the scroll. He would not move the papacy back to Rome. By now he knew the results of such a move, and they were not particularly good for his faction of the church. Besides which, King Charles had been seriously weakened, both by his brother's trafficking with demons and now by Roger McLean's stunt with the sword.

The church had its own sources. Between what Giuseppe Savona sent him and what was available in the papal libraries, they had a college of church wizards right here in Avignon. No one had tried to call a titan and no one would so long as Gregory was pope, but angels of the Lord had been called on to offer advice.

He pulled another sheet of vellum from his desk and began to write.

Giuseppe, my friend,

Be of what help you can to the twenty-firsters. Our best information is that the Lord is quite pleased with them, especially Roger McLean who, though greatly tempted, turned aside from that temptation.

I think we will need the twenty-firsters soon, for a great plague is rising up from the East. I fear it will soon sweep over the Holy Lands.

I am coming to Paris myself to discuss the matter with King Charles. Whatever else, make sure the royal temper does not lead him to do something rash that we will all regret.

Gregory, Vicar of Christ

Dungeon at the Bastille
July 18, 1372

Everyone else was asleep and Jeff was missing Catvia. He touched Coach and suddenly he was in the grove. Really in the grove. And then Catvia appeared.

Dryad's Grove
Time Not Really Applicable

"Look there. Can you see it?" Catvia pointed, her cat ears cocked and her tail twitching.

Jeff followed her finger. In the distance, rising up out of the mist, was a hill with a road circling around it up to the top of the hill. And on the top of the hill was a garage with big signs, looking not quite like it needed a paint job but a little dirty and well used. *Pucorl's Garage. Gas, Ass, and Grass.* Jeff laughed. "Boy, you can always count on Pucorl to smart off, you know."

"Yes, but see how close we are getting." Catvia reached out and hugged his arm.

Jeff hugged her back and things progressed from there in a natural and predictable manner. This time was a bit different. He was physically in the grove, not dreaming. And that meant he provided more than power. He left a little bit of his substance there in the grove.

Near the Dryad's Grove

Some cycles later

The sapling grew as the light increased. Pucorl's Garage and machine shop was migrating from underhill to the Elysian Fields and in its wake came the dryad's grove. It wasn't the only dryad's grove that had been underhill in France, but now it was unique. It had a touch of mortal essence in it, and the seed was growing. It was growing because of the extra energy that the dryads, or succubi, had gained through the dreams of mortal men and women. It gained energy as it slowly floated from underhill to the Elysian Fields.

The Elysian Fields had been declining for the last thousand years and more, but the process had been extremely slow, at least as mortals measure such things. It was still very much a Camelot sort of place, full of gentle breezes and even more gentle sunlight. As Pucorl's land and the dryad's grove approached it, the light grew from the twilight of underhill to the gentle sunlight of the Elysian Fields, and a sapling grew.

The sapling had a shape and a structure that was partly human, partly demonic. It had a name and the form of a tree, because its mother was a dryad. It had data ports and an ethernet connection, because its mother's body was a computer, and it had genes provided by its father. The genes gave it a naturally greater physical constancy. In the course of time, it grew a bud, a flower, and a fruit. When the fruit opened, a dryad crawled out from it.

And that was a very strange thing, for in the normal course of events dryads came from their seed pods as adult creatures, capable of assuming the form of male or female as needed and not tied to any species.

But this was a cute little baby girl with cat's ears and a long silky tail.

The little girl grew, as little girls do, and she danced and played in the grove of the dryad and was educated by her mother, just as her tree had been. With giggling talks and data dumps. She was also educated by Merlin, Raphico, Pucorl and Enzo, as well as the

336

dryads and trees of the grove.

There were, from her perspective, occasional visits from her father, and every time he came to visit he remarked on how much she had grown. It was true, for while only a day had passed for Jeff in the mortal realm, months or even a year might pass in the grove.

Then one balmy afternoon while she was playing in her tree, jumping from branch to branch chasing demonic squirrels, there was a bump. And Kitten Martin fell to land on her feet on a one lane blacktop road that now stretched between Pucorl's Garage and machine shop and the grove of the dryads.

Looking about, Kitten changed her fur into coveralls because Enzo insisted that mechanics wore them. Every dryad knows that you must be properly dressed for the occasion. At this point, Kitten was approximately the same age as Paul Grady, though, of course, home schooled by dryads, demons and an angel, so her education was a bit different than Paul's. And that was before you even got to the dataport behind her left ear and the direct data dumping it allowed.

Dungeon at the Bastille
August 3, 1372

Jeff woke as Coach vibrated on his wrist. It had been a long night. The grove was getting quite close to Pucorl's Garage, which was bringing ever closer the dreadful day when he was going to have to confess to Mrs. Grady that he had a daughter. He had known it was going to be necessary for two weeks now, but Jeff was not yet nineteen, and in some ways a young eighteen. Mrs. Grady was *in loco parentis* and she was sure to scold him. Knocking a girl up was serious business. Even if it had been her idea and she hadn't even told him about it until the tree sprouted.

The time in the Bastille had not been all that bad. The guards were quite familiar with the concept of noble prisoners, and Jennifer owned a village in Normandy. Tiphaine hadn't rescinded the grant, even after King Charles had seized the day planner along with the rest of the computers. Jeff spent his nights with Catvia in the grove, watching his little girl grow up into a person.

Jeff smiled. He couldn't help it. Kitten was cute as a kitten and bright as a new penny.

Jeff decided that he'd just wait and introduce Kitten to Mrs. Grady. That way she couldn't yell at him. Kitten was so cute. Who wouldn't love her? Besides, for the moment, Jeff was the only one who had any direct contact with the demons.

The Rooms of Doctor Delaflote
August 3, 1372

Archimedes looked at the mortal, cocking the head of the crow whose body he shared. The crow, by now, was at least fairly well trained. It knew that it was eating better than it ever had and had grown accustomed to Archimedes' presence so it didn't try to fight him. "It's time, or near enough."

"That's good," Gabriel said, looking up from the scroll he was copying. They both knew the plan, having been visited by Catvia and Asuma in their dreams. Asuma, as it happened, made a very fetching lady crow.

Archimedes cawed. "You need to buy a horse."

"No, I need to rent a horse. If I buy one people are going to ask why." Gabriel got up and moved to the bookcase. He opened it and slid the scroll back into place. Then he opened a much less obvious panel and pulled from it a pouch full of silver coins. He counted out several of the coins and put them on the desk with a note saying that they were to pay the stable keeper for the horse.

Perenelle Flamel's Stable

"I'll get old Brownie ready for you," the groom said.

In the past weeks Gabriel had been taking rides in the country on his off days. Usually with a picnic lunch. Now he looked around the stable. It was daub with wood stalls. There was horse shit in the stalls and a stable boy in patched, worn clothing was mucking them out. The sun was shining and Gabriel could ignore the smells of Paris.

Dungeon at the Bastille

Jeff sat down next to Wilber. "Get everyone ready."

"Have they worked out how we get Pucorl out of the stable?" Wilber, like Gabriel Delaflote, had received dreams from Asuma, since Catvia had proven reluctant to visit the dreams of men whom Jeff might know. Wilber wasn't sure that Jeff realized that Catvia did visit the dreams of other men and women. Well, Wilber wasn't going to tell him. It would do no good, and might do considerable harm.

"They have a plan," Jeff said. "It involves Archimedes."

"Archimedes. That makes sense, if he can get to Pucorl's place in the netherworld."

"Coach says it's time," Jeff said, holding up his smart watch. The face was showing the face of a clock when the hands pointing at H hour. Considering that the face of Jeff's watch could show anything that could fit on the inch wide screen, that was pretty clear.

"Okay, okay," Wilber said. He got up and went over to talk to Mrs. Grady.

Dryad's Grove

Jeff arrived in the grove and heard Kitten shout.

"Daddy! Daddy! Pucorl has a lathe! Come see, come see!"

Jeff turned to his right and saw a blacktop road circling around the grove, heading off for a couple of hundred yards till it went around Pucorl's garage. Then Catvia was there.

"In just a minute, honey bunch," Catvia said. "Daddy has to run an errand first. But Uncle Coach will go with you."

The watch on Jeff's arm was no longer on his arm and the four and a half foot faun was standing next to him. "You hurry up now. There is this one guard at the treasury who keeps trying to play with us."

"You should have given him a nice shock," Jeff muttered.

"Can't. Our bodies are designed to avoid doing that sort of thing," Catvia said. "What it means is we are going to have to hurry, and we're probably going to be discovered sooner than we would like."

"Okay," Jeff agreed. He took Catvia's hand and suddenly he was standing in a royal strong room. He had been here before because Catvia had insisted he rehearse the breakout. He knew where the sack was and quickly turned it over and emptied its contents—about four pounds of gold and silver coins—onto the floor. It made a horrible racket, and Jeff almost slipped on the rolling coins. He started shoving computers, phones, and other electrical devices into the sack and heard a key turning in the lock. He kept going.

The door opened and Jeff was looking at a big, burly man in the uniform of a royal guard. By now Jeff was fully aware just how big a deal uniforms were in the fourteenth century. It was a point of status to wear the king's colors. But that wasn't what caught Jeff's eye. It was the pistol in the guy's holster that really grabbed his attention.

Jeff grabbed another computer and put it in the bag. The guard drew his gun. Then Jeff remembered that Catvia was in the bag in computer form, and though he knew that the magic of the demons had strengthened the vessels, he didn't trust it against a pistol round. He swung the sack behind him and the guard fired.

Jeff felt the red hot poker through his right chest and reached for another computer.

He didn't get it.

Catvia transferred them back to the grove. Jeff looked at the trees and the gentle sunlight, then he looked at Catvia and smiled. She was out of the dungeon. He had done that much. But then he remembered the others. "Coach!" he yelled, or tried to. It came out a cough and blood came out of his mouth.

He looked over at Pucorl's Garage and saw Coach running for

him with Kitten on his heels. Jeff was caught. He wanted to hug his little girl more than he had ever wanted anything in his life. But at the same time, he didn't want her to see him like this.

Coach reached him, fell to his knees, and dropped the sack full of computers on the ground of the grove. Kitten, not waiting for permission, grabbed him around the neck.

Dungeon in the Bastille

At the sound of a grunt and a child's voice, Wilber turned. "Oh, shit. Help me." There was Jeff, bleeding from a hole in his upper chest, with blood coming out of his mouth. Wilber was a bright kid who, because of his medical condition had spent more than his share of time in hospitals. He knew anatomy, and from the position of the wound and the blood on the mouth, he knew that Jeff's right lung had at least been nicked.

The good news, such as it was, was that the wound was nowhere near Jeff's heart. A really good trauma center and Jeff would be just fine. Of course, the nearest trauma center—of any kind: good, bad or so-so—was centuries away.

Raphico could fix him. There was an app for that. But Raphico was with Monsignor Savona and also might as well be centuries away also for all the good it was likely to do Jeff.

"Everyone, grab hold," Jeff tried to say, but it came out a blood-soaked croak.

"No," Mrs. Grady said. "Someone get me a piece of leather and everyone stand back. We have to bandage that wound or he is going to die."

"Daddy can't die!" cried the little girl with the cat ears and the long tail who was dressed in coveralls that had *Pucorl's Garage* stenciled on them.

"Give me room." Mrs. Grady said. Again.

"No time!" Roger said, and Wilber knew he was right even as he hated him for saying it.

"No time," Jeff croaked.

Roger grabbed Jennifer and, dragging her, reached for Jeff. In an instant, they were gone, along with the little girl who was still holding Jeff around the neck.

"What?" Mrs. Grady looked shocked.

"He was right," Wilber said as Jeff and Roger reappeared. Roger reached out and Wilber tossed Paul to him. Mrs. Grady leapt for them and Roger, Jeff, Paul, and Mrs. Grady disappeared.

There was a short pause and Wilber could almost hear the argument between Roger and Mrs. Grady. Then Jeff and Roger reappeared. Wilber grabbed Annabelle, who grabbed Liane, and they were in the grove.

"Lakshmi," Jeff tried to say and disappeared again.

It was no more than two seconds later that Jeff returned with Lakshmi. Then he collapsed onto the grass.

CHAPTER 27

Grove of the Dryads
August 3, 1372

Under a sapling of indeterminate sort, a young man bled out his life, feeding it all unknowing into the soil of the netherworld. His seed and even a bit of his substance were already there. It was that seed from which the sapling sprouted.

He looked up into the eyes of his fantasy lover and his impossible daughter and he felt the grove and the sapling that was his son. His life—all not quite nineteen years of it—seemed to flow out of him with the blood. All his memories, all his hopes and fears, feelings of inadequacy, and moments of fun were pouring out of him too. Not into nothingness, but into the grove, and especially into the sapling. He remembered the struggle to memorize his lines and the even greater struggles with math and science which had never seemed to make sense. He remembered the games and usually being the last one to get the joke or solve the riddle.

It hadn't been a great life. Not the sort of life that you might read about in books. He was no Edison or Einstein, that was for sure. And that hurt, especially since both his parents were really smart people. Life had started to get good only after they had been brought here by Pucorl. A giggle of juvenile delight bubbled up at the thought of Sieur Pucorl in a van. He really was now, Jeff realized, a true chevalier, knighted by the king of France for gallantry. Jeff wished that he was brave like Pucorl, Liane or Roger, or smart like Jennifer, Wilber, or Bill. Good with his hands like Annabelle, quick witted like Lakshmi or his parents. But he was just Jeff.

"No!"

Ilektrismós, the retired lightning bolt of Zeus, spoke in Jeff's mind and aloud as well. Everyone heard the thunder in that voice. "I have known heroes, lad. Many of them. Compared to you, Achilles was all heel."

It was with those words floating in his mind that Jeff Martin passed away. But not all the way away. For the netherworld is a cyclic place and death is only the bottom of the cycle. His presence was still there in the grove, a part of the trees and the grass, even the air. Like Arthur Pendragon, Jeff would return in the course of time, when he was needed again.

****

Paul looked at Jeff lying there on the ground and started to cry. Amelia reached out to her son and held him close, noting that Catvia was doing the same for the little girl who had called Jeff "Daddy." Jeff was dead and it wasn't Catvia who had done it. It was grim necessity and the needs of survival. In order to save them, Jeff had put off help for too long. Maybe it wouldn't have made any difference. It wasn't like they had Monsignor Savona and Raphico here to cure him with a miracle, but there might have been something they could do.

Even as she stood there looking at the body, it was not decaying. More like fading away, feeding into the grove in a nimbus of golden light that brought every tree in the grove to full bloom. Dryads were sitting up and yawning all over the place.

Catvia was shaking her head. "This is nothing to what he would have done in a full life."

Amelia wanted to slap her for the cynicism in that comment, but there were tears in Catvia's eyes, as well as those of the little girl. Amelia couldn't tell and doubted if Catvia knew how much of that regret was for the loss of Jeff and how much was for the loss of support. Which, Amelia realized, didn't make Catvia all that different from most people.

****

Wilber looked around and his grief was a muted thing. Partly that was because he had Merlin whispering in his ear. And, from that, he recognized that Jeff truly wasn't gone. His spirit filled

344

this place and affected everything in the grove. It extended through the connection between the grove and Pucorl's lands, to the garage as well, adding a sheen and a luster that wouldn't be there without it.

Jeff was here and you could feel him, breathe him in the air.

Wilber looked around again. The grove was in full bloom. The trees had flowers and fruits, pinkish-white trunks with golden leaves. From the fruits, new people emerged, naked girls and boys, looking rather like Japanese anime, but with a touch of Jeff's chiseled good looks.

Off to his left, the blacktop led off to Pucorl's Garage and there were power lines that went from the trees to the garage and back again. Ilektrismós reached out to the grove now and, looking, Wilber saw data ports growing out of the trees.

"We need to move, people," Roger said roughly. There was a burr in the big young man's voice. Grief set aside to get on with business. And Wilber thought that was as good, at least as accurate, a monument to Jeff as there could be.

Wilber sniffed and nodded. He went over and put an arm around the little girl's shoulders. "Try not to be too sad. He's still here, you know."

"We need to get over to Pucorl's Garage," Merlin whispered in his ear. "That is where Archimedes is coming."

Catvia picked up the little girl and, carrying her, she set off on the road to the garage. Wilber followed and so did the rest.

Royal Stables, Hôtel Saint-Pol
August 3, 1372

Pucorl heard the commotion before he got word from Merlin. He waited, uncertain of what to do.

A captain of the king's guard came running into the stable. The man stopped at the sight of Pucorl and sighed. Then he walked over and opened the passenger door. Pucorl had been cooperating since the arrest. Letting his doors be opened, even letting the guards watch movies or cartoons on his screens. That was both his choice and part of the plan. Pucorl was his own van, free to make his own choices, and he had chosen to avoid a confrontation with King Charles.

Charles had, in turn, been cautious. Fully aware that Pucorl owned Pucorl, Charles had not put himself in a position to be carted off to the netherworld and left there.

Now Pucorl had a captain of the royal guard in his middle seats. "What happened?"

"I don't know," Captain LeFevre admitted. "We heard that someone got into the royal treasury and absconded with the king's enchanted computers."

"They aren't—" Pucorl started, and Captain LeFevre waved it away.

"The king says they're his, and he is my liege lord, not Themis or Zeus."

It was then that Pucorl got the call. It was Merlin, telling him to get out now. Muttering dark imprecations about the proper timing of warnings, Pucorl did. Pucorl, his armor, and Captain LeFevre were suddenly sitting in Pucorl's garage.

"Pucorl, take us back." Captain LeFevre drew his enchanted pistol and pointed it at the dashcam.

"That's not a good idea, Captain," Pucorl said. "There are a bunch of people coming up my road and they aren't going to be happy that you're here. If you shoot out my dashcam, Annabelle is going to take a crowbar to your head."

They both heard the voices. Not excited voices, but angry voices. Meanwhile Pucorl was learning what had happened to Jeff Martin from Merlin. He was also filled in on the fact that Wilber's computer, along with Jennifer's, Mrs. Grady's and Paul's, were all left in the royal treasury, thanks to the guard who shot Jeff.

"Royal guards aren't popular with the twenty-firsters at the moment," Pucorl told Captain LeFevre. "One of your number killed Jeff Martin. And by the way, the dryads of the grove are not likely to be sending you fellows good dreams for a while. Like a couple or three centuries."

"I didn't kill Jeff, and even the guard who did was probably just doing his duty. It is not fair of you to blame us all for one man's actions."

"Do you think they will care? Would you, in their place?"

Captain LeFevre put his gun away as the crowd entered the garage.

Village West of Paris

Gabriel Delaflote climbed down off the horse with creaking muscles. The morning had been spent in hard riding. His horse was spent and so was he, but there was a correlation between places in the mortal world and places in the netherworld. It wasn't exact, but it was there. It was easier to return to the netherworld in a different place if your vessel in the mortal world had moved to a corresponding place. Archimedes had ridden on Gabriel's saddle for most of the trip, and though not quite so worn as he would have been had he flown on his own wings, he was not in great shape either.

Gabriel pulled a pouch from the saddle bag. It contained seeds, bread, and small fragments of jerked meat. This he fed to the crow, for what was to happen next would come as a shock to the bird part of Archimedes. Before the veil had been torn asunder, this would not have been possible outside dreams, but now an enchanted item or animal could return to the netherworld. It was not common even with items, and more rare with animals, for what if a mortal animal were to get loose in the netherworld? But Archimedes was prepared to try it with the crow that was his vessel.

However, it was going to take some preparation. Gabriel pulled a trowel from his backpack and started cutting lines in the earth. It would be easier to tie the transfer to a location in the netherworld near here if he used a pentagram.

It was almost two hours later and the sun was well into the late afternoon by the time Gabriel indicated that Archimedes should fly to the center of the pentagram.

Archimedes directed and the crow flew. Gabriel started the incantation.

Netherworld

The crow's brain wasn't equipped to translate the impulses of the netherworld into an understandable structure. It would have gone insane, even catatonic, in the first instant of its presence here, but Archimedes, the demonic underlord, translated and filtered. What the crow saw was a wild, barren plane, clouds, thunder, lightning, and updrafts, downdrafts, in a cacophony that while terrifying was still at least sort of what it was used to.

The crow squawked, spread its wings, and flapped for height. As it moved, there was surrounding it a winged woman on a flying horse. Surrounding it, and a part of it. Not exactly a valkyrie, nor yet a muse of Greek mythology, this was the true form of Archimedes, to the extent that Archimedes had a true form. It surrounded the crow and blended with it as they flew.

And they were flying in a very specific direction. West and up to a higher level of energy gradient, from what the mortals would call underhill to what they might call Elysium.

They flew on, through time and space, toward a particular location in both.

Pucorl's Garage

"Archimedes is coming," Wilber said. "Merlin can feel him."

He turned and walked out the open garage door into the parking lot. The parking lot had a reserved slot for Pucorl with a wagon and hand cart sitting there. Wilber looked up and the sun was shining on the blacktop. The sky immediately overhead was a deep blue, but to the east there were roiling clouds.

Out of those clouds flew a somewhat amorphous woman with wings, riding a horse that flew even though it had no wings. Wilber watched as it flew in, circled the sign, and landed in the driveway. There was a body inside the body, the body of a crow that could barely be made out.

"Welcome, Archimedes." Wilber bowed, slightly more than a nod but not much more. There was a hierarchy here and Wilber had his own place in it, as did Archimedes. Merlin was not so poor an adviser as to fail to coach Wilber in its use.

The woman dismounted and Wilber had the feeling that part of the crow was now with the woman and part with the horse. That brought home in a way that Pucorl's Garage and even the dryad's grove hadn't that they weren't in Kansas anymore.

****

The group was loading into Pucorl when Kitten said, "I'm going too!" By now they had all been introduced.

Catvia stopped stock still, then turned to her daughter. She didn't, as Annabelle thought she would, say no. Instead she asked, "Why?"

Kitten's tail lifted, curled over her shoulder, and the tip came to her mouth. She chewed at it as another child might chew her nails. "I want to see my daddy's world. I need to see the world that made him and made part of me."

That was rather mature for a kid, Annabelle thought. But then this wasn't exactly a kid. Kitten was a dryad, and a dryad with a dataport behind her left ear. Something Paul had demanded as soon as he saw it. One thing was for sure, Kitten was smarter than her daddy. Annabelle felt guilty as soon as that thought came to her. It was true, but it was the least part of Jeff Martin. Character is not always dependent on intellect, and Jeff had proved beyond any reasonable doubt that he had character.

Now disarmed, Captain LeFevre stood and watched with a bemused expression on his face. That was the other issue. Whether to take him back with them, or leave him stuck here. Leaving him here might not be the best thing for his survival prospects. The dryads of the grove were quite fond of Jeff in the somewhat cynical way of dryads. But that was before he died in their grove. For to die in the netherworld was to be absorbed by it. Not just the blood and bone, not even just the life force, but

349

the character. Jeff might have been a sucker and a sap. Annabelle was convinced that he was, but he was also brave, generous— and when it came down to it—self-sacrificing. That, too, was part of the grove now and mixed with a character that made its living sucking the life force from more powerful demons by making it enjoyable. How that would work out over time was impossible to predict, but right now all it meant to the dryads was an understanding of how much they had lost with Jeff dead.

They were pissed. And, for that matter, so was Annabelle. There was a part of her that wanted to let them do whatever they wanted with LeFevre, but she didn't want his essence corrupting Jeff's grove. "We should take him too," Annabelle said.

"She's right," Pucorl said. "I don't want him polluting my grease pit."

Captain LeFevre started to heave a sigh, then Pucorl said, "We can always shoot him after we get back to the mortal lands. Or I can run over him a few times."

Captain LeFevre's expression was priceless.

Wilber said, "You go ahead. Drop Captain LeFevre in a village somewhere, then come back here. Merlin and I need to do some stuff."

"What do you need to do?" Mrs. Grady asked.

"Merlin is still half in the custody of the king. It's bad enough for the rest of you whose computers didn't make it out, but Merlin is a special case. He's half here with me and half back in Paris. And, bad as that is here, it's going to be worse in the mortal realm. The Bluetooth connection between my implant and my computer is not going to reach fifty miles, even with a magical assist. Besides, that computer is mine. All our computers and stuff belong to us, not to King Charles. We need to get them back."

There was general agreement on that score, but Annabelle asked, "So what are you going to do about it?"

"Merlin and I are going to make a pentagram in bay three." He pointed at the red garage door. Pucorl's Garage had been evolving over time. Now it had three bays, two gas pumps, and a store attached. The store sold Twinkies and Snowballs, hot dogs and microwave hamburgers. The food content of those things had come from the mortal realm over the course of the last few weeks. But the shape and taste was a product of the magic of Pucorl's Garage.

Annabelle looked at Pucorl. The van's lights came on and went off in a pattern that Annabelle knew was Pucorl's way of drumming his fingers on a desk or cracking his knuckles. Just one of those quirks that people had while they thought hard about something.

She looked back at Wilber. "You know that's a pretty big deal, right? Pucorl letting Merlin have a door into his realm."

"I know, and so does Merlin," Wilber agreed. He went over and sat on the bench by the door to the store part of the garage. "But we need some sort of strong link to Pucorl's lands. Either that or Merlin and I need to go back to his lands."

Merlin's territory was located in the netherworld, in a place roughly analogous to the cathedral at Notre Dame, but a few energy states below it.

"Demonic geography lessons," Annabelle muttered.

"Yes, but important," Wilber agreed. "Look, Pucorl, I know you've been coming up in the world lately and Merlin isn't trying to ride your coattails, in spite of what it may seem."

"I understand that," Pucorl said. "But you know that whatever the intent, a gate like that is going to leak."

"I do know that," Wilber said. "And so does Merlin."

"You guys know the answer, don't you?" Roger said. Roger hadn't said more than a word or two since Jeff died. He was doing the stone-face routine well enough to make Bertrand du Guesclin jealous.

"No, Roger," Wilber said, "I don't."

"Themis."

"What about Themis?" Wilber asked. "She's way off to the east, analogous to Greece or Babylon."

"Not all of her," Roger said. "Her sword is in Paris."

"I understand that, but how does that help us?"

"Because it's her sword. If we bring it here Themis can put in a gate that won't leak." That was true. Themis was at a slightly lower level than Merlin was, but Themis was a titan. She could make and control gates with much greater control, not to mention power, than Merlin could manage.

"You're saying we need Themis' sword? You think she will agree to that?"

Roger shrugged. "I don't know. She left the sword enchanted and in spite of how it seemed, I don't think it was because she had to. All we can do is ask, and to ask I'm going to need to put my hands on the sword."

"That means we have two options. We do a snatch and grab of all our stuff including the sword, or we negotiate with King Charles."

"Do you think we can trust him?" Annabelle asked. "He killed Jeff. It might have been one of the guards who pulled the trigger, but it was Charles who gave the orders that made it happen."

"Frankly," Catvia said, "I'd rather turn him into a eunuch. And I'm just the cat to do it." Her fingernails turned into claws, which retracted and extended.

Mrs. Grady held up a hand. "Catvia, we can't live here in the netherworld indefinitely, whatever has happened to the veil. We have to be able to operate in the mortal realm, and being outlaws in France won't make that easier. Just or not, we are going to have to come to some sort of an arrangement with King Charles."

"You can't live here," Catvia said. "But I can. My daughter can."

"No, Mama. I need to go to the mortal realm. At least for a time," Kitten said. "I need to learn that part of my name."

CHAPTER 28

Pucorl's Garage
August 3, 1372

The van faded into nothing and Wilber turned to bay three. Pucorl had agreed to a temporary link so that Merlin could remain in contact with himself through the link in Pucorl's land. Wilber started laying out the pentagram and soon enough had an audience. The dryads wandered in, sat on benches, and watched as Wilber worked.

Western France
August 3, 1372

Gabriel Delaflote looked up as Archimedes returned, bringing Pucorl and most of the twenty-firsters with him.

Archimedes was sitting on the roof of the van, his talons around the luggage rack. The bird left the van and flew to Gabriel's shoulder, then the door opened.

Captain LeFevre climbed out and Gabriel realized that he would not be returning to the University of Paris. Having been of material aid in the escape of prisoners of the crown, he was going to become acquainted with the king's headsman should he return.

Captain LeFevre was not looking well. He wasn't physically harmed, but there was a haunted look in his eyes. The creatures of the netherworld had taken note of him and that was a chancy thing to have happen in the best of circumstances. Then the rest piled out, and for some little time Doctor Delaflote was becoming reacquainted with his friends and being introduced to Kitten, who carried Jeff's computer under her arm.

Gabriel's attention was arrested. He had never before seen a little girl with cat's ears and a tail, or with a wire running from behind her ear to a computer.

Royal Treasury, Île de la Cité
August 4, 1372

There was a beeping, which brought the armed guard to a standing position. After the escape, the rest of the devices had been moved here and an armed guard placed permanently in the room.

The computer beeped again. "Open me!" it commanded.

Instead the guard called for his sergeant, the sergeant for his captain, and the calling went all the way to Baron Emanuel de Gloster, who was in charge of the actual physical treasury and just under the exchequer in rank.

Baron de Gloster considered calling the exchequer, but that worthy was at his estates outside Paris just now. He considered calling Constable of France Bertrand du Guesclin, but he couldn't stand the puffed-up peasant.

So he pulled up his nerve and went to the computer. It took him a couple of tries and some additional instruction, but he got the computer opened. And there on the screen was one of the twenty-firsters, who appeared to be in a building of some sort, with a demon or angel sitting beside him. The apparition had the wings of a bird sprouting from his back. The feathers of those wings glistened in every color of the rainbow, but the overall effect was of glowing white wings.

"Hello, Baron," Wilber Hyde-Davis III said. "We need to talk to your boss."

"Boss?"

"We need to speak to the king of France," said the apparition.

After that things moved rather slowly. Baron de Gloster was unwilling to disturb the king, but did inform the chamberlain. The chamberlain came to see what was going on. Then, rather than the king, he called the king's lawyer, Nicolas du Bosc.

All of that took most of the rest of that day.

Pucorl's Garage
August 5, 1372

Wilber opened the plastic wrap and stuffed a snowball in his mouth. Not the ice, the coconut-covered cake. Then he went to the cooler and got a coke. It didn't exactly taste like a coke. The flavor was a combination of their memories of how a coke was supposed to taste, and Annabelle drank diet coke, so there was a bit of an artificial flavor to it. It wasn't bad, though. It beat the heck out of sour wine.

Then he went back out to the garage, where a dryad was doing a bump and grind to try and entice Merlin, who wasn't buying. The lines of the pentagram glowed in golden fire and the demon, muse, whatever, was in the middle of it, sitting in a recliner with a beer in one hand and a hamburger in the other.

That was an illusion, of course. Well, sort of illusion. The link to Merlin's domain was real, and here in the netherworld the illusion had substance. Though it was locked into the pentagram, there was a virtual camera floating in a special little niche in the pentagram and Wilber walked over, carefully not stepping on the lines. He sat down in his recliner and had another drink of coke. Merlin called up a whiteboard and magic marker, and a minion of his started to draw a set of runes on the board.

Wilber shook his head. "That should be a theta."

About then there was a beep from nowhere, and Wilber and Merlin faced the camera, waving the imp out of the way. Merlin made a complex gesture that by now Wilber could almost read and a flat screen appeared in the air, showing them what Wilber's computer's camera picked up.

"Welcome, Monsieur du Bosc," Wilber said.

"His Majesty is quite upset with you, young man," Nicolas du Bosc said severely.

Suddenly, Wilber was furious. "Jeff Martin is dead through the greed of your king, du Bosc. You don't know the meaning of upset. But push me just a little, and you're going to find out."

Wilber took a breath. "I apologize, but do not assume that because your boss wears a crown, he has all of right on his side. If he is displeased by us taking back just some of our goods that he stole, think how displeased we are at the loss of our friend."

Du Bosc bowed his head. "I am sorry to hear of Jeff's death." Then his head came up and his eyes hardened. "But breaking into the king's treasure room is an invitation to such a fate. The issues of ownership are the king's to determine."

"Calmly, please," Merlin said. "You assume that in dealing with the twenty-firsters and the demons that enchant their goods you are dealing with subjects of the king of France. In fact, most of them are Americans, nobles of another realm. And even the girl who is a citizen of France is not a subject of the king of France, but a free citizen of the French Republic. If the king had the right of this, then all he had to do was reach out and pull the sword from the stone.

"How, by the way, is the presence of the sword in the floor of his throne room affecting his relations with his subjects? Not to mention the representatives of other nations."

Wilber really enjoyed Du Bosc's expression then.

Royal Palace, Île de la Cité

Charles sat in the throne room of the palace. It was a large, well-appointed room with chandeliers filled with candles and tapestries on the walls.

It stank.

It was located on a small island in the middle of the Seine and downstream of much of the sewage that emptied into the river from both banks. The plans for an improved sewer system worked out with the help of Jennifer Fairbanks had yet to be implemented. In large part that was because they were very expensive plans. It was much cheaper to put a palace upriver and some blocks from the Seine. A palace that he already had. Except now it had a highly visible sword sticking out of the throne room floor. The stink upset his digestion and the bad air was going to make him sick, whatever the twenty-firsters said.

Another merchant approached the dais and the king's clerk brought him the scroll. Charles looked at it. The merchant was seeking a license to enchant his carts. He was tempted to deny it. Paris was overrun with demons these days, enchanted wagons, enchanted cranes, enchanted ovens, and all manner of devices. But it wouldn't do. If he refused, the merchant would enchant them anyway. Besides, he needed the money from the fees and taxes.

Petition granted.

There was unrest in the city and more in the countryside. Almost all the good will he had gained from defeating Philip's army of the dead had been lost because of Roger McLean's gesture.

Another merchant. This one a scribe asking that the new printing presses that Nicolas Flamel was producing based on discussions with the twenty-firsters be banned. There were a lot of scribes in Paris and most of them made their living, at least in good part, by copying books. Flamel had printed a breviary which he was selling for one-tenth the cost that a scribe would charge for it.

Petition denied.

Nicolas Flamel owned four stables in Paris outright, and had interests in a dozen other businesses. As well, Flamel was paying the crown a fee for each breviary he sold and he had sold a lot of them. Again, Charles needed the money.

A clerk came in and went directly for Count Laroche. Charles held up a hand and the next petitioner waited. One look at Count Laroche's expression and Charles knew it was bad. He waved the petitioner back and leaned over to listen.

"Monsieur du Bosc reports that the computer that is the vessel of Merlin has awakened on its own and is acting as a phone to contact the twenty-firster witch Wilber."

"Don't use that term," Charles said. Angry as he was, he understood the effect of an accusation of witchcraft. For if Wilber was a witch for having a demon, then so were several of his advisers. Not to mention Monsignor Savona—and at least two cardinals of the church, from what he had heard. This was a fight he didn't need right now.

"I humbly beg forgiveness, Majesty. The twenty-firster Wilber Hyde-Davis."

"What do they want?"

"To negotiate."

"Negotiate?" Charles said, rather more loudly than he had intended. "They are fugitives and— Have Monsieur du Bosc meet me in the private audience chamber and inform the petitioners that this audience is suspended for the moment."

Private Audience Chamber

Du Bosc bowed low, then faced the king and said, "Jeff Martin is dead from wounds given by your guard, Majesty. The twenty-firsters and their demonic allies are one wrong word from declaring war on you."

"They will lose!"

"Yes, Majesty, they will. But not without doing the crown of France severe, even irreparable, harm. They are respected among the demonic kind. That gives them a power well beyond their numbers, even without the knowledge they bring. And they are seriously enraged. They are only nine mortals now, Majesty. One of their number is dead, a tenth part of their whole. How would you react if Edward III of England killed a tenth part of your people, from peasant to noble?"

Charles sat back. He trusted Nicolas du Bosc as he trusted few other men. In large part because Nicolas, like Bertrand, unfailingly told him the truth—even when he would prefer a polite lie. So now he thought about how his actions must have seemed to the twenty-firsters. Thought about it for really the first time since Roger McLean ran off with that cursed sword. He must have seemed as treacherous as Philip to them. He rather regretted his anger now, but that didn't change anything. If they were that angry . . .

"Very well, Nicolas. Tell me, how angry are they? Can we ever trust them again?"

Nicolas considered a long moment then slowly shook his head. "No, Majesty, I don't think we can. They are few in number and the death of Jeff Martin is not something they can or will forget. They will never again trust you, no matter what you say or do."

Charles nodded. That was his assessment also. He was tempted to have the guard who killed the boy punished—but to what end? The man had simply been doing his duty, however unfortunate the end result. If he was punished for it by Charles, the twenty-firsters would only see further proof of the king's treacherous nature.

"So it's war then? However disastrous for the twenty-firsters and for France?"

Nicolas stroked his beard. "Perhaps . . . not necessarily war, but separation, certainly."

"What do you have in mind?"

"In all truth, Majesty, I don't know yet. Some sort of exile might be enough to prevent war. *Might* be."

"I trust, Nicolas, you mean *them* to be exiled, not me?"

"Yes, Majesty. But I do not think that will be quite enough. That is, I don't think they will go without the rest of their possessions, at least most of them."

"What about the sword?"

Nicolas looked at him and his expression was most peculiar. "Majesty, I do not doubt that they will willingly leave the sword of Themis *right where it is*, if that is Your Majesty's desire."

Charles thought about the Hôtel Saint-Pol with its pearl

359

tapestries, inlaid walls . . . and fresh air. And the sword of Themis sticking up out of the mosaic floor of his large audience chamber. "It isn't," Charles said. And thought again.

What he wanted was the sword of Themis in his hand. At least, that was what he had wanted at the end of the battle of Paris. Since then, he had reconsidered. Well, at least he was reconsidering now. Holy relics and magic talismans were much easier to deal with if they didn't have minds of their own.

"I want it gone. Not in the treasury, not in France."

"And the rest of their equipage, Majesty? The enchanted computers?"

Yet again Charles considered. "I want a computer and a phone." He grimaced. "I will pay for them. A reasonable amount, but they will legitimately come into my hand and be the property of the king of France from now until the end of time. And I want the computer to have *all* of their books."

"I will return to the treasury and relay your position. I think they may well accept."

"I will need something else," Charles said, holding up a hand. "I need their—especially Roger McLean's—public acknowledgment that I am the true and legitimate king of France."

Nicolas winced and Charles almost laughed. Then he frowned. "This is, as the twenty-firsters would say, a deal breaker, Nicolas. After what he did in the throne room, I have to have that."

"Yes, Majesty, but it will not be easy."

****

Bertrand du Guesclin came into the chamber unannounced. He was one of the few men in France who had permission to do so, but he rarely exercised the privilege unless the matter was of critical importance.

"There is a new development, Your Majesty," the Constable said. "The pope is here."

Charles stared at him. "Gregory? *Here?*"

"Yes. And he insists on speaking with you immediately."

Charles looked at Nicolas. Du Bosc shrugged. "It might be helpful. And in any event, you can hardly refuse."

"Yes, I know." He felt a bit overwhelmed, but there was nothing for it. "Have him brought in. Nicolas, you stay. You too, Bertrand."

French Countryside
August 7, 1372

The hedgerows were nice and the road was quite good, Pucorl decided, by medieval French values of good roads. They weren't paved and they were barely wide enough for Pucorl to use. If he ran into a wagon or even a hand cart, someone was going to have to get off the road. But at least they weren't mud. He saw the rock and readied his right wheel to lift. This was a trick he was still learning. It was a matter of spatial awareness and timing. He had to spot the rock so he would be ready, then start to lift his wheel as it touched the rock. He felt the rocks through his tires, but if he hit one while he wasn't ready, it poked him in the tire before he could react. If he started lifting his wheel a hairsbreadth early, it was more comfortable, both for him and for his passengers. At that, Pucorl was doing better than might be expected. He was averaging eight miles an hour. And he was going that slowly only so that Gabriel Delaflote's old nag could keep up.

He did miss his Global Positioning System, though. He missed it in spite of the fact that he had never had a working GPS since he inhabited the van. But he remembered what it was like to know precisely where he was. His memory, in a strange way, reached back to before Pucorl had become the van.

A wagon came out of a side road and Pucorl stopped.

Annabelle pushed the button and Pucorl obligingly lowered his driver side window. Annabelle leaned out and hollered, "Can you get out of the way, please?" in passable *Langue d'oïl*. "We go faster than you do."

The peasant on the wagon looked back at them and jerked on the reins, then he slapped the reins against the rump of the cart horse and ran off down the way.

Unfortunately, that put the wagon in front of them on the road they were using and the hedgerows meant that they couldn't just go around through a field. For the next couple of miles, they went slower still.

Sunset found them about twenty miles northeast of Paris, but that was just a guess. Between the lack of maps and the lack of GPS, Pucorl didn't know where they were, exactly, aside from the fact that they were in front of a farmhouse. It was a largish stone farmhouse, two stories tall, with the stable below the house.

Jennifer rented them a night's lodging, and then Pucorl returned to his garage, taking Annabelle, Catvia, and Kitten.

Kitten was enjoying the world, when she wasn't arguing with Paul. They were age mates of a sort, and each other's only playmates of a similar age. But they were eight years old and Paul was a boy, so things were not entirely peaceful.

Pucorl's Garage

Wilber came out of the bay and said, "We have an offer from Charles."

"What sort of offer?" Annabelle asked, climbing out of Pucorl and stretching—which Wilber watched with interest, Pucorl noted.

He told them.

"I don't know," Annabelle said. "I don't like the idea of any of us in the hands of the king. And even if Roger is willing, whose computer and whose phone?"

"That's a whole other negotiation," Wilber agreed. "And it won't be Merlin."

"What about Igor?" Annabelle asked.

"No," The voice was Merlin's from inside the garage. "The demon called Igor is one of my servants, effectively related to me. I will not leave him in the hands of Charles of France."

Wilber turned to go back into the garage. "That's going to be a problem with most of them, Merlin."

Annabelle followed and Pucorl pulled into the center bay of his garage. He didn't like the way Wilber looked at Annabelle. In the third bay there was a large pentagram drawn in golden fire. Pucorl examined it. It was well made; there was some leakage but not that much. And there, in the pentagram, was Merlin in all his stuck-up glory. Pucorl knew what to look for and saw clearly that Merlin was using the computer to support his form. In the netherworld that didn't eliminate the need for concentration as inhabiting a mortal world vessel like the van did, but it did make maintaining a form a great deal easier. Pucorl could use the computer in the van the same way, though not easily. The computer network in the van was a specialized, not a general use, system. It wasn't set up to run VR programs.

Maybe he should ask Wilber to help him. Then he remembered the way Wilber was looking at Annabelle and decided that perhaps he should ask Catvia instead. Meanwhile, Wilber and Merlin were talking about who might be willing to inhabit a vessel that was owned by the king of France and which of the twenty-firsters might be willing to give up a computer or a phone. It was a "complex question of group dynamics," as the advanced placement sociology text put it, and complicated by what might be offered in exchange. Something that would have to be settled with King Charles, or at least du Bosc.

"Perhaps we should let that rest for now," Pucorl offered. He listened with his radio receiver and noted that in spite of the fact that Merlin's vessel was in the treasury in Paris, he was getting a good signal. The signal went from the computer to Merlin's lands and via the pentagram to Pucorl's lands, where it was picked up by the antenna that was part of the garage and transmitted to Pucorl's vessel. Since Pucorl owned the vessel, he was much more comfortable putting more of himself into it. It was almost like having a body, he guessed. But he could only guess. Demonkind didn't have bodies in the sense that mortals did. Pucorl was land

and puck, just as Themis was both land and titan. "I have a good signal, and we can set up a link across to pick up any calls that du Bosc should make."

"What's the problem, Pucorl?" Annabelle asked.

"No, he's right," Merlin said. "Time runs differently in the netherworld, even with the stronger connection now. It is better if mortals spend as little time here as need be."

"Good point," Wilber agreed, heading for the van. They made the transition back to the mortal realm and the farmhouse.

Farmhouse in France

The farmer and his family didn't seem to be making much of a distinction between the twenty-firsters and the demons. They treated them all with the sort of wary caution normally offered to a ghost or a madman. A well-armed madman. The rest of the group had cots set up in the lower floor of the stable section of the stone farmhouse. The cows and oxen were in the pasture, as was Doctor Delaflote's horse.

In the stable, Paul was sitting on a cot, talking to Green Lantern, his phone. All the phones and the other small devices had made it out of the treasury. The computers, being the largest, had been the last items Jeff started pushing into his bag. Mrs. Grady was talking to Shakespeare through her phone, Laurence. She looked up as they came in. "We heard. If necessary, Shakespeare can be given to the king. I can use Paul's computer. What I don't want is to give up Paul's inheritance from the twenty-first century."

"Batman's bored, Mom," Paul said. "He doesn't like enchanting my computer that much. We should sell my computer to the king and tell the king to call his own demon. I want a good horse."

"We aren't selling your computer for a horse," Amelia Grady told her son. "It would be like trading the house in Paris for a candy bar."

Kitten laughed. Paul's face hardened, and Wilber knew that the issue was decided, at least as far as the computer was concerned. Paul Grady was a stubborn little guy once he got his back up, and there was no way he was going to give up on the idea now that Kitten had laughed at him over it. The way Amelia was looking at Kitten, she probably realized it too. She could use parental authority and force the issue, but that would leave very bad blood between mother and son.

"It doesn't really matter, Mrs. Grady," Wilber said. "The way it's going to work out is that whichever one of you gives up their computer, you're both going to be using the other one. And if something happens to you, Paul inherits."

"See," said Paul, with a sidelong glance at Kitten. "And I never said *just* a horse. We can get other things too. Money and stuff."

Mrs. Grady looked at Wilber, then at her son, then at Kitten, who was looking down at the ground, apparently being talked to by her mother. Then she sighed. Rather theatrically, Wilber thought, and gave in. "Very well. But we aren't giving up both computer and phone."

Lakshmi laughed. "Well, that's not a problem. The only reason that Marilyn wanted to be in my phone was because she was starving in the grove."

Both Lakshmi's phone and her computer were occupied by companions of Catvia's from the grove of the dryads. Marilyn was a succubus, and DW—named after D. W. Griffith—was an incubus. Lakshmi had not handled the transfer all that well and DW was the director of her dreams as she acted in movies and on stages of fantasy. "Marilyn won't starve in the grove now, and she's willing to go back, leaving my phone empty for Charlie Fancy-pants. Besides, it's not like there is anyone for me to call. I just want a lot of frigging money for it."

A Small Room in the Palace of Île de la Cité

Merlin had been moved the next time he was opened. He was placed on a table of darkly stained oak in a library, and in his camera's view was the king of France. Then Nicolas du Bosc and Bertrand du Guesclin walked around Merlin and went to stand beside the king.

Merlin called Pucorl and Wilber's phone, and also Roger's phone, Clausewitz. Roger was going to be needed. He divided the screen of his computer into six sections. He was in his place in the netherworld in the first section, then there was Wilber and Roger. Pucorl's interior was empty, but word had already been sent, and shortly Annabelle, Amelia, and the rest of the group climbed into the van and took seats.

Merlin spoke. "The twenty-firsters have tentatively agreed to your offer, Your Majesty—assuming that we can come to an agreement as to the price of the phone and computer and appropriate sureties of Roger's safety can be arranged."

Charles' face got red, then Roger spoke. "I will accept the king of France's given word as to my safety."

That was, Merlin thought, a nice turn of phrase. Both showing respect for Charles' honor and tacitly confirming that Roger accepted him as the king of France.

The king was visibly mollified by Roger's statement and nodded solemnly. "I have just been visited by Pope Gregory. He wants me to send an embassy to Constantinople."

Nicolas cleared his throat. Charles gave him a glance that was not entirely friendly.

"Perhaps I should say, he wants me to provide a military escort for an embassy that will mostly be composed of his own representatives. The emperor of Byzantium, John V Palaiologos, has indicated some interest in a reunification of our churches." The king raised his hand in a forestalling gesture. "I am skeptical that much will come of that. So is Gregory, for that matter. But it gives us the opportunity to begin a discussion with the Greeks concerning the supernatural forces that have come into the world lately."

Now it was Charles who cleared his throat. "I raise this because the pope feels strongly that it would be of great assistance to the mission if you—all of you twenty-firsters, that is—participated in the mission also. By now, rumors concerning you will have certainly reached Constantinople and Gregory feels—and I agree—that it would be best if the Byzantines saw you in person."

The king leaned back in his chair. "I assume you will want some time to discuss the matter. I will wait while you do."

Merlin shut down so the twenty-firsters could talk privately.

****

The discussion didn't really take very long. All the twenty-firsters thought getting out of France was a good idea, given the state of tension that existed. And Gabriel Delaflote added another attraction when he said, "I have a friend in Constantinople, Theodore Meliteniotes. Well... Theodore is not so much a friend as a correspondent. We've never met in person."

"Is he an expert on magic?" asked Amelia.

"Insofar as anyone is, I imagine." Delaflote shrugged. "His specialty is astronomy, but he's a great scholar on many subjects. We could go and see him. He may know something of what caused all this."

The clincher came when Roger had Merlin ask the king who would be in command of the military escort.

"Bertrand du Guesclin," Merlin reported. "He'll have to resign his position as Constable, of course, but he's already agreed. And apparently Tiphaine plans to accompany him."

"That settles it, as far as I'm concerned," Roger said. "I don't trust Charles, but I do trust Bertrand."

Amelia frowned. "He's still the king's man, even if he's not the Constable any more."

"Yeah, sure. But he won't stab us in the back once we get out in the countryside somewhere. By which expression I mean *literally* have us stabbed in the back, in good old medieval fashion."

"That is probably why King Charles gave du Guesclin the assignment," pointed out Delaflote. "He surely dislikes losing the Constable's services, but he knows that Bertrand is someone you would trust not to betray you."

A short round of discussion followed, in which everyone indicated their agreement with that assessment.

"Okay," Roger said. "Merlin, get back in touch with Charles."

****

Then they got down to it. What they needed—aside from some horses which the royal stables would provide—was copious quantities of ready cash. Of course, in the fourteenth century that meant gold and silver coins. Also some supplies. More than would fit in the van. It was going to be a slow caravan that left France for Constantinople.

They needed the military escort not just to protect them but to protect all the supplies they'd need to bring with them. If it was just them in the van—which would pretty much fill Pucorl up anyway—they couldn't carry enough. Especially, they couldn't carry enough gas. While Pucorl could run his additional systems magically, even move the van through his will to an extent, he couldn't do it for long without using up a great deal of his substance. He needed diesel. It could be biodiesel, but he needed diesel. They needed to take wagon loads of diesel with them.

"We are going to need a small army to accompany us," Roger said, "or we will be beset by bandits every mile of the way."

"I will give Bertrand a sizeable enough force," Charles agreed.

Further negotiations followed. How much gold, how much silver? How many enchanted guns?

"We won't have access to the alchemists of the University of Paris," Wilber said. "That means flintlocks or enchanted guns, and we have already seen how unreliable flintlocks are."

"The alchemists have proved ineffective in producing a usable primer," Nicolas du Bosc said. None of the twenty-firsters had the knowledge to develop a primer. Jennifer had some hard science courses, but they were in physics, not chemistry.

"They will," Wilber said.

"More importantly, the unreliability of flintlocks is less important in larger forces." Roger said. "In a big enough military unit at least some are going to fire, and you can make a good guess at what percentage of misfires you will suffer. But we are going to be a smaller force."

"All the more reason we need enchanted weapons," Bill Howe said. He was sitting next to Jennifer. In what was probably a gross violation of royal custom—not that Roger was in any mood to give a damn—the two of them were holding hands. Since the end of the siege of Paris, Bill and Jennifer had stopped pretending that they weren't seeing each other. Mrs. Grady was concerned about the matter, Roger knew, but what could she really do to put a stop to it?

The real issue was, of course, money. A flintlock cost a lot for a peasant, but an enchanted rifle cost as much as a charger. You not only had the cost of making the rifle, you had the cost of enchanting the rifle. It was easier to enchant a rifle that was artistic than a plain rifle. Scroll work inlays and other fancy work made the demon feel that the job was important, and uniqueness made the connection between the demon and the device stronger.

With a drop forge, a basic flintlock could be made in a few days, but a properly enchanted rifle with the necessary scroll work was weeks in the making. Then that was topped off by paying a wizard a small fortune to call the demon into the rifle. It wasn't cheap. Not even for the king of France.

Eventually, though, they reached agreement. Wilber got Meurtrier because he was the only one who could ride the horse. Roger and Bill got stallions from the king's stables. Paul wanted one too, but his mother settled for a gelding. So did Jennifer after she insisted on a horse of her own, even though everyone knew perfectly well she'd be riding in the van most of the time.

"It's the principle of the thing," she'd say later. "Why should only the guys get a horse?"

"Why should only the guys get a stallion, then?" asked Lakshmi.

Annabelle provided the answer. "Because stallions are a pain in the ass to ride and only guys are dumb enough to want one in the first place."

They also got a chest which contained several pounds of gold and even more silver, to go into Pucorl's storage compartment.

Five minutes later, Roger—who had been shifted to Pucorl's Garage and from there to the domains of Merlin, and hence to Merlin's location in the mortal realm—appeared in the palace on the Île de la Cité, bowed to the king and, escorted by Nicolas du Bosc and a platoon of royal guards, started on his way to the Hôtel Saint-Pol.

Themis, The Netherworld

The being that men call Themis was in three places at once and three forms at once. She was a woman, seated on a throne hearing petitions and making judgments. She had the scales of justice ready to her hand and now she had a book of laws next to the scales. She also had a sword and next to the sword a torch. The sword was the sword of punishment and the torch was the torch of freedom. The book and the sword were new.

She was also the land on which sat the castle she occupied. A land damaged by the mortals and the uses she had been put to.

Finally, she was a sword in the mortal realm. A sword set in the stone floor of a throne room in the mortal realm. The sword that sat at her right hand was its mirror.

A hand touched her hilt and she recognized it. It was the hand of Roger McLean. That hand could not compel her. No hand could compel her now. Roger was the reason that was so. She examined him between one heartbeat and the next, and in the examination she didn't find perfection or anything close to perfection. What she did find was basic decency and a concern for others. A concern for her when she had been unable to compel that concern.

She also saw through his eyes and heard with his ears the presence of the king's guards and Nicolas du Bosc. As well as Clausewitz, his phone. She discussed matters with Clausewitz and Merlin, catching up on the matters of import to her in the time since she had been released back into the netherworld. She weighed the issues on her scales and considered the rights and the necessities.

Roger pulled and she came free in his hand. But she left a ripple in the floor of the throne room. A clear mark that she had been there. She lit the blade with fairy fire and rang it like a bell, but the vibrations that made her song didn't touch the hilt. Instead, she whispered in Roger's mind that he should lay her over his back as though there were a sheath there.

Roger did as he was told and the sword rested on his back without weight and without quite touching his coat. Roger turned and smiled at the expression on the faces of Nicolas du Bosc and the king's guard. Then he walked out and they formed up around him.

Themis was still in three places at once.

Throne Room, Palace of Île de la Cité
August 9, 1372

King Charles sat on his throne, and Bertrand was standing behind him to his right. Roger knelt and looked at Bertrand first. Bertrand was his mentor, the man who had taught him to be a soldier. He was also the sworn man of the king of France, and that would keep a certain distance between them, at least for a while. Still, Roger was glad—very glad—that Bertrand would be going with them.

Charles was looking impatient. Roger bowed and took Themis from his back. "King Charles of France, I bring you greetings from Queen Themis of Themis in the netherworld and come before you as her mortal ambassador." This wasn't the speech they had agreed on, but Themis had her own idea of how things ought to go. Roger was a lot more willing to piss off Charles than Themis. Her kingdom was bigger than France and full of magic.

Charles didn't say anything. He just looked at Roger for a long five seconds or so and waved for him to continue.

"Queen Themis holds no grudge against France for the actions of Philip the Bold. Those actions were acts of treason against the crown of France, as well as acts of war against Themis. Let there be peace between Charles of France and Themis of Themis. Her sword, her earthly presence, is not now owned by any mortal and will never again be owned by any mortal, but she will accompany her ambassador on the quest that you and the twenty-firsters have agreed to."

Slowly, as though he were working it out as he listened, Charles V nodded his royal head.

Roger bowed again, then stood, and rather than backing out of the royal presence as protocol would normally demand, turned and walked out. This wasn't an insult. He was here as representative of Themis who, by any standard, ranked as high as any mortal king.

EPILOGUE

Pucorl's Garage
August 10, 1372

Roger, with a sack of computers on his left arm and Merlin in his left hand, appeared in the pentagram in Pucorl's Garage. Merlin had moved them to his territory, and from there to Pucorl's.

The sword was no longer on his back. Instead, Themis in her aspect as a woman stood in the pentagram with him. She looked around critically, not quite pleased with something.

"What's wrong?" Merlin asked.

"The pentagram is a bit sloppy, don't you think?" It wasn't really a question. She looked at the computer, and it seemed to Roger that she was looking right into Merlin himself. Then the sword, or its mirror, appeared in her hand, and she used it to inscribe what looked to Roger to be an integrated circuit of considerable complexity into the lines of the pentagram. Roger decided that he didn't need to be kibitzing in this discussion.

"How'd it go?" Annabelle asked.

"We're here." Roger shrugged. "I'd introduce you to Themis, but I don't want to interrupt."

"I'm finished, Roger," Themis said then, and stepped out of a pentagram that seemed now to be more solid.

Farmhouse in France
August 12, 1372

Bertrand du Guesclin, formerly the Constable of France, arrived at the little farm house at the head of a military force of some eighty men. Behind them was a not-so-small line of wagons. His wife Tiphaine rode at his side.

Roger came out with Themis on his back to greet them.

Bertrand dismounted and then helped Tiphaine do the same. Once she was on the ground, Tiphaine gave Roger an imperious

373

look.

"Turn around," she commanded, making a twirling gesture with her hand. "I need to see this famous sword for myself."

Roger obeyed, smiling.

"Just as I thought," Tiphaine said. "The horoscope was quite accurate."

Roger chuckled, trying not to sound too sarcastic.

The sword seemed to shine a bit brighter.

"What do you think is so funny?" Themis demanded. Or at least, that part of Themis that still resided in the sword.

Roger's smile vanished.

"At least there will be someone on this expedition who knows what she's doing. I foresee great prospects. Well, better ones, at any rate."

CAST OF CHARACTERS

14th Century

Commissaire Pierre Dubois, of the Grand Châtelet, Fictional

Charles V, King of France, Historical

André Hébert, aide to the Commissaire of the Grand Châtelet, Fictional

Count Moreau, Provost of the University of Paris, Fictional

Gabriel Delaflote, Doctor of Natural Philosophy and collector of writings on the occult, Fictional

Louis, Duke of Anjou, brother of Charles V, Historical

John, Duke of Berry, brother of Charles V, Historical

Philip the Bold, Duke of Burgundy, youngest brother of Charles V, Historical

Nicolas du Bosc, lawyer for Charles V, Historical

Perenelle Flamel, wife of Nicholas, Historical

Nicholas Flamel, scribe, Historical

Joanna of Bourbon, queen of France, Historical

Father Augustine, murdered, Fictional

Bertrand du Guesclin, Constable of France, Historical

Tiphaine de Raguenel, wife of Bertrand du Guesclin, noted astrologist, Historical

Gregory XI, Pope in Avignon, Historical

Bishop de Sarcenas, bishop in Paris, Fictional

Bishop Baudin, bishop in Paris, Fictional

Cardinal Jean de Dormans, cardinal in Paris, Historical

Filberte Renard, doctor of medicine, Paris, Fictional

Olivier de Clisson, general of France, Historical

Demons, Fictional

Pucorlshrigin/Chevalier Pucorl de Elesia, puck, haunts the van

Merlin, muse, haunts Wilber's implant and computer

Igor, puck, haunts Wilber's phone

Catvia, succubus, haunts Jeff's computer

Coach, faun, haunts Jeff's watch
Asuma, succubus, haunts Jeff's phone
Enzo, puck, haunts Annabelle's phone
Rolls Royce, puck, haunts diagnostic tool for van
Batman, puck, haunts Paul's computer
Green Lantern, brownie, haunts Paul's phone
Ishmael, puck, haunts Bill's iPod
Clausewitz, puck, haunts Roger's phone
Laurence, muse, haunts Amelia's phone
Shakespeare, haunts Amelia's computer
Sophocles, haunts Amelia's book reader
DW, incubus, haunts Lakshmi's camera
Marilyn, succubus, haunts Lakshmi's phone
Silvore, puck, haunts Jennifer's phone
Themis, titan, trapped in Philip the Bold's sword
Beslizoswian, demon lord, murderer
Pookasaladriscase, two foot tall brownie in French village
Pucslenstece, puck, called by Father Thomas
Raphico, angel of the Creator, haunts phone given to God
Amiee, puck, haunts de Clisson's parrot
Archimedes, muse, haunts Delaflote's crow
Others named and unnamed

The Twenty-firsters, Fictional
Amelia Grady, drama teacher, driver of van
Paul Grady, 8 year old son of Amelia
Wilber Hyde-Davis, English, 17, has cochlear implant
Lakshmi Rawal, Indian raised in America, 16, cinematographer.
Annabelle Cooper-Smith, American, 17
Jennifer Fairbanks, American, 17
Liane Boucher, French, 17
Roger McLean, American, 18
Jeff Martin, American, 18
Bill Howe, American, 18

Made in the USA
Lexington, KY
04 April 2018